THE

MOON PRINCE

Emilia Mondragón

ISBN: 979-8-218-69089-2

Book Cover by Mintaii

First edition, 2025

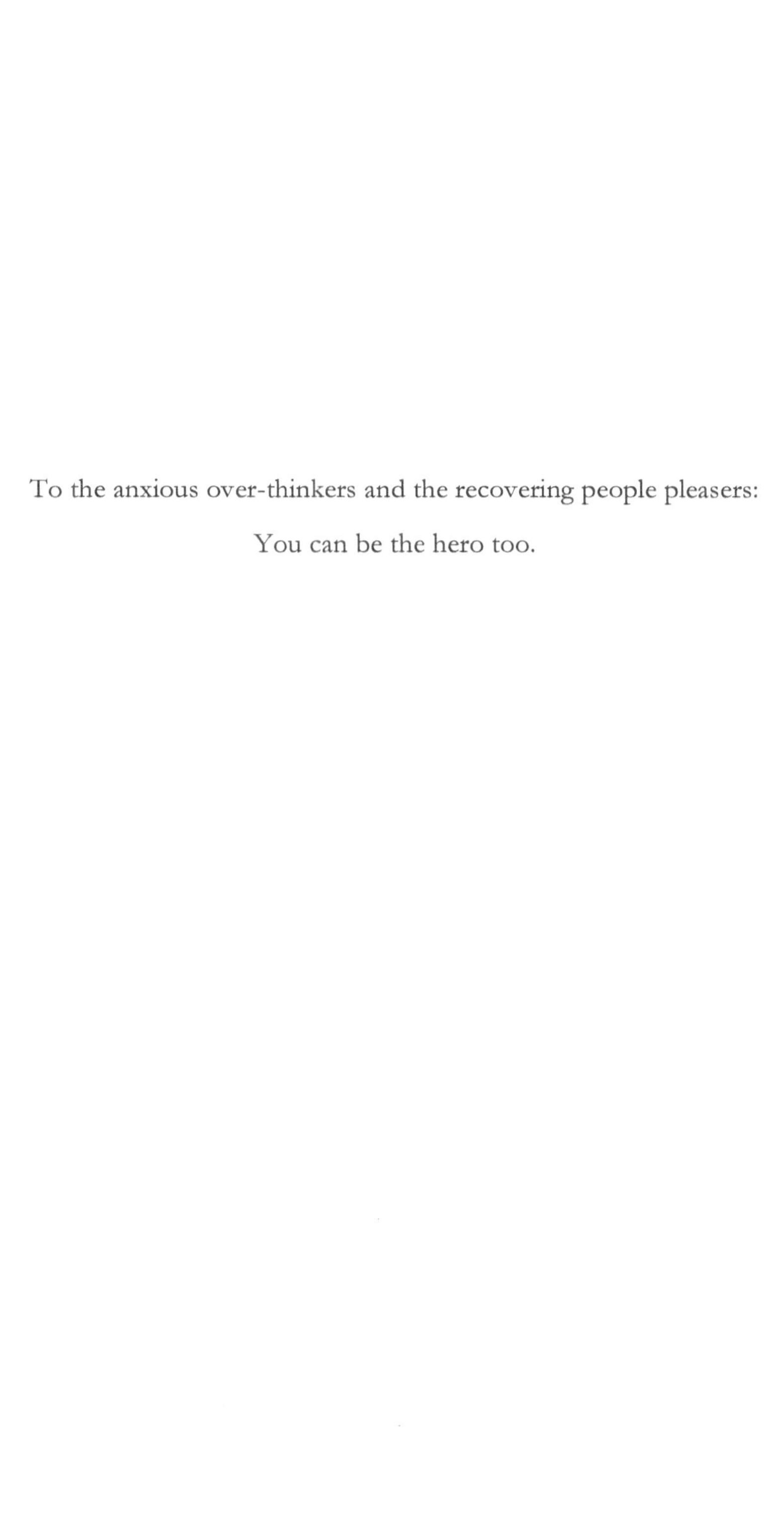

To the anxious over-thinkers and the recovering people pleasers:

You can be the hero too.

"Since childhood, I've been faithful to monsters. I have been saved and absolved by them, because monsters, I believe, are patron saints of our blissful imperfection, and they allow and embody the possibility of failing."

"The way I love monsters is a Mexican way of loving monsters, which is that I am not judgmental. The Anglo way of seeing things is that monsters are exceptional and bad, and people are good. But in my movies, creatures are taken for granted."

-    Guillermo del Toro

Content Warnings:

The Moon Prince has mature content of violent, sexual, and paranormal nature. If you are not comfortable with:

- Blood & gore

- Body horror

- Ghosts

- Demonic possession

- Consensual, open door sexual content

- War, violence, murder,

then read at your own risk.

The world and the characters in this story are not real, but the themes very much are. As I always say, use critical thinking when it comes to any form of media you choose to indulge in.

THE
MOON PRINCE

Prologue

It was the day the God-given would come to regret.

It happened in the heart of Avilonía, past acres of lush, vibrant orange trees in the capital city of Dragona. The capital sat like a golden oasis of stone, bronze, and stunning domed buildings. Palms and mesquite dappled the streets, and various cacti surrounded the outer walls in a beautiful yet threatening boundary. Stoic guards stood tall on the ramparts in their red and gold desert armor, holding obsidian-tipped spears, watching the land like hawks. Beyond them, past the city streets, lively neighborhoods, and the Temple of Fire, stood Tona Palace, home to the Sun King. It was a large dragon against the backdrop of the towering eastern mountains. Its domed steeples were decorated in an intricate pattern of red stone scales, glittering like rubies in the daylight.

Dragona wasn't known for its quiet nature, but today the energy was particularly high, for not only was the Sun King home, but his compatriots—the other God-given—arrived in the early morning. Every month, the champions of the gods convened at the capital to discuss the progress and issues of their ever-growing country. They gathered around a circular stone table, each in their respective seat: Leandro Eliódor, ruler of the Sun Kingdom; Marino and Victoria Markaél, rulers of the Moon Kingdom; Montserrat and Sierra Damiá, rulers of the Earth Kingdom; and Saévio Vórtice, ruler of the Air Kingdom.

For the most part, the meeting was business as usual, save for their very special guest:

Leandro Eliódor's older brother, Sebastián.

The Sun Prince stood apprehensively before the council table, with books and rolls of parchment before him. Compared to his brother, the Sun King, Sebastián had a vacillating energy about him. Leandro stood tall and was built like a warrior, with broad shoulders, sleek, jasper red hair, and bronze skin. A tattoo of red flames covered his throat—a symbol of kingship. And with the golden circlet of metal flames atop his head, he was every bit the regal, confident, and mildly arrogant champion of the sun god. Sebastián, however, was thinner; his red hair was unkempt, and dark crescent moons hugged his under-eyes behind spectacles. The lack of warmth in his skin was further proof that he spent his days indoors poring over books, maps, and parchments when he should've been asleep. But behind the exterior was another powerful God-given with a sharp mind.

"The floor is yours," Leandro said, shooting his brother a reassuring smile.

Sebastián clasped his hands behind his back, taking a wary look around the room. He knew the monarchs well and had grown alongside them since childhood, yet the inadequacy was still there.

With a clearing of his throat, he straightened his spine and began, "*Sus Majestades*, as you know, these last few years following the war, we've been looking through the wreckage of what's left, digging up old ruins and rebuilding what's been taken from us. I've also been cataloging any artifacts that we've found, and within that wreckage, there seem to be some... *items* of value."

Rey Saévio spoke up.

"What sort of items?"

He was the eldest of the monarchs, with graying hair that still contained streaks of its former lilac color. He wore sleek vestments of violet, blue, and silver, with a cape made of silk and owl feathers. A crown made of polished quartz crystal sat atop his head, and his face showed little expression, emulating an air of frigid intimidation.

Sebastián hesitated before answering, "Books, tomes, artifacts, stuff left behind."

"More stuff for the museum, then?" *Rey* Marino chimed in.

The Moon King sat up in his chair now, his golden face lighting up for a moment. He was *Rey* Saévio's opposite in demeanor and tone, but he looked every bit as warrior-like as the Sun King. He donned more leather than velvet in colors of cream, silver, and gold, with a sapphire blue cape patterned with fish scales. Swirling blue tattoos peeked out from beneath the cuffs of his sleeves, and his crown was silver, forged in the shape of waves, dappled with moonstones. His hair was as white as moonlight.

Príncipe Sebastián grimaced. "Not exactly."

The room fell silent for a moment, trepidation filling everyone's hearts.

Marino shared a look with his wife, *Reina* Victoria, whose bore a leery scowl. She wore a cream dress embroidered with gold and blue, but the cape that fell around her shoulders was deep violet, many shades darker than the lilac hair that cascaded down her back. Owl feathers adorned her shoulders, and her crown was a mixture of raw quartz embedded in silver.

Just as she opened her mouth to pose a question, Leandro beat her to it.

"What are you talking about, Seb?"

His golden crown of flames and red stones glittered in the firelight. Leandro may have gotten his brother the audience, but he did not know the extent of his request.

"It wasn't from our people," his brother replied. "They were found in the northern mountains, in a mausoleum of some kind... and it bore the mark of the Black Death."

Gasps and curses danced around the room at the sound of the infamous conqueror's moniker.

"There was more?" Victoria exclaimed.

"Much to everyone's surprise, yes."

"Burn it then. Burn it all," she hissed.

The Air King clicked his tongue, which she ignored.

"I agree," *Reina* Montserrat scorned. "We should destroy that place and everything in it. You said it was in the mountains? I'll do it myself."

The Earth Queen wore a black dress with red embroidery and a cape of the richest emerald silk. Raw obsidian jutted out from her shoulders, melded there by magic. Her hair looked black at a glance, but in the light, the color shifted with a glint of green like a beetle's wings. It was wrapped around her head in a braid beneath a circlet of bronze with a set of bull's horns sticking up from the sides. A tattoo of black ink marked the side of her face and neck with a pattern that resembled marble or smoke. Beside her was her wife, *Reina* Sierra. She wore a teal dress, her brown curls down her back, and her skin a rich brown. Her crown was pure obsidian.

Around them, were resounding statements of agreement. The Sun Prince attempted to quell the cacophony, but to no avail.

"Everyone, will you please—"

Noticing his brother's expression, Leandro slammed a fist against the marble table.

"Hey!" he shouted.

The burning candles in the room turned a cool blue, pulsing and flickering with magic. The temperature momentarily rose as heat radiated off of him, his eyes glowing yellow. Everyone's words died on their lips as they looked towards Leandro Eliódor, rather peeved, but with no argument.

When the Sun King relaxed, the flames turned back to normal, and his eyes reverted to their warm amber color. He then motioned to his brother, speaking in a stern voice.

"Seb has more to say. Let him finish before we make any decisions."

Victoria rolled her eyes and sighed, "Fine. Seb, please continue."

El Príncipe eyed his brother, equal parts thankful and irritated, before turning his attention back to the room. His throat bobbed as he swallowed hard.

"You might not like what I have to say, but I have to say it. I wish to study the items before they are discarded."

More gasps and louder outcries erupted before him.

"What?"

"Are you insane?"

"Why would you ever want to touch them?"

"Because it could be of value!" he exclaimed, cutting through the fray.

His frustration was escalating; that much was certain. The lights around the room flickered once more, though the color remained the same.

"He managed to take over cities and countries with his magic," he continued. "Maybe we could find something to help us rebuild. Perhaps we could use it for good. It's a part of our history!"

Victoria put her hands on the table and leaned forward, thoroughly riled.

"That's what books are for, Sebastián! Write it down, paint a pretty picture, sing a silly song, and pass it down, but we don't need to keep them like trinkets! Cursed items or not! Have you learned nothing?"

"We can't just erase what happened!"

The Queen of Storms scoffed, "Who said anything about erasing what happened? Do you think *any* of us has forgotten what happened? You think our people will?"

"There's no need to be aggressive, Victoria," *Rey* Saévio derided.

She tensed but didn't look him in the eye as she hissed through her teeth, "I don't recall asking for your opinion on the matter."

The monarchs looked between them carefully but didn't address it.

"What happened to honoring the dead?" Sebastián asked.

"You think that applies to someone responsible for millions of deaths? A man who tampered with death itself and used the bodies of our people against us?"

"All I'm asking is for a small window of time to look into them, take what we can use, and then you can do what you please."

Victoria growled as her husband put a gentle hand on her arm. She sat back against her chair, taking slow, even breaths to still her heart.

Reina Montserrat took it as her turn to speak.

"I refuse to believe that the pursuit of your knowledge is that important," she spat. "It reminds me a little too much of those religious heathens who followed that demon around. You're better than them, Seb. If you ask me, I'm glad he died the way he did—at the bottom of El Toro."

The Queen of Storms smirked with satisfaction while Sebastián snapped his head towards the Earth Queen in horror.

"You have no respect. You never have," he muttered.

Everyone in the room froze. Victoria's eyes widened, and Montserrat's face twisted into something vicious. Her foxlike eyes darkened with a glint of volcanic red, and the ground shook just enough to make the hanging fixtures sway and the goblets bounce. At the same time, Marino and Sierra grabbed her shoulders to hold her back.

"Montsé, don't."

The Earth Queen growled, "You—"

"Easy, easy," Marino whispered.

"Seb, even you know that was unnecessary," Leandro said. "This doesn't need to turn into another battle. Not between us."

His brother grumbled, pinching the bridge of his nose. "I apologize, Montsé. That was uncalled for."

His tone wasn't particularly genuine, but it could have been exhaustion working away at him. At the very least, it was enough to appease the Earth Queen.

Montserrat harrumphed. "Apology accepted. For now."

It was then that Leandro asked, "How much time do you need, Seb?"

"Wait, seriously?" the queens exclaimed.

Even the Moon King sputtered. "Leo, you're genuinely considering this?"

The Sun King met council's eyes one by one, saying, "The sooner we let him kill the curiosity, the sooner we can get rid of it."

"He's right," *Rey* Saévio agreed. "We don't need to be children about this. If he believes that there can be something valuable, then perhaps there is."

Victoria groaned and rolled her eyes once more.

"Everything of value that man took from us," she whispered.

Marino ran his hands over his face and hair before reiterating, "How much time *do* you need?"

The Sun Prince shrugged. "I don't know. A month."

"A day," Victoria countered.

"A week."

"Three days."

He let out a long, vexing exhale but didn't argue further.

"Fine. Three days."

Three days was all it took.

1

The Great Divide

Esmé

Coáraluna, New Avilonía—Present

I could hear the murmurs of the audience beyond the curtains as they awaited the second half of the show. The performances the winter solstice were some of the most anticipated throughout Avilonía. We were on our last few shows, which meant the theater was fully packed. No detail was spared, and the most talented performers in all of the Moon Kingdom had a place on stage tonight. Including me.

My chestnut brown hair was slicked back into a tight, low bun, with red flowers affixed to either side of my head. A layer of charcoal lined my brown eyes, and my lips were stained scarlet. The dress itself was a beautiful, ruby brocade monstrosity with a scooped neckline, thick straps, and a giant skirt with rose detailing. It was one of many vibrant costumes I wore for the opera. Only at *Teatro Paraiso* would I ever look like this, and only at the theater could I ever be such a bold, passionate caricature of myself. Yet, by some stroke of luck, it is the part I get to play.

The night was going smoothly, but compared to the liveliness of the audience, the energy backstage was fraught with anticipation and stress. As soon as one of us exited into the wings, our bright smiles and poise were swiftly exchanged for tired sighs and a panicked need to get ready for the next number. It was easy to get lost in the thrill of it all, but now and then there would be a lull, and my nerves would kick back in. Nerves and thoughts of other things I was trying to keep away from my mind.

The memory of a beautiful young man with dark eyes made my anxious heart ache, as if a hand reached into my rib cage and squeezed. Smiles, laughter, and a sparkling gaze. Kisses and hands holding hands, skin on skin—

I clenched my jaw as warmth spread across my cheeks. No matter how many times I tucked such thoughts away in a box, he always came sneaking back to forefront of my mind.

What have you done to me?

A body collided with my shoulder, knocking me out of my thoughts. I let out a small yelp and felt large hands gripping my waist— a jarring sensation. The scent of tobacco and sweat filled my nostrils.

"Oop—"

"Sorry!" I said instinctively.

It was one of the stage crew, Marco, who was much older than me. He was tall and broad-shouldered, with long black hair and brown eyes. When we made eye contact, he wiggled his eyebrows and let his hands linger a little too long as he moved past me.

"It's okay, *hermosa*," he drawled.

I put my acting skills to use and pasted on a sweet smile, letting out a nervous chuckle. He gave me a firm squeeze before turning and walking away to the opposite wing. My face burned once more, except instead of feeling butterflies or any sort of infatuation, I felt sick. And as soon as he was out of sight, my smile fell away.

Marco, like a lot of the men I tend to encounter, was simply a bit too…*friendly*. While I may have found it flattering at one point, it was starting to get incredibly tiring, frustrating, and uncomfortable. In their eyes, I was a pretty little thing for them to look at and touch because they felt like they could. It was even more aggravating how all I seemed able to do was choke and not speak up for myself. I wanted to believe they meant well, even if it didn't feel that way at all.

It was a force of habit. When you're an immigrant and an orphan, you learn to keep your head down and stay quiet lest you lose your job, money, or housing. I've come a long way from struggling the way I used to, but some things were hard to shake. And behind my dresses and makeup, I felt like an impostor.

"Handsy, that one."

The voice startled me, making me jolt, but only momentarily.

"Camilo," I gasped.

He was a tall young man with dark curly hair. He wore black pants and nothing but a vest over his shirtless body. He was a longtime friend as well as one of the crew members in *Teatro Paraiso*. We spoke in whispers as we always did when a show was running.

Camilo chuckled at my reaction. "Sorry. Didn't mean to scare you."

"You're fine."

He raised an eyebrow, motioning with his head in Marco's direction.

"Do you want me to talk to him?" he asked.

"No. You don't have to do that," I replied, shaking my head.

"Fine. Where's your boy? Is he here tonight?" His lips curled into an impish smirk, his green eyes burning bright.

I scoffed and swiftly clamped my mouth shut. My heartbeat quickened, and blushed all over again, making me grateful for the stage makeup. Though I'm sure it was still obvious his question affected me. It was my downfall, really. Still, I tried playing coy.

"Boy? What boy?"

Camilo rolled his eyes. "Come on. You know who I'm talking about."

I did know what "boy" he was referring to, but the situation, for many reasons, was hard to explain. All I knew was how *he* made me feel, and even *that* was too terrifying and complicated to put into words.

I glanced down at my gloved hands and thought back to the sea of faces I managed to catch in the audience tonight. I would be lying if I said that I hadn't hoped to see a familiar one among them or that I hadn't scanned the crowd when the performance allowed, only to be met with disappointment. Again.

"No, he's not," I whispered.

Camilo frowned. "What does he look like? Maybe I can find him for you."

I narrowed my eyes at him and the cheeky grin he gave me.

"No. I know what you're doing, and it's not going to work," I told him as I smoothed out my gown and adjusted things that didn't need adjusting.

"Hey, I know you're a private person, so I won't annoy you too much, but you can't blame us for being curious. We hardly know anything about the guy," he said.

My heart tightened with dread.

"I know. It's complicated, Milo. He's gone most of the time, and I rarely get to see him."

"He's from the Air Kingdom, right?"

"Yes, so it makes things difficult. Long distance is hard."

"Does he at least write?"

"Sometimes."

Not really.

"Maybe he should hurry up and propose then, huh?" he joked.

My jaw dropped. "Milo!"

"What? It wouldn't hurt," he said with a giggle. "Maybe then we'd finally see him. Otherwise, it's just drawn-out, unnecessary pain."

I know.

That very pain ate away at my marrow. It was galling considering I didn't want to feel that way at all.

A different, more physical ache hit me on the side of my head then. It was sharp as a needle and was followed by a harsh ringing in my right ear. My hand flew to my temple as I closed my eyes with a wince.

"Esmé?" Camilo sounded distant.

After a few moments, the pain spread throughout my skull, duller but still present. When I was able to open my eyes, a dark shadow passed out of the corner of my vision. With a racing heart, I followed its movement, but there was nothing there. No matter how hard I stared into that dark, empty corner of the stage, it was completely empty.

It always was.

"Hey…"

Camilo's voice cut through the ringing that was now ebbing away. He was at my side, his hand resting gently on my shoulder in concern.

"Are you alright?" he asked.

"Yes," I responded breathlessly, after a dazed moment. "Just another migraine."

"Did you take your medicine?"

I groaned, remembering that I still had one more task to do after this long day.

"I ran out, but I'm going to get some more soon. I'll be fine until then."

He furrowed his brow. "Are you sure?"

I smiled softly. "Yes, I'm sure."

"Okay, well, Flora called places," he said, pointing to the stage. "If you're sure you're okay, you should get ready."

I perked up, putting on the brightest face I could muster. My friend smiled at me before disappearing to join the rest of the crew. The wings filled up as the music swelled. And just before the show commenced, I took one last glance behind the set, expecting to see the shadow, but the darkness all looked the same to me.

❋ ☽ ○ ☾ ❋

After every show, the entire cast and crew gathered at the producer's house down the street from *Teatro Paraiso*. He was a middle-aged man named Fabian, and our current director, Teo, was his husband. I met both of them during my audition over a year ago after hearing about the casting call through my friend Dulce, who used to be the company's costume designer. They were very particular, not to mention perfectionist workaholics, but I assumed that this was how most people in the performing arts were. I was just fortunate they took me under their wing.

This time of year, their house was decked out with decorations for the solstice, like garlands of sliced oranges and rosemary, bundles of poinsettia on the mantle above the fireplace, and several candles that brightened the sitting room. By the wall was a table with a wide array of delectable foods, drinks, and desserts that I happily helped myself to after a taxing day.

I was now out of my extravagant costume and back in my casual attire, which was an embroidered white shirt and lavender skirt with colorful ribbons ringing the bottom. My hair flowed past my shoulders in loose waves, which I thanked the gods for because it helped with the migraine.

Fabian, Teo, Camilo, Flora, and a few other members of the cast and crew were draped on different pieces of furniture, holding alcoholic drinks and plates of food. Marco and his friends were among them, making jokes and flirting with whoever was in their line of sight. I wasn't much of a talker myself, but I did like to listen to everyone's ramblings and laugh at their stories. Of course, the one thing I most certainly did not partake in was the consumption of liquor. No matter how many times it was offered to me, I respectfully denied it.

"Come on, you need to let loose a little," Marco sang, draping his arm around my shoulder.

I chuckled, slowly sliding out of his grasp. "No, thank you. I think I'll be alright."

"You're just afraid you'll tell us about your boyfriend," Camilo teased.

"Am not," I said defensively.

Of course I am. It didn't exactly help with my ailment either.

Flora smacked him in the arm. "Leave her alone, Milo."

Marco, however, was surprised to hear that.

"Wait, you have a boyfriend?"

"No, I don't," I replied, staring daggers at Camilo.

My friend's face lit up, his eyes bearing mischief.

"Yes, she does, actually. He's from up north. He goes hunting in the woods for fun."

"Camilo!" I chided with a strange look.

"Seriously?" Marco asked.

"Yeah, he's really big and scary-looking. I'm surprised she's even with him."

"Hold on. You've met him?" Flora blurted out.

Camilo nearly stumbled then but managed to keep his cool. "I saw him once by accident. It was brief."

I put my face in my hands, partially mortified but mostly to keep myself from laughing. Even if Camilo did know anything about *him*, none of what he said was remotely true. In fact, it was comical, but Marco didn't know that, and he seemed to buy every word. And even if I hated that it took the mention of another man to scare him, the look of apprehension in Marco's face had me biting back a smile.

Regardless, the last thing I wanted to do was talk about my love life, so I took it as my cue to go. I grabbed my blue shawl with yellow stars, wrapping it around my shoulders. Flora, my stage manager and friend, frowned.

"Wait, where are you going?"

"Home," I lied. "I'm getting tired, and I have a headache."

It wasn't completely untrue. The migraine was weighing down on me even now, which is why I needed to deal with it.

Flora pouted but didn't protest. Instead, she gave me a big hug and a kiss on the cheek, her emerald eyes sparkling as she took me in.

"Have a good night, Esmé."

"You too, Flora."

Camilo grumbled in discontent as I gave him, Fabian, and Teo the same farewell. Before leaving, I stopped by the snack table and scooped some of the leftover food and pastries into an empty box to take along with me.

"Do you need someone to walk you home?" Camilo asked.

I smiled softly. "I appreciate it, but no. I think I could use the time alone and the fresh air."

❋ ☽ ◯ ☾ ❋

Emilia Mondragón

Coáraluna is a town off the southwestern coast of New Avilonía made of a white, blue, and sea-green collage of stone houses with red shale roofs. To the east were the inland beach neighborhoods and farmlands sitting against the backdrop of the roiling green hills. Then, across two bridges made of fortified quartz crystal, was the main island itself, which is where I currently reside.

The island city was built into the side of a large hill and was divided into different levels going upward like a giant set of stairs. The base tier was where the bridges connected and consisted of fishing ports and docks for shipments and military vessels. With its ascent, there were varying degrees of residential homes, with their quality and cost rising with the hill. There were marketplaces, restaurants, schools, temples, and the arts district, which is where *Teatro Paraiso* was. Each level was accessed by tunnels, stairways, cobblestone streets, and pack mules, or could even be passed through by manually operated gondolas. But of course, everything paled in comparison to the crowning jewel at the very top—the marble structure of *Castillo* Paricia, home to Markaél's.

Even at night, I could see its familiar exterior from the arts district right below it. The golden firelight illuminating the palace allowed me to faintly see the blue-scaled tiles adorning the domed tops. Its towers peeked out from behind the wall, looking like giants watching the city. Despite all the power it held, some part of me couldn't help but think that it looked unbelievably lonely up there. Or perhaps it was the familiar yearning wound around my heart like a thread that kept pulling in a direction I had no sight of.

I tore my attention away from the castle and focused it in the opposite direction, down the slope. The short heels of my boots clicked softly against the stone as I followed a small, thin canal, doing down the same path. Jacaranda trees adorned the winding streets, now practically bare from the colder season and looking more and more like thin hands reaching up to the darkness. Upbeat music filtered out of a restaurant smelling of delicious Avilonían dishes—sweet, spicy, and savory all intermingled. The scent nearly made me stop in my tracks. A few familiar citizens waved in my direction—some asking me how the show was, and others congratulating me on my performance. Most of the time, I was barely recognizable out of my costume, but the handful of people who saw me to and from work always knew my name.

Eventually, I reached the edge of a low marble wall where the tier ended and the canal dropped to a waterfall below. A man in a blue uniform waited next to a steel gondola hanging from a thick, twisted wire. I greeted him and paid him some silver before boarding the box. He closed the door behind me and, using a crank, sent me off on my descent down to the lower levels of the island.

I leaned out one of the small windows, letting the salty ocean breeze kiss my cheeks as I toyed with the ring on my finger. It was an opaque green stone with a wavy pattern to it called *malaquita* or malachite. From what little I knew, *malaquita* was a crystal believed to be used for protection. My friend Canela even told me that if it were to break, it was a sign that it had used all its power to guard the user from dark energy. I couldn't say for certain whether it was true or not, but it was all the more reason to keep it close—that and the fact that it was a gift from my parents.

I don't remember much about them. I was too young when I lost them to have anything but a last name and a city—Vespertín and Anelante. They gave their lives to save mine by sending me on a ship across The Rift to get me away from Old Avilonía and the one they call the Sun Killer. And I am not the only one. Many refugees shared the same fate. Because before there was such a thing as Old and New Avilonía, there was simply *Avilonía*—one land to be shared by all— until great devastation occurred.

It all began with the Black Death.

Also known as the Undying King, Casímir Gedeón was a conqueror from the east. Out of the kindness of their hearts, the people of Avilonía welcomed him with open arms, only for him to plunder and pillage the country using his followers and an army of undead. Avilonía's land was fertile, beautiful, and steeped in magical energy, but at the time, the only ones who harnessed its power were witches and wizards. And Gedeón was determined to be the strongest. He used dark rituals against Avilonía's fiercest warriors and made himself practically immortal with his necromantic ties. Before the Aviloníans knew it, their land was taken, thousands of lives were lost, and the Black Death ruled without mercy.

The gods, seeing this, decided to turn the tide and do something they had never done before: bestow gifts on Aviloníans they saw as worthy. The first to be granted a gift was a man who became known as Sol Eliódor. Sol had been a great warrior who prayed to the gods for help against the Black Death. He was a leader and an honorable man who was revered by those who knew him. And after years of no response, Solistó, god of the sun and bravery, answered the warrior's prayer. He chose him as his champion and bestowed upon him a fragment of his magic, which gave him powers no human had ever possessed. Sol's brown hair turned jasper red, his eyes took on a golden glow, and he gained the power of light, fire, and courage. Thus marking him as the first ever Sun King of Avilonía, a title and a gift that would be passed down for generations to come.

Following Eliódor's prayer, the magical energy of Avilonía's land was unleashed, breaking a barrier between the world of men and the world of gods. More deities followed suit, bestowing gifts on those they deemed virtuous. Eliódor, Markaél, Vórtice, and Damiá. Sun, Moon, Storm, and Earth. Every single fighter and their bloodline were blessed, and they fought until their last breath, passing the legacy on to their children, and so on. Their descendants grew strong until they were able to cut Gedeón down, take every last bit of land back from his grasp, and reclaim it as their own.

After generations of suffering, the Black Death was no more, and Avilonía was divided into four kingdoms: Sun, Moon, Earth, and Air. Together, the descendants of the God-given were able to rebuild, and for years they ruled in peace. Or so it seemed.

They say it happened in three days.

That was the thing about souls—if one of them was tainted or evil enough, then it warped into something else. Some souls were lucky enough to find peace and cross over. Others became lost and were doomed to roam forever. However, there were those who became something akin to beasts. And the Black Death became just that—a demon that cursed what it left behind. He lingered, waiting in hopes of latching on to the first poor soul that was either weak or willing enough to do his bidding. Sebastián Eliódor—Leandro's brother— was that soul.

Once a prince with the power of light, Sebastián became a dark and poisoned version of himself who corrupted the world around him and burned what remained. He murdered his family in cold blood, eliminating everyone but himself from the Eliódor bloodline and earning him the title of the Sun Killer. One by one, monarchs and their families fell, and with the Black Death's followers by his side and an army of dark magic, Sebastián Eliódor continued what Casímir Gedeón began.

Kingdoms were evacuated, citizens fled, and the monarchs who survived split themselves between fighting and providing sanctuary. Sebastián continued to conquer the land and advanced towards the then capital city of Dragona with a choking grip, leaving the God-given to take drastic measures. And one winter day, Montserrat Damiá, champion of the earth, and Marino Markaél, champion of the moon and tides, used their abilities to split Avilonía in half and flood it until there was nothing but a vast sea between them—The Rift.

This is known as The Great Divide.

Of the former empires, the moon and air kingdoms remain. The Earth Queen disappeared, never to be seen again, leaving *Rey y Reina* Markaél to rebuild and rule over what they had left, while *Rey* Saévio ruled to the north. Though our side of the country has been safe from the Sun Killer's clutches so far, a war against Sebastián Eliódor still rages on at The Rift and Old Avilonía's borders in hopes of taking back what was once ours.

As I watched the hills from high above, I half expected to see The Rift or any sign of battle, but there was none. There was no fire, no magic, and no darkness but the starlit sky. There was no smell of fire or pollution, just sea salt and earth. All was well on this side of the world. Yet, with a glance at the southwestern port, I couldn't help but notice that all the military ships hadn't come back in weeks. It worried me.

I'm not a fighter. Far from it. I'm lucky enough to end up in such a beautiful city like Coáraluna. But I also knew that I lived in a world that could fall apart at any moment. It almost felt wrong to be here, living in such blissful ignorance, when I knew what happened on the other side. Still, what else could I possibly do? I felt helpless, but if I thought about it too much, then I'd spiral.

I turned back towards *Castillo* Paricia, the house of the Moon King and the Queen of Storms.

They've gotten us this far, haven't they?

I winced as another sharp pain in needled at my skull, this time between my brows. I massaged the skin there as the ringing came and went once more.

Focus on your own problems first, Esmé.

2

A Prayer For Death

Esmé

My stop was on the second level of Coáraluna, at a place called *Distrito Obsidiana*, or the Obsidian District. This time of night, it was more animated compared to the upper levels of the city, but highly precarious. The homes were smaller and stacked up next to each other, and there were numerous food carts, bars, and markets that stayed open well past midnight, closing right before the witching hour. Above all else, it was a place for the strange and unusual, whether it was because you were looking for something of the sort or because you were strange and unusual yourself. I was seeking something specific, but often wondered if I fell into the latter by default.

I clutched my bag and kept my shawl wrapped around my head as I walked through the shadowy streets. By all accounts, a girl like me didn't belong in a place like *Obsidiana* (whatever that meant), but I don't go as often as I used to. Still, I kept it a secret from nearly everyone in my life. I didn't need them prying around the dark corners of my world that even I understood little of. At the very least, I wasn't up to anything nefarious. I simply came for one thing and one thing only: a potion from a witch—and a friend—named Canela Montenegro.

Canela ran a shop in *Obsidiana* where she sold charms, potions, spell components, and performed magic for a price. I met her when I was doing odd jobs, and even served as her assistant for a short time before joining *Teatro Paraiso*. While I am not a witch, she showed me the practical usage of herbs, and when some of the warships came back from The Rift, she taught me everything about treating wounds. She never pressured me to do spells, but I was well-versed in the meanings behind every single item in her shop. She was the closest thing I had to a mother or a *tia*, and if it weren't for that, I wouldn't have risked going back to the Obsidian District at all.

To put it simply, I suffer from extreme migraines or *episodes*. They happen at random times and have plagued me for years. They started as an occasional ache but worsened into a sharp pang in my skull, followed by a dull ringing. That turned into seeing shadows that swiftly disappeared without a trace. It became such a hindrance that I went to an apothecary for help. They told me I must have sustained an injury when crossing The Rift and gave me simple tinctures for the pain. But since the episodes were so unpredictable, they did very little in the end. It wasn't until Canela offered help that I acquired a solid treatment.

I found myself down the familiar path to Demuerto Street, following the shape of the hillside, until I spotted Canela's shop. Before approaching the door, I cast a glance up and down the road, my eyes searching until they caught onto a familiar figure. Up at the corner, just out of range of the firelight, was a man sitting on a blanket with a clutter of items around him.

I took the box of leftovers from my bag and made my way towards him.

"Oh, look, the little bird's back," he mused with a low chuckle.

I hummed shyly, stopping just a few feet before him.

He was a middle-aged man with skin that was scorched from too much time in the sun. His long black hair was unruly and striped with gray, and his eyes were as black as the district's namesake. He wore dirty, tattered clothes, no shoes, and a weary smile on his face.

"*Buenas noches*, Ignacio," I greeted.

"*Buenas noches*, *Mija*," he returned warmly. "How are you?"

I shrugged. "Tired. How are you?"

"Surviving," he replied with a shrug of his own. "Happy to see you again, though."

"Happy to see you too. I brought you some leftovers."

With a crouch, I held the box out to him. Ignacio's eyes lit up, just like they did every time, and he took it carefully, placing it on his lap like it was precious cargo. Upon opening it, his expression became equal parts delighted and confused.

"You're too good to me, Esmé. I don't know how I'll ever repay you." His words were a bit slurred, and the scent of liquor emanated from his breath, tickling my nose.

I shook my head. "You don't have to. Your kindness is enough."

He sighed, his eyes glistening.

I met Ignacio around the same time I started coming back to *Obsidiana* for my headaches. I knew how dangerous the district could be, so I was used to practicing vigilance. Even so, on that particular day, a strange man tried to mug me. Ignacio heard my screams and knocked the man down, scaring him away. Since then, I have brought him back whatever extra food or money I could give. It was my way of thanking him, but I also knew he had so little. From what he told me, he used to serve in the Sun King's army before *El Rey* was killed. Like many others, Ignacio lost his family and his home and then eventually ended up in Coáraluna with nothing. It broke my heart to think about it, but the fact that he was still alive had to mean something.

"You're an angel," he said. "You know, I think my daughter would've been about your age."

"I wish I could've met her," I whispered, feeling suddenly emotional.

"Me too."

After a brief pause, I said, "Enjoy the food, Ignacio. Have a good night," before straightening up and heading towards Canela's shop.

Like many of the stone buildings in Coáraluna, the rock pattern on the outside was inlaid with chunks of blue stone and raw quartz amid gray. The wooden door bore a wreath with orange slices adorning it in a beautiful pattern.

Upon entering the familiar space, a bell announced my arrival, and I was hit with a mixture of scents that seemed to both welcome and envelop me. Incense, eucalyptus, lavender, sage, and a plethora of other herbs were all too familiar at this point. On many tables were crystals of various sizes, ranging from small, coin-sized ones stacked in a bowl to ones as big as my head. There were candles, multicolored threads, jewelry, ready-to-go potions, and shelves of jars holding anything from animal bones to seashells to dried plants for teas and spells. At a glance, it was overwhelming, but there was a hominess and protectiveness to Canela's shop. Perhaps it had something to do with the magic she wielded, or maybe it was the familiarity of it all.

As always, the altar drew my immediate attention. Rather, it *demanded* it. On a piece of red velvet, among a smattering of black and white candles, was a statue of a beast with three distinct heads—a crow, a snake, and a jaguar in the center. Its eyes were twinkling red rubies, and one of its clawed paws rested on a skull. He had many names, but the one everyone knew him by was Micqui, the God of Death. The statue didn't scare me like it used to, but there was something in its powerful stare that made me feel like it was gazing into my soul.

My belief in the gods, though unwavering, was still quite casual compared to most in Avilonía. I didn't have an altar in my house or pray every day, but I did honor them in smaller ways and have visited the Moon Temple a few times. I was also well-versed in their stories and the realms they ruled over. Most of the gods were fearsome in their own right, but the God of Death instilled a certain level of intensity like no other.

The people of Avilonía had much respect for the dead and were familiar with the afterlife itself, but not many actively worshiped its deity directly. Death was something many took at face value and feared due to the havoc the Black Death wreaked with his necromantic magic. People prayed to gods for guidance, help, or gifts, but to pray to a god of death for anything of the sort was like asking for death itself. Before I met Canela I used to feel the same until I met Canela. Perhaps it was an idea rooted in ignorance, but to have his effigy and to channel him for magic, you either had to be into the dark arts...or you had to be brave.

"Have I ever told you that death is a symbol for change?"

The sudden voice made me jump, and my breath caught in my throat. A woman chuckled, and my attention was drawn to the witch coming down a set of wooden stairs, holding a dried bouquet of lavender. It was none other than *Magistra* Canela, standing in a dark blue dress with embroidered flowers at the neckline. Her black curly hair framed her tawny face like a beautiful lion's mane as she flashed a smile in my direction.

"*Buenas noches*, Canela," I said breathlessly, giving her a soft smile of my own.

"*Buenas noches*, my sweet girl," she sang.

She set the flowers down on the counter and kissed me on the cheek before wrapping me in her embrace. Her hair tickled my nose and smelled of cinnamon—a welcome scent. When she pulled away, she tucked a piece of hair behind my ear.

I frowned. "A symbol for change?"

"Mhmmm." She let go of my shoulders and wandered behind the counter. "People think that death is merely the finite definition of the word, or in Gedeón's case, something to be tampered with. But really, death is just a stepping stone."

I eyed her curiously as I rested my hands on the counter, my fingers brushing the polished surface.

"A stepping stone for what?" I asked warily.

"Transformation. To transform and improve, we must let past versions of ourselves go. Like how farmers scorch the earth to prepare it for the next harvest, or how caterpillars destroy themselves to become butterflies. It's a natural cycle of life. Change, like death, is inevitable. And if you fight it, it will fight harder."

My eyes flitted to the statue of Micqui once more, feeling an odd mixture of trepidation and ease. After all, change was terrifying, and you often didn't have a say in what kind would be served to you.

"Have the headaches continued?" the witch asked suddenly.

I snapped my attention away from the God of Death as my painful reality came rushing back to me. My reply came in the form of a somber nod that had Canela pursing her lips grimly.

"But the potion helps?"

"For as long as I use it, yes," I answered.

Canela sighed, "At least that's something."

She bent down, disappearing for a moment as she continued to speak.

"Are you still seeing that boy?"

Seeing as I had a bad memory, I forgot if I ever mentioned my romantic life to Canela or if she simply sensed it somehow. Either way, she would've found out one way or another, considering she was one of the few people who knew me well, *truly* well. She had seen a lot in her life and knew so much more than I, yet bore no harsh judgment. It was why many flocked to her, including me.

My reaction, however, was the same as it was with Camilo: dreadful. My cheeks burned hot, except this time there was no makeup to hide my flush. I ran my hands over my hair nervously, clinging to it at my shoulders. I thought of those dark eyes and that smile, always at the forefront of my mind, no matter how hard I tried to focus on anything else.

I must have hesitated for a moment too long, because Canela popped up from behind the counter with a skeptical expression.

"Oh…are you not…?"

I released my hair and fidgeted with my ring, saying, "No, it's not that. It's just… it depends on your definition of 'seeing'."

The witch raised an eyebrow. "With your eyes?"

I chuckled. "With my eyes, not that often. He lives up north."

"Ah. Well, have you thought about visiting him?"

If only.

"I *have*… but it's complicated. He's busy," I replied.

"Let's hope that means busy doing business and not 'busy doing other people,' otherwise I'll have to hex him," she sang, flashing a dark smile.

"I'll let you know if I find out. Though I'm not keeping my hopes up," I muttered.

"We can always do a love spell."

I gaped at her. "Canela!"

"I'm kidding! You know, I would never recommend that… to people I care about."

I snorted in response.

Canela then raised her hand with a smile, a small, black bag resting in her palm. I perked up, all thoughts of my romantic life going out the window. From the bag, she pulled out a vial about the size of my palm with a silvery liquid swirling inside. She slid it over to me, and I took the glass bottle in my hands, turning it over seriously. It was a concoction that had a pungent smell and tasted rather bitter, but what mattered to me was that it served its purpose by alleviating my migraines. I took a spoonful a day, every day, indefinitely.

"I had hoped your ailment would be gone by now, but it seems that some maladies don't go away so easily, especially those of the mind," the witch said.

I looked into her eyes, my insides twisting. "Is there nothing else you can give me?"

She shook her head. "As of right now, I've done what I can, but I'll keep looking."

A wave of frustration and exhaustion crashed over me, and I heaved a long sigh. The feelings took root within me long ago, and their vines were growing, wrapping around my bones, weighing me down every day. And that wasn't taking into account the burden in my skull.

Canela put a hand over mine, her long nails painted black and her fingers adorned with rings of different stones.

"You're not the only one, little songbird," she reassured. "I have many people come to my shop who are plagued by addiction and visions of war. Like our friend Ignacio out there. People who come from Old Avilonía, just like you, who were affected by the Sun Killer's magic."

"So the man in the apothecary was right? I sustained some kind of injury at The Rift, and now I'm here?" I fought the urge to whine like a child as the words came out of me.

My friend wavered as if trying to deliver the news gently.

"It could be that... or it could be that you simply came from a land poisoned by dark magic. You do not need to be within touching distance of a demon for it to affect your soul, or, in your case, your head. It affects the water, the earth, and the air, and it is not easily filtered out. Not when the source is still alive. If you saw Old Avilonía now, you would know."

I looked back down at the potion, my frustration now feeling more like a flame that threatened to burn me alive from the inside out. I clenched my teeth to fight back tears.

Unfair.

It seemed so unfair that even though I managed to escape the clutches of the Sun Killer, he somehow still managed to brand me. I and everyone else who wanted to get away.

"Do you think it could get worse?" My voice came out in a broken whisper.

"Maybe, maybe not. As long as you take the potion, you should be fine."

"How long do you think I have to take it?"

When my eyes met *Magistra* Canela's again, her expression full of sorrow, I wanted to cry even more.

"Do you want the truth?" she asked.

I swallowed thickly before answering, "Yes."

"For life... or until the demon is dead."

My lips quivered as tears watered my vision. I looked away once again, towards the statue of Micqui. Though I fought against my emotions, a few tears managed to escape and run down the skin of my cheeks.

Taking a potion wouldn't have been so terrible if it actually worked the way it was meant to, especially when the inverse meant completely falling apart. Each bottle only lasted so long, and the second I ran out, it was a race against time and my mind. Otherwise, the episodes came back in full swing. It was such a burden. *I* felt like such a burden, and the fact that I have done everything I can and it still isn't enough devastated me. Magic could not save me, and even then, the best could not be sacrificed for one girl with bad headaches when there was a war.

As the God of Death's feline face stared back at me, there was a dreary pain in my skull yet again. I've never prayed to the God of Death before, but tonight I did, saying that if change was truly inevitable... then I hoped for my and everyone else's sake that it came with haste.

3

Something In the Water

Río

The glittering city of Coáraluna loomed overhead as the shipping vessel neared the port from the Marisláni Ocean. I leaned against the railing, watching from beneath the hood of my cloak as it grew nearer. The sight of my beautiful island practically made me cry with joy.

Home.

Dark gray clouds circled above the marble palace, but I couldn't tell if it was a natural storm or if it was something else. Surely, I'd find out soon enough.

I owe the gods a big one for the fact that I made it here at all.

I didn't mean to be gone so long. I hadn't planned on it, but much to my chagrin, things turned out more complicated than anyone expected. A day turned into two, which turned into a week. Maybe a little more. Considering I had never been absent for more than a few days, it was a new record, but things were different this time. The stakes of the challenge I took on were monumental, and I was lucky to have come out of it alive. Perhaps I had been a little in over my head, and I'd be lying if I said I wasn't at least a little shaken. I took pride in the fact that few things did that to me. Some might call it arrogance, and maybe they were right this time.

I gripped the ship's edge in shaking anticipation with scratched and bruised knuckles. Though I did my best to disregard the ache in my side, it flared up every time I moved tersely. That and the other minor injuries I sustained would be a lot harder to hide or explain this time around. Even worse was the sound of screaming. They echoed from distant yet vivid memories. The scent of the salty sea air morphed into that of blood, thick with the smell of iron. Darkness, fire, and running. I am running and fighting for my life all over again, and then—

The ocean responded to my turmoil with a gentle spray of seawater against my skin that I quickly wiped away.

I had seen battles from afar, but this was different. Even my father went out of his way to make sure I was alright before I made my return.

It was worth it. It has to be.

My attention went to the obvious heat radiating from my pocket—another thing I was trying to ignore. It was the very reason I went missing in the first place. Perhaps it was a trick of the mind, but I swore what lay within was ready to burn a hole through my clothes and skin. Still, I knew that if I stored it anywhere else, it would be too easy for someone to find it. I just hoped it was concealed enough so I could get it into the right hands.

It's been more than three days. I'm fine.

I let my gaze trail up towards *Castillo* Paricia, and my heart swelled with such intense yearning I thought it might burst. Then my eyes traced down the hill of the city, stopping at the familiar domed building with white pillars. *Teatro Paraiso.*

Esmé.

Her face flashed in my mind for the millionth time over the past few weeks. That brown-eyed girl with the shy smile and beautiful chestnut hair. She was all I'd been able to think about in brief moments of calm. It was funny how that worked—how someone can infiltrate your thoughts even in times of chaos. I held on to the last time we kissed and the sound of her saying my name like a lifeline. I had never craved to touch someone more than I did her.

The ocean sprayed me again, making me chuckle. Before me, the loading dock got closer as we approached the port of Azulí Bay, and my heart beat even faster.

I *wanted* to see her again, yet I couldn't help feeling unbearable guilt. I disappeared for so long and didn't even get a chance to tell her before it happened so suddenly. Then again, how could I? She has no part in what I do. I made sure of that for her own sake, and I was but a fragment in her undoubtedly busy life. Was I a fool to think she waited for me this whole time? She was a gorgeous, talented girl who drew a lot of attention to herself. I shouldn't expect her to wait for me, even if I wanted her to.

Not that she'd like the attention. She's shy.

A smirk pulled at the corner of my lips at the thought.

Still, she was a good friend, if not more. Although now, after everything, I've been focusing a lot on the "more." *Gods, what I would give for that.* Even if my life makes the mere idea nearly impossible, especially now.

Sitting on top of a crate next to me was a bouquet of small blue flowers. I picked them intending to visit her, even if they were a little withered from the journey. All things considered, I should be heading straight back home, but there was a force pulling me elsewhere—a voice in the back of my head saying:

Go find her, you idiot. Tell her you're alright.

I suppose I could make a quick stop before things worsen. It was only fair. What's a little more arrogance? I just hope she can forgive me. I'll find a way to make it up to her.

4

Tide Bender

Esmé

The gondola gently swayed as it made its way back up the hill towards home. The other people in the box with me were two couples who were damp from taking a dip in the ocean. I eyed them with a soft smile before focusing my attention out the window.

As soon as I took my first spoonful of Canela's potion, my migraine immediately abated. The bottle was now in my satchel, wrapped safely in the velvet bag it came in. All that was left was a broad heaviness in my soul. The witch did her best to comfort me before I departed, but our conversation still left me incredibly disheartened. I'd like to think that sleep would be the solution, but that's if my racing mind allowed it.

Everyone exited halfway up the hill at a place called *Distrito Larimar*. After thanking the guard, I split off to the right while the couples went left. Now that it was well past midnight, the streets were a lot quieter, and everything was a lot darker, save for the flaming lampposts illuminating the way.

Emilia Mondragón

Above me, lightning flashed, followed by rumbling thunder. I slowed my pace to look up at the once starry sky, now covered in dark clouds. The rainy season had long since ended, but everyone who lived in Coáraluna was used to the unpredictable weather. It came with the territory of living in a semi-tropical city that was ruled by a storm queen like Victoria Markaél. And while I loved the rain, the last thing I wanted was to be caught in it this late.

I moved at a brisk pace, but about two blocks before my destination, I felt a faint drizzle against my skin. I pulled my shawl over my head, hoping it could provide some cover, but the drizzle turned into droplets, and all at once there was a downpour.

The shrill sound of a cat's meow caught my attention, and I looked up just in time to watch a small black form skitter across the street, a bell jingling in its wake.

I gasped. "Midnight!"

Midnight was a stray cat that lived in my neighborhood. He belonged to everyone and no one, though I had taken the liberty of bringing him into my home most nights. I put a bell around his neck to keep tabs on him at all times and to make sure that no one with a loathing for cats got any ideas. The thought of him being out in the rain by himself made me feel horrid.

Before chasing after him, I searched my bag for a parasol, but of course, I was ruefully unprepared tonight. My shawl was already soaked through, my hair getting damp. The gods, or the queen herself, had it out for me. I clicked my tongue in annoyance and debated making a run for it before a voice cut me short.

"Need an umbrella?"

It was a male voice. My head snapped up, looking around for the source and growing wary when I couldn't find it. I clutched my bag, thinking it was some thief wanting to rob me or worse. But just as I was about to call out, I noticed that the rain had mysteriously stopped.

Rather, it stopped just about a foot above my head. I stared up in complete shock, mouth open, as the droplets fell onto what looked like an invisible dome around me, but continued to pour everywhere else. I inhaled sharply, understanding exactly what it meant. There was only one person I knew who could do such a thing.

A cloaked figure came out of the shadows and into the firelight, approaching me from across the empty street. The rain fell around him in the same fashion, without touching him at all. A dark bundle rested in his arms, and a soft jingle came from it as it licked its paw, but I was more focused on the man himself.

I stood rooted in place, my heart racing, but not in fear. It was something else. An amalgamation of shock, yearning, and anticipation. My fingers tightened around my bag as he stopped an arm's length from me. Midnight continued to lick his fur, unfazed by the human holding him.

"Still taking in strays, I see," the figure said in amusement.

He held the cat out to me, and I blinked a few times before I registered the action. I took the soft feline in my arms, lightly petting his head before trailing my eyes back up to the cloaked man. Even in the dark, I could see the features of his face—a playful grin and dark eyes I knew too well.

"You," I whispered.

"Hey, Esmé."

He reached into his cloak and pulled out a makeshift bouquet of little blue flowers. I raised my eyebrows in surprise, my expression softening. They were beautiful, dainty, and sweet, albeit a little withered. They were also not a plant you could easily find in these parts of the country. I knew because he had picked them up for me before. *Recuerdos*, they were called. Memories. A reminder to never forget the person who gave them to you. I would've picked them out myself regardless of the name, yet it felt incredibly apt, all things considered.

I took them warily, our fingers brushing together, making my heart stutter. I stared at them with fondness, trying to hide my smile, yet they did nothing to alleviate everything I had felt in his absence.

Two weeks. Nearly three.

Of course, I had been counting. This whole time, I was torn between longing, concern, and grief, wondering if I should give up and move on or continue to wait. And now that he was here once more, proving that he hadn't disappeared forever, I had so many burning questions. Though I doubted he'd answer them at all.

"Is this your way of apologizing for being gone for so long?" I asked. There was no venom in my voice, but the query made my emotions clear.

Midnight squirmed in my arms, and I readjusted my hold on him. When I looked back up at the cloaked figure, I could see the remorse in his eyes.

"I know. I'm sorry. I tried writing to you, but got caught up in a mess. I came straight here when I arrived. Can we talk?"

He looked nervous. Even now, I was never entirely convinced it was *I* who made him feel that way. It was hard to deny him when he looked at me like that or when he went out of his way to give me flowers. And it was also hard to deny that I couldn't stop thinking about him every day he was away. Though I may not admit it.

Still, I regarded him for a hesitant moment. No matter how many times we spoke, he made me anxious. It wasn't a cautionary gut feeling. No, he was dangerous in a different way. My mind seemed to scramble in his proximity, and I knew I couldn't say no to him and therefore second-guessed everything. Yet, beneath all of my self-doubt, I knew how undeniably I missed his presence, and now that he was here, something felt right for once.

"Okay. Let's get out of this rain."

＊ ☽ ○ ☾ ＊

Once I was financially stable enough, I was able to afford my apartment in the Larimar District. My place wasn't grand, but it was enough for me and much more than I used to have when I had so little to my name. It was in a two-story building inlaid with blue-green stone that housed a number of living quarters. My neighbors were kind, but they were about as nosy as the average Avilonían, which is why when my *visitor* came around, I had to resort to sneaking.

I rushed inside, releasing Midnight as I kicked off my shoes and threw off my shawl. I swiftly set the flowers down as I made for the bedroom window to unlatch and lift it open. I stepped back, and a moment later, a pair of hands gripped the window sill, and the cloaked figure pulled himself up and into my apartment with a soft groan. My hand flew to my mouth to suppress a laugh.

He smirked at me from beneath his hood.

"I bet you missed that, huh?"

"I think you're out of practice," I remarked, rolling my eyes, but my smile fell when I noticed him clutching his side.

"Are you alright?"

"Yeah, yeah, close the curtains," he urged, sliding the window shut.

With a dubious frown, I rushed around the apartment and pulled all the curtains closed lest any prying eyes get a look inside. The entire time, I could feel his watchful as he followed me around, my heart hammering against my chest. When I whirled around to face him, I nearly gasped.

There, standing in the middle of my living room, with the hood of his cloak now pulled down, was a tall young man not much older than me, with messy hair the color of moonlight. Dark brows sat above his equally dark eyes, and stubble peppered his jaw. He wore leather armor underneath his cloak, and small gold hoops hung from his earlobes.

Príncipe Río Maximiliano Markaél. The Moon Prince.

Not even that long into our reunion, and I was already flustered because he—The Moon Prince of Avilonía—was *smiling* at *me*.

In a long breath of silence, we both took each other in for the first time in weeks, with unspoken words stretching between us. I had no clue where to start or how to put words to my feelings, but did not need to when I noticed a cut above his left eyebrow. His knuckles were scraped up as well.

"What happened?" I asked with a frown.

"What? Oh, this?" he said, motioning to the injury. "It's nothing. I'm fine."

My mouth twisted in discontent. Despite the plethora of inquiries sitting at the tip of my tongue, I knew I couldn't ask them. It was part of this unspoken agreement between us, and if I *did* ask, he always told me it was of no concern. It was "business of the crown," and I was nowhere near that level of authority to even hear whispers of what *Príncipe* Río was up to. Whatever it was, he got his hands dirty pretty often for a royal.

"Are you sure about that, *Alteza*?"

When he caught me eyeing his side, he shook his head and took slow steps towards me.

"Please don't—"

He hissed mid-sentence, clutching his side once more. With wide eyes, I rushed to his side but did not touch him. He lifted his head to meet my eyes with his own.

"Please, call me Río," he stressed for what seemed like the thousandth time now.

I pursed my lips but dropped the subject.

"Actually, I think I might need those magical hands of yours because I may or may not have torn my stitches getting here," he said with a chuckle.

I scoffed, "Stitches? Oh, Gods, take a seat, please."

Leaving the prince behind, I rushed to the washroom to fetch a box containing what I often used for occasions like this: needles, thread, ointments, and gauze. This was yet another reason why I visited *Obsidiana* as often as I did. Ever since I became acquainted with the Moon Prince, I have found myself needing to restock my first aid kit more often than not. As long as I reassured Canela that it wasn't for me, she didn't badger me about the whole ordeal.

We met at *Teatro Paraiso* earlier in the spring, after a performance for *Príncipe* Río's birthday. He and the entire royal family were in attendance, and I vividly recall it being one of the most exciting shows I had ever done. Teo was especially extravagant with the visuals so that the princess, who was deaf, could enjoy the show. The Markaél's requested to meet both Teo and me afterward, which was the highest honor I had ever received in my career. They complimented my talent, telling me that they looked forward to seeing me again. It was such a whirlwind, and I almost would have thought it was all in my head if proof of that night wasn't with me now.

Nothing in the world could have prepared me for *Príncipe* Río Markaél. He was the son of the Moon King and the Queen of Storms, and his personality lived up to his name. Playful, sarcastic, charming, and intimidating all in one. When our gazes met for the first time and he kissed my hand, his eyes seemed to swallow me whole, and I couldn't ignore the spark I felt within me. An *intrigue*. I blamed it on the fact that he was a prince and that was all, and sometimes I still do.

I thought nothing of it until we ran into each other at the Obsidian District. I didn't recognize him in his cloak and leather attire at first, but somehow he recognized *me*. What he was doing there, I didn't know, but he revealed his identity and told me he had seen me at Canela's shop before. Without hesitation, he offered to pay for the gondola and accompany me back home. Once I managed to process my complete and utter shock, I offered to treat the scratch on his arm in exchange. One thing led to another, things escalated, and now I had a prince following me around like a lost puppy.

But who am I to complain?

When I returned with my supplies, the prince was sitting at my kitchen table with nothing but his pants on, completely shirtless except for some bandaging around his torso. My breath hitched as my eyes roved over his muscular body, and when he caught me staring, a smirk played on his lips. I tore my eyes away, my face and body blazing as I focused on the task at hand.

"How's Canela?" he asked.

I was grateful for his ability to fill the tense silence, because I struggled with my words when I was so electrified in his presence.

"She's great. As always." I walked up to him and pointed to the bandage. "May I?"

He straightened up and nodded. "Yes, of course."

I sat across from him and unwrapped the bloody dressing. All the while I tried to ignore our proximity, the way it made me feel, or the other nights it reminded me of. The sensation of his eyes boring into my face made it worse, but as I pulled away the remainder of the bandage, I became too preoccupied with the large gash on the side of his ribs.

Everything I ever patched up for the prince seemed like mere scratches in comparison to the wound before me. It was clear that a large blade caused it, and he was lucky to be breathing at all. Some of its stitches were torn, and the wound was bleeding once again. And despite how scared I was to find out how deep it was, I would surely see in a few moments.

I gaped at him in horror.

"Don't worry about it," he said, shaking his head.

With anger flaring in my chest, I put the gauze down, grabbed a small pair of scissors, and started cutting at the stitches with care.

"You always say that," I muttered, "but not all wounds can be fixed, *Alteza*."

Despite my polite tone, my irritation still bled through. For some reason, he never seemed to mind.

"Río," he repeated.

Again, I didn't say it.

"I still don't know why you keep coming here instead of getting healed in the castle," I told him.

I'm sure *Castillo* Paricia had far better resources than I did.

He hummed. "But then I wouldn't get to see you."

My heartbeat skipped a beat, and I had to pause lest I cut a piece of his skin.

"Now, you're just saying things," I whispered.

"I'm really not. I mean, I am, but it's not anything I don't mean."

When I finished removing the old thread, I cleaned the wound and prepared the needle and thread to close it again.

"How are your headaches?" he asked.

A heavy sigh fell from my lips as that disappointment from earlier returned.

"Still there, unfortunately," I replied.

"Have they improved?"

"As much as they ever will."

With a brief warning, I pierced the needle through his skin. I always expected some sort of dramatic reaction, but all I ever received was a grimace or a hiss. I often wondered if he was made of metal, because I had seen men cry about much less. The prince, however, never complained.

Somehow, he was also the only person who knew about my business with Canela. It seemed only fair to tell him after he found me in *Obsidiana* and showed me who he was. He's witnessed a few of my embarrassing episodes himself. And while he never interrogated me over such things, he did reveal his worry now and then.

"Maybe I can help," he urged. "We have a wizard at the palace who might know something."

I looked up from my work and to fix him with my own version of a stern look, as this wasn't the first time he said something like this.

"I appreciate it, *Alteza*, but no, thank you."

"Why not?" he asked indignantly.

"I don't need you or your family wasting time on my silly little problems. I can manage on my own."

When I finished closing up his wound, I put down the needle and grabbed a jar of paste made of herbs. I smeared some of it over the wound and wrapped a new piece of gauze around his torso. The prince argued with me the entire time.

"You always help me, Esmé. It's only fair that I help you."

"I have my medicine. I can help myself just fine. There's nothing more to be done," I contested.

Without looking at him, I packed up the first aid kit, threw away the old gauze and stitches, and washed my hands in the kitchen sink. Again, I could feel him lingering behind me the whole time. It would've been suffocating if it wasn't oddly comforting.

Perhaps it was stupid of me to deny the prince's help, but it didn't feel right to waste such precious resources, even if I was grateful for the offer. And after what Canela said, I didn't think I could afford to have any more hope that might be ripped away. I had gone so long trying to figure out what was wrong with me and how to fix it, and I was simply exhausted. There was nothing to fix, only live with, and talking about it was a little too painful at the moment.

When I turned back around, the prince was leaning against the kitchen doorway, still shirtless, his eyes trained on me. I had to look down at my hands lest my heart implode.

"I am sorry for being gone for so long," he uttered softly. His voice was like a warm fire, its heat washing over me and beckoning me towards him.

I fiddled with my ring as that tense silence returned. Thoughts cycled through my head like a swarm of bees, but whenever I tried to speak them, my mouth did not move. My words and feelings were caught in the back of my throat, their weight a pressure on my chest.

"Why are you here?" I asked finally.

He smirked and shrugged one shoulder. "I wanted to see you. I said, I wanted to talk."

No matter how sweet it sounded, I wasn't entirely certain how truthful he was being. Boys and men said things all the time that weren't true.

"Did you really?" I asked in a small voice.

He frowned at that, the playfulness leaving his eyes.

"Of course I did."

I gave him a shrug of my own before the words started tumbling out, "I don't know. I guess it's hard to believe when you disappear so often and then don't come back for long periods of time. I was starting to think you'd grown bored of me, which I would've expected. To be honest, I'm surprised you came back at all."

The prince blinked a few times, taken aback. "You think I'm that kind of guy?"

I don't know. I think it's too good to be true. How do I know the man beneath the cloak is real?

I stood a little straighter, looking at him seriously. "I think, *Alteza*, that you have power, and there's no desire you can't easily get your hands on. Who's to say you don't have other people waiting for you in other parts of the country? Or even the city?"

He laughed in dismay. It was a sound that gave me butterflies, but also confused me at the moment.

"I don't know if I should be flattered or offended, but if it makes you feel better, that's not true at all. I don't have the energy for that. Also, *please* call me Río. Or call me Max if it's more comfortable."

"Why?"

"Well, it's a shortened version of my middle name—"

"No, I mean, why do you insist on my calling you by your given name?"

The first few times we spoke, all I could do was call him "*Alteza*." It was how everyone addressed royalty. However, the Moon Prince very adamantly wanted me to call him by his name. I did my best to avoid it entirely when able. In a way, it kept me from getting hurt, because saying it made everything between us more real and complicated. After all, there was power in a name.

At first, he hesitated, and in that breath, I thought all my fears might come true.

"Because I like you. A lot," the prince answered.

My eyes widened a fraction as he went on.

"I don't blame you for thinking that about me, Esmé. I haven't exactly been open about my life, and I know people like to talk. Some people in power like collecting others for their pleasure, but not me. I'm embarrassingly monogamous, contrary to what others might think."

There were many rumors surrounding the prince and his family. They were told by those who loved them, hated them, wanted to be them, or some mixture of the three. It was easy to get carried away by hearsay when you didn't know any better, but it was different when you knew *Príncipe* Río personally.

A giggle bubbled in my throat. "'Embarrassingly monogamous'?"

The prince smiled. "Yes, it's a heavy burden for a prince, really."

"I bet."

The phrase equal parts amused and endeared me. It whittled away at my shell just a little more.

"Well, if it makes *you* feel better," I said carefully, "I don't let rumors sway my judgment if I can help it."

He stared at me wistfully. It made my breath catch. We both watched each other from across my kitchen, neither of us saying anything for a moment. But the thing about *Príncipe* Río Markaél was that he didn't break eye contact so easily, even when I wrestled with it so much. It was enough to make me squirm until I tore my eyes away.

"Can I kiss you?"

He uttered the question in a steady yet gentle voice, and that tone alone was enough to make me falter. His eyes were full of sincerity and longing, making me melt.

One of the traits I liked about the Moon Prince was that he kept his distance. He never touched me without asking, or if I didn't want him to, even if I usually did in the end. We *had* kissed before, and maybe a little more, but there were days when we didn't do anything like that at all. And right now, as he asked that question, I could see that perhaps I *was* wrong. Maybe he did miss me as much as I missed him.

Every emotion I fought hard to contain behind politeness and poise broke free from its box.

"Please," I whispered.

With my confirmation, the prince pushed himself away from the doorframe and closed the distance between us. He took my face in his warm hands, letting our eyes meet briefly before crashing his mouth against mine. I sighed as he parted my lips and brushed his tongue with mine. Every fiber of my being sang with the taste of him and the feeling of his very touch. I pushed myself to my toes, clinging to him greedily, wanting him closer. There was so much hunger in his kiss, as if he had been craving me as much as I craved him. It was toe-curling, sending a wave of heat through me.

No matter how much I pretended, I knew I *wanted* him. I've desired his kiss for days—*weeks* since he was gone. I missed his firm yet tender touch, his warm breath on my skin, and his dark eyes consuming me with their depth. He unlocked something within me that nothing else quite did, and it was a dangerous addiction.

We only pulled away when we were out of breath, and the prince rested his forehead against mine.

"I fantasized about that," he panted, "every day."

I giggled in response, utterly dazed.

His hands touched my face, then my shoulders and waist, as if unsure where to rest his hands. That nervous energy returned, but he didn't back away, and neither did I.

"Do you…" He began hesitantly, but then willed some stability back in his voice. "What would you like me to do?"

I frowned. "What do you mean?"

"Do you want me to leave? Do you want me to stay? Do you want me to kiss you again? Do you want me to do more? *What do you want*, Esmé? Whatever it takes to make it up to you. I'll do anything you want."

The sound of my name coming from his mouth sent a shiver down my spine, but the urgency in his voice caught me off guard. It was new for him.

"You don't have to—"

"Esmé," he said, pushing a piece of my hair behind my ear. "*What do you want?*"

He was being so gracious that I fought against the internal need to please that threatened to hold me back, and I said the first true words that came to the top of my head.

"I want you to stay. Even if it's just for a little while longer."

His face softened. "Okay. I promise."

"And Río?"

His eyes flashed at the sound of his name. "Yes?"

"I want you to kiss me again."

With a grin, he obliged, and I allowed myself to get lost in his lips.

This was forbidden. I knew that. It was frightening, yet when the prince was here, it didn't matter. None of my fears did. All I knew was that he was here. He came to me and offered himself on a silver platter. He was *mine* for the night.

His hands skittered against my waist and hips as he kissed my lips, my cheeks, and my jaw. I moaned in response, already too far gone.

"Keep kissing me," I whispered against his ear. "Don't stop kissing me. Kiss me everywhere."

I let the desire seep into my words.

"Happily," he replied.

Río maneuvered me towards the bedroom. He planted wet, hot kisses against my neck, palming my breast through my blouse, and I was putty in his hands. Though he was a man of the moon and could bend water at will, he made me feel ablaze. We stripped each other of our clothes, leaving them scattered like leaves in autumn. And he kissed me. He kissed down to my thighs and then between my legs until I found myself unable to say anything but his name. And then he crawled towards me until I was pinned beneath his body, only stopping to let his eyes linger on my face. To my dismay, a tormented emotion lay within them.

"Are you alright?" I asked.

He blinked a few times, shaking his head. "Yeah. Yeah, you're just… you're so beautiful."

I wasn't entirely convinced, but any thoughts faded away with his lips. Then he was inside me, stretching me and fucking me into the mattress as I clung to him for dear life.

No headaches. No shadows. No burdens.

For now.

5

The Black Diamond

Esmé

"I'm surprised you didn't rip your stitches again. Didn't that hurt?"

After noticing some blood had seeped through the bandage, I double-checked the wound, but to my wonder, it was completely fine.

"Eh, it was worth it," Río said.

I snorted in reply.

The prince cleaned us up and brought some glasses of water from the kitchen. His familiarity with my apartment warmed my heart a little bit, almost as much as his attempt at making *chocolate caliente*. Somehow, he managed to burn the milk, and I had trouble holding back laughter. It seemed that the God-given did have their limits (in the form of warm beverages), and it was endearing how much he blushed over it. With Midnight curled up next to us, we drank our hot chocolate (that

I made) and ate ginger cookies on the bed with barely anything on until the mugs were empty.

It was so domestic, it almost seemed normal, and in that space of time, I thought this *could* be normal. There were no titles or lack thereof; there was no chasm between the classes we were born in, no secrets, no duty, and no image to uphold. But in the end, that seemingly impenetrable bubble burst when the inevitable moment came when *Príncipe* Río had to go. Because this apartment was *not* the palace on the hill.

While he started getting dressed, I sat at the end of the bed, mindlessly braiding my hair as I cast secretive glances at him. He may have been a prince, but he was every bit a trained fighter. From what he told me, not only was he proficient in water magic, but he was also an expert swordsman. The cut of his muscles reminded me of the multi-faceted crystals in Canela's shop, and the few scars against his skin were natural imperfections that added to his beauty. I had a hand in stitching a number of them, and seeing them stirred something in me. He was tanner from his time overseas, making his pearlescent white hair stand out more. Most of the people of Avilonía had varying shades of bronzed skin and dark hair, but the God-given always stood out with their bright-colored locks. It was so magnificent to me, as if witnessing the living embodiment of magic.

As if sensing my staring, his eyes flitted to mine. I averted my gaze, which was ironic considering what we had just done.

He chuckled. "You drive me crazy when you do that."

"Do what?" I asked innocently.

"Look at me like that and then get all shy. You make a guy like me have *very* dirty thoughts."

I scoffed, "Well, I don't do it on purpose." *But maybe I should.* "Perhaps you should get your mind out of the gutter, hmm, *Alteza?*"

I tied off my hair and threw it over my shoulder as I raised my eyebrows at him.

The prince snorted, stalking over to me. "Perhaps."

He leaned down so his nose grazed mine, and he took my chin with a light touch. If I had been standing up, my knees would have surely buckled. He kissed me softly, and I grabbed the collar of his shirt, keeping him there for a moment. I half-expected him to do something more, but I knew better. He already kept his promise by staying longer than usual. And when he broke the kiss with a sudden sadness in his eyes, I already knew what he was about to say.

"I have to go."

"I know," I whispered, dropping my hand.

I looked down at my palms and twisted the malachite ring, trying to distract myself from my stupid disillusionment. The sudden swell of emotions flooding my chest and tears springing to my eyes worsened my foolishness. As if sensing this, Midnight jumped on the bed and crawled onto my lap. I stroked his fur dejectedly as the prince continued to hover.

"Hey," he called to me, barely above a whisper.

I said nothing, nor did I meet his eyes, scared I would break. When I didn't respond, he crouched down before me, finding my gaze. He put his hand over mine.

"Esmé."

When he noticed my expression, his face went grim. He shook his head, brushing his fingers over my cheek.

"Don't look so sad. I'll be back, I promise."

"Will you?" I asked in a small voice, but then backtracked. "I mean, I know you will, but I guess it's a matter of when, isn't it?"

"This time was different. I won't be gone that long again. Not without telling you or making sure to reach out somehow. I'll use magic if I have to."

"But even if you do come back, what does it even mean?" I blurted out.

The prince furrowed his brow, and to be quite honest, I surprised even myself. I could've snapped my mouth shut like I always did, but then I remembered what Camilo had said back at the theater. About drawn-out, unnecessary pain. Now that I had come down from the high of my night with the Moon Prince, reality was much clearer to me, and with the weight of the world, my ailment, and this situation, the room was suddenly too small.

I took the prince's hand away from my cheek and pushed myself off the bed to get some space. Midnight jumped off of me and scurried to the living room. I went by the window before turning back around to face the prince, who was watching me with bewilderment. My heart was beating like a hummingbird's wings, and things poured out of my mouth like never before.

"*Príncipe* Río, you have been lovely, more than lovely, but I am so confused," I started. "I don't know what we are or what I can even be for you, considering who you are. You come in here at night, sometimes bleeding and bruised. You bring me flowers and fruit and say such sweet things, and then you leave without saying when you'll be back. I enjoy your presence, but... I don't know how to feel."

I gestured with my hands as I rambled, pacing back and forth.

"You know, some people fantasize about meeting a handsome prince or princess and getting swept away to a beautiful castle, but prince or not, do you know what they imagine?" I asked, stopping to look at him expectantly.

Río stared at me from the edge of the bed, wide-eyed, and simply shook his head. I answered for him.

"Courtship! Courtship and being wooed. We imagine dates, flowers, dancing, and pretty dresses. Sunshine, love notes, and marriage." I spouted it all until I had no breath left. With a deep inhale,

I went on with more calm, "And though I don't expect those things from you at all, you've done…*some* of those things…and I don't mind…well…everything else…"

I trailed off apprehensively, somehow unable to politely name our nightly trysts.

"Mhmmm…" he hummed with a smirk.

I rolled my eyes at his expression, but my next statements filled me with dread to say.

"But to be honest—and please forgive me for saying this—if this is all it's going to be, then I don't think we should be seeing each other anymore. I don't know if I can handle the pressure of being a secret, and I don't know if I *want* to be a secret. It feels uncomfortable and like you don't actually care about me, and I don't take delight in being used, no matter who you are."

I put my hands over my face, my voice coming out muffled as I continued, "And I've tried keeping my expectations realistic, but you make it so hard—"

"Esmé."

"Hmm?"

"*Esmé.*"

Río's hands gently wrapped around my wrists, and I gasped. I hadn't even heard him make a move towards me, having been lost in my maunderings. He pulled my hands away from my face with an expression of utter bewilderment, though there was always a faint smirk on his lips. I turned bright red, suddenly awash with embarrassment.

"Oh…no. I don't know what came over me. I'm so sorry. That was so stupid."

"No, *no*, not stupid at all." He shook his head with a chuckle. "That was probably the most I've heard you talk the whole time I've known you."

I gave him a strange look. "You're not angry?"

"No, of course not. Why would I be angry?"

"I... I don't know," I stammered, my shoulders falling.

Río regarded me curiously, as if debating whether or not to go on a tangent and press the issue, but didn't.

"If either of us should be angry at anyone, it's *me*," he said seriously. "Esmé, I didn't know you felt that way. I didn't mean to make you feel like I didn't care or like I was using you. I would never, *ever*, do that. It's the opposite. I wouldn't..."

He closed his eyes and sighed, running his hands over his face in exasperation. When he looked at me again, he took my hands in his, stupefying me with his demeanor.

"Esmé, you deserve the fucking *world*," he said. "I've been a fucking idiot, which wouldn't be the first time. But the truth is..." He looked down for a moment before gazing into my eyes and saying, "I think about you all the time."

My face softened at that.

"I come here even when I'm not injured because I like seeing you," he said. "I'd probably injure myself more often if it meant you would stitch me up again."

"Please don't."

He laughed. "I won't. But I *do* care about you, and I want to keep seeing you when I can. My life is way too complicated, and you're the one thing that's not, even if you don't think that's true. That's why I don't want to make *your* life more complicated than it already is. But if ending this would make you feel better, then...so be it, I guess."

The prince choked on his final words, as if it hurt to utter them out loud. Even I felt my heart on the verge of breaking at the mere thought of never seeing him again. I wish I could take back everything I said, turn back time until we were lying in bed again, and then freeze the moment forever. My rotten mouth got me here.

"But if you gave me one more chance, I could make it up to you," he added urgently.

He cupped the side of my face, his eyes alight with desperation, and I felt some relief in knowing he didn't want to walk away either.

I nodded vigorously, saying, "Okay."

The prince sighed, his lips spreading out into a boyish smile that moved my heart. He glanced around, as if searching for something, and I watched him warily as he reached into the collar of his shirt. From it, he pulled out a necklace and slipped it over his head. It had a crescent moon made of aquamarine, with a small silver star hanging from the bottom.

"Take this," he said.

"What? Why?"

In all my time of knowing him, he never took off, which was why it was a shock that he was doing so now.

"This means a great deal to me. More than you know. So, if I give it to you, then I have to come back for it, don't I?" he explained cheekily. "It's a promise... and collateral."

Before I could protest, the prince slipped the chain over my head and let the aquamarine fall over my heart. I was at a complete loss for words, and all I could do was take the charm in my hands and marvel at its beauty.

"I don't know whether to think you're insane or admirable," I told him.

The corners of his lips turned down as he nodded. "That about describes my entire personality, I think. But it's a promise that, *even when you don't need my help*, I'll always be here. I'll always come back."

I glowered at his poignant words and then pushed myself on my toes to kiss his cheek. He then turned his head to kiss me softly on the lips.

As the prince went off into the washroom, I stared down at the crescent moon, still in disbelief that it was in my possession. I ran my finger over it with a smile before tucking it into my nightdress and heading off towards the living room.

I picked up the flowers that Río gave me and went into the kitchen to put them in a small vase of water. And as I set them down on the table, I spotted his satchel and cloak crumpled on the floor. With an amused huff, I went over to pick them up, and there was a clatter on the floor. I searched around with a confused frown and saw that a small wooden box had fallen out. It was engraved with a filigree pattern and had a red velvet interior that was now wide open. Right beside it was a strange item wrapped in a white handkerchief.

I set Río's clothes on the back of a chair and crouched down to take the box in my hands. As my hand hovered over the wrapped item, I paused, sensing a wave of *warmth*. It was odd, making the tips of my fingers tingle. Though wary, I scooped it up anyway, and when I held it in my hand, I could see the facets of a perfectly cut black diamond nestled in the fabric. Dizziness overcame me. And as I beheld the mysterious stone, a sudden *urge* settled inside, telling me to touch it. It was strong yet so natural that I didn't think it was much outside of normal curiosity. It just looked so gorgeous—the way it seemed to have a red pulse in its center, like a heart.

Putting the box on the floor, my fingers reached out, wanting to feel it against my skin, when Midnight scurried across my feet with a hiss.

No!

"Don't!"

Río's voice was strong enough to break me out of my trance with a jolt. The diamond fell out of my hands, clattering violently to the floor. I spun towards the prince, who was by my side in seconds. His hands went to my face, my hands, and then my face again, his eyes wide with terror. His expression alone was enough to instill fear in me.

"Di-Did you touch it? Are you okay?" he demanded.

"No, I didn't touch it. I swear," I stammered, shaking my head.

"Are you sure? How do you feel?"

"Yes, I feel fine," I argued, pushing myself away from his suffocating grasp. "What is that?"

Río grabbed the handkerchief from the floor and meticulously picked up the black diamond without touching it. He then wrapped it back up and placed it in the box before stuffing it in the satchel, which he secured on his hip.

"It's a cursed item," he muttered. "You shouldn't be near it."

"A cursed item?" I exclaimed. He shushed me, making me scowl. "Is that what you disappeared for?"

"Yes."

"And you're just carrying it around like it's nothing?"

"I can't trust anyone else with it, clearly," he snapped.

I craned my head back. "Well, how was I supposed to know? You're the one who brought it here."

The prince sighed, "I plan on destroying it with the proper magic. Which I personally don't have."

He finished putting on his clothes and then wrapped his cloak around his shoulders, tying it around his neck. All I could do was watch him in complete astonishment.

"Now, if you'll excuse me, I have business to attend to," he said.

I felt myself shrink at his sudden coldness and hugged myself as he headed back towards the bedroom window, slowly following but doing nothing to stop him. I clenched my jaw as a lump formed in my throat.

Río pulled up his hood and lifted the window open, then suddenly froze. He peered over his shoulder at me, and as soon as he saw my expression, his shoulders drooped.

"Shit."

The prince strode back toward me, heavy boots on the hardwood floor. I gasped as he grabbed my waist and gave me one last gentle kiss on the lips.

"I'm sorry. I'll be back," he said, softer now.

He motioned to the necklace, and then, with a kiss to my forehead, went out the window and disappeared into the night.

As I stared after him, a single tear ran down my cheek. I wiped it away, taking out the chain he gave me and holding the aquamarine in comfort. In a whirlwind of events, Río Markaél managed to reassure me and confuse me all in one night, and now all I wanted to do was rest.

And in those moments before sleep, I thought about the cursed item and what the prince had asked me. As far as I could tell, I didn't feel anything different. The heat and the urge to touch it were gone, and everything was seemingly normal. Yet in that place between dreaming and waking, there was a distant sound in the back of my skull. It was faint but present, like the sound of glass cracking ever so slightly.

6

The Oncoming Storm

Río

I feel like such an asshole.

I know Esmé didn't mean to touch the stone. If anything, it was my fault for having it on me in the first place when I went to see her. I don't know what I would do if something happened to her because of me, but I'm glad she's alright. Or at least she *seemed* to be.

I've dealt with magic my whole life and the only darkness I felt was from the stone itself. There was no malevolence in her eyes, only confusion. Even worse was the gut-wrenching expression on her face right before I left. It wasn't like me to snap at her the way that I did. I was just scared and angry at myself.

That fucking stone.

It was too powerful in the wrong hands, no matter how good their heart was. Even one like hers, as unnerving it was to think about. All I knew was that I had to get it away from her as fast as possible.

With my magic to shield me from the rain, I crept around the streets of Coáraluna, using the downpour and darkness to remain as invisible as possible. I made my way up the slope of the hill using the many passageways that I knew by memory.

Many tunnels ran through the hillside that were used for supply, military, and royal transport. There were also secondary and tertiary tunnel systems underground—one was in case of emergency, and the other, in my instance, was for sneaking in and out of the castle. Only select people knew about the latter, and the way to access the entrance was by following the canals that ran through the city.

The canals carried fresh water from a series of aqueducts that led from Lake Cisné. Using a filtration system, they supplied usable water for our people in Coáraluna as well as the surrounding cities and farmlands. They, of course, came in handy for a God-given such as myself should a crisis arise. It's never come down to it, but with our history and the current war raging on, it was better to be safe than sorry.

Making sure I wasn't being followed, I walked alongside one of the canals in the Arts District until I was well past the neighborhoods and into the natural greenery of the island. I pushed through a canopy of trees to find the mouth of a smaller tunnel, where the water rushed out. With one more sweeping glance to confirm I was alone, I lifted my hands and connected to the current. It was second nature at this point, as if operating another limb. I could feel its familiar vibrating energy in my fingertips, palms, and arms. My dark eyes took on a stormy sapphire glow as the water parted before me, revealing the stone bottom. I carefully stepped down, reaching into my satchel to take out a long chain with a teardrop moonstone.

I held it to my lips and whispered, "*Luz*."

With a hum, it came to life in my fingers, now emanating a bright white light. Using it to illuminate the way, I began my journey into the hill, creating a path in the water as I went.

THE MOON PRINCE

✳ ☽ ○ ☾ ✳

Eventually, the tunnel opened wider, leading me to the mouth of an arched stone pathway with burning sconces. Stepping out of the canal, I let my influence on the water drop and continue its natural flow. With my eyes on the darkness beyond, I pulled down my hood, running my hands through my hair. A soft breeze whistled by along with the sound of drizzling rain. Moonstone in hand, I walked down until I was out in the open, amid the dark greenery of a small valley. Then, with the rain still at bay, I looked up.

Above was the silhouette of *Castillo* Paricia, a behemoth made of marble, towering over me from the top of the island. It was once a place I found too suffocating, but recently missed it. I often did, but there was something about nearly dying that made me feel, for the first time in a long time, *relieved* to be home.

I raised the teardrop light, closed my eyes, and rubbed it twice between my fingers. When I opened them again, I stared at the stone in anticipation. A breath later, the light flashed twice in response, giving off a soft hum. I sighed, an equal sense of joy and melancholy filling me.

Ela. She's probably furious.

There was a set of stone stairs carved into the side of the hill that I used to make my ascent. The aching wound at my side made the journey more laborious, but with Esmé's help, I at least felt better than before. My heart was pounding, but that had less to do with my injury and more to do with the nerves that rattled my bones with each step. My return was different this time, and it could mean anything.

Though I am the Moon Prince, I wasn't always able to live my life the way I do now. In fact, I have less influence or power than I would like. While I adored my mother, she ruled with an iron fist, and ever since my father left for the war front some years ago, everything has been thrown off balance. Knowing what I do, I didn't blame her, but I ultimately grew tired of all the rules and restrictions to the point where I'd leave the castle in the middle of the night. It started as something stupid and fun—a means of escape to pretend I wasn't myself—which turned into getting involved with the cause.

It was my father who pushed me in that direction. On one of his visits, he caught me in the middle of an escapade. Without telling my mother, he pulled me aside, and we had a long conversation. I told him that being holed up in the castle made me feel useless and that I had every right to leave when I desired. I wanted to be my own person. I wanted to prove myself. And instead of berating me, my father told me that if I was so restless, then I should put the energy to good use.

It started as short visits to The Rift. I'd spend a few days at a time with my father showing me around a warship and teaching me about strategy. But on my mother's request, I was never allowed anywhere near Old Avilonía itself. It was too dangerous, and putting half the family in harm's way was too high a risk. So, alternately, my father had me focus on sleuthing and infiltration. Whether it meant going to the kingdom's edge to listen for anything of value, keeping tabs on allies, or sneaking onto enemy supply ships and blowing them up. All I had to do was get in, do what I needed to do, and get out.

It was never an impossible task, and save for a few altercations, I returned with my life. It was a source of worry for everyone around me, but I knew what I was doing. They didn't understand. My entire youth, I've only ever been the Moon Prince, son of the Moon King and the Queen of Storms. My future was sealed from the moment I was born. There was nothing more thrilling and freeing than getting to defy every part of that image by pretending not to be me and doing something other than being a royal, something *worthwhile.*

We were warriors before all of this, so why can't I?

My mother says that my father and I are the same way in that regard. Perhaps that's why it was only a matter of time before our ambitions got the best of us.

At the top of the stairs, I arrived at a tangle of trees behind the castle wall. There was no paved trail, but it was very clear that many had walked through here before and carved a path with their feet. I followed it until I came upon a part of the marble exterior that was covered in a curtain of ivy. Still using my light, I felt around the surface with my hands until I found a space that was hollowed out. Behind the vines was a wooden door, barely visible in the dark unless you were looking for it. With a deep breath, I rubbed the pendant once more. Three times this time. Except instead of receiving a response, there was barking. The lock on the door clicked before swinging inward.

A large black dog nearly knocked me off my feet. It got on its hind legs and pawed at my chest, whining and licking my chin. I scrunched up my face and laughed through the pain shooting up my abdomen as I patted his head and tried defending myself against the aggressive affection.

"Echo! Hey, boy!"

I got down on one knee to give him a proper hug, running my hands over his slick fur as I muttered incoherent baby-talk praises. He was a large hound that could easily bite someone's face off, but his mouth was currently spread out in a happy grin, his tongue hanging out as his tail wagged back and forth. I was so distracted by him that I almost didn't notice the person standing in the doorway.

Almost.

My eyes lit up at the sight of my little sister, *Princesa* Mariela Markaél. Ela for short. She was four years younger than I and looked more like our mother every day, save for the moon-touched hair.

Ela hugged a robe against herself with tears in her eyes, her hair tied up loosely behind her head. I warily got up to my feet and stepped around the dog with my hand out. Before I could say anything, she rushed forward and threw her arms around my shoulders. I caught her with a pained chuckle, stumbling a little from the sudden weight.

Gods, I hope that didn't tear my stitches.

We held onto each other for a long moment, our magic protecting us from the rain, before she let go and dropped to her feet. Her face fell into a glare right as she punched me in the arm, marking the endearing moment over.

"Ow!" I hissed, throwing her a questioning look.

Using her hands, she scolded me in sign language. Though she didn't speak, she was still very loud.

"Where have you been?" she demanded. "It's been weeks! I thought you were dead!"

I grimaced before signing my response back to her, "I'm sorry. I thought Dad would call you guys."

One of the ways we communicated over long distances was by using a frosted mirror. One of them was in our war room, while the other was on our father's ship.

"He did, but he was pretty vague about it. And he also didn't say you'd be gone so long!" she replied.

"This mission was harder than I thought, alright? Again, I'm sorry."

She raised her hands quizzically. "Where did you go? Where did Dad send you?"

Ela's dark eyes scanned my face, briefly catching on the cut above my brow. She then glanced towards my hip, where Echo was nosing at my satchel with a growl, as if already sensing what it held. I put my hand over it and gently shooed him away. My sister tapped me on the shoulder, drawing my attention back to her.

"Río?"

I hesitated, scared of telling her the truth and knowing how she would respond. But I knew I couldn't hide it from her. I didn't want to.

"Past The Rift," I said.

Her jaw dropped.

"Past The Rift?" she repeated more aggressively. "As in, Old Avilonía?"

I gave another confirming nod. A strangled noise came out of her as she gaped at me. I was getting a lot of those looks today.

The only outsiders who ever stepped foot in Old Avilonía were aligned with the Sun Killer or those fighting at The Rift. Everyone else was forbidden, and for obvious reasons, people never wanted to go in the first place. It was polluted with dark magic, and nobody wanted to risk falling back into the hands of Sebastián Eliódor. As of late, I was the first in a long time to go *past* The Rift willingly. Granted, I didn't get very far inland. The black diamond I stole was in a small fort by the southern coast, covered in dense fog. But the mission wasn't without sacrifices. The reminder made me sick to my stomach.

My sister signed more frantically now, "How are you still alive? Are you okay? What did you even go there for?"

As I was about to answer, I heard a voice I knew all too well.

"Is that you, Río Maximiliano?"

There was a crack of thunder, and I stiffened at the sound of my name. Ela and I both looked back through the door, towards a figure standing in the dimly lit courtyard. With a wary glance at my sister, I stepped past her and into the castle grounds. Only then did the figure become clear to me.

My mother. Victoria Markaél Vórtice, the Queen of Storms.

She stood before the stables, the rain having stopped. Her lilac hair was tied in a braid with bits of gray striping through it, falling down her purple robe. Two guards flanked her on either side, though

I hardly thought she needed them at all. I half-expected her to look livid or disappointed, but instead, there were tears in her eyes.

Guilt overwhelmed me, replacing my unease.

"Hey, ma," I uttered, stopping a foot or two in front of her.

Her eyes roved over me, taking me in fully. She then clicked her tongue, shaking her head.

"Come here," she whispered, holding out her arms.

With a soft smile, I hunched over and let her wrap her arms around my shoulders. I rested my cheek against her hair with a sigh, taking in the familiar scent of vanilla as my eyes fluttered shut. Severe melancholy and longing threatened to break me, but I held them back with all of my will. All the while, my mother squeezed me like a coiled snake, as if afraid to let me go.

"Ma," I choked out. "Ma, you're gonna break my neck."

"After disappearing like that, I just might, Río Markaél," she snapped.

A nervous chuckle rumbled in my throat. It was a motherly threat, which she made a lot of. I wasn't always convinced she wouldn't deliver on them.

When she finally let me go, she crossed her arms and glared at me. *There it is. That's the look I was expecting.*

Mariela came around now and stood behind her.

My mother looked over at her and signed, "Did you know he was coming home today?"

Ela clasped her hands behind her back and simply nodded.

"Only for a few hours," I said with my hands and my words. "I gave her a signal when I was getting close."

My mother whipped back around, her eyes flashing. "A signal? And you didn't bother to let *me* know? Your own mother, who's been worried sick about you?"

I grimaced, my face hot with shame. Mariela pressed her lips into a thin line. There was a reason I kept things from my mother, but in hindsight, I should have made her aware of my safety.

My gaze fell to the ground seriously. "I'm sorry."

"You should be," she said. With a gentle hand, she reached out and brushed my hair away from my forehead, her brow furrowing at my injury. "What in Gods' name did your father send you off to do this time?"

I faltered, sharing a look with my sister, who still looked struck by what I told her. And Echo, who was by her side, had his eyes locked on my satchel, where the black diamond was.

Our mother glanced between us with deep skepticism, and suddenly her face hardened. She raised her chin, her expression turning to stone with that iciness that instilled fear in grown men.

"Ela, go to your room."

Mariela gave a silent scoff. "What? Why?"

"Because I need to speak with your brother. Alone."

"I want to know why he was gone, too!"

"Not right now. This is between me and Río. I don't need your two cents. Now go," my mother signed sternly.

Ela crossed her arms with an irked sigh but didn't protest any further. Instead, she came over to me and gave me another brief hug around my torso. I happily accepted her embrace and felt her trace letters on my back with her finger, spelling:

Talk later?

I pulled away and signed a simple "yes" with a soft smile.

As she started making her way towards the castle, with Echo as her partner, she threw one last look at me. She pointed to her eyebrow and then mine before saying,

"I'll fix that for you later."

I chuckled. "Okay."

When she was far away enough, I looked at my mother, and with that same seriousness, she took my arm gently.

"Let's go upstairs."

✹ ☽ ◯ ☾ ✹

At the peak of one of the large towers of *Castillo* Paricia was a war room. It served as a gathering chamber for political conversations, strategy talks, and sometimes even family meetings. The room itself was made of white stone, with a raw quartz table that was smooth at the top. It was littered with maps, books, and a variety of parchments, both belonging to either of my parents. Historical literature and magical tomes filled bookshelves in a corner next to a large frosted mirror. And across from the table itself was a hearth, with upholstered chairs gathered around it.

The fire in the hearth crackled as my mother and I faced each other on opposite ends of the quartz table. She stood with her arms folded, waiting expectantly, as I leaned against the stone.

"Well?" she said impatiently. "Out with it."

My palms were slick with sweat as I searched for the proper words to explain myself. I went over the entire story in my head many times, down to the last detail, but I was too eager to get to the point. There was no use in long-winded introductions, so instead of speaking, I decided I could simply *show* her.

I reached into my satchel and, with caution, took out the wooden box. Though small, its contents were heavy and radiated a pulsing heat. As if handling explosives, I brought out the white bundle within and placed it on the table before us.

My mother frowned, moving to take it. "What is this?"

"Don't," I said urgently.

She instantly retracted her hand, shooting me a bewildered look. I reached down and, finally unwrapped the white cloth, revealing the black stone within.

All at once, my mother's cool demeanor vanished. She inhaled sharply, and horror overtook her features. Her hand flew to her mouth as she backed away, almost hitting the wall of the chamber. Lightning flashed above the skylight, followed by the sound of nearby thunder.

Despite what I knew, her reaction still took me by surprise. I had never seen her so scared before. She didn't even look at me for a long moment, only stared at the black diamond as if it were a living, breathing monster about to devour her and everything around it. It sent a chill down my spine.

I was a toddler when The Rift was created, so I have no solid memory of the horrors my parents endured because of Sebastián Eliódor or even The Black Death. All I knew was what I was told through stories and songs, and what I had seen with my own eyes at The Rift. Even then, I could only imagine the nightmares my mother was undoubtedly reliving now, because this stone was no ordinary gem or cursed item. This was known as the Eye of Gedeón.

One of three in existence, Casímir Gedeón created them to increase his power. Legend has it that he used to wear them on a crown of thorns but managed to scatter them across the land before he was slain. For years, they were nowhere to be found, presumably destroyed when he was. That is...until Sebastián Eliódor got his hands on one. Its influence instantly took hold, and with his newfound abilities, Sebastián managed to find another. The third was yet to be found, still lost in the wind, but he was smart enough to keep the ones in his possession where only he could find them. One, he wore one around his neck, and the other... I managed to take myself.

After a choking moment of silence, my mother gaped at me in disbelief.

"Where did you get this?" she whispered sharply.

"Fort Adelfa," I responded.

"*Fort Adelfa?*" she reiterated incredulously. More thunder. "Not Old Avilonía!"

"Yes, Old Avilonía."

My mother grasped the back of a chair until her knuckles turned white. If she had the strength, she would've crushed it in her hands.

"I specifically told you not to set foot in that godsforsaken place," she hissed, raising a reproachful finger. "That was my *one* rule! One rule that I gave you when you decided to go running around playing vigilante for your father!"

"'Playing'?" I blurted out, suddenly angry. "What I've done has helped *your* efforts immensely! No one expects *El Príncipe de Avilonía* to be sneaking around. Not when everyone thinks his mother keeps him locked up in a tower. Not far off, to be honest."

My mother scoffed, narrowing her eyes at me. "I've kept you safe, Río Markaél. You and your sister. You should know why."

I gritted my teeth as old war stories cycled through my mind. There were none that I had lived through myself, but I was well aware of the people that were lost back then—the people *my mother* lost.

"I do. But I'm not the same child I used to be, Mom. I'm trying to prove myself. I *have* proved myself," I stressed, pointing to the diamond.

Neither of us moved near it out of fear of its influence.

"How did you get it anyway?" she asked.

"Dad's army, explosives, and some extra help," I replied with a shrug.

"Help from whom?" she demanded, crossing her arms once more.

I found myself hesitating, already anticipating a negative reaction, but within that hesitance was a flicker of hope.

"Sea nymphs."

My mother looked taken aback. "Sea nymphs? Since when have *they* given a shit about our cause?"

"Since their water has been contaminated by Sebastián."

Many creatures and beings lived across Avilonía—sea nymphs, werewolves, sprites, dragons, and various others. Legend has it that before The Black Death, we used to coexist and share the land, but in the battles and wars that followed, a lot of species were wiped out. By the time the Sun Killer came to reign, they retreated to their homes and wanted nothing more to do with humanity, God-given or not. My parents sought an alliance with the kingdom of the sea nymphs for years, but after many vehement rejections, they gave up on their efforts.

She raised her eyebrows. "You spoke to the king?"

"No, he still hates us," I chuckled darkly.

"Of course he does," she said with a roll of her eyes. "He doesn't think a human should be able to control the tide. By default, he hates all of us."

"But there are people in his kingdom who want to help, who want to fight back. Ma, we have one of the stones!" I exclaimed, motioning to it again. "Do you know what this means? We can destroy it and get the nymphs to join our side. We can get the other stones, and we can end this once and for all!"

Despite my passion, the queen rubbed the bridge of her nose in exasperation.

"How can you be so sure that *he* doesn't control them, hmm? Like those half-beasts?"

She was referring to Sebastián's werewolves.

Nearly two decades ago, when I was just a child, he kidnapped a select few in human form. He bent them to his will, forcing them to bite enough innocent souls to build his own hunting pack. While not all werewolves were under Sebastián's control nowadays, it was easy to be wary of them. In certain parts of the country, it's even highly advised to stay out of the woods after sunset, especially around a full moon. But according to my father, if you were familiar with magic, it was easy to tell who was being manipulated and who was not.

"No. I would've known. Besides, everyone at that fortress fought hard to protect that stone. The nymphs would've sabotaged us if they were under his command."

If it weren't for the nymphs, it would've been a massacre. Many from both their army and my father's fell, some of whom I saw with my own eyes. One of them even saved me from getting sliced in half, and for that, I would be forever grateful.

My mother sighed and scowled at the Eye of Gedeón. She bit her lip, pondering severely as I clasped my hands behind my back, waiting with bated breath.

This was a ray of hope—not just for me, but for everyone in Avilonía. Ever since The Black Death arrived on our coasts, it has been a constant back-and-forth of murder, pillaging, fighting back, reclaiming, and back again. If it weren't for The Great Divide, our country would have been in total ruin long ago. Of course, the war never truly stopped, but my parents fought hard to protect our people and land. Still, with Sebastián Eliódor and his followers still alive, ravaging everything in their wake, there would never truly be peace. He and what remained of Gedeón needed to be obliterated.

Finally, the queen straightened up.

"Obviously, we will destroy it," she said.

"Of course."

"But I wouldn't get my hopes up about finding the other two."

I furrowed my brow. "Why not?"

"You forget, Río, that one of them is around that bastard's neck. It's a suicide mission."

"So we find the third one, then," I contested, "before he does."

My mother huffed a breathy laugh. "No one's ever been able to find it, my love. Not even him, thankfully."

"That means it's only a matter of time before he does. There has to be something we're missing."

"Río, you can't just make impulsive decisions—"

"I'm not saying we do it now. I'm saying, just...think about it, okay?" I implored.

I thought of the legends behind the stones—their dark influence and ability to poison the earth. I saw what they were capable of when I went past The Rift. Everything was a horrific scene of blood and tar with water so dark no one could see through it, and plants that were rotted to the center. The very sea was riddled with creatures unlike anything I had ever seen.

In that same breath, Esmé crossed my mind. The vision of her from earlier this evening, holding the very thing that threatened to corrupt her essence. With the way my heart was beating so fast, I may as well have been in battle. I saw no sense and simply knew I had to get it out of her hands and keep it that way. I couldn't let her become another horror story. Not her or anyone else.

My mother looked between my eyes with an earnest expression until she finally gave in.

"Fine. I'll talk to your father about it, and we'll strategize."

My shoulders instantly relaxed. "Thank you."

"In the meantime," she said poignantly, "the annual winter solstice ball is in a couple of days—"

I groaned, slumping over the back of a chair. My mother ignored my dramatics and raised her voice to speak over me.

"—which I'm sure you were hoping to avoid. But it means every noble, witch, or wizard of importance will be there. People from your grandfather's kingdom have been invited."

I raised my head to share a distasteful look with her before moving on.

"It's best we strengthen our relationships that way, since it's the closest and easiest form of action."

"I hardly think either of those things is in the same realm at all," I argued.

What was a ball compared to what went on at The Rift?

"I know you think they're foolish, Río, but handling the politics behind the scenes is just as important as fighting battles, if not more. What do you think I do here while your father is away? Sit on my ass? You want people to support you? Root for you? Fight by your side when the time comes? You need to *talk* to them. It's not just dancing and dressing up. We're also celebrating 20 years since The Great Divide, so what better time than now?"

I pulled myself up a little straighter, nodding dejectedly. As much as I wanted to kick and scream about it, I wasn't a child, and I could see her point. Even though I found menial politics extremely boring.

"The thing is, a lot of the people who attend are traditional and archaic. Talking to them is like talking to a brick wall," I said.

My mother chuckled.

"I don't disagree with you, darling, but there's only so much we can do without antagonizing them. Believe me, I've tried. But if you really want to change that, you can always start now. You might be a good fighter, but your image is still questionable."

"I haven't done anything in years," I grumbled vexedly. "They need to get over it."

"You can help them get over it by talking to them," she told me honey coating her words. "You're charming, my love. I'm sure you can handle it."

I snorted. "I'll try."

When we both fell silent, our attentions were inevitably brought back to the Eye of Gedeón. Even though we kept our distance, its hot, oppressive energy radiated through the room like its own hearth. It was as if it could sense us and was growing angrier with every passing second that we didn't give in.

"Río…"

My eyes met my mother's intensely. There was a touch of fear in them that unnerved me to see.

"What?" I asked.

"Do you know what this means?"

"One step closer to killing him."

"No. Not just that."

I frowned. "What do you mean?"

"Things are only going to get worse before they get better."

Uneasiness crept into my soul. I knew that by doing this, things wouldn't be the same, but that was the last thing I wanted to hear from my mother.

Worse?

Before I could get the word out, the queen raised her hand in the air and closed her eyes. Rain came down in thick droplets once more, beating down on the glass skylight. Lightning flashed once, twice, and three times, and thunder shook the tower. When she opened her eyes, there was a silver thunderstorm within them. Knowing what was about to happen, I backed away from the table.

My mother then threw her hand down, finger pointed to the stone, and a thunderbolt crashed through the ceiling. Broken glass came down everywhere, and I turned my back to it as I covered my ears from the booming sound. Rainwater splashed on my skin, and the air was tense with crackling energy. When all that was left was the sound of rain, I turned around to find my mother standing before a charred table with rain pouring down before it, the black diamond completely obliterated. Her lilac hair was soaked, and her fingers were now covered in charcoal.

She flashed me a smile, her eyes wild and her chest heaving. All I could do was gawk at her with a mixture of awe and fear.

"I've been wanting to do that for years."

✳ ☽ ○ ☾ ✳

I left the war room mildly damp, a little charred, and no less shaken than I was before. For once, I was starting to wonder if I was incredibly in over my head.

I'm not afraid of a challenge, and I never have been. It's not the way of my family, and it's not the way of my people, even with my mother's restrictions. Still, for my entire life, the Sun Killer was a little more than a ghost story. Yes, I knew he was real. I have seen what he has done, and I have heard the tales from my parents who knew him personally. He and Gedeón were the reasons we couldn't go out late at night, why we couldn't trust strangers, and why we burned our dead. He's the reason for superstition, for the deaths of many, and for The Great Divide, but now, he seemed more real than ever. It was hard to think about amid the chaos of it all, but my mother was right.

I took the Eye—me—and I don't know whether I should be proud of that or not. There's no wondering what could happen next.

On my way to my room, I stopped by my sister's door, seeing as I promised we'd talk. I could hear Echo whining and scratching at the wood as I approached, and just as I raised my hand to knock, Ela's door swung open. She stood on the other side expectantly, with Echo pushing past her legs to get a look.

I burst out laughing.

"Have you been waiting this whole time?" I signed.

"Of course."

"How did you know it was me?"

"Echo hasn't done that since you left." She then gave me a quizzical look. "Why are you wet?"

I shook my head. "It's a long story."

"Well, you look horrible, so you should probably get some rest."

"Didn't you want to talk?"

She waved away my question with her hand. "We can talk in the morning. But first!"

With a motion for me to wait, my sister looked over her shoulder and outstretched her hand. Like many rooms in this palace, there was a small fountain in the corner that served a decorative and practical purpose. She made a pulling motion, and a small trail of water rose into the air, following her fingers as she guided it back towards me. As it floated before my face, I moved my hair away from my forehead and closed my eyes. I felt the cool water touch the spot above my brow. It didn't hurt much anymore, but I could feel Mariela's magic soothe the area. She did the same to my knuckles, which gave me a view of the water stitching up my skin until it was brand new. No cuts or bruises were left. Not even a scar.

Variations in magic weren't uncommon among the God-given. Much like personalities, each champion's strength could differ from their siblings, parents, and beyond. Save for my mother, my entire family could control the tides, but it came more naturally for my father and me. The goddess blessed Mariela by giving her the magic of healing and it matched my sister's personality beautifully. I, on the other hand, had an affinity for freezing things, which was both ironic and useful when living in a coastal town.

Mariela made a gesture with one hand, asking if there was anything else that needed healing. My hand unconsciously went to the wound at my side that nearly took me down in Fort Adelfa, but stopped in midair.

Esmé patched this one up for me today. I could see her vividly before my eyes. Her closeness, her hands working diligently and carefully on my skin, the way her hair fell down her face, and how she furrowed her brow intensely as she put me back together.

Not yet. Not this one.

There were some wounds I didn't *want* to part with. Crazy, I know, but they were always the ones Esmé tended to. Yes, pain wasn't fun, but not turning to magic for everything made me feel more human, as did the scars. They were reminders that I survived something, and in a way, they were also reminders of nights spent with a beautiful brown-eyed girl with a big heart that I simply could not let go of.

My sister waved a hand in my face, snapping me out of my daze.

"Are you okay?" she asked.

I nodded. "Yeah, I'm fine. Just exhausted."

With the thought of Esmé still, an idea struck me like lightning in the war room, and a large smile widened on my face.

Mariela watched me in befuddlement as she returned the water to the fountain.

"What?"

I narrowed my eyes at her thoughtfully before asking, "Can you do me a favor?"

Maybe there *could* be something good before things get worse.

7

The Invitation

Esmé

The day after the prince returned, I received an envelope at the door with a life-changing letter inside.

**The Markaél Family Hereby Invites You To
The Winter Solstice Ball
An evening filled with magic, performances, dancing, and more
to celebrate the rebirth of the sun, the start of winter, and 20 years
of remembrance since The Great Divide.**

I stared down at the piece of parchment, frozen in place. I did my best not to crush the beautiful invitation with my trembling hands, which was written in clean, elegant calligraphy. The parchment itself gave off a faint scent of lavender and vanilla. But that wasn't all that was inside the envelope.

I flipped to the next page in the small stack, which had a letter with a longer message on it.

Miss Esmé Vespertín,

I gasped at the personal use of my name.

As you may remember, my family and I had the privilege of watching one of your performances on the day of my son *Príncipe* Río's birthday, and we met backstage after the fact. To reiterate our thoughts from that evening, your voice is absolutely wonderful, and we thoroughly enjoyed your show. So much so that we would like to formally invite you to perform during the winter solstice celebration at the royal palace, *Castillo* Paricia.

My knees wobbled beneath me, and I had to sit in one of the breakfast chairs as I continued to read.

There, you would perform no more than three songs with instrumentalists who will be provided for you. Afterward, you may mingle and partake in the festivities as you please.

Of course, I must apologize for the last-minute notice. To make up for it, I would be more than happy to provide transportation for you as well as the resources to acquire an outfit for the night. Simply present this letter to any well-known seamstress, stylist, or shoemaker as a waiver for the expense and to put you at the front of the queue. Your carriage will arrive in the evening at your residence to pick you up.

I look forward to seeing you and watching you perform once again.

THE MOON PRINCE

Reina Victoria Markaél

The queen? I wanted to scream. *The queen remembers* me*? She knows my name? And wants* me *to perform at the castle?*

Part of me wanted to believe that it was a joke or a prank that one of my friends was playing on me. But the more I inspected the invitation, the seal on the envelope, and the signature with the stamp at the bottom, I knew something like this couldn't be easily forged.

I was invited to the winter solstice Ball at *Castillo* Paricia.

As far as I knew, only people of higher status were invited, whether they were the reigning nobility from across the country or practitioners of magic. Artisans, warriors, and even performers were often invited as well. Of course, never in a million years did I think *I* would be one of them. It was a life-changing opportunity, albeit an absolutely terrifying one.

Me? Go to a ball? By myself? In the face of so many powerful people that I didn't even know? My heartbeat quickened. *Yes, it is very terrifying.*

I looked down at the sapphire wax seal on the envelope. It was the crest of the Moon Kingdom and the Markaél family, which bore the image of a rabbit circling a crescent moon. Imagery that I associated with home, but also the prince.

Still holding the parchment in my hand, I took out the necklace he gave me from the shirt of my dress.

Was this his *doing?*

It couldn't be a coincidence, could it? Not with him. If he were anybody else, I would've marched up to his house and questioned him about it, but alas, I'd have to wait until the next evening he graced my windowsill. Until then, I'd have to find someone else to blather on about my newfound predicament, because clearly, I had an event to process and prepare for.

Fabian? No. Camilo? Maybe. Perhaps Flora. No…

Emilia Mondragón

Dulce.

✻ ☽ ◯ ☾ ✻

Dulce and I met during my very short stint as a barmaid, and after learning that our families were both from Anelante, we had an instant connection. She offered me a place in her apartment for the better part of a year until I had a stable enough income to move out. At the time, she was working part-time as *Teatro Paraiso*'s costume designer and was the one who urged me to audition for the latest show. Not long after I became an opera singer, she left her job at the theater and opened up a business of her own in the Jade District that grew in popularity seemingly overnight.

The Jade District was a fashion district on the same level as *Teatro Paraiso*, and people from all over the city went to Dulce for ribbons, sewing supplies, and—most importantly—her custom-made dresses. Whenever there was a big royal celebration, such as the Winter Solstice Ball, even people of high stature went to her for gowns. She was a hidden gem for many and has been doing quite well for herself in the last year or so. She's made a few of my favorite clothes, but I've never needed anything as grand as a gown until now.

When I arrived at her shop, Dulce was busy doing a fitting for a client who also seemed to be attending the royal event. She was an older woman, and her dress was made of beautiful red satin. When I managed to catch my friend's eye, her face lit up, and she gestured for me to wait. With a nod, I lingered among the rolls of ribbon and fabric until she finished up. As soon as the shop was empty, Dulce locked the door and flipped a sign to say it was closed. She then turned to me with a wide grin.

"Esmé, hi!" She rushed over to hug me.

Dulce was shorter than I, so her embrace was around my waist. When she pulled away, she looked up at me with dark, almond-shaped eyes, right beneath a curtain of bangs. Her short hair was dark ebony black and stick-straight, though she usually wore it pulled back for work. She was dressed in a simple white blouse and a burnt orange skirt.

"It's been a while since you stopped by," she said.

"I know, I'm sorry." I winced apologetically. "I thought we'd catch you at the theater."

Dulce clicked her tongue, resting her hands on her hips. "I know. This upcoming ball has been taking up most of my time. It's one of the biggest ones of the year, so I haven't been able to focus on much else. I had to stop orders from coming in a week ago."

My heart dropped. "What really?

Dulce caught my nervous expression immediately.

"What? What is it?" she asked.

I looked down at my hands warily. "Dulce… I was wondering if I could—and feel free to say 'no'—ask you a favor."

"Oh! What kind of favor?"

"Ummm…I may or may not have been invited…to said ball."

Dulce gasped, her eyes going wide.

"Wait, what?" she exclaimed.

I took the envelope out of my bag and held it towards her. Dulce snatched it out of my hands, bouncing on the balls of her feet as she opened it. I watched as she read the invitation as well as the letter from the queen herself, and with every line, her eyes grew larger, her mouth opening in shock.

When she finished, she looked at me and blurted out, "Esmé, this is amazing! This is the queen's handwriting and everything!"

"I know!"

"Anyone who's anyone is going to be there!"

"I know," I reiterated anxiously.

Her lips fell with a frown. "Then why don't you look happy?"

"I am happy! I'm just nervous," I told her, holding my cheeks anxiously. "I've never done anything this big before. I've only ever performed at the theater."

Unless you requested a private audience, only nobles were allowed in the palace. There was also the fact that this was most likely Río's doing, and I couldn't tell her about it.

"But you've performed in front of the royal family before! She said it herself, they loved you!" Dulce argued.

"I know," I sighed. *Oh, don't I know.* "But what if I get so worked up that I forget the words and embarrass myself? I highly doubt there will be a spotlight to help wash out their faces."

She rolled her eyes. "You won't embarrass yourself. I don't think I've ever truly seen you mess up while singing in the entire time I've known you. I you'll be fine."

Dulce put her hand on my arm in reassurance, and we shared a soft smile. I was lucky to have come to her first and was even luckier to have a friend like her.

She glanced back down at the letter and eyed me skeptically.

"So… about that favor…"

"I was hoping you'd be willing to...make me a dress?"

My friend scoffed, "Of course! Are you crazy? This is by order of the queen! She gave you a waiver!" She waved the page around for emphasis. "It puts you at the front of the line! Only really important people get these."

"Really?" I marveled in disbelief.

"Really," she affirmed with a nod.

Dulce folded the pieces of parchment and handed them back to me before taking a sweeping look around her shop. She tapped her chin thoughtfully, then all at once, sprang into action.

"Alright. Three days. That means I need to get started immediately if we're going to make you the best-looking opera singer *Castillo* Paricia has ever seen."

"You don't need to—"

Dulce ignored my protests.

"Gods, I wish I had some extra hands right about now," she muttered.

"I could help," I offered.

"No. Absolutely not. You have a ball to prepare for, and you need to rest. The only things I need from you, my friend, are measurements and design preferences. I'll just send for Milo and Flora and hope they're not busy. They're usually willing to help in a rush. For now, get in front of that mirror."

I couldn't help but chuckle. "Yes, my lady."

I did as I was told and rushed to a small platform towards the back of the shop in front of three mirrors as Dulce grabbed a measuring tape, a pencil, and some paper. Not only did my friend take measurements, but she also helped me pick my favorite fabrics out of her collection. She questioned me about necklines, sleeves, skirt shapes, and everything else that had to do with the anatomy of a gown. It was truly a testament to how good Dulce was at her job because there was only so much I knew about fashion design on my own. It was confounding, but I felt like I learned so much in just a short amount of time. It did a lot to quell my unease over the event, especially with Dulce's sheer excitement rubbing off on me. I could hardly stop smiling the whole time.

After sending a messenger, Camilo and Flora appeared towards the end of the process, and they were about as ecstatic about the whole ordeal as Dulce was. She sketched a few ideas for me, but as soon as she had everything she needed, she practically kicked me out of the shop, saying that she'd send for me if she needed me. So, with my ideas and preferences given, I left the artistic interpretation up to her and gave my friends the space to make my very first dress for my very first ball.

When I was back on the familiar cage of the gondola, the sun had just set on the horizon. The last bits of orange fell behind the ocean as the sky took on a dark violet color. This time of day, the hues of the city looked especially beautiful and golden. Beneath its sapphire domes, *Castillo* Paricia itself looked solid gold in this light. The prince was in there now, and in a few days, I'd get to see what it was like for myself.

I ran my fingers over the aquamarine moon fondly. The mere thought of him made my heart ache. Even though I saw him yesterday, I wanted to see him again. I wanted to make sure he was alright, and some part of me wanted to make sure *we* were alright. He was wounded and left in such a hurry, with an uncharacteristic expression. And despite his apology, it was hard not to believe it was somehow *my* fault for almost touching the stone. The *cursed* object. Yet he still left this token with me, which meant something. He said it was important, so I will treat it as such, like treasure.

Once I arrived in Larimar, I continued my usual route home past the many jacaranda trees. In the darkness of the night, the giddiness started to settle in. I was going to a ball at the palace. I was going to wear a dress that *I* helped design. I was going to perform in front of the royal family and the nobility of the Moon Kingdom and beyond. And *Príncipe* Río was going to be there. As much as I hated the attention, I wanted to announce it to the world.

Hugging my shawl around myself, I was smiling ear to ear when something strange caught my eye. There was a woman in a nightdress standing on the terrace of a multi-story home. What drew my attention was her soft humming, or at least, what I thought was humming. Eventually, it became clear that she was crying. I slowed my pace, and with growing concern, I let my feet carry me in her direction. And the more I grew near, the more the woman seemed featureless.

Strange.

Thinking my eyes were deceiving me, I blinked a few times. There was a sharp pinch at my temple, like the tip of a knife. Considering I took Canela's potion the day before, it confused me. Shivers ran down my spine, and then, without warning, the woman jumped off the terrace. A horrifying scream ripped out of me, my blood turning to ice in my veins as she plummeted to her imminent death.

"No!"

I ran forward, as if I could stop her, but before her body even reached the ground, she vanished into nothingness. I choked on my breath as I stopped still in the middle of the cobblestone street. Light flickered on in some windows, and there were questions from balconies. For a long moment, I was unable to move, my eyes glued to the spot where the woman's corpse should have been. Only when a man came out with a questioning look did I manage to stammer out a few words.

"S-Sorry. I saw a rat. Two of them. One crawled over my foot, going that way."

I pointed off toward another small street to further the lie.

The man cringed. "Ugh. Guess I have to get rat poison again," he grumbled. "You sure you're okay?"

No.

"Yes, thank you!"

"Alright. *Buenas noches.*"

"*Buenas noches,*" I whispered.

He closed his door, leaving me alone on the street once again. I clutched my shawl, desperately trying to keep my hands from shaking. Dizziness overcame me, and bile rose in my throat, but I held it in.

Not wanting to stay in the setting of such a horrific image, I pulled my shawl over my head and all but sprinted home.

8

Little Star

Esmé

If I didn't think there was something wrong with me before, I certainly did now.

It didn't make sense. It *shouldn't* make sense. I had seen the woman with my own two eyes, hadn't I? She was there, and then she jumped, and then... she was just *gone*. Perhaps it was a trick of the mind—another effect of my migraines and the poison following me from Anelante. But I took Canela's potion, and it never steered me wrong before. What changed?

The black diamond.

No.

No, I didn't even touch it. I *know* I didn't touch it.

I was so shaken that I hardly slept the nights leading up to the winter solstice. I stayed at home as much as possible to avoid another supernatural altercation and only left for the theater or to get fitted for my dress. Even so, in the in-between, I swore there were strange faces in the night and people who mysteriously disappeared. I chalked it up to my imagination—figments brought about by stress or anxiety. I *wanted* it to be. Maybe I was just scaring myself over the whole cursed stone debacle. Or maybe I *am* just losing my mind.

❋ ☽ ○ ☾ ❋

The prince stopped by two nights after I saw the woman jump from the roof. I pondered telling him about the incident, but thought better of it. I didn't tell any of my friends either. I didn't want any of them to worry, especially not with the big event approaching and not when Río was already so worried about my ailment. Instead, I focused on interrogating him about the invitation.

"Did you do this?" I demanded, holding up the parchment.

He put his hands on his hips and said, "I'm great, Esmé. Thank you for asking. My wound is healing well, thanks to you. How are *you*?"

"I'm happy to hear that, *Alteza*. I'm doing spectacularly. Please answer the question."

His lips spread out into a big, mischievous grin. "I did."

"W-Why?"

"You said you wanted courtship. You know, dates and pretty dresses. What better time than now? What better date than a ball?"

My heart swelled at the romantic gesture.

"I guess I didn't think you'd actually do it, or so soon."

"I don't see a point in wasting time," he replied with a shrug. "Besides, it's another way to make it up to you. Not just for being gone, but... for the other night."

His expression turned somber and apologetic as he reached for my hand. I slipped it into his, and he traced his thumb over my skin.

"You're still okay, right? You seem okay."

I faltered before answering, "I mean... I think so. Would it be obvious if I weren't?"

"Oh, yeah. From what I hear, possession's pretty hard to miss."

"Possession?" I exclaimed in horror.

THE MOON PRINCE

The prince laughed, taking my face in his hands.

"Yes, but you're fine," he reassured. "You'd be physically ill, and you wouldn't even be talking to me right now. You'd be out of your body, saying weird things, and acting against your will. You wouldn't be you. *Trust me.*"

That, at the very least, stilled something in me. Nothing of the sort has happened. I was still myself. I hadn't changed at all, but it did nothing to explain what *was* happening. I just had to make a mental note to visit Canela after the ball when I wasn't so preoccupied.

❋ ☽ ◯ ☾ ❋

Everyone had the day off for the winter solstice, and many came from further inland to share in the celebrations the capital city had to offer. While Coáraluna was often a beautiful painting of white, blue, and gold, in the weeks leading up to the holiday, it slowly became a sunset of red, orange, and green. People decorated their homes and the streets with golden banners and ribbons, baked orange slices, and rosemary. Symbols of the sun were painted on walls or hung from roofs and lampposts, and events at the Temple of Fire were held all day. Fire and smoke ceremonies were hosted in the main squares, and musicians performed on the streets for people to listen to and dance to. The restaurants were closed, but everyone's families would be cooking up a feast of their own within their homes. And because they were a high expense these days, many saved up their money to afford pastries and jams made of the few orange trees that still grew in Avilonía. This year, I had been saving up for one, but of course, plans changed.

I usually spent the winter solstice with my friends at Dulce's house. Camilo would cook one of his mom's recipes, Flora would bring sweet bread that looked like fluffy shells, and I'd bake sun-shaped ginger cookies. Dulce would make the strongest alcoholic

94

drinks known to man as she helped Camilo where she could. I knew I'd miss partaking in the sweet tradition, but any sense of bittersweetness was alleviated by what was to come.

As expected, I hardly slept the night before and was buzzing from the minute I woke up. Even though we wouldn't be celebrating the holiday the traditional way, all of my friends still gathered together for the momentous occasion. Camilo, Dulce, and Flora squeezed into my apartment, intent on helping me get ready for the night. I didn't even have to ask them. They simply arrived a few hours prior with hair and makeup supplies, shoes, and a large box that contained my dress. I had yet to see the final product, and I was on the edge of my seat with excitement.

Every possible measure was taken to make me look prim and proper. I bathed, washed my hair, put on a face mask, and waxed my face and legs with Dulce's help. Flora applied makeup while Dulce did my hair, and Camilo made me tea, both for my voice and to relax me. All the while, I warmed up with some vocal exercises. Otherwise, I was at the mercy of my friends, which, to be honest, I was very grateful for. It was the first time any of us were going to be a part of something this grand, so it was safe to say that we all shared the same enthusiasm.

When my hair and makeup were officially done, Dulce ushered me into my bedroom with Flora, locking the door behind us. Upon entry, I caught a glance of the gown on my bed and gasped, but before I could stop to admire it, Dulce blocked my view.

"No! Save your thoughts! Let's get it on you first."

She and Flora helped me assemble the outfit, starting with the underskirt. I then slipped into the dress and was squeezed into the corset and laces. They hung jewelry from my ears and tied a choker around my neck before helping me into my shoes. Only then was I maneuvered in front of a tall mirror on the wall, and as soon as I saw my reflection, I was struck speechless.

Dulce's design was inspired not only by the sun but by the turning of the season. The winter solstice marked the longest night of the year, with days that promised to be longer as the year progressed. Many took it as a symbol of resilience and rebirth, and somehow, my friend managed to capture just that. The gown had a heart-shaped, off-the-shoulder neckline with a skirt that was a proper, wide ball gown. From the bottom, the dress began as rich, black fabric that was adorned with golden rose petals. They started in a sparse pattern, like stars dappling the night sky, and became thicker towards the bodice until they almost resembled armor. As for my accessories, everything was gold. My hair, which was half up with big curls going down my back, was decorated with golden star-shaped pins. My earrings were dangling sunbursts, and the necklace was a black ribbon that hugged my throat with a matching sun charm. My bracelets were gold as were my shoes.

I looked breathtaking.

"Dulce," I whispered in awe.

"Yes?" Her expression turned dubious. "Oh, no. Do you hate it?"

"No, no, no! Quite the opposite. Dulce, this is amazing. I think it's your best work," I mused.

Her eyes sparkled. "You think?"

"Yes! How did you make this so fast?"

It was so well-crafted; it boggled my mind how quickly she finished it on such short notice. I was almost too afraid to touch it.

"Well, it's a design I've had in my sketchbook for a while. The dress itself wasn't that hard to make. It's the petals that took forever, but with Flora and Milo's help, it was less difficult than it could've been," she explained.

"You make it seem so easy."

"Well, I think you make singing look easy, so I guess we're on the same page," she said with a shrug.

I hummed in response.

Dulce was no witch, but I swear, looking at this dress, there was magic in it. I'd say I looked dressed to impress, but it was beyond that. Part of me thought I looked like a character in an opera, but grander. Yet, with the way I was floating, being on stage seemed more real than what I was about to do. I couldn't believe it was *me* standing in the mirror, about to go to a ball that the *prince* had invited me to.

The prince. My *date*. At least that's what he implied. And somehow, the thought of *him* seeing the dress excited me more than anything else.

"Oh my gods, where did you get this?"

I was so busy digesting it all that I didn't notice Dulce approaching the bedside table. When I glanced over my shoulder, she was holding Río's necklace in her hands. My stomach dropped.

"W-Wait—"

"Oh, that's stunning. What is that?" Flora asked, rushing to her side.

"It's aquamarine," Dulce uttered dubiously. "Where did you get this?"

My face warmed, and I stammered, trying to find the right explanation. At the very least, I could attempt to bend the truth.

"My, ummm... the *boy* I've been seeing. He gave it to me."

Flora smiled with glee. "Did he? How romantic!"

Dulce raised her eyebrows. "Really? So he came back?"

"Yes, but only for a little while. It all happened so fast," I said.

"Well, Esmé, you know this stone is expensive, right?"

That took me by surprise.

"Is it?"

"Yes. Most of them go to the Markaél's, so it's a hard thing to get without the proper money. Your boy must be rich," Dulce said.

I opened and closed my mouth in shock.

A precious stone? He didn't tell me that. I've been carrying it around like it's nothing!

I never had the urge to strangle a prince until now.

"I... I didn't know that," I uttered out loud.

"I'm surprised he didn't blabber about it. Most people do. But I guess that means he really likes you," she sang with a cheeky grin.

Again, I blushed.

"Is he going to be there?" Flora asked excitedly. "At the ball?"

I chuckled, "I can't imagine why he would. He didn't mention it, but maybe he might."

"Well, if he doesn't, he better hope the prince doesn't fall in love with you tonight."

Flora and Dulce giggled, much to my detriment. It only flustered me more. Falling in love was a dangerous request to ask of a royal. Even I knew that.

"Stop it," I chided.

"He just might. He'd be stupid not to. Especially in that dress," Flora sang.

"Although I wouldn't get too close to the Moon Prince if I were you," Dulce warned.

Both Flora and I shared an odd look.

"Why do you say that?" I asked.

"When you work with the people I do, you hear a lot of hot gossip," she explained. "I don't know how true it is, but one of the ladies told me that he almost killed a kid once."

It was as if the air had been sucked out of my lungs.

Out of all the rumors I knew about *Príncipe* Río, I never heard *that* one before. I knew that some people thought him rude and stuck up, while others thought he was alright. To the outside world, he's either a mystery and a recluse, or he's partying somewhere in the Air Kingdom. There was something wrong with him because he hadn't publicly dated anyone in years, and some go so far as to question his ability to carry on his father's legacy. It didn't help that with half the God-given gone, the morale and faith in the gods' champions went down significantly. Overall, opinions were greatly split. Canela told me that rumors like that came with every generation. Even so, compared to attempted murder, everything else seemed tame. Even Flora looked shocked.

"How?" she asked.

Dulce shrugged. "I don't know. It was a lord's kid, and I think it happened years ago, but considering he's a God-given, I can only imagine what *that* looked like. I mean, if we can't trust *them*, what then?"

I have seen the prince use his magic before, but it was always for small things. I didn't know the extent of his abilities, but everyone knew what his father could do, so it wasn't hard to envision. In truth, being on the wrong side of a God-given's magic sounded like a nightmare, yet part of me refused to believe that Río was capable of such a thing. At least not off the battlefield.

"Maybe it was self-defense," I offered.

"Maybe. I'm sure it's just a rumor," Dulce said casually, unaware of my sudden turmoil, "but staying away from people with too much power isn't a bad idea to begin with."

Just as she was about to return the necklace to its place, I raised my hand to stop her.

"Wait. I think I'd like to take it with me."

"Oh, of course!"

Instead of wearing it, I tucked it safely in my skirt pocket. Now that I knew its value, the last thing I needed was to draw more attention to it, but I couldn't bear to leave it behind. This event would mark the first time I'd see Río in public, which, in a way, made it the perfect time to give it back.

Following Dulce's lead, I walked out into the living room with Flora in tow, where Camilo was waiting patiently. He bolted up from the couch, and as soon as he laid eyes on me, his jaw dropped. Ever the dramatic person, he started clapping and whistling.

"You look amazing," he said.

"Thank you, Milo."

A knock came at the door, and everyone gasped. Camilo rushed to answer it, and on the other side was a uniformed coachman dressed in white, gold, and blue.

"We have a carriage for Miss Esmé Vespertín."

My breath hitched, my heart hammering against my ribs. I almost forgot to breathe until Dulce put her hands on my shoulders and bore her eyes into mine.

"Inhale and exhale. It's time, my friend."

I nodded vigorously and worked extra hard to put air into my lungs.

"You're going to be great!" Flora cheered, and Camilo shouted, "Break a leg!"

Already shaking, I gave everyone a big hug before approaching the door. The coachman offered me his hand, and I took it politely so he could lead me down to where a sapphire blue carriage pulled by white horses awaited. A few of my neighbors were either outside on the street or looking through windows, gawking at the scene as they no doubt wondered who from the Larimar District had the privilege of such a ride. As we approached the carriage, another coachman opened the door, revealing a gold interior. With the first coachman's help, I went up the steps and sat on the comfortable plush seat. It was then that I noticed Dulce had been trailing closely behind, holding the back of my dress so it wouldn't get ruined.

She then clasped my hands in hers, beaming at me.

"I'll come to check on you in the morning to see how it went!"

"And check on Midnight before you go, please," I said.

"Of course. You're going to do great things, little star. Good luck!"

My heart swelled, and before I knew it, she was letting me go. The coachman closed the door, and then I was by myself in the royal carriage. It jostled as the coachmen climbed on, and a few seconds later, my body lurched as we started moving up the street towards *Castillo* Paricia. I pushed aside the window curtains, waving and watching as my friends and home became smaller and smaller in the distance.

9

From the Ashes

Esmé

As we made our way to the top of Coáraluna, we passed by many neighborhoods that were already active with boisterous festivities, bringing a smile to my face. The residential streets disappeared as we entered a dim tunnel illuminated by burning embers, that led to a dirt road lined with thick trees. Through the greenery, I could see the endless ocean to the west, where the sun was disappearing beneath the horizon.

We rounded the hill, and my mouth fell open at the sight of the crowning jewel that was *Castillo* Paricia itself. I nearly pressed my face against the glass window, watching as the giant structure got closer and closer, its various towers growing ever taller. From this angle, I could see its true vastness. It was not simply built on the hill but into the *side* of it, on a cliff overlooking the sea. Its many arches, tall windows, and domes made of glass and blue stone were even more beautiful from up high. It briefly disappeared from view until we came upon the exterior wall. It was made of textured marble, with a giant arched gateway leading inside. Guards in sleek aquamarine armor stood at the ramparts, watching overhead with golden spears. Two aquamarine flags hung from either side of the gate, depicting a white rabbit circling a silver crescent moon.

Our carriage fell in line to the right with the arriving guests, while the empty carriages filtered out on the left. We crossed a bridge arcing over a small chasm. My instinct was to avoid looking down, but was glad I didn't. Otherwise, I would've missed the sparkling waterfall cascading below. It too left my view as we followed the line under a portcullis onto a wide pathway lined with blooming jacarandas. It opened to a large courtyard built in a semicircle where, right in its center, was a golden statue of Marisláni, the goddess of the moon and tides. She was holding a sword toward the night sky, and white flowers decorated the ground at her feet. We circled behind her until the carriage came to a sudden stop.

My heart leapt into my throat at our arrival. There was rustling, and then the door to my right swung open.

The coachman bowed his head and said, "We have arrived, *señorita*."

He reached his hand out, and, with a hesitant nod, I let him assist me down the carriage as I clutched my skirt on the way down. I thanked the coachman with a smile as I smoothed myself out before turning towards the castle itself.

Paricia's facade was like a small mountain, towering both over the guests and the statue of the goddess. It was made of marble and quartz with details of gold and varying shades of blue crystal. A magnificent set of stairs led to beautiful white stone arches, and the steps themselves were tiled in a collage of blue. Above the entryway was a large, scallop-shaped window made of stained glass depicting an image of ocean waves beneath the moon. And even in the dim light of dusk, I could make out the blue tiles of the large dome resembling mermaid scales. Ivy climbed up the pillars and walls like spidery green veins.

Guests were already filtering in, wearing their best winter solstice attire for the evening. I couldn't help but notice that a few of them were stealing glances at me. Some even paused to stare, point, and whisper. It didn't know if it was out of judgment or curiosity, but it felt rude regardless of the fact. One would think nobles had manners, but it seemed I was wrong. For my own sake, I didn't stick around to let any self-doubt fester and instead grabbed my skirt with both hands and went up the stairs towards the entrance. There, the guests filed in a line at the double doors, holding their invitations. I took mine out of the pocket of my skirt and presented it to the guard, who let me in with no hassle.

Upon entry, there was a massive foyer with a big double staircase and two guards positioned at both ends. The tiled floor was designed in a blue and white spiral with a massive fountain sitting in the center. Hanging above it was a chandelier in the shape of a multi-pointed star. Following the current of guests, I went down a hallway with cream walls and vaulted ceilings with a mosaic pattern of curling waves. Everything else, from the carpets, curtains, and fixtures, was either blue, white, or gold. Large woven tapestries of major deities hung on either side, and the tall windows had more stained-glass images of the moon, stars, ocean, or even Marisláni herself. On top of it all, several garlands, ribbons, and flowers had been hung up for the night's event. No detail was spared.

Eventually, I arrived at a pair of doors manned by another guard. The sound of music and chatter from inside reminded me of being backstage at a show, listening to the audience beyond the curtain. I couldn't tell if the butterflies in my stomach were from anxiety or excitement. Perhaps a bit of both. In an attempt to stay calm, I pretended like it was just another night of performing.

Just find the prince, and you'll be fine.

The grand ballroom was vast, with tall, layered walls of intricately carved stone and blue and gold detailing. Tall windows with woven blue curtains ran parallel to each other, stretching close to the ceiling, and they were pulled open to give a view of the island and the ocean beyond. There was a vaulted ceiling with another tiled mosaic depicting moon phases and constellations. Three chandeliers made of aquamarine and moonstone lit up the space, with a massive one hanging in the middle.

I peered over the banister, looking down from a smaller double staircase to a small fountain below and the sea of guests that were gathered in the chamber. There was so much to take in, so much beauty. And I was so busy marveling that I almost forgot what I came here for. I didn't even notice that they were announcing people's names… and I was next.

"*Señorita?*"

The voice was enough to snap me out of it and look over at a steward in a dark blue suit. His hair was perfectly done, and there was a polite smile painted on his face.

"Sorry, yes?" I asked breathlessly.

"Name and where you're from, please."

"Oh! Of course. Esmé Vespertín. From Anelante."

Coáraluna was all I knew, but my family was from Anelante, and if there was any time to honor them, it was now.

The man nodded, looking mildly surprised, and as I stood at the top of the stairs, he shouted in a loud voice, "Miss Esmé Vespertín of Anelante."

As if a spell were cast upon the room, the once constant chatter was reduced to whispers as soon as my name was called. I glanced at the crowd, catching the curious eye of many. I had a sneaking suspicion that these people didn't meet many from Old Avilonía these days, especially not in a place like this. It made the fight to remain poised that much more difficult, yet I continued down the steps towards the rest of the party, clutching my dress like a lifeline. I maintained a cool expression, despite feeling like an exposed nerve. I held my shoulders back, my spine straight, and my head high, channeling the energy of one of the many characters I played in the opera. All the while, I used my discretion to scan the many faces for a familiar one...but to no avail.

Once on the main floor, I continued to search the procession as I moved into the space. I smiled at the surrounding guests, bowing my head and giving some of them a simple greeting. This was so similar yet so different from being onstage. There were so many of them, but where the stage often provided distance, these people were so close to me it was uncomfortable. Their probing gazes trailed from my face down to my dress, and, once again, I wasn't sure if it was negative. It wasn't until I took one good gander around the room that I made a horrifying realization:

In a ballroom filled with hues of poinsettia red, I was the only one wearing something black and gold.

Oh, gods. Dulce, what did you do?

"Miss Vespertín."

A familiar voice split through the noise, cutting my path short. Behind my mask, my heart leapt with joy and relief. I glimpsed around for the source, but I didn't need to look very far. He was pretty hard to miss, as he came from the center of the room, with the guests parting for him and their whispers growing louder. He too stuck out in his blue attire, but without his cloak, he would have stuck out regardless.

Río.

But it wasn't Río as I knew him, no. This was every last bit, *Príncipe* Río Markaél of Avilonía. His face was clean-shaven, and his hair was perfectly styled. Gone were the cloaks and black rogue attire; for now, they were replaced with a beautiful, deep sapphire blue jacket with a high collar that reached below his chin. The shoulders were embroidered with tiny beads of different shades of blue in a swirling watery pattern, and a silver chain made of small crescent moons ran from his right shoulder diagonally across his chest. He wore a matching pair of pants that went down into black boots. On top of his head of white hair was a silver crown—a thin band forged to look like crashing waves.

He looked spectacular, like something out of a storybook, and I had to exercise every last bit of control to keep myself composed in front of hundreds of people.

The prince stopped a short distance before me, and it wasn't until he bowed that I remembered exactly who and where I was. With a hitch of breath, I curtsied, and we shared a soft smile. There was a hush around us, bringing more attention to the moment than I would've liked.

"*Alteza*," I greeted him.

"Miss Vespertín," Río repeated. His eyes were alight as they roved over me discreetly. His throat bobbed as he swallowed hard. "You look absolutely stunning."

Even in public, he never tore his eyes away from mine. I almost wanted to avert my gaze but stood my ground instead. I had a feeling playing coy didn't win me any favors here.

"Thank you. If I had known there was a strict theme, I would've dressed accordingly," I replied nervously.

He scoffed, "Strict? No, I think you've captured the spirit of the holiday quite perfectly. You're a special guest after all."

He sounded so formal, and his voice took on a smooth, enchanting tone. I didn't think it was possible, but apparently it *was* easy to forget just how much of a prince he truly was when in the privacy of my home. Seeing the difference was startling, but I knew how to play along.

"Thank you for coming on such short notice. It's an honor to have you here," he added.

"Of course. It's an honor to be here at all. I would never turn down an invitation from the royal family."

"We're excited to see you perform. I know my mother will be excited to see you. Why don't I show you around? Take you to her?"

He motioned with his head and held out his elbow to me. I tried not to look too eager as I took it.

"Yes, of course... *Alteza.*"

The prince escorted me through the crowd, which required little to no effort as they made a path for us without question. Being with him, I almost wanted to exhale in relief, but with so many eyes watching, I was also incredibly aware of myself. As a performer, I thought I knew what it was like to be watched and ogled, but never to this degree. Most people only liked you while you were entertaining them, but they hardly cared about who you were afterward. When the act fell away, so did the magic. I wondered if it could've been the same for someone like Río. The circumstances were simply different.

"I've got you," he whispered, as if sensing my unease.

I gave him a thankful squeeze.

He walked me over to the refreshments table, which was filled with an assortment of cheese, fruits, pastries, and small foods, as well as a chocolate fountain. The prince explained every decadent pastry out loud, some of which I had never seen before. Even though it was partially a rouse, I was genuinely engrossed in what he was saying. In fact, I rather liked hearing him talk. My attention was especially latched onto the tray of orange jam pastries. They were much smaller than the ones sold down in the city, and I had to resist the discomfiting urge to sneak one into my pocket.

"You can have one if you like," he said.

I looked up at him in surprise, not realizing he was watching me the whole time. There was an amused smile on his lips, and I so badly wanted to roll my eyes.

"Are you sure?" I asked.

"That's what they're there for, and in my honest opinion," he leaned in close to my ear and whispered, "the food's the best part of the whole thing."

A giggle bubbled in my throat, and I bit my lip to repress it as well as the shudder brought on by his breath.

Río grabbed a small plate, placed a rolled-up cake on it, and handed it to me. I graciously accepted and, trying not to look overzealous, took a careful bite of the pastry. I hummed merrily as the combination of sweet, moist cake and delectable citrus jam filled my mouth.

The prince chuckled. "You've never had one before?"

I shook my head in response as I finished the remainder of the small dessert and cleaned myself off with a napkin. He took the empty plate from me and handed it to the nearest steward to take away.

"Remind me to send some to your apartment."

"Don't," I scolded under my breath.

Even though the offer was very enticing.

He giggled softly before saying, "You look beautiful, by the way. Like a sunrise."

My cheeks warmed at the lovely compliment. "Thank you. You look incredible too. You clean up nice for a rogue in hiding."

Our eyes met briefly as crimson bloomed across his cheeks.

"Thank you," he whispered.

His all-consuming fervid gaze had me squirming where I stood. I tore my eyes away and took a sip of some bubbling cider to distract myself. I even let myself become mesmerized by the golden effervescence in the beautifully crafted glass.

"I'm really glad you're here, Esmé."

I finally looked at him then. There was something so vulnerable and much deeper to his words that, if I didn't know any better, I'd say butterflies were fluttering in my stomach.

"Me too. I'm happy to see you," I replied.

His cool, royal demeanor continued to fall away, and what remained was an expression I only ever saw in secret. I had to take another sip of cider lest I catch fire in the middle of *Castillo* Paricia.

The prince cleared his throat and, loudly, in his professional voice, said, "Shall I introduce you to my mother now?"

I pasted on a smile that mirrored his. "Of course! I wouldn't want to keep her waiting."

We left the refreshments table, heading towards the far end of the grand ballroom, where the room itself ended in a semicircle of large bay windows overlooking the back of the island. Here the guests were crowded in denser clusters, and when they parted the way, it was easy to see why. In front of the windows was a raised dais with three tall thrones made of gold. The first one was empty, and the other two were occupied by two indelible women who were hard to miss.

One was *Princesa* Mariela Viviana Markaél, dressed in a beautiful light blue dress decorated with a waving pattern of sapphire and gold beads. Her hair was pinned up in an extravagant braided updo with a silver tiara sitting among white flowers. A large, black dog sat by her feet, wearing a chain with a crescent moon hanging from it, looking vigilant.

The woman next to her was older and more striking. Her hair was predominantly lilac, worn straight and sleek behind her back. The body of her dress was the richest violet fabric while her flowing sleeves were sheer lavender, falling off her shoulders. The gown hugged her form, with a train that swirled around her feet and a slit that was adorned with clear rain drops. Her crown was silver embedded with raw quartz crystal. Swirling clouds marked the back of her neck and back with black ink, which I only briefly caught a glimpse of.

Reina Victoria Lluvia Markaél, the Queen of Storms... and *Príncipe* Río's mother.

This felt very different from our last meeting.

Her gaze first went to her son, her dark eyes softening before falling on me suspiciously. She scanned over my dress in one fell swoop, and I did my best not to visibly shrink in her intense presence.

"Mother, this is Esmé Vespertín, the opera singer that you invited from *Teatro Paraiso*," Río explained.

The queen's skeptical expression dissolved, replaced by an award-winning smile.

"Oh, Miss Vespertín, yes! It's a pleasure to see you again."

I let go of Río's arm and curtsied before the Queen of Storms, saying, "The pleasure is all mine, *Majestad*."

"This is my daughter, Mariela. You've met her as well," she said, motioning to the princess beside her.

I curtsied in her direction. "*Alteza*."

The young girl waved at me and made signs with her hand that I didn't understand.

"She said that it's nice to meet you," the prince deciphered.

My first and last meeting with her was brief, but I did recall her father, the king, translating her words through sign language. That night, I made a mental note to learn a few key words, but it completely slipped my mind by the time I met the prince again. Now, I couldn't help but be embarrassed at my lack of knowledge, even though I knew I wasn't the only one.

To think I could've asked for lessons.

"It's nice to meet you, too," I said, making sure not to mumble.

Río then motioned to the dog by her feet. He was predominantly black but had patches of brown fur around his mouth, chest, and paws.

"This is Echo, her guiding companion. He's on duty right now, but he's a softie, I swear."

The dog flashed a smile with his tongue hanging out, and I couldn't help but giggle. The princess signed something again, and Río translated.

"You can pet him if you like."

I perked up with excitement. "Really? I'd love to."

With my skirts in hand, I bent down as best as I could, running a hand over Echo's soft head. He wagged his tail merrily, making me smile. Despite him being a dog, he reminded me of Midnight.

"Most people are terrified of him, but for some reason, I think he likes you," the queen mused.

Straightening up, I opened my mouth to comment, only for my words to catch in my throat at the sight of a boy standing right behind the hound. He appeared no more than a teenager. Lilac hair framed his forehead and fell around his ears. He wore a suit much like Río's, except his was made of deep purple fabric, with clouds embroidered on his shoulders and a chain of teardrops hanging across his chest. Though the suit was tailored to his figure, it still looked slightly too big for him. He winked at me with dark eyes, making my breath catch. Despite the strange feeling in my gut, my instinct was to greet him until my attention was taken elsewhere.

"She says she likes your dress," the prince told me.

I snapped my attention back to *Princesa* Mariela, smiling brightly at her.

"Thank you."

"Yes, your dress is very beautiful," *Reina* Victoria remarked. "Where did you get it on such short notice?"

"My friend is a seamstress in the Jade District. Her name is Dulce Cabral," I replied.

"Oh, I think I know of her. She's very talented. I'll make sure she gets paid for her work, and I'll keep her in mind if I need anything in the future."

My heart swelled with pride. "Yes, I think she'd like that very much. Thank you."

I took a quick glance towards the boy in the purple suit, hoping to get his name, only to find that he was gone. I stole a look around this side of the room, yet he was nowhere to be found. Not even the people around us seemed bothered by his absence at all.

"Miss Vespertín, the floor is all yours, whenever you're ready," the queen said, drawing my gaze back to her once again. "You can talk with my son about the accompaniment beforehand."

My eyebrows shot up. "Oh?"

"Oh, yes, both he and Mariela will be accompanying you with their instruments. Won't you, darling?" Her words were coated in honey as she spoke to the prince.

Río returned her smile, but his eyes and his tone told me it was a forced expression.

"Yes. Yes, I will."

"Good. Now, get ready. The guests are waiting."

As I hid my befuddlement, Río whisked me away once more, with his sister at his other side. He steered us to the right side of the ballroom, where a grand piano stood next to a golden harp. The princess sat down by the latter and started plucking away at the strings, as if testing them out.

"I thought she couldn't hear," I said to Río in a hushed tone.

"She can't, but there are certain instruments she can feel. Others she can almost see," he explained.

I furrowed my brow. "How?"

"She says each note has a different color. It's easier on something like a harp or a piano," he explained.

He ran his hand over the large percussion instrument and flipped it open so the hammers and strings were exposed.

"Which you can apparently play," I added in dismay.

He smirked. "One of my best-kept secrets. Mostly because I don't like doing it in front of people anymore. Mom abused that privilege for many years before I stopped."

"And you're doing it today because..."

The prince dropped his voice low, so only I could hear. "It was the... the *price* I had to pay for getting you here."

My jaw fell open. His lips curled deviously, and I had to bite back a grin of my own.

"You bribed your mother to get me here?" I asked.

He took a hesitant glance over at his sister, who looked over and gave him a thumbs up. He held up a finger, as if telling her to wait, and she nodded before returning to her harp.

"Well, actually, I bribed my sister. It would've been too risky to bribe the queen. She's not happy with me at the moment," he said.

I hummed. "Of course."

"Anyway," he said a little louder, "what will we be playing with you tonight, Miss Vespertín?"

I was unaccustomed to talking to Río so professionally, but he made it easy so we were on the same page. Fortunately, the princess was incredibly kind and assured me that she was very familiar with the music I presented to them. I even found myself enraptured by the way Río translated the entire conversation as she watched him intently. There was something about his attentiveness towards his sister that attracted me to him even more, which didn't help this whole forbidden aspect at all.

The songs chose were "A Hummingbird's Wings," "Call to the Light," and "From the Ashes." The first was the honorary Avilonían anthem that had been written in the first war, and the next two were seasonal songs that originated from the Sun Kingdom. They were perfect for tonight's celebrations of both the winter solstice and the anniversary of The Great Divide.

When we were all ready, the queen got out of her chair and called the attention of the room with a swirling breeze.

"Ladies and gentlemen of Avilonía, in honor of tonight's winter solstice celebration, I have an esteemed performer from our very own *Teatro Paraiso*. I've had the pleasure of witnessing her talent myself, and it's only fair that I share it with you today to celebrate the magic and resilience of our people. May I present to you, Miss Esmé Vespertín, as well as my children, *Príncipe* Río and *Princesa* Mariela Markaél!"

The guests gave a resounding clap as they gathered in a semicircle. I fiddled with the ring on my finger, feeling that familiar pre-performance buzz. My eyes flitted between *Princesa* Mariela and Río, who flashed me a comforting smile. When I was ready, I gave him a nod, and with a sigh, he raised his hands over the keys and began to play. His sister followed along in an enchanting string melody, leading me in as I started to sing.

The singing was always easy. I've been able to do it for as long as I can remember. If anything, what was difficult was the inability to stop and admire the Markaél's immaculate skills. *Princesa* Mariela's talent with the harp was hypnotizing, and there was something unapologetic about the way *Príncipe* Río played the keys. Dare I say, he played even better than the accompanist for our shows. It hit me with the realization that I only really knew a fraction of the life of the rogue prince that came stumbling through my window at night, and I had this burning desire to know more.

Each song seemed to flow from my soul. I let my emotions fuel my art, and when it was all over, the ballroom erupted in thunderous applause. I was overjoyed, the reaction nearly moving me to tears as I took a bow before my audience. Still beaming, I motioned to the princess, who bowed, and I turned to Río to do the same thing. My heart lurched in my chest when our eyes met, his expression one of complete and utter awe. Catching myself, I motioned to him, and he quickly stood up and bowed before the crowd with a charismatic grin. And our eyes connected again, I was overcome with the capricious desire to kiss him.

✳ ☽ ○ ☾ ✳

A brief mingling period followed the performance. Río took me around the room and introduced me to a few of the lords and ladies of Avilonía. There were a few witches and wizards who were invited, some of whom ruled cities of their own. I couldn't say if they were apt, but they were a little more refined than I was used to, and I found myself missing Canela.

Eventually, was pulled away, which meant I was left to entertain people who were oddly curious about me. I always gave them the same spiel: My name is Esmé Vespertín. I'm 21 years old, and I'm a refugee from Anelante. I don't remember my family, but I found a home in Coáraluna and made a place for myself at the *Teatro Paraíso*. Among other details. It was easier to keep my mind on track that way.

Soon, it became time for our next event:

The Winter Solstice Fire Ceremony.

Essentially, a fire pit is set up, big or small, and on a piece of parchment, people write the things in their lives they wish to let go of.

Then, they fold the paper and place it in the fire to release it into the smoke and sky. I've done one every year and often wrote down things that had to do with finances, loneliness, or wanting to release the anger I had over my life. But this year, I found myself focusing on none of that.

For tonight's ball, the queen had a small pyre set up on one of the ballroom balconies. And as I stood by the doors with my charcoal and parchment in hand, I was having a hard time thinking about anything at all. The ceremony began, and I watched the royal family go first—the queen, the princess, and then the prince—and as I caught Río's eye, I couldn't help but wonder what the fire could burn for me that didn't feel completely selfish.

When I inevitably found one, I wrote it down in bold letters, folded the paper, and walked over to the fiery pit, its flames licking at the inky sky. The people around me stepped aside, making space for me with more appreciation than before. I curtsied to the royal family, my eyes lingering on Río. His own eyes, which were like volcanic glass, seemed to reflect the fire perfectly within them. I then held the parchment in my hands and closed my eyes, focusing on it—because Canela said that everything was about intent—and when I opened them, I let the message fall into the flames. I watched it turn into ash and smoke, imagining it going up, away from the pit, the ballroom, and from me.

Fear.

Fear was what I had written.

10

Dance of the Dead

Esmé

After the ceremony, I was truly on my own. Being the introvert that I am, talking wasn't exactly my strong suit. My performance wasn't a failure and the prince provided some comfort, yet I was still very much a fish out of water. I may have looked the part, but it was complex task trying to connect with nobles who had a very... *limited* view on life. These people existed above the surface with their lavish lifestyles and power, and despite their well-mannered exterior, they were remorseless. They asked about my life, my friends, my family, and even my association with *Príncipe* Río. I used discernment when answering their questions, but couldn't help my awkwardness. And when they ultimately realized I'd give them nothing of value, they became bored.

My mind was swamped from the theatrics of it all, and I inevitably strayed to the refreshments table to get away. I helped myself to a glass of water and some slices of fruit as sources of energy and solace. There were simply too many people, so much social interaction, and so many *whispers*.

My peace didn't last very long.

"Esmé Vespertín, is it?"

My body tensed, and I had the urge to hide under a table or crawl out of my skin. Instead, I smoothed my features, put my refreshments down, and looked towards the man who addressed me at my left.

"Yes, *buenas noches*."

He was a young man about Río's age with a slender face and black hair that was neatly slicked back. His eyes were dark, coffee brown, and he wore a crimson suit with gold detailing, going with tonight's theme.

"*Buenas noches*," he replied, bowing his head. "I am *Vizconde* Silas Calicó. I'm from the city of Valerta."

Valerta was a city in the forest of the Air Kingdom, home of *Rey* Saévio. He was *Príncipe* Río's grandfather, though he never mentioned him at all. Outside the castle walls, people said that he was cold and unforgiving, but the Air Kingdom itself was said to be vibrant and spectacular. Curiously enough, I had never personally met someone from the Air Kingdom until tonight.

Amid my surprise, I bowed my head.

"A pleasure to meet you, Lord Calicó."

He flashed a charming smile, his canines sharp. "The pleasure is all mine. I came over here to introduce myself and compliment your immense talent. If I had known that such a precious gem was hidden in Coáraluna, I would've slipped away sooner."

"That's very kind of you to say, sir. Thank you," I replied with a shy smile.

"Of course. I hear you're from Anelante. I can't remember the last time I met someone from the Earth Kingdom. I don't mean to pry, but... do you remember much of your home before crossing over?"

"No, I'm afraid not. I was too small."

"Ah, I see." He put his hand in his pocket and casually leaned against the table. "It's a shame to grow up without one's culture. I can't imagine not being able to go back home when you want to."

It wounded me to hear him voice the very thoughts that brought me great sorrow.

"It's not easy, but I make do. Lucky for me, there's not much for me to miss other than what people tell me," I said.

From what I read in books and heard in passing, the Earth Kingdom was equal parts stunning and severe. It was known for its red rock cliffs, jagged mountain ranges, and the famed volcano known as El Toro. They were the largest producers of obsidian crystal and top-of-the-line steel. Anelante used to be the capital—a mountain city not far from the volcano itself, with snowy winters and evergreen forests. Sometimes, I tried picturing myself there, existing in the snow. It was always strange.

"I think I'm more of a coastal woman anyway. I rather like Coáraluna," I mused.

The viscount huffed. "Well, wait until you visit Valerta. Spend a year there, and you'll see just how beautiful it is to watch the seasons change."

It was such a lovely thought. Our beach town only ever had two seasons: sunshine and rain. Sometimes both at the same time. It could be a bit much for some people, but more often than not, Coáraluna was known for its beautiful weather. It was one of many reasons people came from far and wide to tour the place and spend vacations here.

Of course, I would be a liar if I said I wasn't eager to know what the Air Kingdom was like. I almost fantasized about such a thing, but that innocent idea was quickly muddled by the way the viscount's eyes trailed over me. It sent a sudden, uncomfortable shiver down my skin as he continued talking.

"I see you're also acquainted with the Moon Prince and his family," he said when his gaze found mine once more.

"We met once at the theater. They were very kind to invite me here. I'm simply a guest," I replied, nervously toying with my jewelry.

"Well, based on his attentiveness towards you tonight, I would argue otherwise."

I hadn't been holding eye contact for very long, letting my attention wander to the ballroom as we spoke, but when he said those words, I snapped my gaze back to him.

"Whatever do you mean?" I asked.

People whispered around me, making me self-conscious.

"Well, the prince rarely shows his face around these things, let alone gives anyone the time of day."

My face fell slightly. *So that's why everyone was so curious tonight.*

Heavy footsteps approached from behind, and suddenly, I felt someone's body heat at my back. The smell of sea salt, jasmine, and familiar musk filled my area as a shadow cast across Silas's face. The viscount's brown eyes went above my head, his mouth curling into a cold grin.

"Ah, speak of the devil."

"What the fuck are you doing here?"

The vicious whisper over my shoulder almost made me jump. I whirled around, and as if summoned, the Moon Prince was standing right there, except he didn't look quite like himself. A burning, malicious scowl replaced his charming, boyish demeanor. But it wasn't directed at me... it was directed at the viscount.

Silas Calicó looked unperturbed.

"I was invited, obviously," he retorted. "Father couldn't make it, so *I'm* here. Miss Vespertín and I were just having an interesting conversation."

The prince scoffed, "What interesting thing could *you* possibly have to say?"

"I was just about to ask her if she'd save a dance for me."

My eyes widened at that, but I had very little time to even consider the offer before the prince put his hand on my waist and moved me aside. I let out a tiny squeak as he planted himself between us.

"No, you weren't," he said as a matter of fact. "Miss Vespertín is *my* date. Fuck off."

I bit back the strangled noise that wanted to come out. In other circumstances, I would've smiled at the admission, but the hostility put my feelings on pause.

"Ah, so she *is* your date?" Silas Calicó smirked.

My stomach churned as I glanced between them. Everyone around us had gone quiet as they focused on the altercation, but the men didn't seem to care or notice.

"Don't you have a *wife* to get back to?" Río spat out the word with unexpected bitterness.

"Unfortunately, Lorena couldn't make it, but she sends her regards." Silas cast a glance. "Why everyone wants to marry *you*, I'll never know."

My body got red-hot, but instead of embarrassment it was from bewildering anger. The prince was quicker with his words than I'll ever be.

"Bold words for someone who can't hold their breath for very long. You're just angry because all you have to offer is money."

Silas's face hardened, his amicable expression freezing over. "And what about *you*, Markaél? You weren't even chosen by a god. You're just a product of the ones who were."

I and a few guests in proximity gasped. Río's muscles tightened. The air was so thick, it could be cut with a blade, and it was hotter than any pit the queen could light. I bit my tongue for as long as I could, unaware of what I should or shouldn't do, but I could bear it no longer. A brawl at the winter solstice ball was different from whatever the prince did overseas.

Letting go of some of my restraint, I put a hand on Río's arm.

"*Alteza*, I think we should get some air, don't you think?" I suggested gently, the apprehension clear in my voice.

The prince twisted around to look at me, and his hostility softened before my eyes. He took me in for a beat before he finally nodded and tried schooling himself back into his mask of nobility.

"Yes, Miss Vespertín. I think you're right."

He held his elbow out to me, which I took with a smile. The prince then turned back to Silas Calicó with a rigid look.

"Have the night you deserve, *vizconde*."

As he maneuvered us away from the table, I thought that was the end of the interaction. But it seemed Silas wanted the last word, and he said it loud enough for many to hear.

"Be careful with that one, Miss Vespertín. The sea is just as deadly as it is beautiful."

My stomach lurched. *Príncipe* Río stopped in his tracks, and I peered up at him warily. His jaw was clenched, his eyes straightforward, but I could see him contemplating whether turning around was worth it.

I gave him a soft tug.

"People are watching," I whispered.

With an irritated sigh, he continued, taking us up the stairs and away from the ballroom.

✳︎ ☽ ◯ ☾ ✳︎

We exited into the cooler, much quieter hall, striding past the stained-glass windows, the hanging tapestries of the gods, and even past the main double staircase to an empty gallery. Only when the doors shut behind us did we let out a deep sigh of relief and drop the masks we'd been wearing all night.

I let my hand fall and whirled around.

"Are you alright?"

"Yeah, I'm fine," he muttered, giving me an apologetic look. "I'm so sorry you had to see that, Esmé. I swear that doesn't usually happen."

"Who was that?" I asked.

The Moon Prince rolled his eyes. Even now, the viscount agitated him.

"Silas Calicó. He's from my grandfather's kingdom, and his father is currently on the front line. We go way back," the prince explained.

"I take it you don't like him. I've never seen you so angry before," I said, hugging myself.

Even that night with the black stone, he was nowhere near as disdainful towards me. This was miles from it. Not that Silas was any better. His words toward the prince ruffled my feathers more with every passing second.

Río nodded. "I despise him, yeah."

"Why? And why does he hate you?"

"*You weren't even chosen by a god. You're just a product of the ones who were.*"

How hateful, I thought.

The prince faltered. His eyes held an ocean of wretchedness, as if seeing memories I couldn't. He looked angry, frustrated, and guilty all at once. But when he spoke, he didn't give the explanation I hoped for. As per usual.

"Stupid shit that happened years ago. Back when we were still friends. Nothing you need to worry about," he assured, moving closer to me.

A thought I had often needled away at me.

When am I allowed to worry about you?

Instead, I said, "Okay…who's Lorena?"

It didn't escape me, the way he mentioned Silas's wife with underlying rancor.

Río's throat bobbed as he swallowed thickly. His long silence only confirmed the inkling in my gut.

"She's Silas's wife—a lord's daughter from the Air Kingdom. We used to be together."

My chest flared with a furious feeling I could only assume was envy. Even though it was obvious that someone like Río could and would have had other lovers, his reaction unsettled me.

"Oh," was all I managed.

"We were teenagers, Esmé. It was a long time ago," he said. "She's married to Silas now."

And if she wasn't?

It was another reason they loathed each other, I assume. It didn't help my turmoil, but I pushed it down.

"Okay," I replied simply.

"Just stay away from him, alright?"

I frowned at his tone. "Is that jealousy talking, or…?"

I was aware of my hypocrisy when I asked that question.

Río snorted in amusement.

"I have a feeling he's not your type." I must have made a face because he laughed, before getting serious again. "It's more than just that. There's a reason we're not friends anymore. He's not a good person. Trust me."

"Alright."

I couldn't help but feel like there was something vital he wasn't telling me. Maybe it was what Silas said before we left, or even what Dulce told me back in my apartment. I didn't want to believe the rumor, but after that last interaction, I wondered if something *had* happened years ago.

Like countless times before, I tried telling myself that I shouldn't care. I knew better than to go poking into the prince's life, but things felt different since he last returned. Especially tonight. He was so protective over me in the eyes of so many people watching. It was something new between us. Then again, with the nature of our late-night meetings, he didn't have the chance. Every day, he made the possibility of letting go that much harder.

We stared at each other for a long, aching moment. The energy was so intoxicating between us, and I had to look away because, inherently, I am a coward. Instead, I traipsed around the gallery, taking in what it had to offer. The walls were covered in massive pieces of art, from still lives to landscapes and portraits of old monarchs. Around the open space, there were statues and old artifacts like daggers and black clay pots.

A soft smile played on my lips as the prince lingered behind me, stopping next to me when I stopped. His shoulder brushed mine, and in a daring move, I let my hand drop beside his as I lingered before a family portrait of the Markaél's. It was *Rey* Marino, who looked like an older version of Río, with a beard and silver-scaled armor. He was broad-shouldered and had swirling tattoos on his forearms. *Reina* Victoria was pressed into his side with a grin, and his arm was around her waist. In front of them sat their children, *Princesa* Mariela and *Príncipe* Río himself. I admired everyone's faces, but mainly the prince's. Even in this medium, he still had that mischievous look in his eyes. It was a look that he shared with the king.

"Marisláni, save me," Río groaned.

I glanced over to see him scowling at the painting in discomfort.

"What? You don't like it?" I asked with an amused giggle.

"I certainly don't like staring at it."

"I, for one, think the painter did a great job, but I prefer the real thing."

He smirked. "Do you?"

"I do."

His knuckles brushed against mine, sending tingles across my skin.

"Did you mean what you said about me being your date?" I asked, studying the painting.

He hummed lowly. "I did."

"What would your family think?"

"I don't care what my family thinks. At least not about this."

My cheeks warmed, and my heart skipped a beat as our pinkies locked together. Again, I couldn't tell if he bold or out of his mind.

"But aren't princes supposed to be with princesses or some noble's daughter of the highest degree? I think I miss the mark in a lot of ways," I whispered.

"Who told you I wanted any of that?"

My head snapped up in surprise, and the look in his eyes took my breath away. In this room dedicated to art, he looked at me as if I were a painting worth admiring. And the scary thing was, I could say the same about him.

The prince laced his fingers with mine and leaned in a little closer. Suddenly, I was in a daze, my knees getting weak, and if he wasn't touching me, I fear I may have floated away.

"You really do look beautiful tonight," he whispered, with a timid glint in his eye.

"Thank you. I didn't get a chance to tell you, but you play the piano beautifully."

He smiled sheepishly and I bit my lip. He rarely blushed, and it made me giddy.

"Thanks. It means a lot coming from you," he said.

"Of course. I appreciate you inviting me. It's overwhelming with all these people…"

He grimaced. "Yeah, I know."

"But I'm glad you're here."

I'm always glad you're here.

Río inhaled, and suddenly he was pivoting to cup the back of my neck. His fingers gently caressed my skin, and I unconsciously shivered. He inclined his head close enough so our noses brushed together, but he didn't bridge the gap just yet. The proximity and the feeling of his breath against my skin made me burn with anticipation and desire. I was clay in his hands, eager and waiting to be molded.

"Can I kiss you? I've been wanting to kiss you all night," he murmured.

My words came out like a sigh of relief: "Have you?"

"Yes."

"So have I."

He pulled me toward him and devoured my lips in a kiss. It was ardent and sensual, and I didn't realize how much I craved this until I moaned into his mouth. As if our nights in my apartment weren't already forbidden, doing something like this in the middle of a palace event was even more so. I feared a god might smite me, or worse, the queen.

I pulled away for a moment, mumbling, "We probably shouldn't be doing this."

"Probably," he said against my jaw.

"Someone might find us."

"I don't care."

He captured my lips once more, and all my protesting died with his kiss. His hands went to my waist, pulling me flush against him. With a soft sigh, I curled my fingers into his hair, willing the private moment to never end. The prince had a habit of roping me in with his unapologetic nature and rubbing it off on me as if it were my own. I almost believed that none of it mattered and that we were safe within these walls.

A door creaked open, and the room filled with the sound of barking. The prince and I disconnected from each other with a startled gasp, and something metallic clattered to the floor. I jolted at the harsh sound, my heart already thrumming as *Príncipe* Río cursed. We both looked towards the noise to see his silver crown on the floor and then glanced up just in time to watch Echo barrel towards him with a gleeful smile. While the prince fended her off, I was met with the face of *Princesa* Mariela, who was standing by the gallery door. Her eyes were as big as saucers, and her mouth was open in shock.

My stomach dropped, and my skin went beet red, running so hot I could mistake it for a fever. She had undoubtedly seen at least the tail end of what transpired between her brother and me, and I was absolutely mortified.

"*A-Alteza*," I stammered, managing a wobbly curtsy.

Beside me, Río hissed. "Aww shit."

The princess tore her eyes away from me and fixed her brother with a derisive look.

"What are you doing here?" Río demanded as he signed the words to her.

She gave him a voiceless answer, speaking with her hands. They proceeded to have an entire conversation before me that I could only watch but not understand. Whatever it was, it got progressively more argumentative, and I had a sneaking suspicion I was the topic of it.

Echo approached and sat before me with his tongue out and tail wagging. I flashed him a wary smile before my eyes caught on something behind him. The boy in the purple suit again. I choked back a yelp, and just like that, he was gone.

The prince's sigh of exasperation pulled my attention to him, though my bones were still rattled. He put his hands in his pockets, and the Moon Princess crossed her arms as she stared her brother down. She then shot me a merry smile before motioning for Echo to follow with a click of her tongue. The hound padded over to her, and they both disappeared from the gallery.

The Moon Prince picked up his crown from the floor, throwing me a remorseful smile. I dropped my face in my hands as I instantly started freaking out.

"She saw us, didn't she?"

"Only briefly. It's fiiine."

"*Río.*"

"She's good at keeping secrets. I promise," he assured.

"She didn't seem too happy about it."

"Esmé, it's okay. She's just worried."

"I'm going to throw up."

"Please don't."

The prince took my wrists delicately and pulled my hands away from my face. Of course, he was a picture of amusement and consideration. My lips turned with a skeptical frown, brows furrowed.

"How are you so nonchalant about all this?" I accused.

He shrugged. "I stopped caring what people think about me a long time ago."

Unwittingly, the statement aggravated me. I often admired the Moon Prince's optimism and his disregard for other's opinions; yet, right now, it almost made me *angry*. Whether because he was so arrogant about it, or because it was so difficult for me to meet him there sometimes. The words exchanged with various nobles, including Silas Calicó, were doing a good job of hammering into my skull.

"Must be nice, *Alteza*," I whispered bitterly, looking off towards a landscape painting.

Despite his hold on me, the prince became so quiet that I had to look at him to see if he was still there. His expression was grim, and it hit me with a pang of guilt. I almost took it all back until he spoke.

"I shouldn't have invited you here," he said.

My chest constricted, feeling as if it were about to cave in. As soon as my demeanor shifted, the prince took my face in his hands, shaking his head.

"No, not like that. I wanted you here because I wanted to see you, Esmé. I wanted to give you what you wanted. But this…this world…*my* world… It's pretty, but it has a habit of trying to eat you alive."

There was rage and anguish in his eyes as he spoke. I had a feeling that what happened with the viscount was nothing new—the whispers, the ogling, and the questions, too. I took in *Príncipe* Río now and compared him side by side with the version I came to know and the version out there in the ballroom. They were so different, I wondered which parts were real and which weren't. Whatever the answer was, I was starting to understand that there was more to why he spent his nights the way he did. If he could have a modicum of relief, no matter how far it took him, then he was going to take it.

Now, the question was: Do I add to that relief, or do I keep him here? Do I fit into this story, or am I just making things worse?

I placed my hand on his wrist and whispered, "I'm sorry."

"Don't be," he said softly. "You know… We can get out of here if you want."

The offer did seem incredibly inviting, all things considered.

"What about your family? The ball? Didn't your sister come in here looking for you?" I asked.

"I'll probably have to make a quick appearance. Although there was one thing I was hoping we could do before the night was over."

"What thing?"

"Dancing," he sang.

I gasped with delight. "Dancing?"

He giggled at my response. "Yeah, dancing."

I wouldn't mind leaving early if he were offering it, but it would be a travesty if I didn't dance at a royal ball. And with the Moon Prince as my date, at that. A dream come true was in my grasp, and I had to take it. Especially when the tricks in my mind were on the verge of ruining this time entirely.

"I'd love to," I replied enthusiastically. "Maybe just a few songs."

"In that case..." The prince stepped back and cleared his throat. With one hand behind his back, he offered me the other and asked, "Miss Vespertín, will you do me the honor of being my dance partner this evening?"

"You're really taking this whole courtship thing seriously."

"Of course I am. I am a gentleman, after all," he grinned.

With a roll of my eyes, I curtsied and took his hand.

"Why yes, *Alteza,* I would be delighted."

He tugged me towards him, eliciting a small yelp.

"Out here, you can call me Río."

"Río," I repeated poignantly, and his smile widened.

He placed my hand on his elbow and led me toward the door. As we passed by the few remaining paintings I missed, one in particular nearly made me trip over my own two feet. Río made a noise of confusion beside me as I came to a sudden stop, and my attention was glued to the image.

It was a portrait of a young boy I had seen before with lilac hair dressed in violet attire and a crown made of quartz.

"What's wrong?" the prince asked.

"Who is that?" I asked, my voice small.

"Oh, that is—*was*—*Príncipe* Saévio Vórtice. He was my uncle and my mom's younger brother. He died before I was born during the war with The Black Death," he explained grimly.

I wanted to scream.

Had I seen *Reina* Victoria's younger brother, the fallen Air Prince? I knew of him from stories and was vaguely aware of his fate. He, like many others, was killed at the hands of Casímir Gedeón in Old Avilonía. He was supposed to be dead, yet I saw him before my very eyes, and he saw *me*. He smiled and winked at me, and he disappeared just like that woman who jumped off the terrace. How was that possible? I never even knew what he looked like.

The world started closing in. The whispers from beyond the gallery and the ballroom seemed to grow louder and louder. A dull ache pressed against my head, as if something wanted to break out.

Río brushed my cheek softly with his hand. "Hey… are you okay?"

No.

"Y-Yes."

I looked around, seeing shadows, only for them to vanish in the blink of an eye.

No, not again.

"J-Just a bit of a headache," I lied.

He frowned seriously. "Are you sure you want to go back in there? Maybe we can—"

"Yes!" I exclaimed, but then cleared my throat as I recovered myself. "Yes, I want to. I could use the distraction."

The Moon Prince eyed me curiously but didn't argue.

As soon as we descended the ballroom stairs, all eyes were on us. Even the guests who were already dancing paused briefly to get a good look. I more importantly caught the attention of the queen, whose skeptical gaze struck fear in me. Despite how excited I was in the gallery, I was terrified I might be standing a little too close to the fire when it came to *Príncipe* Río Markaél.

He took my hand, leading me into the middle of the dance floor, and gave me a wide spin. The skirts of my dress twirled and gave off a faint shimmer in the firelight. He pulled me towards him so that we were chest to chest, eliciting a sound of surprise in the back of my throat. Like a proper partner, he clasped my right hand in his left and rested his right on my waist. I put my left hand on his shoulder, my fingers tracing the beaded waves on his jacket.

This closeness felt so different in this setting.

The guests talked with palpable novelty. I could hear them wondering why the prince was giving the opera singer such undivided attention. Silas Calicó was among them, watching me like a hawk. I couldn't help but give the crowd a nervous glance as we were officially the center of attention.

"Hey," Río uttered, giving my hand a soft squeeze.

I looked into his dark eyes, somewhere between black coffee and midnight.

"Look at me," he said. "Just look at me. Don't worry about anyone else, okay?"

I answered with an apprehensive nod, and for once, I kept my eyes on Río's as we moved across the dance floor in time with the music.

To my dismay, the prince was the sturdiest and most confident dance partner I've ever had. And I've had many. It was another one of his hidden talents that I'd have to prod him about later. In true Río Markaél fashion, he threw in some surprises, like spinning me around or dipping me at random intervals. There came a point where I could hardly contain my laughter, and he couldn't contain his smile. It did a good job of taking me out of my head, and we both seemed to forget that there were others around. We were so focused on each other that it somehow didn't matter how potentially dangerous this all was. I blamed it on his contagious optimism. I told him what I wanted, and he gave it to me, so I was reveling in it. I was flying.

At the end of the song, the prince lifted me by the waist and spun me around. Everyone applauded until the next song began, and as Río took me in his arms again, I noticed something strange over his shoulder. *Him.* The boy in the purple suit—*Príncipe* Saévio Vórtice. My eyes almost popped out of their sockets as a chill ran down my spine. I quickly returned my focus to Río and tried holding my composure, but the terror on my face must have been evident.

"What's wrong?" he asked, looking over his shoulder, but it was clear he didn't see what I did.

"Ummm…"

We kept moving across the dance floor at a slower pace, but the Air Prince was still there. It wasn't just him in the sea of guests either. No, there were others—people I had mistaken for partygoers but now knew otherwise. Family members, lords, and ladies, I had seen in the many portraits in the gallery. There were servants and warriors in armor, all without faces, just like the woman on the terrace. The whispers became a clamorous cacophony that drowned out the music and my thoughts. And then there, in the back of the room with the queen, stood a tall, armored man with broad shoulders and white hair.

The whispers reduced to a singular, masculine voice that said, "Run."

Río stopped and put his hands on my shoulders.

"Esmé, look at me. Talk to me. What's wrong?"

I didn't know that I was having a physical reaction until then. My chest was heaving, and my hands were shaking. Tears blurred my vision. The people around us watched silently, and the other dancers had slowed down as well, but I was too scared to feel any kind of embarrassment.

I shook my head vigorously, telling him, "I-I don't know."

Echo barked and snarled viciously. A crack came from the ceiling, drawing Río and I's attention upward. Above us was the largest chandelier, the crystals rattling against each other as it shook.

The prince looked at me in horror and then at the crowd before shouting, "Run!"

The prince's arm circled my waist, and he pulled me away just as there was another crack and the chandelier came down with a resounding crash. Everyone screamed and scurried out of the way. Río and I fell to the floor against each other, and he shielded me with his body as bits of shattered crystal and debris flew around us. When the noise seemed to quiet down, we both looked up in utter shock towards the carcass of the beautiful chandelier that now lay broken in the spot where we once stood.

Echo's barking remained incessant, and then a low, guttural growl came from behind me. With a shaking breath, I dared look over my shoulder, but nothing could have prepared me for what I was about to witness.

There, standing in a corner, was a server in dark blue attire, his eyes glowing red as he twitched in place. His muscles then rippled, his bones cracked out of place, and his face took on an inhuman shape. He grew larger and larger as fur bloomed out of his skin and sharp teeth jutted out of a long snout until, within a matter of seconds, he was no longer a man... but a half-beast.

A werewolf.

11

In Sheep's Clothing

Río

The werewolf's eyes glowed a bloody red, mist emanating from its sockets. My body froze as cold, unadulterated terror coursed through me.

This was dark magic.

How is this happening? How did it get in here?

There was more than just one. All around us, the sound of cracking and growling filled the room as more servants transformed into large, black beasts. Echo was going feral across the room. Guests let out blood-curdling screams that chilled my veins. Esmé scrambled back against me, gasping in terror. Her body shook as I held her protectively, my eyes trained on the werewolf closest to us. As if sensing my gaze, it cocked its head in my direction, and I swear it smiled before it threw its head back in a howl. The others answered in tandem, creating a haunting sound.

Despite my fear, my instincts kicked in.

"We need to go," I whispered in Esmé's ear.

In the distance, my mother shouted, "Everybody out!"

I helped Esmé to her feet, keeping her hand in mine as I broke into a run towards the stairs. My mind was intent on taking her to safety and getting to a source of water as fast as possible. I couldn't command the ocean from this far, but I could make it to the fountain on the other side of the room. Or at least I tried.

The wolf jumped overhead and landed right in front of us, blocking our way. Its weight cracked the wooden floor beneath its feet. Esmé screamed, and I pushed her behind me to shield her from it. The monster reached forward with its large paw and wrapped it around my throat, lifting me into the air and pulling me from Esmé's grasp. I choked out a strangled gasp as she shouted my name.

"Río!"

The werewolf swiped at her with its claws, as if shooing away an insect. Esmé cried out in pain, and out of the corner of my eye, I watched her collapse in a heap on the floor.

My heart dropped.

"Esmé!"

I struggled in the werewolf's clutch, trying but failing to see if she was alive. Anger overwhelmed me as the werewolf took me in with its big, scarlet eyes, its fangs bared. I held onto its paw, trying to give myself some leverage, and with a snarl of my own, I pulled my leg back and kicked it square in the snout. It shook its head but looked otherwise nonplussed.

"Don't touch her!" I hissed through gritted teeth.

In my head, there was a biting laugh and a voice that was not mine.

Don't bother fighting, Río Markaél.

My movements stopped, my eyes widening. The voice wasn't aggressive, but it was deeply *unsettling*.

You took something from me, it said.

It was as if two people were speaking at the same time. One was softer and smoother, while the other was a demonic rumble. At first, I thought the voice came from the werewolf itself, but the more it spoke, the more I knew this was something different. There was only one thing he could be talking about, and only one person who would go this far.

Sebastián Eliódor.

"Y-You," I stammered.

You didn't think I'd take a hit without hitting back, did you?

My insides turned, but I didn't let this horror silence me.

"If you came here looking for it, you're too late," I choked out. "We destroyed it."

I know, he snapped. *That's precisely why I'm here. That was very disrespectful, wasn't it?*

I looked around frantically, searching for his face in the crowd.

"You're here?"

The voice chuckled. *No. Not yet, but I will be. In time. I've been waiting for the excuse, and now I have you to thank for that.*

"You can't cross The Rift. Not while my father's still alive," I argued.

Oh, trust me, he's not a problem anymore.

The blood drained from my face, and for a moment, I was underwater. The sound of screams, shouts, and angry hounds became a horrible conglomeration in my ears. The insinuation was clear, yet I didn't want to believe it. I refused.

No, I thought. *No, he can't be dead.*

"You're lying," I spat.

I'm afraid not. You know, it's hard to forget the sound of a man getting torn to shreds.

I felt like I was falling.

THE MOON PRINCE

And now...now, it's your *turn.*

12

Whispers

Esmé

The world was a blur, and the only feeling was the searing pain in my right arm. It was different from a migraine and was similar to— what I could only imagine—being on fire. I reached to cradle it, but my mere touch was enough to make me hiss. My fingers came away slick with blood. When I dared to look at it, I saw three jagged claw marks tearing through my skin, oozing crimson. The sleeve of my dress was torn, and the gold was now splattered ruby. I almost couldn't believe it was *my* arm.

The screaming was constant and so much whispering. The metallic smell of blood filled the room. Through it all, I could make out Río's voice as he talked to someone I couldn't hear. I searched for him, only to gape in horror to see him still in the werewolf's grasp. It opened its jaws, ready to eat him alive. The whispers rose to a crescendo and I screamed.

"No!"

The voices left me, shrieking the same word over and over. The werewolf stumbled backwards. Río was released, and he fell to the ground in a coughing fit. I sat there, wide-eyed, unsure of what transpired. I took a glance to check if anyone else was doing it, but everyone, including the God-given, was either running or fighting for their life. Others were being torn to shreds. The beast clutched its head before shaking it and turning its attention to me. Its eyes glowed brighter, and as our gazes met, pain seared through my head, making me recoil with a groan.

With the beast distracted, Río called the water from the fountain. It flew over my head towards him until it was close enough to wrap around the werewolf's neck like a rope. The prince forced it back and away from me with a grunt. Then, with a motion of his hands, Río formed a frozen spear and threw it into the monster's heart. Its eyes rolled back, and it dropped lifeless to the floor, its large body causing the room to rumble and the ice to shatter on impact.

The prince pointed behind me.

"Esmé, move!"

Another beast came barreling in my direction, making me its target. I dashed to the left just in time for Río to attack it with his magic.

"Run! Get out of here!" he commanded as he proceeded to fight it off.

There was a part of me that wanted to stay with him. I didn't want to leave him at the mercy of these monsters, but I knew better. I was too scared and had no magic to offer. So I listened to *Príncipe* Río and bolted. I let my shoes fall away as I sprinted through the broken glass and bloodshed, aiming for the stairs from whence I came. Werewolves were everywhere and they were laying waste to the guests in the vicinity. More water flew around the room, commanded by the princess in a shield of protection. And to my right, there was a loud, thunderous crack as *Reina* Victoria put a hole through another werewolf. Her eyes were wild and full of rage, her dress torn.

The swarm of screaming guests carried me away, towards the stairs and my freedom, only for a clawed hand to pluck me out of the crowd. I let out a loud shriek as it pinned my arms to my sides and lifted me into the air.

Tears streaked down my cheeks as I stared into another werewolf's fiery eyes. The wound in my arm burned arduously from the constriction that I nearly passed out. I was ready for the beast to eat me or kill me like the rest, but instead it tilted its head inquisitively. Such a strange expression for a creature that I would have pondered further if my skull didn't feel like it was about to split open. I bit back a sob, awaiting my imminent death as I heard Río shout my name once again.

13

Fallen Star

Río

I wrapped the water around the werewolf's face, pulling him down and suffocating him in the process. I quickly picked up a spear off the ground from a fallen guard and jumped onto its back. It tried clawing at me and shaking me off, but I was furious and unrelenting. I plunged the blade into its back once, twice, and three times into his heart as I screamed until he finally collapsed beneath me. My chest burned from the exertion, sweat running down the side of my face.

From the top of the werewolf's body, I saw my mother putting a bolt of lightning through one of the two beasts she was warding off. And my sister was shielding some guests as she ushered them to safety. Echo was chasing off monsters and risking his life to do his job. Many were falling dead as an entire pack of wolves tore into them. Innocent people. People I grew up around my whole life.

My body shook.

Emilia Mondragón

This is all my fault. He's not planning on letting anyone leave this room alive.

A familiar shriek called my attention to the center of the ballroom. Another hulking werewolf held Esmé in its claws, her face contorted in anguish. My stomach dropped.

"Esmé!"

I picked up a sword and ran headfirst towards it, the voice speaking to me once more.

Interesting girl you have here, little Moon Prince.

Esmé whimpered, shrinking away as if in pain.

I don't think she can hear me.

My steps wavered, the statement catching me off guard. I flitted my gaze between the werewolf and Esmé. It was easy to tell which ones were actively being controlled by the Sun Killer. Not only was it the glowing eyes, but also the change in demeanor. While the others were animalistic, this one was inspecting her. And his words terrified me.

What does that mean? I asked myself.

The wolf looked at me and said, *You won't mind if I keep her, will you?*

I scowled at him, tightening the grip on my sword.

"Let her go!"

No, I don't think I will.

I lunged. He took a swipe, but I slid between his legs, slicing at his ankles. The werewolf lurched, and as he did, Esmé fell from his grip. I took the opportunity to reach out to the now-empty fountain, begging and pleading with all my rage. It cracked and sputtered as I bared my teeth, forcing my magic to reach out, latching onto it. Then, with a sigh of relief, a huge wave of water broke through the stone. I honed its energy and threw it at the wolf with a scream, slamming it right into its body and sending it flying. With both hands, I froze the water in place, encasing the werewolf in icicles that pierced right into him. Blood oozed from its immobile body onto the ice and floor.

But, *he* wasn't going to stop until he was finished.

14

The Stepping Stone

Esmé

Stars danced before my water pooled around me. When I managed to recover, I looked up to see Río warding off werewolves left and right, with his mother not far off. He fought with an ease and fury that was marvelous despite the circumstances.

With the water floating around him, the prince's eyes met mine across the room. I could see the intention in his eyes and wanted to tell him to stop for his safety, but he was already dashing toward me. In that moment, another half-hound was already on his heels, as if they were all intent on taking him down.

"Río!" I cried.

The prince looked over his shoulder just as the black werewolf crashed onto him, knocking him to his back. Río groaned and tried drowning it with the water, circling them both in a shining blue orb. I stared through the warped surface as the monster continued to snap at him with its teeth, on a mission to devour. In an attempt to shield his face and neck, Río raised his arms, and the creature sank its teeth into his skin. The prince cried out, and the hold on his magic released, flooding the ballroom at my knees.

In the seconds leading up to that moment and the ones that followed, my vision seemed to darken around the edges as the whispers returned. In the recesses of my skull, there was the cracking of glass. It was as if there were a fiery pit of my own deep inside my chest, begging to be released like a dragon's breath. I couldn't tell if it was anger, grief, fear, or something else, but it was unlike anything I had ever experienced before. When I saw Río at the mercy of such a wild beast, all I could think was, *Get away from him.*

That one thought echoed all over me in a million voices coming together, and then it morphed with my scream.

Get away from him. Get away from him. Get away from him.

Get away from him. Get away from him. Get away from him.

Get away from him. Get away from us!

As the monster bit him, there was the sound of rustling and bones cracking. Gasps cut through the cries, pulling me out of my mind and back to reality. At first, I thought it was the werewolves proceeding with their terror, but no, something much worse had elicited such a reaction.

The corpses of the dead had somehow risen.

Some of them stood over me, their eyes crackling with violet embers. I shrank away, my hands covering my mouth, muffling my blood-curdling scream. The beast that was attacking the prince stopped its movement to look around in shock. Río himself, who was now sopping wet, clutched his bloody arm in disbelief. Those running for the door were either too stunned to move or were moving faster than ever.

I tried pushing myself to my feet to run away, but kept slipping on the damp floor. Tears fell my face, convinced that whoever sent the werewolves summoned another wave of creatures to obliterate us.

Instead, they rushed forward towards the back of beasts, and paid no mind me, the prince, or anyone else.

Río rolled out of their path, and we all watched, petrified, as they tore the beasts to shreds with an inhuman strength that no dead body should have. Even the Queen of Storms seemed at a loss for words.

At long last I got to my feet, but teetered from a sudden immense fatigue. My head weighed like stone, but I tried pressing forward at a sluggish pace towards the prince.

"Río." My voice was hoarse as I said his name.

He turned towards me, his face lighting up as our eyes connected, only to fall into a strange, appalled expression.

"Esmé?"

The world spun around me, and stars spotted my vision once more as the weight of exhaustion pushed down on my body.

"Río?" I slurred.

My legs gave out, and the last thing I remember was the prince shouting my name one last time.

15

A Broken Promise

Esmé

The hard surface of the ballroom floor turned into something softer and warmer beneath me as I came back to consciousness. The sound of roaring thunder brought me back to my body and my awareness to the resounding downpour beating against a nearby window. There was no screaming, no growling, no whispers of the dead. It was otherwise utterly quiet, which was eerie within itself.

My eyes slowly fluttered open, but the room was pitch black. Without even needing to move, my body seemed to ache. There was pressure in my head, and my right arm throbbed. But the strangest thing of all was the weight on my wrists and the feeling of something covering my mouth. The condensation from my warm breath made it even more suffocating.

What happened to the ballroom?
Where is this? Where is everyone?

Emilia Mondragón

I reached over to scratch my itching arm, and chains rattled with my movement. I gasped, but it was a muffled sound. I felt around my face and my fingers found leather—a muzzle strapped to my jaw. I sat up in a panic, pain shooting up my arm as more rattling ensued. The source, to my horror, came from a pair of manacles seizing and weighing down my wrists. No matter how hard I tried, they couldn't be removed. And as my body trembled, I started to scream.

Did one of the wolves take me? Is everyone dead? Am I being held captive by an evil sorcerer somewhere where no one can find me? Are they going to kill me? Is Río dead?

"She's awake," a male voice said beyond the door.

I clung to that voice, and though stifled, I cried for help, pulling at my restraints as tears streamed down my face. Many agonizing minutes passed, and still, I received no response to my pleas. Yet I screamed with all my might until my lungs gave out, and all I could do was sit there with my knees tucked into my chest, shaking from my sobs.

Just as I was about to lose hope, I heard the rustling of armor and the jangling of keys. Something clicked, and a door creaked open. A dark figure moved across the room and pulled the curtains apart at a far window. I whimpered as the harsh daylight cut through the darkness. I lifted a manacled arm to shield my eyes, and that was when he spoke.

"Esmé."

I dropped my hand and sat upright with a wince. I almost thought I imagined it or that perhaps I was in some dream, but there he was, plain as day, standing before me.

Río.

His bright sapphire suit was long gone, as he was now dressed from the neck down in all-black vestments—the color of mourning. The contrast between it and his hair made him look striking and cold.

Yet despite how clean and well-dressed he looked, I could see how battered he was. He was alive, but there were a few bruises above his collar, and a brokenness in his eyes that wasn't there before.

The prince stood frozen in place as his gaze scanned over my entire being with a haunted expression. I moved toward him but was once again stopped by my chains. I tried saying his name, but only incoherent sounds came out. He cast a furious look at the guard who was standing by the window.

"Get that thing off her," he growled.

The armored man stood straight and addressed the prince respectfully: "I'm sorry, *Alteza*, but the queen insisted she wear it until we know how her magic works."

My eyes widened. *Magic?*

"*She's* not the animal here. I think she'll be fine," Río snapped.

The guard stiffened at the veiled threat, and I eyed them both warily. The prince's shoulders drooped, exhaustion and irritation encumbering him.

"She can't talk if she's muzzled. Remove it, or I will," he ordered with more composure.

The guard gave a curt nod. "As you wish, *Alteza*."

I stood stock still as the man made his way to me with a ring of keys in hand. He approached with an air of unease and skepticism that was strange to me. Nevertheless, he reached behind my head, and there was a faint click. The muzzle loosened, setting my jaw free. I sighed and proceeded to rub my face, taking deep breaths.

"Leave us," the prince told him.

The guard hesitated once more but didn't object. With the muzzle in hand, he exited the room, leaving Río and me to ourselves in the small chamber. The authority quickly left the prince's demeanor, replaced by worry, sorrow, and guilt as his eyes met mine.

"Río. Río, you're okay," I stammered, my voice hoarse.

I moved as far as my restraints would let me, realizing then that I was no longer wearing the gown Dulce made for me but a white nightdress that was not mine. I tried not to let my mind linger on who could've put me in it.

"Esmé," he whispered. "Esmé, I'm so sorry."

"What's going on? What happened? Why am I here? Why am I in chains?" I asked, my voice quaking.

He moved to the edge of the bed, resting his hand on the frame.

"You don't remember anything?"

"I mean…" I trailed off as I went through the events of the ball. "I remember the chandelier falling and breaking. I remember the werewolves and getting injured. I remember you getting attacked and then it bit you…"

I gasped as a new kind of horror struck me. Río pulled up the sleeve of his right arm, revealing a white bandage beneath. My fearful gaze met his grim eyes.

"You were bitten by a werewolf," I whispered sharply. "Doesn't that—doesn't that mean—"

"Yes."

My hand flew over my mouth.

Aside from breeding, the only way to pass on the werewolf curse was through a bite. A scratch like mine would only ever leave a scar, but if someone were to get bitten, they'd transform by the next full moon. No doubt, the one who bit Río didn't intend on letting him live, but things turned out differently. His life was spared in exchange for a curse.

"Well, isn't there anything you can do?" I rambled anxiously, "I'm sure there's a cure somewhere. A way to break the curse—"

"Esmé, trust me. We've had hundreds of years to look for one and still haven't found anything. It isn't that simple," he said, shaking his head.

I frowned. It pained me to see such a burden fall on him.

"What else do you remember?" he asked.

I recalled the bloody scene in the ballroom. The massacre, the blood, the screams, and then...

"The corpses," I uttered. It gave me goosebumps just thinking about it. "The corpses came alive, and they killed them all."

Río nodded, his brow furrowing curiously. "Do you know *how* they came alive?"

I shrugged. "No. It just happened. Whoever sent those werewolves must have done it."

The only other person who could raise the dead was Casímir Gedeón. He's been dead for many years, but if there was anyone who could be capable of doing such a thing now, it was Sebastián Eliódor. But if he figured out how to raise the dead, what hope did Avilonía have?

"That's what I thought at first," the prince said.

"At first?"

He went quiet for a moment, staring down at the bed intensely. His knuckles turned white as he gripped the bed frame before meeting my eyes again.

"Esmé... do you remember what happened before the chandelier fell?"

Now, it was my turn to go silent. I worked my jaw as I looked down at my hands. I instinctively tried playing with the malachite ring, but found that it too was gone. My lips pouted in disappointment, and I tried not to let the thought of losing it overwhelm me.

"You started to *panic*, remember?" the prince continued, "Can you tell me why?"

It was hard to erase what I had seen on the dance floor from my memory, both before and after the wolves appeared. I remembered the faces of people who weren't even alive, looking right at me—the queen's brother, and the very clear figure of the Moon King. I didn't know what it meant, but it couldn't have been anything good. I did what I could to ward off my condition, and after my last visit to Canela's, I thought it was at least under control, but now nothing made sense.

Talking about it out loud scared me. Río knew about my headaches, but he didn't know about the shadows. He didn't know what Canela said about me being poisoned or about the woman who jumped from the roof. He didn't know how mad I truly was. It choked me to try and speak.

"You're going to think I'm crazy," I said, my eyes brimming with tears.

Río scoffed, "Sweetheart, I'm turning into a monster by the next full moon, and the dead rose last night. Try me."

When I looked into his eyes, there was nothing but care there. It warmed my heart, even if for a moment.

With a harsh swallow, I finally replied, "Spirits. I saw them. I *heard* them... *everywhere*, and I couldn't make it stop."

He tensed. "What did they say?"

"To run."

Río worked his jaw, his expression one of concern.

"Have you always been able to see spirits?" he asked.

"No. It started with the migraines," I admitted in a small voice.

He furrowed his brow. "The migraines? The ones Canela helps you with?"

"Yes. I've been going insane for years trying to figure out what's wrong with me, and then all of a sudden, I started seeing things that weren't there. At first, it was shadows out of the corners of my eyes, and then... well... The potion helped me for a long time. Until now, that is."

The Moon Prince straightened up, and for the first time in our entire relationship, the worry dwindled, now replaced with foreboding.

"I knew you would think I was crazy," I whimpered.

"I don't think you're crazy," he contested.

"Yes, you do! You're looking at me like you do!" I exclaimed.

"I'm *worried*! Not just anyone can see the dead, Esmé," Río stressed.

"You don't think I know that?" I blurted out. "Why do you think I never told anyone?"

"Since when did the potion stop working?"

Again, I faltered, the words sticking to the back of my throat as I recalled that the pull of the black diamond and how he reacted to me finding it.

"Esmé…"

"Since the day you returned," I muttered in shame.

Río sputtered, his eyes flashing. "The stone. You said you didn't touch it."

"I didn't! I swear!"

"Then why did the dead rise last night, Esmé?" he shouted in the same tone.

I blinked suddenly, completely taken aback by his question. There was a very clear insinuation there, and I almost didn't want to believe that it was directed toward *me*. But there was no humor in him at all, only accusation and a sliver of betrayal. It crushed me and made me sick to my stomach.

"You think *I* did that? You think *I* used dark magic?" I demanded.

"Unfortunately, all signs point to that, yes," he replied seriously.

I got up on my knees, trying to make myself taller and to make him understand.

"Río, I'm not even a witch! I've never practiced magic a day in my life!"

"You drink a potion for your headaches. You go to Canela's frequently. She taught you how to patch people up. She must have taught you more."

"That's simple first aid! I don't perform spells or rituals. You know this. I don't make the potions myself. I wouldn't know how!" I was so riled up. I couldn't remember the last time I shouted so much. "I'm from Anelante! Sebastián killed my parents! He destroyed my entire kingdom! Do you really think I would even dare to touch the same magic that he or The Black Death used? You said the signs of possession were obvious."

Instead of continuing to shout, Río took a step back in anguish. It was more confusing than anything else.

"Your eyes were glowing, Esmé," he said weakly.

My anger was put on hold as I fell back onto my heels, the chains rattling around me.

"W-What?"

"Your eyes were glowing," he repeated with more firmness. "They were the same color as the corpses. Violet. I saw it just before you passed out."

I restlessly carded my fingers through my hair. I couldn't believe what he was saying. I didn't want to. How could *I* have done that? I never even touched magic before, let alone something as dark as *necromancy*. Weren't rituals required for such a thing? Could it have truly been the stone? Was its pull so strong that I didn't need to touch it at all? Was I slowly being possessed and controlled against my will without my knowing it?

"I-I didn't-I didn't know. I couldn't-I've never—"

"Listen," the prince said gently, "maybe you're telling the truth, and you don't know what you did or how you did it... but that makes you even more dangerous."

I gave him a sharp look. "*Dangerous?* But I *am* telling the truth. I don't want to hurt anyone!"

The prince grimaced, his voice wavering as he spoke, "I know. I know you don't, and I'm sorry, but...until we know more..."

He eyed the manacles on my wrists, and it sent me into a spiral.

"No, no, no, Río, please," I begged, fighting against the chains. "Don't leave me here! I didn't mean it! I'll prove it! I'll do anything! Río, please let me go!"

The prince backed away, his face full with torment.

"Esmé, you have to understand. The only other person who could do what you did was a monster. I can't just let you go," he stressed, his voice breaking.

"What are they going to do?" I demanded.

"I… I don't know…"

My heart broke the further he got from me. Río, my rogue prince, who was often so eager to help me, refused to do it when I needed it most.

"But you promised!" I wailed. "You said you'd always be there, but you lied! I knew this would happen! I never should've trusted you!"

The Moon Prince winced, turning his back to me. He put his hand on the door, his shoulders rising and falling as he tried to still himself. I heard him sniffle, and without saying another word, he wrenched the door open and abandoned me in my prison.

"No, please! Río!"

I heaved a sob as the door slammed shut and fell against the bed, my heart completely shattered.

I felt so stupid and naive to think that I could live some fairy tale or that someone like *Príncipe* Río would ever truly be on my side. All those nights and so many words exchanged... for *this*. It all meant nothing. *I* meant nothing. I was a prisoner with nowhere to go and no means of escape, and all I could do was curl up into a ball and succumb to my tears until the well was dry.

16

Life Ruiner

Río

The tower door closed behind me with a heavy thud, separating me from Esmé indefinitely. I made it two steps before I stopped and stared at the stone with a tear falling from my eye. I could still hear her cries from the beyond, and it was a sound that hollowed me out more than I already was.

She was right. I *had* broken my promise. This went against everything I wanted, and there wasn't a single thing I could do about it.

I wiped my tears away before descending the tower stairs to where my mother and her guards had been listening to the conversation. The queen was ever the picture of poise and regality, donning an embroidered black dress to match my suit, yet I could see the desolation in her eyes as clear as day.

Earlier this morning, we received a message that my father's ship had been attacked and that he and everyone on it had been killed. Considering how the werewolves managed to sneak in to the palace,

Sebastián had been planning this for a while. My stealing the Eye only hastened the process. There was still a question of how exactly it happened, which we were investigating. The rest of my father's ships were still on the front lines, but without his magic, it was only a matter of time before the Sun Killer broke through. Esmé being caught up in all of this was simply the cherry on top of it all.

I couldn't find it in myself to be kind about any of it. None of us did.

"Are you satisfied?" I asked, looking my mother in the eyes.

She gave me a vicious, tight-lipped smile.

"No, of course I am not satisfied," she spat. "Your father is dead, as are many of our people. My only son got bitten by a werewolf because he managed to piss off the most dangerous man in the world. Not only that…he's also brought a girl that he's infatuated with—who has mysterious necromantic powers—right into our home. I have to do damage control, including for the stunt you pulled on the dance floor. Shall I keep going?"

Feeling as if I've been slapped, I swallowed hard, finding no other words worthy of an argument.

"Are we doing this or not?" I whispered.

My mother nodded. "The carriage is waiting at the front. You will be riding separately with the captain."

"Won't people talk?"

"They're already talking. Right now, I care more about safety than words."

Giving in, I held my arms out banally to Captain Dominic who brought out a pair of handcuffs. I kept my shoulders square and my head high as he secured them to my wrists despite the tumultuous sea of emotions I struggled to ward off. They manacles were attached to a thick chain that the captain wrapped around his fist like a leash. It was a precaution now that I was on my way to being more monster than human.

My mother led the way as I was dragged along to the main floor, past the destroyed ballroom. It unsettled me even now. The iron stench of blood never seemed to leave my nose, and the sheer terror still rocked me to my core. I fear I may relive it until the day that I die.

Once we were out on the driveway, I heard a soft grunt and a bark from the carriage beside mine. I locked eyes with my sister, who looked puffy from crying, and nearly burst into tears myself. She ran towards me, evading both my mother and the guards, to throw her arms around my shoulders. I couldn't hug her back, not this time, but I still kissed the side of her head. Something in me cracked and I feared I wasn't strong enough to keep myself from truly breaking.

When Mariela let go, she was crying all over again. I reached out with my bound hands and wiped her tears away before my mother ushered her towards their carriage. My sister tried arguing with her, to which I signed that we'd see each other later. It was enough to calm her down and give me something to look forward to on this bleak day.

We silently jostled down the island in our carriages across the quartz bridges until we arrived at a domed building made of marble and moonstone. It was a place dedicated to worshiping Marisláni called *El Templo de la Luna.* Every temple for the moon goddess was built at the edge of a body of water, and the moon temple of Coáraluna was the grandest of them all, facing out towards the western horizon. Many people were baptized there in the ocean's waters, rituals were performed at different moon phases, and the God-given held their coronations. And it was also a place where people were put to rest.

Today, a crowd gathered outside the pillars, waiting for the funeral ceremony to start. Not only were we mourning my father today, but all the lives that were lost on the winter solstice. The surviving nobility and their families were among them, as were many others who wanted to pay their respect. Through the carriage window, I tried to see if Silas showed up, but thankfully, I couldn't find him.

Upon arrival, Captain Dominic removed my manacles and opened the door to let me out. As I stepped into the clouded gloom, my eyes swept across the many crying faces. I simply nodded in greeting as their sobs needled away at me. While I would have donned a charming smile any other day, it didn't feel right this time. I didn't have it in me to muster a single smirk. I was mourning many things today.

Mariela immediately rushed to my side with Echo and my mother following behind. We shared a pained smile before they each took my arm and entered the temple.

Unlike the exterior, the inside of *El Templo de la Luna* was decorated from floor to ceiling in a colorful mosaic of tiles. It told a story of Marisláni's birth, her story, and the legend of the first champion of the moon goddess, Perla Markaél. The arched windows were pushed open, letting in the salty ocean breeze. Up ahead, on a raised dais, was a statue of Marisláni beneath a circular skylight with a smattering of flowers, candles, and offerings at her feet. Behind her were large stone arches overlooking the sea. Occasionally, a wave would crash; its spray would fly into the sky.

Before the statue stood a priestess and three other devotees. They were dressed in flowing iridescent robes of sheer fabric and fish scales. Headpieces of gold, moonstone, and aquamarine adorned their hair and faces. They bowed as the three of us stopped before them, and then we all bowed our heads towards the effigy.

What began was a ceremony for the passing of my father and the victims of the winter solstice. Since we found no body to decorate or burn, we could only honor his spirit. My mother gave over one of his moonstone-laden crowns, and the priestess placed it before the goddess' feet. The devotees handed us flowers to place around it, and I managed to do so with shaking hands and silent tears. They then proceeded to sing and dance around the statue as the crowd sang along.

My sister curled into me, sobbing as I held her close. Our father was her hero just as much as he was mine and this loss would forever leave a rift in our lives.

I took a glance at my mother, expecting the same thing, but she was stock still. Her eyes were vacant. To an outsider, she may come across as frigid and unfeeling, but I knew better. A light had been snuffed out in her, and it broke me. It broke all of us.

Eventually, the devotees encouraged others to place flowers around the statue in honor of the fallen. As they lined up in the center of the room, I let my eyes trail up towards the statue of Marisláni. I wasn't one to beg, yet I pleaded for some sign or reassurance. My faith in her never wavered. After all, my magic was hers, but I had difficulty finding the meaning behind what had happened. There was no clarity in the future either; there was only fear, and I couldn't help but wonder if I was being punished. I also wondered if my father's death affected her, too. Did she mourn her champions when they passed? Was it like losing a child or a creation? Did she regret giving us this gift? Was she disappointed in our inability to complete what we set out to do? Because the way I see it, the country only seemed to break more and more every year.

✶ ☽ ◯ ☾ ✶

Back home, I gave my sister a final embrace and went into my room one last time to change into something more comfortable. In the hallway, I was restrained anew. Because we didn't spare a single second in this place. I was then taken down like a dog to slaughter through the many levels of the palace until we were below the main floor, in a dimly lit stone dungeon.

My mother stopped before a vacant cell and turned to me with a stern look. I worked my jaw, unable to look her in the eyes.

"This is for your own good, darling. I hope you understand," she told me.

I hummed angrily. "Is it now?"

"With your father gone, I have to do what's best. Not only for our people but for our family. We just took a massive hit, Río. And from what you told me, Sebastián has taken quite an interest in you, which is not good. Until I get this mess cleaned up and until I figure out our next move, you should stay here. The last thing we need is another werewolf loose in the castle."

"I guess I just didn't expect my mother to treat me like an animal so quickly," I said, throwing her a glare.

She narrowed her eyes. "You saw the way those beasts acted last night. The way they massacred everyone. Even if they *were* controlled by Sebastián, we don't know enough about them. They're not typical werewolves, Río. We don't know how much control you might have when you turn. We don't know how powerful *his* influence is. If not for me, then think of your sister. Think of the guilt you'd have on your conscience if something happened to her."

The mention of Mariela hit me to my core, poking at my lingering, unresolved guilt.

"It's just until the full moon passes. Six days, and then we'll see what happens," she reassured.

"What if I can help?" I suggested. "With the mess. The Rift. I've spent plenty of time with Dad and am familiar with his strategies. I know Esmé better than you do. I can help!"

My mother raised a hand to stop me. "After what you've pulled, the last thing I need is your input on what should be done."

I rolled my eyes, burning with frustration. My mother motioned to the captain, who opened up the cell and ushered me within its metal bars. He wrapped the ends of the chain tightly around a ring on the wall and locked them in place before exiting the cell and sealing me in.

My mother grabbed one of the bars and looked at me between the steel earnestly.

"Until the full moon passes, my love."

She walked away, and my heart began to race.

"Wait!" I shouted, rushing the bars.

The chains tugged on my wrists, preventing me from touching the door. My mother came back with a questioning brow.

"What are you going to do to her?" I asked urgently.

"I'm going to question her and then have her tested to see the true origin of her abilities," the queen replied.

"And then…?"

My mother eyed me thoughtfully, not saying anything for a moment. The silence was deafening, worsening the dread I've been feeling since this entire debacle started. I knew how ruthless my mother could be, and I didn't blame her. But when it came to Esmé…

"You're not going to kill her, are you?" I whispered.

"That depends," she replied with a sad shrug.

The queen disappeared again and I instantly panicked. And it was in that panic that I remembered something from the bloodshed and chaos of last night. Something extremely vital.

"He said she couldn't hear him!" I blurted out in desperation, my voice echoing in the stone dungeon.

My mother looked over her shoulder at. "Who?"

"Sebastián." I panted as my heart pounded in my chest. "When he was holding Esmé, he said she couldn't hear him speaking in her mind. He wanted to keep her because of it."

She furrowed her brow, crossing her arms. "Are you sure?"

"Yes, I'm sure," I stressed. "He called her an 'interesting girl' and refused to let her go. He didn't even know who she was."

"Well, then… I guess your little girlfriend might be more intriguing than I thought."

17

Mother of Storms

Esmé

My cell was a small, circular room made of stone with a high ceiling that rounded out into a dome. An iron-wrought chandelier hung from it, though no one had the courtesy to light it. Other than the bed, there was a small bedside table, a chamber pot, and a chair by a lone arched window, which provided my one source of light. Not that I could use any of it at will, as I was still muzzled and chained to the bed.

I was a shell of a human being or like some kind of caged animal. I must have cried every last tear that was left in my body until I was numb, staring at the walls for what could have been days. My arm throbbed and itched from the werewolf's claws, making it hard to think. Eventually, exhaustion took over and pulled me into dreams filled with werewolves, blood, and screams. In some of them, Río died, and in others, *I* died. In one dream, undead corpses tore me to shreds, and in another, Río morphed into a dark half-beast and pulled me apart with his teeth. Every time, I woke up screaming, and while the nightmares fell away, I could never shake the reality of what happened in that ballroom.

Some broken part of me hoped that this was all some hallucination, a dream within a dream that I had yet to wake up from. Perhaps I was still asleep in my home in the Larimar District, and the ball hadn't happened yet. I'd wake up, get ready, and enjoy a night of no horrors, and my friends would be waiting for me when I got back, begging for juicy details. Or perhaps I'd wake up never having known *Príncipe* Río Markaél at all. Yet, regardless of everything, the last idea filled me with despair. And my heart ached at the thought of my friends. Even though I was sure nothing would come out, I wanted to cry again.

Dulce. She said she'd check up on me today. She's probably worried sick. They all probably are.

But I had no way to contact them at all. I had no power or freedom anymore.

I'm no expert at lock-picking, but even if I were, I'm sure I wouldn't get very far. They took all of my hairpins and jewelry to keep me from attempting such a thing. I had no idea where I was. I had no grasp of the layout of the castle, but most importantly, I was in the home of the God-given. Río and Mariela could drown me if they pleased, and the queen would put a hole through my heart if I even *tried* to escape. Although jumping out the window didn't sound like a horrible last resort. After all, if they truly thought I was some monstrous necromancer like Gedeón, then my days were already numbered. There was no guessing what would happen next.

I torpidly watched the rain dappling against the glass of the window when again there was shuffling outside my door. Thinking it was Río coming back with good news, I hastily sat up. Unfortunately, when the door swung open, a different Markaél walked inside.

My eyes grew as *Reina* Victoria entered my chamber with a guard in tow.

"Remove her muzzle, please," she ordered.

Unlike with the prince, the guard did not hesitate once with her request and deftly removed the leather binding from my face. I massaged my cheeks as I eyed her warily, my heart already racing with anticipation.

"Leave us," she told him.

A cold, pressing silence fell as I was left with the Queen of Storms. She glanced up at the light fixture, and with a touch of a ring on her finger, the candles lit up with orange flames. A simple charm, no doubt. She then clasped her hands in front of her, regarding me with icy skepticism that cut like a knife.

The monarch looked even more fearsome than she did in the ballroom. Her lilac hair was half-up in braids, while the rest fell sleek behind her back. The almost amethyst color stood out against her obsidian, long-sleeve dress. Her crown was still on her head, a clear symbol of status and authority, as were a smattering of rings on her fingers. The look she gave me in the ballroom had been enough to put me on edge, but it was nothing compared to the expression she had for me now. She was imposing, coiled like a snake that was ready to strike at any given moment, and I was her prey.

Again, I didn't know whether to shrink away or not. It wasn't exactly easy to look put together in front of a queen when I was in shackles and a shoddy nightgown. Still, I exercised the skills I honed over the years and at the opera, resting my hands in my lap with my back straight. Despite my best efforts, I spent more time looking anywhere but at her piercing gaze.

"*Majestad*," I whispered.

"Esmé Vespertín, is it?" *La Reina* asked in a clear-cut voice.

"Yes."

"Do you know why you're here, Miss Vespertín?"

I swallowed thickly, remembering my shouting match with Río and his horrifying revelation.

"Only what the prince has told me," I said.

"And what has he told you?"

I toyed with the fabric of my gown. "That I raised the dead."

"And do you agree with that accusation?"

"No, I—" I began defensively before clamping my mouth shut. My face turned red, and I took a deep breath before answering with more tranquility. "If that's true, then I don't recall it. I've never done anything like that before, nor would I ever want to."

She glowered. "Are you sure about that, Miss Vespertín? Because, from what I heard, you can see spirits."

It was jarring to have her know my dark secret, especially since I had no defense for it.

"It's not something I have control over, *Majestad.*"

"We'll see about that."

Her mockery was like a slap in the face.

The queen crossed her arms, looking somewhat warrior-like as she raised her chin seriously.

"Are you truly from Anelante?" she prodded.

"Yes, I am," I answered firmly.

"And when exactly did you cross The Rift?"

"When I was a child."

She raised an eyebrow. "And what of your parents?"

"They... *died* just before crossing the sea. All I have of them is my name and, well, a ring they left behind."

"Ah, yes." She reached into her skirt pocket and took out the familiar green ring. "I had to make sure it didn't have any secret enchantments. Lucky for you, I found none."

The Queen of Storms tossed the piece of jewelry towards me in a lackadaisical manner. I took it with eagerness as it landed within my reach, and as soon as I placed it back on my finger, a sense of comfort washed over me.

"We also found this on you," she said.

Río's aquamarine necklace dangled from her and my heart dropped. It completely slipped my mind that I brought it with me at all. I was supposed to return it to the prince by the end of the night, before things took a turn. There was a look of disapproval in the queen's eyes as she held it. I stammered, trying to find some excuse, but I didn't know what was worse: explaining why Río gave it to me or letting her think that I stole it.

"I... I d—"

"This was a gift from his grandmother, on his father's side. Did you know that?"

A gasp caught in my throat, coming out strangled. "He mentioned it was given to him, yes."

"She got it for him before The Rift was created. My son was born on a blue moon, you see, and she wanted to commemorate that," she explained casually.

This was another piece of Río's life that I knew nothing about, and while I was intrigued, I wasn't entirely certain why the queen was sharing it with me at all.

As if reading my mind, she said, "Which means this item is of great value. In nearly 20 years, he's never lost sight of it. So, I wonder, Miss Vespertín, how in the world it got into *your* hands?"

My rambling got worse.

"I-It was only temporary. He said he'd take it back."

"Temporary? Why?"

"Uhh…"

When I didn't give an immediate answer, the queen stepped closer to me and I nearly scrambled back.

"What is my son to you?" she demanded.

The nights between Río and me danced through my memory. Talking, not talking, patching him up, kissing, and being naked. Never in a million years did I think I'd have to explain my relationship with the Moon Prince to his mother. At least not like *this*.

I cursed him in my mind for not preparing me for this somehow. *What* is *Río to me?*

All of my friends called him "my boy." *My boy*. Except Río was less of a boy, and whether he was mine was not entirely up to me. What we had was forbidden and doomed to end the way it did, but at the very least, we could agree on one thing.

"He's my friend. I care about him greatly," I answered.

The queen huffed, unconvinced. "That's all?"

"I…" I trailed off, my voice unsteady. I focused on my hands as I said, "We've never really put a name to it. I know that he's a prince, and I know that makes things complicated, but—"

"He is more than just a prince," she cut me off coldly. I snapped my attention to her, startled by her sharp tone. "He is *the Moon* Prince. A *Markaél*. Do you know what that means?"

Of course, I knew *exactly* what that meant.

"He's powerful," I responded.

The queen nodded. "And most people would do anything to have or snuff out that power, especially those like Sebastián Eliódor. Which is why I think it's convenient that someone like you, who can not only see and hear spirits but can also raise the dead, somehow made her way into my son's life."

The blood drained from my head and I shook my head vigorously.

"It's not like that at all."

"Then, please, enlighten me."

"With all due respect, *Majestad, you* came to *my* performance. I met you by chance. I had no idea we'd be formally meeting backstage."

"That doesn't mean you couldn't have seen it as an opportunity. Perhaps you were waiting for the right moment to go after him."

"I did no such thing," I argued, feeling defensive. "It was *he* who—"

My hand flew over my mouth. I didn't mean to throw Río out in the wind, but it was too late.

The queen's eyebrows shot up. "Ah, so it was *Río* who sought *you* out?"

I looked away, saying nothing more, but I'm sure my silence was enough. At this point, I was practically vibrating out of my skin, my heart like a growing flame in my chest.

Reina Victoria heaved a long, weighted sigh that turned into a soft chuckle.

"My son really loves going after what he shouldn't, doesn't he? How long have the two of you been seeing each other?"

To spare Río, I didn't want to answer, but I was in the presence of a God-given, and he accused me just as much as she did.

"Since a little after his birthday," I whispered.

"And what is it that you want out of a relationship with him?"

Thinking of the answer hurts me now, because "more" is what I would have wanted to say once, but that was too personal and mortifying to share with the queen.

"His companionship and kindness are all I could ask for. Which he's already given without me even asking," I replied simply.

"That's it?" she scoffed. "Bedding the Moon Prince isn't on the list?"

That burning in my chest grew brighter, and just like with Silas Calicó in the ballroom, I felt a sudden spark of *anger*.

What an audacious question.

"Moon Prince or not, I hardly think that matters," I contested.

"In this world, *little girl*, everything matters," she hissed, her stormy eyes narrowing. "Do you know how many girls like you *dream* of being in your position? With the attention of a powerful royal at your beck and call? I'm sure many would commit crimes. Who's to say you wouldn't?"

Her condescending tone and use of "little girl" to belittle me only aggrieved me more. While I had a habit of holding back, I felt urged to stand my ground in the face of the Queen despite my restraints and her authority. If I had nothing, I could at least fight for my dignity.

"I haven't bewitched him, if that's what you're insinuating. I've already told him that I'm not a witch. He has the freedom to come and go as he pleases. More often than not, he does come back. Perhaps you should ask *him*."

"I saw the way the two of you acted around each other all night. Even the blind would've sensed it, so don't tell me that you don't know when I know that you do. Did you truly think that what the two of you had would last? Did you think there would be more after the ball? That, with the state of the world, he'd sweep you away, and you'd get to live some fantasy? Miss Vespertín, either you had a plan or you are way in over your head because you have no idea what you're in for. What goes on in this castle is more than just swooning and playing dress-up."

Her words struck something so deep and painful within me that I had to clench my jaw to fight back tears. Yes, I told Río that was what I wanted, or rather, what I would've *liked* to have. I knew how outlandish it was to think it could happen in a world like ours, especially for a girl like me, but Río insisted. And if there was one good thing that came out of this horrible mess, it was that he granted me just that. Even if it was only for a few hours and it was all over now. Even if it wasn't entirely real.

"No, *Majestad*," I said with a shaking voice. "I come from nothing—a poisoned world that I can never go back to, and dead parents that I can't even remember. I know just how lucky I am to be alive. I am just a pretty girl with a pretty voice won the Moon Prince's attention for the time being. Nothing more. I knew it was only a matter of time before it ended. And I assure you that there is nothing you can say to me that I don't already know or that I don't say to myself every day. If it's that much trouble, then the palace can have him back. I don't need him. I never have."

My face was damp with tears as I looked right into the queen's eyes. Her expression seemed to soften, but I wasn't completely certain it wasn't pity.

"Río said you were shy. Either he was wrong, or he's rubbing off on you," she said.

My eyes flashed in surprise, and I swear I caught a hint of a smirk on her lips.

"My son... is to be king," she continued.

I gasped, straightening up at this bit of news. "*King?*"

"I assume you didn't know?"

"Know what?"

Apprehension broke through her facade. She let her eyes go to the wall, working her jaw as some painful memory passed over her eyes. Thunder cracked outside my window, making me flinch.

"The Moon King has fallen."

The air seemed to be stolen out of my lungs. Immediately, my heart ached for Río. Not only was he next in line to take the throne, but he was bitten by a beast and lost his father to The Sun Killer.

No wonder he looked so broken.

"I will be taking the weight of the kingdom for now, but eventually, should something occur, Río will take my place," the queen explained severely. "In the meantime, I will be doing everything in my power to destroy the man responsible, as well as anyone who might be remotely tied to him. Do you understand?"

I nodded silently in response.

"Were it not for the fact that your...*corpses* literally tore apart our other suspects... this would be much easier, but I'm afraid most of this rests on you. I will be having you evaluated to see just how much of the truth you're telling and to find out how your magic works. Until then, and until the full moon passes, you will not be allowed near the prince, for his safety and the safety of others."

The queen knocked on the door, and it swung open not a moment later. She lingered by the threshold as she continued to speak.

"I will have food sent up to you, and after that, we'll begin the process. Then we'll see if you truly are just a pretty girl with a pretty voice, Miss Vespertín."

18

The Queen's Court

Esmé

I was given a simple plate of yellow rice, beans, and flatbread for my first meal. I didn't realize I had been starving until it was put before me, and I ate every bite like an animal. The only other courtesy I was given was fresh bandages, which a maid replaced. It was the first time since the attack that I had seen the mark the werewolf gave me. It was still appallingly swollen and jagged, causing my arm to smart with any movement, but at the very least, it wasn't bleeding profusely. After that, I was muzzled once again and put into a different pair of manacles with a long chain attached. Wearing nothing but my nightgown, I was pulled down a spiral staircase by an armored guard. At the base of the steps was the queen who, with a swift motion, led the way through various cream and blue hallways.

Now and then, we'd pass by a steward, and the only way I was able to discern whether they were real or not was if they acknowledged the queen. It was an unsettling guessing game to play. And now that I wasn't overwhelmed by a crowd, I realized that the whispers I had been hearing were not normal at all and followed me everywhere still.

Eventually, we came upon a large wooden door with a dove carved into it. The queen knocked twice before entering, and I was dragged into another cylindrical chamber, but more than double the size of my cell. The walls were lined with bookshelves going two stories high, with ladders to access the highest ones. Two tall arched windows lit the space that was littered with books and papers, shelves with jars and crystals, and chairs that seated more literature than people. A few of the books and parchments themselves had to do with charting the stars and tracking moon phases, which would have piqued my interest in other circumstances. It reminded me of a more academic version of Canela's shop, and with fewer dead things.

In the center of the room was a curvy woman with raven hair that was half-up in two knots above her head. She wore a skirt of sage green and a corset of deep teal around the waist of her white blouse. A pair of round spectacles sat on the bridge of her nose, and her fingers were stained with ink and charcoal. She smiled at the queen, bowing her head as she greeted her with respect. When her eyes trailed over to me, her smile faded, and the light in her eyes dimmed.

Before all of this, if you were to ask anyone in my life—Río included—if I, Esmé Vespertín, could ever instill fear in *anyone*, they would surely laugh at the idea. Yet, here I stood, bound and treated like a criminal.

"I assume this is the one?" the woman asked.

"Yes," the queen nodded. "Is it ready?"

"It is."

Majestad motioned to the guard. "Put her in the chair."

The bespectacled woman stepped aside, revealing what looked to be an iron chair with restraints for the wrists and ankles. My throat tightened as the guard tugged me forward and sat me in it, sparing no kindness. He removed my manacles and then, with the help of another armored man, grabbed my wrists and secured them into the iron braces with a harsh click. They did the same to my ankles until I was trapped and immobile in what very well could be a torture device. The removal of my muzzle didn't make me feel any better.

My ability to remain calm diminished with every second. My breathing was ragged as I fought the overwhelming urge to break down. In my discomfort, I found myself wanting to fidget but couldn't due to my new restraints.

"No funny business, Miss Vespertín," *Reina* Victoria said sternly. "All the bodies from last night have already been burned, so there will be no raising the dead anytime soon. Still, you try anything, and I *will* kill you."

I didn't think there was anything I *could* do—at least, not anything that I was *aware* of.

"What are you going to do?" I asked in a small voice.

The queen looked to the other woman, who held a small bottle in her hands. It was similar to the ones Canela used, except the liquid in this one was crystal clear.

"This is Paloma," the queen said. "She's the family's wizard, and what she has here is truth serum."

My eyes widened, lingering on the vial cagily.

I've heard of truth serum in legends and from Canela. According to her, criminals and people of high authority used it. She refused to sell it because she didn't want to be responsible for putting it in the wrong hands. Of course, people like the God-given had the power to make it as they pleased. Today, I was their next victim, and I had an audience to witness it.

La Reina bore her eyes into mine and said, "Normally, I don't ask suspects for permission, but my son seems to care about you, and you've been cooperative thus far. So, I will only ask this *once*... Miss

Vespertín, do you consent to taking this truth serum so we may properly judge you?"

My gaze snapped between the serum, Paloma, and the queen. I didn't like the idea of being held against my will and forced to tell someone my secrets. It was an invasion of not only my privacy but my mind and free will. Regardless of my feelings, I had an inkling that the only other option was death. And I suppose if this was the way to prove that I was not working for the Sun Killer, then so be it.

"Yes," I replied, despite how much my body was screaming against it.

By order of the queen, Paloma uncorked the bottle and walked up to me with diffidence. She told me to open my mouth and then poured the contents onto my tongue. I cringed at its bitter, perfume-like taste but swallowed it whole. Everyone in the room observed me carefully, waiting for me to either spit it out or for it to take effect. Almost instantly, a strange tingling sensation made its way down from the top of my head to my fingertips and toes. A lightness took over me, as if I had taken a shot of liquor.

La Reina wasted no time asking questions.

"What is your full name, and where are you from?"

"My name is Esmé Vespertín. I'm from Anelante, but I currently live in the Larimar District."

The answer seemed to tumble out instantly, my mouth moving before my brain could process it.

"And what exactly do you do?"

"I'm an opera singer for *Teatro Paraiso*," I said.

"How long have you worked there?"

"A little over a year."

"What did you do before then?"

"I worked as a merchant's assistant, a cleaner, and a barmaid. My last job was with a witch named Canela."

I gasped as soon as the words came out. I didn't mean to express my incriminating connection to Canela, but the magic of the serum was so effective that I couldn't stop it.

"I didn't mean—"

"I know who she is," the queen interrupted with a roll of her eyes. "She's a powerful witch, but she's posed no major threat so far. Unless you have a reason to believe otherwise."

"No, absolutely not," I told her, shaking my head. "Canela helps people with her magic. Nothing more."

"And what exactly were you doing while working with Canela?"

"I tended to the counter, helped customers, and restocked items."

"Did the witch teach you any magic?"

"No, not like that. She taught me about crystals and herbs and how to tend to people's wounds. That's all."

"Do you still talk to Canela?"

"I do. She's the one who makes the potion for my headaches."

She rumbled a thoughtful hum. "Have you *ever* practiced magic, Miss Vespertín?"

"No. Never."

"Are you sure? Not even dark arts such as necromancy?"

"I'm very sure."

There was a strange comfort in knowing that the serum was helping push forward my truth. I only hoped it would be enough to sway the queen of my innocence.

She went on, "Are you aware that you potentially raised the dead last night, Miss Vespertín?"

I faltered at the thought, as I still had a hard time grasping it.

"Río—the prince—made me aware of it, yes. Before that, I thought someone else had done it."

The queen folded her arms and ran her tongue over her teeth with a furrowed brow.

"But you said you could see spirits?"

"Yes, I did."

"Pray tell, what spirits have you seen?"

"I watched a woman jump off a roof on my way home. There are people whom I see for a moment and then disappear. There were all kinds of people from portraits in the ballroom and then..." I almost didn't want to say it, but the potion won, "Your brother."

The queen's eyes flashed, her cool demeanor breaking. "What did you say?"

"I saw your brother," I replied more clearly. "I didn't know who he was at first until Río told me. He was wearing a purple suit, and he had hair like yours. And then I saw the Moon King in the ballroom before the attack."

"Did they say anything?" she pressed.

"Only the king said anything and it was a warning to run."

"Saévio has been dead for decades. What could they possibly want from you?" the queen demanded.

"I don't know. I'm sorry," I replied meekly.

She stared at me long and hard, as if trying to force knowledge that I didn't have out of me. But above all, I could see in her eyes that there was more than rage there. There was grief, and it riddled me with guilt that I couldn't give her more. I watched her mentally reel herself back in before continuing with the task at hand.

"When one uses magic, there is often a feeling you get—whether it's emotion, energy, or something like fire within you. You may not have done it on purpose, but you must have felt *something. Did* you?"

I recalled the moment before the bodies rose, and all I could picture was the werewolf biting Río and how terrified I was. The memory of the entire ballroom being ripped apart, bodies and blood scattered on the floor. And I was next.

The serum did a better job of formulating my response than I did.

"I didn't want Río to die."

Despite her frostiness, *Reina* Victoria almost looked surprised by my answer.

"And earlier too," I continued. "After the chandelier fell. A werewolf was about to kill him, and I felt the same thing. I screamed, and then the monster let him go. I didn't know why, and I still don't know why, but it can't be a coincidence, can it?"

"No, it cannot," she said. After a moment of silence, she asked, "Do you work for Sebastián Eliódor?"

"No," I scoffed.

"Have you ever *met* Sebastián Eliódor?"

"No."

The Queen of Storms leaned forward. "But you've seen the black diamond, haven't you?"

"Y-Yes."

"When?"

"A few days ago. When Río came to my apartment," I whispered in shame.

"And you swear that you didn't touch it?"

"I swear!" I blurted in desperation.

"Do you know exactly what that stone was, Miss Vespertín?"

"N-No, I don't. He just said it was a cursed item."

"It's known as the Eye of Gedeón. It's one of three stones created by The Black Death to strengthen his power," she explained.

A feeling as if just suddenly doused with ice-cold water washed over me as I gaped in horror.

"He told me it was cursed! He didn't tell me it was—"

"Of course he didn't. It's since been destroyed, but if you had touched it, then destroying it wouldn't have mattered because it would've latched itself to you. Although, based on your relatively good health and your seemingly normal behavior, I'm inclined to say that isn't the case. However…" she trailed off ponderously before saying, "You told Río that you started seeing spirits since that day, didn't you?"

Was she listening to our entire *conversation?*

"Of course I was," she replied with a smirk.

I let out a surprised squeak, unaware that I spoke aloud.

"Other than the spirits, did you hear anything else last night? Did *he* speak to you, the Sun Killer? When the werewolf had you in its grasp, did you *hear* anything? Did you…*feel* his magic? Anything?"

Her endless questions made me feel as if I were being pelted with stones, with no mercy in sight.

"No. I think I would know if the Sun Killer spoke to me. I didn't think werewolves could speak at all," I responded.

The queen straightened up suddenly, her face falling. Paloma gave her an odd look, as did I.

"They don't," *Reina* Victoria uttered. "These, however, were controlled by Sebastián himself. And when under his control, he can speak into people's minds at will. Río heard him. I even heard him. That's why I think it's strange that you, a girl with no magical history, could resist such powerful magic."

My mouth fell open as I choked on air. All my thoughts were at the mercy of Paloma's potion, tumbling out of me against my will.

"I didn't know I was doing that at all."

"Which seems to be the pattern with you," the queen derided. "Did you feel *anything* strange at that moment?"

"Just sharp pain. I didn't think much of it because I get headaches all the time."

"And how long have you had these headaches? Seen shadows?"

"Ummm…three years? But they weren't always this bad."

"And before then?"

As with all of my answers, I expected the truth serum to assist me, but my mind came up blank. No words came out. I thought carefully, trying to remember a time without my ailment, but had trouble producing a memory.

"I don't know," I uttered, furrowing my brow.

The queen pushed further, "Could it be possible that something *sparked* these headaches? You don't remember an event or an injury?"

I opened my mouth, but nothing came out. My heartbeat quickened at the sudden halt of my thoughts. It was as if I crashed into a brick wall.

"No, it's just been that way," I said. "Although Canela speculates that it could be an effect of the Sun Killer's magic, like a sickness."

La Reina exchanged another strange look with the wizard. This time, they both seemed unnerved, and to be quite frank, I agreed with the sentiment. I knew I had a bad memory, but not *this* bad.

"It could be, although I've never known Sebastián's magic to indirectly affect memory," the queen said. "You said you came here from Anelante. I'm assuming on a ship across The Rift."

"Yes."

"Exactly how old were you?"

I was about to say a number, but it came out as a strangled noise. I had no definitive answer, and it frightened me.

"I was—I thought...I was a child," I stammered.

"You're an orphan, which means you would've been put into an orphanage. Do you remember the name? Or who looked after you?"

I grasped for a name, face, or location, but all I had were ideas, not true memories. She was right. I would've gone to an orphanage. I *knew* I had gone to an orphanage, but why couldn't I recall it? I had friends, didn't I? Foster siblings? A caretaker?

My breaths came out heavy, and my head started to throb.

"I-I don't know."

The monarch threw more questions that I couldn't answer.

"Do you remember *anything* from your childhood, Miss Vespertín? Do you remember where you were before Coáraluna? Were you adopted? Did you go to school? Even just a birthday that you remember?"

All I could do was shake my head vigorously in reply. In a sudden panicked state, I squirmed against my restraints as a sharp pain spread across my forehead. I closed my eyes, trying to remember who I am and who I was before *Teatro Paraiso*. Before Dulce, Canela, and Coáraluna, it was all blank. I thought I knew. This whole time, I thought I knew, but I didn't. It was all darkness. Cold nothingness. And it broke me.

"No," I sobbed, tears streaming down my face. My eyes met the queen's in distress, gasping, "No, I don't remember! I don't remember anything! Why can't I remember?"

I wanted to hug myself and curl into a ball on the floor, but I was trapped. All I could do was hunch over the armrest and cry as I repeated everything I knew about myself:

"My name is Esmé Vespertín. I'm 21 years old. I'm a refugee from Anelante and an opera singer at *Teatro Paraiso*. My friends are Dulce, Flora, Camilo, Canela, and Río…"

Somewhere far away, *Reina* Victoria whispered, "That's enough."

A warm hand came upon my shoulder, and a kind voice spoke to me.

"*Señorita?*"

I glanced up and, through watery eyes, saw Paloma standing over me. She smiled softly through her wariness. In her hand was another vial, except this one contained a light blue potion.

"This will counteract the effects of the serum, and it'll help soothe your mind," she explained.

Without question, I let her put the liquid in my mouth, which tasted flowery. As soon as it went down my throat, a wave of tranquility embraced me. It was warm and comforting, like sitting in front of a hearth, wrapped in a soft blanket. My crying immediately stopped, and my lids grew heavy. Above all else, the urge to say everything aloud was gone.

The guards freed me from the chair and put my manacles on my wrists. One of them moved to place the muzzle over my face, but the queen shook her head.

"No, I don't think that will be necessary."

In my dream-like state, I was taken out of the wizard's chamber and back up to my tower. The whole time, I felt like I was floating on a slow current, taking everything around me in with a dazed smile. So much so that I didn't even bat an eye at the figure standing by the base of the tower stairs. He was a tall man, dressed in black vestments with matching raven hair. His face was hazy, with indistinct features, but I could feel him staring right at me. Whereas any other day, I would've been scared, tonight I raised a manacled hand and simply waved at him. Again, he had no face, but I could tell that he was smiling.

It'll be alright.

All of a sudden, I was back in bed with my head on the soft pillow. My eyes fluttered shut, my body growing heavy against the mattress.

"Get some rest, Miss Vespertín," someone told me before I fell victim to my dreams.

19

Champion of the Fool

Río

There was an encumbering weight over my entire being as I sat on the cot of my dingy cell. With my back against the wall, I eyed the empty tray lying a few feet away, bouncing my leg anxiously. I've barely spent more than a day in my new abode, and I was incredibly restless. The damp, underground dungeon was suffocating, and I pitied the poor fools my mother put down here in the past. I'm not used to doing nothing. I'm not used to sitting around without knowing what's going on. All I knew was that my mother was most likely interrogating Esmé at this very moment and it drove me mad.

I couldn't get her expression out of my head—the one of utter betrayal. The sound of her sobbing tormented me even now, making me feel like a complete and utter piece of waste. I knew she was dangerous and that this was how we treated dangerous people, but it didn't hurt any less. I never thought that by inviting her into my home, I'd be inadvertently putting the kingdom in peril and Esmé in chains.

Had I really been that stupid?

The first time I saw her was at *Teatro Paraiso*. It was my 23rd birthday, and I told my mother I wanted the celebration to be a family affair, not a public one. I chose the theater because of my love for music and nostalgia for the many shows I grew up watching. Of course, like everything else, it once it became more of an expectation, I attended them less and less. However, something called me to *Paraiso* for the first time in years. And that something came in the form of a girl—a *star*, right at center stage.

From the moment I laid eyes on her, I was absolutely awestruck. Esmé was beautiful and talented, but there was also an energy about her that shone from within. It was only confirmed by the way she carried herself. It could've been due to her shyness, but she didn't ogle at me or go out of her way to impress me. She simply did so by existing. For once, *I* was the one eager to know more.

I even plotted to attend the theater more frequently with the intent to see her again, but by some twist of fate, I ran into her in the last place for romance to bloom—the Obsidian District. I often went there to purchase supplies for my journeys overseas, and I was very familiar with *Magistra* Canela and her shop. One of those nights, Esmé was there, buying a potion for her migraines.

Esmé is something else. She always was. Like a deity among men. For me, it was always about more than just her hair, her beautiful eyes, that sunshine smile, or even her singing voice. It was the way she interacted with the homeless man by Canela's shop and how she brought in that stray cat almost every night. She even took *me* in when I was bleeding and bruised, when she had every reason to fear me for who I was. It all fed into the magnetism that brought me to her doorstep every night from day one.

Emilia Mondragón

In another time or another world, I would've given her everything. In hindsight, it could have very well been witchcraft. I pondered over the notion a lot over the long, grueling hours, but I've concluded that a spell would have made me perform better than I did. In the end, I made everything worse because we *don't* live in another world, and the time is *now*, and I don't think there will ever be a way to come back from this at all. Even if everything turned out fine and she somehow forgave me, I wasn't entirely certain if she would want me or if she even *should.*

After a life of "playing vigilante," ending up in a cell allowed everything I ran from to come crashing down around me. The memories of Fort Adelfa and the winter solstice ball, my father's death, Esmé's imprisonment, my *curse...* They were like hounds from the underworld that finally caught up, sinking their claws in and dragging me towards my judgment.

Champion of the Moon Goddess? More like a champion of the Fool.

Lorena said that to me once. Perhaps this whole time, she was right.

With a sigh, I looked down at my bandaged arm. The beast nearly bit off my whole limb, or at least it felt like it at the time. The memory was such a blur, a mixture of wrath and terror. When that werewolf knocked me down and opened its jaw, it was the second time in my life when I was almost certain my life was over. Not even my magic could save me. I survived crossing The Rift only to be killed by a monster in my own home.

Like many times before, I unwound the bandage to keep track of the curse's progress. There were large tooth marks all over my forearm that were already healing on their own. The wound appeared weeks old, which was a positive symptom of my impending ailment. Spidery white veins branched out from it, making their way up my skin. It was the venom—or magic—doing its work. Ultimately, when the full moon came, I'd be just like one of those half-wolf monsters that killed our people at the ball. And my father. It felt like a punishment or some kind of sick joke.

The Moon Prince got bitten by a monster controlled by the moon. A God-given turned slave. How apt. I wonder what Marisláni thinks of me now.

I'm not one to give up so readily, but as I told Esmé, I'm not the first to search for a way to break this curse, and I wouldn't be the last. My mother would no doubt do everything in her power to look for one, but I wasn't holding out hope. I had mere days until I turned, and not only was I in a cell, but I was at the mercy of the queen's authority, and with the king gone, there's no telling what she would do.

Gone. The word echoed in the cavern of my mind. *Father is gone.*

Tears welled up in my eyes. The mere thought of him was enough to wrench open a door in me and fill my heart with choking grief.

It didn't make sense. I just saw him not long ago. We spoke through the frosted mirror and talked about whether or not he'd be attending the ball. He was alive, strong, and hopeful. He always was. How was it possible that he could be gone just like that, and that I was never going to see him again? He was the Moon King, one of the creators of The Rift, and a warrior. If he is gone, then what is left in his place?

Me?

I scoffed out loud.

I'm good with a blade, and my magic is strong, but I am nowhere near as powerful as my father was. I can't break apart a country or hold back an entire army with an ocean. At least I never tried. There were still limits to my capabilities that I hadn't yet explored. I've never had the reason to. My mother made sure of that. She didn't want to raise us like soldiers the way my grandfather did to her, so she shielded us instead. I spent a lot of my life being a proper prince until I decided I had had enough, but at the end of the day, I was no general, and I was no king. I may be good at the few things I *can* do, and I always considered myself a fairly confident person...until now.

Ruling a whole kingdom was something entirely different. Having people depend on me to help them, save them, and do whatever it takes to keep the balance was always someone else's job. I knew it would be mine one day, but I naively assumed I had more time. I thought I had more opportunities to learn and rise. But what if my mother was right? What if I *am* still a child? What if I *don't* know shit? What if I've already fucked it all up?

This is what I get for being ambitious, isn't it? We destroyed the Eye of Gedeón, and it cost my father's life. I fall for a girl, and she turns out to be a necromancer. I fight back, and I become a monster. I'm even a failure for a spy, because how could one as "skilled" as me let an entire pack of werewolves into his home with no prior knowledge? How could I have been so distracted? No matter how many times I sifted through every piece of information, it didn't make sense. This was the job my father gave me and I failed him.

"You weren't even chosen by a god. You're just a product of the ones who were."

My old friend's words haven't affected me since I was a teenager. It wasn't like me to care about the things he or other people said, but the happenings of the past week have broken me enough to wonder if maybe he was right. After all, I almost punched him in the face for it, but I also wanted to punch him for a multitude of other reasons.

The creak of the dungeon door and its resounding clatter resounded through the dungeon, dragging me out of my brooding. I wiped away my stray tears and wrapped up my arm as footsteps drew near. My heart hammered in anticipation as the silhouette of my mother came towards me.

"What happened?" I immediately asked. "Is Esmé alright? Did-Did you—"

My mother cut me off, not letting the dreadful thought leave my lips.

"She's still alive. She's asleep in her room," she said, standing before me now.

I nearly collapsed with relief. The only thing stopping me was the unusual expression on my mother's face. She looked not only tired, but frazzled. It was a rare thing to see, especially after an interrogation.

"What happened?" I repeated.

"We interrogated her with the truth serum," she replied.

I scowled uncomfortably. "What did she say?"

"Well, everything she told you was true. She doesn't work for Sebastián, and she's never practiced any sort of magic before, so there's that."

That, at the very least, brought me some comfort. Still, I knew there had to be more.

"But…?"

"But, Río…she has no memory," my mother gasped.

"What do you mean?"

"When I asked her about her life before Coáraluna, she couldn't remember anything. Even with the truth serum, she literally could not recall a single memory before three years ago. Not from her childhood, her life, friends, family, anything!"

I gave her a strange look, feeling a stone drop in my gut. Out of all the outcomes I expected, this was completely outside the realm of possibilities. As far as Esmé told me, she had an established life and identity. It was one thing if she had lied about it, but it was another for the truth to be *this*.

No memory?

"Was she *aware* that she had no memory?" I asked.

"No. She looked more shocked than any of us were, and she…" The queen trailed off for a moment before saying, "She broke down into hysterics. We had to give her something to calm her down."

With a dreadful ick, I ran my hands over my face and hair with a hiss. Not only was Esmé forced to endure the effects of a truth serum, but she was also left to contend with a life-shattering reality that even I couldn't imagine enduring. All I could do was picture her broken face streaked with tears, as I felt on the verge of imploding.

I met my mother's eyes, my next words a desperate plea.

"I need to see her. Please. Let me see her."

She shook her head. "Río, *no.*"

"Why not?" I demanded.

"Because, darling," she said indignantly, "she may be who she told you she is, or rather, who she *thinks* she is… but there are still at least 18 years of her life that are unaccounted for! Her mind is blank! Doesn't that concern you?"

"Of course it does," I snapped. "That's precisely why I want to see her!"

My forearm throbbed under my bandage as my veins went red-hot. The queen cocked her head to the side with a gaze that could see right through me. When she spoke again, it was with surprising placidity.

"My love, the curse is already affecting you, which is another reason you shouldn't see her. In both of your fragile states, do you want to make matters worse?"

My eyes fluttered closed, and I let out a long, exasperated sigh. *I can't even be angry about one thing without this wolf shit getting to me.* The feeling subsided for now, but it was unsettling how fast my mind and body were changing. And I knew my mother was right. The last thing I needed to do was snap at Esmé or do something terrible.

"No. I don't," I answered dejectedly.

She nodded in approval.

"Like I said, based on what she *does* remember, it seems that she is who she says she is. Everything she's told you is true," she reiterated. "And let's say that Sebastián doesn't know who she is, and this has nothing to do with him. Who knows? But to have someone's memory completely wiped clean? That's powerful magic, Río. Either that or a serious head injury, though I have a feeling it's not so simple."

"You think someone did this to her?"

"She has some serious abilities within her. Things no one should be able to do so easily, and she did them with no magical history and no memory. That's more than anything a witch can do. That's—"

"God-given," I gasped, my eyes widening.

"Or quite the opposite," she offered seriously.

I know what I said to Esmé back in her tower. I know that necromancy was inherently evil, yet I remained in denial. Or was I simply viewing the world through rose-colored lenses again?

"If she's not consciously working for Sebastián, then who the fuck allowed those beasts to get in?" I whispered sharply.

"That's what I'm trying to figure out," my mother stated. "I've been questioning the surviving guests who haven't run home yet, but as you can imagine, they're not very happy about it. Many of them were simply here for the celebration and witnessed a massacre instead. And to be honest, none of them seem like the type to do such a thing."

"What about Silas?"

"He answered a few questions before going back to Valerta. He said he wanted to be home...with his *pregnant* wife."

A flurry of emotions hit me, painted clearly on my face as I raised my eyebrows, scowled, and then burst out laughing. My mother shook her head in a mixture of mirth and disapproval.

After an incident that happened years ago, we haven't been on the best of terms with Silas's family. The only person who was ever invited to social gatherings was his father, but upon asking my mother, she confirmed what the viscount said. His father couldn't make it, and seeing as we needed all the political allies we could acquire, my mother allowed him to attend *without* a plus one. It was her one gift to me, aside from a genuine apology for not giving me a warning. Granted, if I had known, I wouldn't have attended at all. If anything, I was more enraged over how close he got to Esmé.

No wonder he was being bold. He's making his father proud by continuing his legacy.

"I don't know who I feel more sorry for, her or the child," I chuckled.

"If you had stayed together, that would've been you," my mother mused.

The thought made my skin crawl, and not because I didn't want any children.

"No, Lorena wanted comfort, and there's no one more boring and comfortable than a northern viscount she grew up with," I shot back.

She always told me that we southern boys were unruly, especially those of us who lived by the sea. God-given or not, we spent our days in the ocean with our feet in the sand and our faces to the sun. Our music was loud, and our cities were dappled in color like no other. And above all else, we wore our hearts on our sleeves, even those of us who had to guard them for our reputation. Considering Lorena always said such things with a smile, I assumed she found it attractive or endearing. As it turns out, it was neither.

"There are certain comforts that get you nowhere fast. That's why I'm here and not there," my mother said.

Way before she married my father, my mother was meant to be queen of the Air Kingdom. However, with the sudden death of her brother, her relationship with my grandfather crumbled, and she chose to marry the prince from the Moon Kingdom she had fallen in love with. I wasn't alive just yet, but I heard that the very act of denying the crown was about as tumultuous as The Great Divide. And with no other remaining heir left, my grandfather was left to continue his rule. To this day, nobody knows what Saévio's plans are for when he passes, but if anyone thought that he'd pass the crown to either me or my sister, then they'd be mistaken.

As I looked into my mother's eyes, I had the urge to ask her how she was truly doing. My father was not only her husband but also her best friend. There was a time when she went so far as to call him her savior, and she was not a woman who gave men such credit lightly. But the Queen of Storms would sooner let her deep emotions show in her magic than in her outward expression. The only person she opened up to so easily was my father, and he was dead. Only the continuous thunderstorms would tell me of her grief.

"About Esmé…" she said. "I found out what triggered her magic. Do you want to know what she said?"

I perked up at that. "Of course I do."

Her face softened, which was surprising all on its own.

"She said that she didn't want you to die."

All at once, my heart was a puddle on the floor.

"She thinks it's why the corpses ripped the rest to shreds," my mother explained. She stepped forward and grabbed the bars to look at me seriously. "She saved you, Río. Her feelings for you are so strong that they unleashed something powerful. Even if it was just for a moment. I've never heard of a dark magic that could be fueled by anything other than hatred or greed."

"Neither have I," I whispered with the same wonder.

My mother took something out of her pocket and held it up for me to see. It was the silver necklace with the aquamarine moon that I knew like the back of my hand. The last time I checked, Esmé had it in her possession.

"It was hidden in her dress, the one she wore to the ball," my mother explained before giving it to me.

I took it in my hands, feeling the familiar smooth stone.

Considering its sentimental value, I knew it was impetuous to give it away so freely, but Esmé's monologue about courtship pushed me to cross a line I had been afraid to. I wanted to give her something that meant more than just the flowers and the late-night visits. I wanted to make her a promise, and somehow, the necklace seemed safe in Esmé's hands. The fact that it was here now proved that. I was supposed to take it back from her before things fell apart.

Another one of my failures.

"She said you gave it to her. Why?" the queen asked.

"It was, uh…it was supposed to be a promise," I answered softly, my heart aching.

"You mean like a proposal?" she exclaimed.

I laughed at her reaction, feeling grateful for the reprieve.

"No, not like that. It was a promise that I would come back for her and that I would always be there for her," I said with a pained smile.

I stared at the necklace before closing my fist around it somberly. All the while, I could feel my mother looking at me, her eyes boring into my face.

She released a tired sigh. "Río, I don't know what will become of your relationship with this girl, but I can at the very least tell that you care about each other. Unfortunately, evil has a way of sneaking up on us when we least expect it."

She was earnestly apologetic. I wondered if she was thinking of my father and the way evil sneaked up on all of us and snatched him away forever.

20

Princess of the Moon

Esmé

18 years.

18 years of my life that I couldn't remember, even under the influence of magic. How can that be? I thought I knew who I was and where I came from, but in a matter of minutes, I was proven horribly wrong. How could I have lived my life in such a way? How did I not question it? Was I so focused on survival that I never stopped to wonder? I never thought there was anything *to* wonder about. My life was what it was, until it was not.

Who am I?

I wanted to scream it from the top of this very tower.

WHO AM I?

Not knowing the answer scared me more than anything else. More than the headaches and spirits. Because 18 years of nothing may as well have meant that I have been comatose for my entire life. As far as I know, I am no one.

Was everything I knew about myself a lie? Where do I come from? Why am I here? Why can't I remember anything? What if I *were* just a pawn for an evil being, and I didn't even know it? What if who I am is so much worse than I could have ever imagined?

So many questions with no answers left me helpless and alone, even more than I already was. Had Paloma not given me a potion to calm me down, I wouldn't have slept through the night. Even so, when I was roused in the morning, I found myself wishing I never woke up at all.

A handmaiden brought me breakfast and informed me that the queen would be stopping by shortly. I resisted the urge to groan. When she left, I stared at my tray, which was a simple serving of eggs, toast, and a tangerine. Unfortunately, the further turning of events made me lose my appetite, and by the time the queen arrived, the only thing I had eaten was the tangerine.

I bowed my head wearily, only to perk up at the sight of Echo and *Princesa* Mariela following closely behind. She was in a short-sleeved periwinkle dress with gold embroidery. Her hair was tied back, with some white and lavender pieces falling down the sides. Echo, her black companion dog, stood guard by the door with his eyes trained on me.

"Oh, hello, *Alteza*!"

My greeting was excitable and genuine, but as soon as I remembered our last face-to-face interaction, my cheeks flamed. I still didn't know what she told her brother after she caught us kissing, but I know she didn't approve. I made a mess of myself in many ways that night. Instead of showing me disdain, she smirked upon seeing my expression, though it was eclipsed by the alarm passing over her eyes. Everyone else in the castle gave me similar expressions, so it wasn't terribly surprising. At the very least, she didn't look as scared as they did, though I'm sure my manacles and attire didn't do me any favors.

Remembering that she couldn't hear me, I waved at her in greeting and she returned the gesture. The handmaiden then came around my bed and set down a water basin on the bedside table before standing aside, waiting. I gave the water and everyone in the room a bewildered look before *Reina* Victoria finally spoke.

"*Buenos días*, Miss Vespertín," she said, signing with her hands.

"*Buenos días, Majestad.*"

"Did you have a decent night's sleep?"

"I did, thanks to Paloma."

"Good. I've brought my daughter here to help with your injury. One of her gifts is her ability to heal others using her magic. Unfortunately, wounds made by beasts will still leave a scar, but I assure you that she'll leave you looking much better than any stitches would."

I raised my eyebrows at that, marveling at the fact that the God-given's abilities could vary between generations. It fascinated me, until another realization dawned on me.

"You have healing magic?" I blurted out.

"Yes, it's one of Ela's specialties. She's rather proficient at it," the queen boasted, making the princess smile.

Meanwhile, I was having an internal war, debating whether to be angry at myself for being naive or at the prince for lying to me all this time.

"Since when?" I asked casually.

"Since she was a child."

I scoffed. *Much better than any stitches would, indeed.*

They both shared an odd look at my behavior, and I swiftly moved on before either of them asked any questions.

"Sorry, this is still so new to me, but that's awfully kind of you."

"Considering the obvious hole in your memory, I'm still not entirely sure how much I should trust you. But... you've proven yourself enough that I don't feel inclined to leave you with an infection. I don't need you fainting in Paloma's tower."

My body stiffened at the mention of the wizard. "Are you going to interrogate me again?"

"No, but we do want to figure out if we can crack into that brain of yours and see what exactly is keeping your memories hidden."

There was a sense of solace in knowing that others wanted to find the truth as much as I did. Though I tried not to think about the ominous fact that almost *anything* could lie within those lost years.

"In the meantime, I have some business to take care of," the Queen of Storms said.

She and her daughter exchanged kisses on the cheek before heading to the door. With a glance over her shoulder, the queen looked between us both.

"You try anything, you die," she ordered before exiting the chamber.

By all means, her threats should've unnerved me, but the thought of hurting anyone, let alone Río's sister, wasn't remotely in my nature. I was the complete opposite of violent. Yet, I somehow found the queen's last threat endearing. She reminded me of Dulce and the way she spoke to men when we went out to the markets.

Princesa Mariela, however, shook her head at her mother's remark before turning her attention to me. With a soft smile, she motioned for me to move closer. I obliged and sat on the edge of the bed, as far as my chains would allow. Only then did I notice the nearly identical necklace to the prince's, except hers had a moonstone crystal with a rainbow shift. A gift from her grandmother, I suppose. I could also see the resemblance between her and her brother. White hair aside, the shape of their brow was the same, and their eyes were the same black coffee shade. They even had similar expressions. However, whereas Río looked like his father, the princess looked a lot more like her mother. She had an angular, pointed jawline and high cheekbones, and she bore that same striking, regal poise that was in her mother more often than not. Yet, in contrast, there was a welcoming kindness to the Moon Princess that was different from her brother's charm. I wasn't sure if it had something to do with her age or if it simply came from within.

She started speaking with her hands while Arabella, the handmaiden, translated.

"May I remove your bandages?"

"Yes, of course," I replied with a nod, holding my arm out to her.

With the utmost care, the princess unwrapped the gauze from my wound, revealing the gruesomeness beneath. Her eyes instantly widened at the jagged injury in its entirety. She shot me a nervous look as she handed Arabella the bloodied gauze.

"Does it hurt?" she asked.

The best answer I could give was a dubious shrug. Yes, it hurt, but my relationship with pain was very different from other people's. I was accustomed to dealing with ongoing aches, and therefore my tolerance for such things was a little broken. My arm burned, but it was a dull constant now, like background noise or the whispers in my head. And I had gone through so much physical and mental anguish these past few days that it all seemed to blend anyway.

"I'm used to living with pain," I told them honestly.

Arabella translated this, and the corners of the princess's lips turned down.

Not wanting her pity, I shook my head. "It's alright."

She twisted her mouth ponderously and signed, "I'll make sure it doesn't hurt anymore, okay?"

That alone filled me with an urge to cry that I had to resist.

The Moon Princess turned towards the water basin, pulling her shoulders back. She lifted her hands over it, and I watched as the water took on a faint blue glow. With a pulling motion, it rose out of the basin, and the princess pivoted towards me with a focused gaze. My face was alight in wonder as it followed her hands in a thin, floating stream.

Arabella propped up my arm with a light touch as the princess enveloped my wound with water completely. The sudden coldness over the gash made me wince and see stars, but I didn't flinch away. Fortunately, the sensation didn't last and soon gave way to a relieving warmth. When my head stopped swimming, I finally looked down, and observed as my wound started to close up through the rippling waves of glowing water.

"Wow!" I gasped.

It was one thing to hear about the abilities of the God-given, but it was another to witness them up close. When we first met, I remember being in complete awe of Río and his ability to manipulate the water around him. It was "small," as he would say, and back then, I thought he was being humble. It wasn't until the ball that I witnessed what he could truly do. The way he fended off each werewolf using the wide range of his magic astounded me. He was as furious as the sea itself. And I couldn't help but wonder what else he and his sister were capable of when given the opportunity.

In less than a minute, *Princesa* Mariela finished her work and returned the water to the basin. The only thing left behind of the werewolf's claw marks was fully healed, spindly scars that wrapped around me like thin branches. They were lighter than the rest of my skin, but were practically smooth. Even better, there was no more pain, and I was able to move my arm again as if the problem never existed.

I ran my hand over the area, still amazed.

Can she do this to the inside of my head?

I grinned at the princess with appreciation and turned to Arabella to ask, "How do you say 'thank you' in sign language?"

The handmaiden made a short motion with her right hand. She placed her fingers on her chin and moved them outward. I repeated the same motion to *Princesa* Mariela, who giggled in approval. I made sure to thank Arabella as well.

As the Moon Princess was taking her leave, she signed something to me, and Arabella said, "She said it's nice to truly meet you and that you're not what she expected at all. She's...*sorry* that her mother put you in here."

Her gracious statement took me by surprise.

"That's awfully kind. It was nice to meet you, too, *Alteza*."

I bowed my head as they headed out, with Echo joining them. In the hallway, I saw the outline of a lilac-haired prince dressed in royal purple vestments.

My breath hitched. That coldness came back, but this time it was more like a soft breeze, and the air smelled like crisp autumn. With it came unbearable melancholy.

Instead of staring and doing nothing, I raised my hand and waved. He smiled and returned the gesture right as the door closed in his face. And as I sat there, completely dumbfounded, I couldn't help but think that for all the fear surrounding the dead, that didn't feel scary at all.

✳ ☽ ○ ☾ ✳

By some miracle, the queen allowed me the luxury of a bath. I was taken away from my high tower and into the most ornate bathroom I've ever seen in my life. It was made of white, gold, and lavender, with a tiled floor, layered, intricate walls, and a vaulted ceiling painted with white and gold clouds. There was a massive bathtub in the center, a changing station, as well as a vanity. There was a beautiful stained-glass window with a design of jacarandas filling the chamber with mid-morning light.

In the vanity mirror, I took the first glimpse of my reflection in days. My hair was as unruly as a tumbleweed, my face was pale, and darkness circled my under-eyes. Fading bruises marked my skin, and there were still remnants of dried blood dappled here and there. I resembled an old, broken doll more than a person.

Arabella immediately offered to wash me, but I insisted on doing it myself. I wasn't helpless, and now that my wound was healed, nothing was incapacitating me from completing such a task. Considering my lack of freedom already, I hoped I could at least have that. Thankfully, the handmaiden didn't push me on it and simply sat by the vanity, reading a book from her apron while also keeping a close eye on me.

I scrubbed myself raw, eager to be rid of any possible reminder of that dark day, even if it was only from my body. When I was clean and resembled some version of my old self, Arabella helped me get dressed in a very simple sky-blue dress as well as simple shoes. She then brushed out my hair and put it in a braid down my back before urging me out the door.

My usual guard eyed me with scorn as he applied the handcuffs to my wrists. Even with his helmet on, he was a recognizable towering man with emerald eyes and a thick beard. Swirling Moon Kingdom tattoos adorned his bare shoulders, setting him apart further.

He dragged me towards the wizard's tower. Anxiety threatened to suffocate me the whole way there, plagued by the dreaded interrogation from the day before. Upon entering, I expected to see the horrid iron chair again, but instead saw a familiar individual with curly hair standing next to the queen and her wizard.

I gasped, "Canela?"

My friend's auburn eyes sparkled. "Esmé!"

She rushed over to me, ignoring everyone's protests, and wrapped me in her arms. I couldn't hug her back, but I still leaned against her shoulder and breathed her in. She held my face in her warm hands, regarding me with maternal affection as my vision blurred with tears. It felt so good to see a familiar face. I almost thought I was dreaming.

"Please don't touch her," the guard growled.

The witch clicked her tongue with a sneer. "Oh, please, Captain. She's harmless."

"I don't know about that anymore," I said warily, and Canela frowned. "What are you doing here?"

"I asked her to come," *La Reina* replied.

We both turned towards the queen, who looked beautiful in yet another black gown.

"Why?" I asked.

"I told you she was a powerful witch, and you said she was able to help you with your headaches. Well, there's a reason for that," the queen said. "I don't know if she told you, but Canela's specialty is the mind."

I craned my head back in surprise, and Canela simply shrugged. In the years I had known her, she never mentioned such a thing.

"How?"

"She can look into people's heads," *Reina* Victoria said.

"With permission and the proper preparations, of course," Canela clarified.

My eyes widened in horror. "As in, you can read people's thoughts?"

"No, nothing like that," the witch chuckled. "Am I good at reading people? Yes. Do I know what everyone's thinking all the time? No. It's a special practice. A form of clairvoyance, if you will."

"Oh…"

In a castle full of magic users, I was starting to feel like the stupid one playing catch-up.

"And she's the only person in this city who can do it well," the queen added. "We're hoping she can help us with your memory problem. Lucky for you, you're the only reason she agreed to come here in the first place."

The witch nodded in agreement. "I don't work for the crown, but I do work for the people I care about."

"Oh, really? And don't you care about the greater good?" *Reina* Victoria argued.

"With all due respect, *Majestad*, the greater good lives within the streets of this very city, not just in high places. I like making myself accessible to anyone who needs me. You're welcome in my district at any time," Canela told her with a sly smile.

"No, thank you. Can you help her or not?"

"I will certainly try my best."

"Good. Let's get started then."

21

The Graveyard

Esmé

Thank Marisláni, I wasn't strapped to the dreaded iron chair this time. Instead, I was told to lie down on a large wooden table that was cleaned for the occasion. The wizard awaited with another bottle in her hand containing a potion of liquid gold.

"What does this one do?" I inquired diffidently.

"It'll open up your mind, darling, and make things a little clearer," Canela answered with a consoling touch.

"Yes," Paloma nodded. "Don't worry, it's not a truth serum. This one helps with memory and makes it easier for Canela to do her magic."

Despite their reassurances, every muscle in my body was tense. What we were about to do could unlock something within me that could very well be beyond my imagination. I was terrified, but my curiosity outweighed it far more, because right now, *knowing* was better than *not.* So, I drank Paloma's potion, which tasted of peppermint. Compared to the other concoctions I'd taken, I didn't feel an immediate difference, so I wasn't entirely certain it worked at all. With Canela's assistance, I got up on the wooden table and lay flat against it, with my eyes on the domed ceiling and burning candles. My guard stood by, holding my chain, as everyone else in the room gathered around, looking down with watchful eyes. I was meat on a chopping block and could look anywhere but at their eyes as my anxiety heightened.

Canela took her place by my head and brushed her fingers through my hair. It was a pleasant, comforting gesture.

"It's alright, little songbird," she said lowly. "This shouldn't hurt, okay? I'm just going to look into your memories. I'll ask you a question, and you think of the first thing that pops into your mind. We'll go from there."

"So... it *is* like the truth serum."

"Only a little bit, but unlike the serum, you don't have to show me anything you don't want to. You have the power to shut me out if it gets too uncomfortable. Tell me to stop, and I will. Remember that."

I let out a shaky breath. "Okay."

The witch looked over at the queen with her eyebrows raised.

"Proceed, please," *La Reina* pressed on.

Canela nodded and rested her fingers against my temples with gentleness.

"Close your eyes for me, Esmé."

I did as I was told. Still, I felt nothing aside from her touch and the hard surface of the table. There was only darkness.

"Can you think of where you work, Esmé?" she asked.

With a hum of agreement, I pictured the interior of *Teatro Paraiso.* I thought of the dressing rooms, the chaos of rehearsals, and what went on backstage. The memory seemed fuzzy around the edges, like a dream, but then, just like magic, the image sharpened before me. All at once, it was as if I were there, in the present.

I gasped as Camilo passed me by, helping carry a heavy crate, while Flora gave orders to the performers. She told me to take my place, and suddenly, I was on stage in a large dress, standing before hundreds of people sitting in velvet chairs. The spotlight was shining on me, and I blinked a few times from the brightness.

"Wow," I whispered.

"Okay, now, can you show me where you live?"

The memory of the theater melted before my eyes until I was standing in the bedroom of my apartment in Larimar, wearing a simple skirt and a white blouse. Midnight passed by my feet, and when I bent down to touch him, he felt solid, soft, and real. I walked out into the living room, taking everything in with a melancholy and nostalgia that threatened to suffocate me. My apartment wasn't much, but it was home, and I missed it terribly.

I wandered into the kitchen, and halted before a small vase of blue flowers. My favorite color. I plucked one of them from a stem and held it between my fingers with a frown.

"Where did you get those flowers, Esmé?" Canela asked.

Her voice was very clear in my mind.

"Río," I replied immediately.

The memory shifted, until I was standing before the Moon Prince in the rain as he handed me the bouquet that night. He was smiling at me timidly, his eyes alight, and in spite of everything, my heart yearned for him even now. The feelings from that evening were so far away yet so present, but unlike reality, I dared to reach out grazed his cheek. He almost *felt* real. I almost wished he was. Except he simply stared with no reaction because he *wasn't* real, and this wasn't how the memory went.

The painful conversation between Río and me was a fresh wound of its own. Many conflicting feelings festered within me now, more than ever before. Back then, I didn't know that my best days were behind me. If I did, I wouldn't have gone out of my way to ruin them. I was soaring through the heavens with the prince until cruel reality shot me out of the sky and sent me plummeting into darkness. And I was partially to blame. No matter how hurtful it was, I could hardly blame him for the things he said and did. This whole time, I thought I was supposed to be scared of *him*, when in reality, I should've feared myself. No longer was I the girl that he met, but some broken person with no past and the ability to do dark, nefarious things.

"Did anything else happen that night?" the witch asked.

My mind drifted before I could think twice, and without warning, I was naked on the bed with Río in between my legs, both of us moaning. I tried squeezing my eyes but couldn't close them.

"No!"

The memory quickly faded, and suddenly the prince was giving me the aquamarine necklace. Then I was back in the kitchen, holding the flowers he gave me. I put them back in the vase when I noticed Río's clothes on the floor. And just like that night, I went over to pick them up, and the black diamond clattered to the floor. I picked it up carefully and started feeling that strange pull, raising my hand to touch it, when, suddenly, Río barged in.

"Don't!"

A strange force dragged me backward, pulling me from my spine. My eyes flew open, and I was back in Paloma's tower, with Canela standing over me. Her face was ashen as she snapped her gaze to the queen.

"The Eye of Gedeón? Your *son* had The Eye of Gedeón?" she exclaimed.

There was a sigh. "Believe me, it was news to me too, until he showed up with it."

Canela stepped back and looked around warily. "You have it here?"

"No, I destroyed it. I'm not stupid."

The witch didn't look too convinced, but the queen didn't have time for her skepticism.

"Did you see her touch it?" she demanded.

"No, she didn't."

"Did you find what the blockage is?"

"Not yet."

"Well, then. Go on," the monarch ordered.

Canela looked down at me disconcertingly, as if thinking of ending this altogether.

"Please," I pleaded. "I need to know."

The witch bit her lip, and after a vacillating moment, she put her hands back on the sides of my head. I closed my eyes again and waited for her voice to come through.

"What happened after you saw the Eye, Esmé?"

Memories flashed before me of the woman jumping off the roof, *Príncipe* Saévio at the ball, and the spirits on the dance floor, the Moon King was looking at me. I thought of the werewolves and the bodies that rose from the dead. The massacre at the ball was particularly vivid and reappeared over and over, as if Canela was combing through it for evidence of something. I tried closing my eyes to block it out, but as always, it did nothing.

I whimpered, and only then did Canela pull back. The memory went backward until I was standing in the middle of the ballroom with Río, both of us dancing right before everything went wrong. I was so carefree back then, but now it was so bittersweet, I wanted to cry. I wanted to cling to him. I wanted to take his hand and run out of that ballroom before it was too late.

"No incantation," Canela uttered. And then she asked me, "When did you know you could raise the dead?"

The bodies rose around me once more, and then I was bound in my tower, talking to Río as he relayed what he saw before I passed out.

"Nothing before?" she asked.

"No," I said. No other memory came to mind.

The witch exhaled in frustration.

"Alright, can you show me your earliest memory, Esmé?"

The first thing I could think of was walking into a local tavern to ask for a job. A few other memories bled together of me working there, customers being rude, and the owner raising his voice at me for being too slow or not speaking loudly enough.

"When was this?" the witch asked.

"Three years ago."

"Okay... Can you show me where you were *before* Coáraluna?"

Much like with the truth serum, I had to do the laborious task of searching for something to present to her. I reached into the recesses of my mind, trying to imagine the orphanage I lived in, but the image was muddied and blurry, quickly dissolving into a puddle. As another attempt, I tried thinking of school or even the day that I crossed The Rift, but they were no more than ideas that turned to dust.

"Strange," Canela whispered. "Can you show me a memory from when you were 10?"

Again, I tried pulling at anything from that time in my life, but the result was the same—a blurred image.

"Hang on. This might be a little uncomfortable," she warned.

A fuzzy memory stood before me, and just as swiftly as it appeared, I was suddenly being pulled toward it. I grunted as my body hit something that resembled quicksand, and a force sought to push me through. With the little strength I had, I tried pressing myself through it in hopes of helping the process. At first, it didn't seem to work until my hand eventually broke past. On the other side, I could feel cold air.

"I think there's something here!" I shouted.

"Good. Go towards it!" the witch urged.

I tried digging through the barrier with my hands, and with the help of Canela's magic, I managed to squeeze through. When most of my body was on the other side, I fell into the darkness below. I screamed as I plummeted before landing on hard stone with a grunt. After managing a brief recovery, I lifted my gaze, expecting to see a scene before me, but instead, I found myself in a cold, dark cavern. Sharp stalactites hung from the ceiling, and the walls themselves were made of black volcanic glass. The full moon stared down from a large opening and flowers bloomed in a circle all around me.

I was all alone.

With timid curiosity, I pushed myself to my feet and approached the flowers. They were beautiful star shaped flowers that glowed bright purple and grew in small bunches from thin stems. They sprouted from the cracks of the stone floor, as if out of sheer spite. I cautiously reached out to touch one, half-expecting something terrible to occur, but instead, a sense of comfort and familiarity blossomed within me.

"What is this place?" I finally asked.

I expected a response from Canela but was met with pure silence. I looked around in confusion and called out to the witch.

"Canela?"

My voice echoed, but no other voices answered in return. Not even a whisper. A shock of panic sliced through me, and I ran towards the rocky cavern wall, intent on looking for the strange entrance from whence I came. But as soon as I reached the edge of the flowers, I ran face-first into what felt like a solid wall. I fell to the ground with a groan and rubbed the sore part of my forehead.

What?

I scrambled to my feet, hands outstretched, and walked to the edge—slowly this time. When my fingers touched the invisible barrier, I felt around and followed its perimeter in hopes of finding some kind of gap, only to find that it wrapped in a full circle, caging me in.

I clutched my hair in distress, and with nothing else to do, I proceeded to pound my fists against the invisible barrier.

"Canela!" I yelled. "*Majestad!* Paloma!"

No response.

I was relentless with my blows until I was sure my hands might shatter. The wall did not budge.

"Canela! Río!" I screamed, a sob ripping through me. And then, to no one, I demanded, "Let! Me! Out!"

I threw a punch with each word, and then there was a resounding crack. My breath hitched, and as I stumbled back, I spotted a fracture in the glass. There were others I hadn't seen before, and a new one was forming right before my eyes.

My stomach dropped, and a force pulled me backwards, dragging me away. The dark cavern vanished, my eyes snapped open, and I was back on the wooden table in Paloma's tower. I was hyperventilating with tears streaming down my face.

Canela came around to the other side of the table and put her hands on my damp cheeks. She looked frantic.

"My gods, Esmé, are you alright?"

"What happened?" the queen demanded.

I shook my head vigorously, saying, "I don't know. I don't know," over and over.

Canela sat me up and took me in her arms.

"I thought I lost you in there!" she exclaimed.

"I tried calling out to you, but you couldn't hear me," I cried into her shoulder. "What happened?"

She leaned away and put her hands on my shoulders. "I was trying to pull at the blurry memory to see if I could uncover it, and you just…*disappeared*. It was like you went to a place I couldn't get to."

"How?" the Queen of Storms whispered sharply.

I tore my eyes away from Canela to look at Paloma and the queen who donned matching expressions of disbelief, which wasn't comforting at all. Even the guards looked on edge.

"Did you go somewhere?" the wizard asked.

"I-I did."

"Well, what did you see?" *Reina* Victoria implored.

"It wasn't a memory," I told them, shaking my head. "It was a…*place*. I landed in this cave with stalactites, and there were these glowing purple flowers. I tried leaving, an invisible wall kept me trapped in there."

The queen's frown deepened with every word. Even the professional magic-users looked at a loss for words.

"I've never heard of such a place. Or such magic." She looked between the witch and wizard and asked, "Have you?" Both shook their heads. She then turned back to me. "Did it look like any flower you recognized?"

In the few memories I *did* have of Coáraluna, I had seen much flora and fauna, whether it was out on my walks or in the markets. But nothing matched the ones in that cavern.

"No, I've never seen glowing flowers before."

The queen groaned through her teeth and started pacing the room. In the meantime, Paloma got me some water, which I thankfully took.

"If you were to see this flower, say, in a book... would you be able to recognize it?" she asked.

"Yes," I replied with a nod.

The wizard picked up a notebook and quill, and I did my best to relay every detail of what I saw, down to the color of the crystal walls. Paloma seemed pleased enough with my description, which was a small solace for me in this worsening predicament.

The cold glass in my hands was a small grounding force as I looked over at Canela, who was biting her thumbnail pensively.

"So... you didn't see anything?" I asked.

She shook her head grimly. "No memories. Just a barrier. Even my magic couldn't go through."

"A literal one, from the looks of it," the queen said, "which doesn't answer any of our questions at all."

"What does it even mean? Who would even put it there?" I whispered, swallowing against a lump in my throat.

"Did you sense any dark magic, Canela?"

"I didn't sense that, no," the witch said and then looked at me curiously. "Did *you*? While you were there?"

The last time I was close to evil, all I felt was pain, whether it was physical or in my head. Before that, it was the black diamond, which seemed to beckon me with a dark hand.

"No, this was different. This place was quiet. I couldn't even hear the spirits," I said.

The queen stood before the table with her arms crossed in a determined stance.

"Well, then I guess we'll just have to keep digging for answers. I see why Sebastián took an interest in you. He probably couldn't get into your mind, either. Which means we have to figure out what's in there before *he* does."

THE MOON PRINCE

✳ ☽ ○ ☾ ✳

The rest of the day was spent trying to pry my skull open. Without fail, it would either result in absolutely nothing or me getting locked up in the cavern once more. Even though I managed to escape it every time, it took so much out of me that I became feverish with exhaustion. I was pushed beyond my limits, and at a certain point, Canela had to step in and put an end to my torture.

"If we keep doing this, we could break her, and she could become catatonic," she protested.

"I agree, *Majestad*," Paloma said.

The queen sighed, "Fine."

I lay on my side with sweat beading down my face and nothing left to give. My disappointment over the dead end came in a close second on the list.

Canela pushed my hair away from my forehead, whispering to me gently, "Everything will be alright, darling. Let's get you some rest."

"But we didn't get any answers," I muttered, my voice breaking.

"We can try something else another day. You're too weak to keep going."

I nodded sluggishly, unable to do much else.

"Are we sure we've tried everything?" the queen demanded.

"We've used everything at our disposal, *Majestad*," Paloma contested. "Allow me to do some research, and maybe then we can try again."

"I just hate the idea of wasting precious time."

"Well, then perhaps you can focus on honing her magic. Have you thought of that?" Canela asked.

La Reina scoffed, "Don't be ridiculous. She can summon the dead. Do you know the requirements for such a thing?"

"If you want to understand what you're working with, it might be the only way," Canela argued. "And I'm not talking about human corpses. Small animal carcasses are easy to acquire, and you can test her connection to the spirit world without getting your hands dirty."

"I don't want any of that shit in my castle. Especially not after what just happened."

"Would you rather I take her to my shop instead? I'd be more than happy to take her off your hands."

"Absolutely not."

The witch clicked her tongue in irritation. "With all due respect, *Majestad*, you're being difficult, and you're clearly at your limit."

My eyes widened at her tone. No one *ever* spoke to the queen that way.

"Difficult?" the queen blurted out. "You think *I'm* being difficult? Have you seen the world lately, *Magistra*? Better yet, did you get a look at the ballroom on your way here? People are dead, including my husband, so excuse me for being a little 'difficult.'"

"I understand your grief, Victoria. And I won't pretend to know what it is to rule a kingdom, but even you must understand that the key to her memory might just be her power. How can she use it if you won't let her? Is this how you treat your children?"

Tense silence fell upon the room. The witch kept her eyes trained on the Queen of Storms, whose stormy eyes were wild and furious. Her hand curled at her side, and a gust of wind burst through the room. In the back of my mind, there was boyish laughter among the whispers of the dead. They were amused, but I was not. I was terrified for Canela, even if the witch herself didn't look it.

The lavender-haired queen lifted a finger and said, "Mention my family again, and I will put a bolt through your heart. You don't know shit."

No matter Canela's intent, the queen took the witch's words personally. Her magic electrified the room, and I felt myself stuck in the middle. A crack of thunder made me jolt. Without thinking twice, I sat up and placed myself in front of Canela with my hand raised protectively.

"*Majestad*, please."

My words echoed around the room, making the candles dance violently.

Please, please, please. Don't, don't, don't.

Everyone gasped, and the queen lurched backward. She shook her head and shoulders, as if brushing off cobwebs, and when she finally looked up, her fury and disbelief were directed at me.

My hand flew to my mouth, realizing what I had just done.

"You," she hissed.

"I didn't-I didn't mean—"

With a metallic scratch, the captain took his sword out and pointed it at my throat. I fell back into Canela with a sharp inhale, and her hands went to my shoulders, keeping me from falling. I shook in terror as the tip of the blade dug into my skin without mercy, the guard's eyes full of rage.

"I'm so sorry," I whimpered.

With swift movement, a dagger made of dark crystal appeared in Canela's hand before she pressed it beneath the captain's helmet. The guard standing by the door shouted and raised his spear, ready to attack the witch. Paloma raised her hands, and green mist emanated from her fingertips, also ready. My blood rushed in my ears as I sat frozen in the middle of it, scared to make any wrong moves.

"Are you seriously going to kill a girl who has no clue how to use her magic? Who could be the answer to everything you're seeking?" Canela demanded. "You saw what she could do. She's powerful. You, of all people, *Majestad*, should know what it is to be born into something you must learn to control. It is both a gift and a burden to have a life tied to magic."

My eyes flitted between the captain and the queen. Somehow, even her Royal Majesty looked scared, but it wasn't because of Canela. No, it was because of me. *I* instilled fear in *Reina* Victoria's heart.

A teenage prince with lilac hair materialized beside her. He swept his gaze around the room with wary delight before setting his sights on me. Everyone else in the room was none the wiser to the royal phantom in their midst.

In the back of my mind, someone spoke.

Hi Esmé. We've met a few times before. My name is Saévio, but everyone calls me Savy.

He sounded young and jovial despite my predicament, pulling me away from my chaotic reality.

The Air Prince turned to his sister with a little more affection and said, "Tell her Savy's here. Trust me."

As if things couldn't get more peculiar, I did as I was told. If only to save my own throat.

I cleared my throat and said, "Savy's here."

The queen scowled at me, completely taken aback.

"What did you just say?"

"Your brother, Savy. He wanted me to let you know that he's here."

"I'm always here," he said.

"He's always here," I repeated. "I see him all the time. He wants you to know that it wasn't your fault."

"What isn't?" she hissed.

The prince looked at me as he explained, "There are things she's seen and done that neither of us should have had to, but it was war and it was our job to vanquish evil. We were both so young when I died. Our father only made things worse. She blames herself for everyone she's lost. I know she does."

"It's not your fault that you lost so many people. That you lost him or your husband," I choked the words out as the sword cut further into my neck.

The queen was struck speechless, but didn't move as she continued to listen. Whatever the Air Prince told me, I relayed to her.

"You're trying to protect the ones you have left by shielding them, because you're afraid of what dad did. But you aren't dad, V. You need Mariela and Río just as much as they need you. Esmé too. Something strange is happening. I don't know what it is, but I can feel it."

It felt too personal to be told this much about the queen's life and speak it out loud the way I was, but my life was on the line and nothing got through to the queen quite like this.

"I'm always here when you need me. I never left. I love you."

With tears in my eyes, I spoke the last words out loud, feeling every ounce of love to the point where I wasn't sure if it was mine or someone else's. I watched as the queen wept before me, and I willed those emotions toward her. At first, I didn't think it worked, but the candles danced again, and the words repeated over and over, leaving me before morphing into a single, *I love you.* His words, not mine.

In the back of my mind, there was another crack.

Reina Victoria squeezed her eyes shut and hugged herself tightly. She turned away from the room as her shoulders began to shake with her quiet sobs. Everyone else remained still with their blades pointed at each other. The nervous anticipation set me on edge.

"Put your weapons down. Take her to her room. We're done for today," said, her voice strained.

When the captain hesitated, she shouted, "I said, get out!"

Everyone snapped to attention and quickly put their weapons away. I slumped with a sigh of relief, rubbing the part of my neck where the blade had stuck me, and my fingers came away red with blood. Canela helped me off the table, and the captain pulled me by the chain towards the tower door. I took one last glance at the queen, who was hunched over a stack of books. Seeing her that way racked me with guilt.

She'll be okay, Savy said.

On the way out of the tower, Paloma gave me another potion to help me sleep.

She lingered for a moment and then leaned in close to whisper, "She has good intentions. It's just… The only other person who did anything like you was…"

"A monster," I finished, nodding in understanding, the calming effects of the potion already taking effect.

On the route to my prison, Saévio flickered between solid and translucent before me.

"Thank you," I whispered.

"Of course. You're very special, Esmé. She'll see that one day."

I frowned. "How? How do you know that?"

He chuckled. "Isn't it obvious?"

"What?" I shook my head in bewilderment. "What do you know?"

"Esmé? Who are you talking to?"

Canela's very real voice startled me back to reality. She was walking beside me with a hand to keep me from teetering. The effects of Paloma's potion were making me see her in double.

"The prince, of course," I sang.

We passed by *Princesa* Mariela and her dog, as well as one of her handmaidens, Mathilde. They were solid and alive. I waved at them, and they waved back disconcertingly. The Air Prince materialized behind the hound and waved as the dog's tail wagged.

Wait…

If I weren't inebriated, I would have been coherent enough to stitch together some thoughts about it.

Saévio muttered something, and I said, "You should go talk to your mother. Give her a big hug."

The princess furrowed her brow as Mathilde translated this, and gave me a nod as we continued our way.

Once in bed, I was put back into my restraints. Canela sat on the edge and brushed my hair out of my face. I was amazed the captain let her stay at all after what she did.

"Why is this happening to me, Canela? Why can I see them?" I asked.

"I don't know, darling. Some people are just more sensitive to these things. Many call it a gift."

"Raising the dead hardly sounds like a gift."

"Yes, that is something else entirely," she mused.

"Why are you protecting me?" I cried. "Maybe you should've let her kill me. Maybe I'm not worth the trouble."

A tear fell out of my eye and rolled over my nose onto the pillow.

"Don't say that, Esmé," she argued softly. "Just because you have something they don't understand doesn't mean you don't deserve a chance. Your life has just as much value as hers and her children's. I told you why I pray to the God of Death himself. I know that people tend to villainize what they don't fully comprehend. But if the Air Prince himself is speaking to you... I have a feeling he agrees with my sentiment. That Moon Prince of yours sees something in you, too. You just have to see it in yourself."

My heart hurt as I thought of Río, causing more tears to fall across my face.

"I don't know if he does," I whispered.

"I saw the way he looks at you, Esmé. Believe me, he does. Something like that doesn't simply go away."

I wanted to believe it so badly, so I chose to. It was a small amount of comfort, at the very least.

Little by little, the fatigue made it difficult to keep my eyes open.

"Canela, can you tell Dulce I'm okay?" I asked lazily.

I don't remember her response.

22

Unbreakable

Río

I was half asleep on the cot when I heard Esmé calling my name. It was distant, but I recognized her perilous tone immediately. I sat up with a start. The hairs on the back of my neck stood on end as I whipped my head around, looking for her, but she was nowhere to be found. I called out her name, expecting her to be somewhere down the way, but there was no response.

Nothing.

Of course not. My mother made sure she was far from reach.

Must have been a dream...or a nightmare.

I tried dozing off after that, but as soon as my mind quieted, I was rudely awakened by the sound of barking. I nearly jumped out of my skin.

"Mother of—Ela!"

Mariela and Echo rushed up to the bars excitedly, and I instantly sprang to my feet.

"How are you? Is everything okay?" I started signing.

We hadn't seen each other since our father's funeral.

"I'm alright, but I should ask you the same thing. You're the one in chains!" she motioned with her hands.

"I'm surviving."

It was the best I could do, considering my circumstances. As my mother said, things were only going to get worse before they got better.

"How's Mom doing?" I asked.

My sister's face darkened, filling me with dread.

"What? What is it?"

"I just saw her," she told me. "She was crying. A lot."

I almost wanted to ask why, but I had a feeling I knew the answer.

"Dad?" I signed.

Ela shrugged. "She wouldn't tell me. I think it was partially that, but I think it was something else."

"Like what?"

My sister wavered before telling me, "We saw Esmé on our way to Paloma's tower. She was with that witch with the curly hair."

I straightened up at the mention of Esmé.

"Canela?"

"Yes, her. It was strange. She told me to go comfort Mom, so I did. Before I went in, Paloma told me there was a bit of an incident."

I frowned. "What kind of incident?"

Ela shook her head. "I don't know. Apparently, there was an altercation. Something to do with Esmé's magic and Mom's brother, but Paloma said it was no one's fault."

"Did either of them look hurt?" I asked urgently, suddenly expecting the worst.

My mother's magic was powerful, and I knew firsthand how capable she was at annihilating a threat. But I also knew that Esmé's magic was dark and unpredictable. My family came first, but I also didn't want Esmé to get hurt if it wasn't her fault.

"Physically, Mom is fine," my sister said. "I stayed with her until she went to her room. But Esmé didn't look too well. She looked exhausted, and I think she was bleeding."

I craned my head back with a scowl. It didn't matter if it was in my mother's honor; the thought of Esmé being hurt at all infuriated me. My curse was exacerbating that feeling, defying all logic. I couldn't control what happened at the winter solstice, but this was different.

My sister reached through the bars to put her hand on my arm, and at the same time, Echo whined. It was a stark difference from his usual cheerful greetings.

"Who was with her?" I asked, looking into her eyes seriously.

"I told you. It was that witch, Canela."

"And the guards?"

"The captain, I think. Why?" As soon as she asked, my sister gave me a stern look. "Río, no."

I raised my hands defensively. "What? I'm not going to do anything. I'm chained up, remember?"

"Still, I know that look. Esmé's fine, and you're already on thin ice," she argued.

I rolled my eyes in response. Though I knew I might fail, I tried not to think about it too hard.

"She's really sweet, by the way," Mariela told me suddenly. "Mom called me in to heal her wound. After catching the two of you in the gallery, I didn't expect it."

I giggled as I recalled the fiasco. My sister harbored no shame for not only barging in but also for chastising me in front of Esmé. She told me I was lucky that it wasn't some lord that caught us, or worse, our mother. Was it stupid of me to do that in the middle of a palace event? Probably. Did I regret it? No, not really.

"I didn't think someone like her was your type," Ela added.

Despite the jab, I found myself unable to disagree.

"Yeah, well, Esmé's different," I replied.

In many dangerous ways.

I unconsciously fidgeted with the aquamarine necklace, and regardless of how desperate I *didn't* want to sound, I couldn't help but wonder…

"Did she ask about me?"

The seemed childish, but I couldn't help myself.

"No. Sorry," Mariela signed remorsefully.

My chest deflated, feeling my heart crack a little bit. Although I didn't know why. I expected anything else after the way I left her. Even before then, I wasn't exactly making her life easy.

The bite on my arm pulsed, filling me with a sudden otherworldly irritation. I let my eyes flutter shut and took deep breaths to contain myself. My condition was worsening as the days went by. More often than not, I was borderline feverish and felt as if I were suffering from a long hangover. I was angry at nothing and everything, and if I thought about Esmé, my father, or even my situation too deeply, it only lingered. I hated it.

When I opened my eyes, Mariela was eyeing the scar on my arm. Rather, what remained of it. I removed the bandage once I realized how useless it was. The wound was no longer a wound at all, and the white veins were only becoming more visible as they quickly crept past my elbow. Even my chest bore the marks of my future transformation. In due time, my body and mind were never truly going to be mine ever again. The looks I was getting from my family didn't help.

"Does that hurt?" she asked.

"No," I responded, shaking my head. "No pain. Just anger."

"Paloma's been looking into a cure, you know. But most of her research is stuff we've already learned. Werewolves existed long before the God-given. Along with most of the magical beasts around here."

I ran a tired hand over the growing stubble on my chin and signed, "Disappointed, but not surprised."

Mariela reached into her skirt pocket and took out a small vial of black liquid. I instinctively cringed in disgust as she handed it to me through the bars.

"She told me to give you this. What is it?" she asked.

"It's some bullshit concoction she made that's supposed to make me feel better."

In rapid succession, I popped the cork, held my breath, and downed the entire bottle in one go. This was the second time I had taken it. Even if there wasn't a cure so far, there were still plenty of treatments for the werewolf curse. I'd gladly take anything that would help alleviate the symptoms, and Paloma was a great wizard. Unfortunately, she didn't specialize in curses like mine. Animals and magical creatures, perhaps, but dark curses were something entirely different, so whatever she made was based on new research. And because my mother never trusted anyone else with her family, I was at the mercy of experimental remedies.

This one tasted like licorice and tar. It was a disgusting mixture, and I've drunk plenty of disgusting things overseas with my father. I cringed even more at the salty aftertaste, resisting the urge to gag. And when the bottle was empty, I threw it over my shoulder and heard it shatter on impact as it hit the wall.

"If it's bullshit, then why do you drink it?" my sister asked derisively.

I shrugged. "It helps with the rage for a few hours."

A few seconds later, the burning feeling in my arm subsided. Even if my inner turmoil didn't go away, the red-hot urge to lash out was now tranquilized. For the short duration it lasted, anyway

"Well, maybe she can make you more, so it can last all day," Mariela offered.

"I wish, but she said if I take too much, it could either stop working or make me worse."

Werewolves were known to become addicts as a way to deal with their ailment, which wasn't encouraging at all.

My sister scowled. Not at me, but at the situation.

"I hate this. I hate that you're in here," she signed angrily.

"Me too," I replied dejectedly.

Mariela looked at Echo, who gazed up at her with a troubled whine, as if feeling what she was. I watched my sister's fury turn into fear, and when her eyes met mine once more, they were bloodshot with tears.

"What's going to happen to you after you turn?" she wondered, her mouth quivering. "Is Mom going to let you go or keep you here forever? What about the next full moon? And the next? People hate werewolves! Especially after what happened at the ball! What if you get killed because of it? What if Sebastián tries to kill you again? I can't lose you, too!"

A soft sob came out of her as tears fell from her eyes. My chest tightened, and I had to fight back tears of my own. Echo nudged her legs in a comforting gesture, and my sister bent down to give him a hug before straightening up again.

I stretched my hands out to her as far as I could, palms up. She sniffled before reaching through the bars and putting one of her own hands over mine. I clasped it gently and gave it a reassuring squeeze.

Being here in this dungeon, isolated from everyone else, I wasn't able to be there for my family after my father's death. My mother was intent on keeping her emotions in check, but Mariela wasn't like that. She was still a teenager, and she was even more glued to my father's side than I was when we were growing up before he started leaving for long periods.

Every time he came back, he'd sweep us up, shower us with gifts from his travels, and tell us how much he missed us. He was always like that. No matter how ferocious he could be as a king and a warrior, he never spared an ounce of love for his family or his people. He was funny and clever, and he was not afraid to *feel*. No matter how many years passed, he adored my mother like no other man loved his wife. He was powerful and rich in many ways that had nothing to do with magic at all. And now... that was viciously ripped away.

How fucking unfair.

I took in my little sister now, as grief-stricken as I was. I pictured my mother crying in Paloma's tower, and I thought...

I can't let that die, too. I can't let that die with him. Even if I am a monster, I can't break. Not now.

I pushed past the tears burning behind my eyes and let go of my sister's hands to say, "You are not going to lose me. Alright? I will do everything in my power to make sure that doesn't happen. My job is and has always been to keep you and Mom safe… and I can't do that if I'm dead, can I?"

My mouth curled with a soft smirk, trying to lighten the mood. Mariela rolled her eyes at me playfully.

"Right now," I continued, "keeping you safe means dealing with this bullshit of a curse and figuring out what we're going to do about that asshole who did this to us. Yeah?"

My sister wiped her tears and nodded.

"I just hate feeling so useless," she said. "I wish Mom would tell me things, but she never does. I can't even eavesdrop. Otherwise, I would."

"I know," I sighed in exasperation. "I wish she'd stop being so overprotective. Now is not the time to keep us in the dark."

"I know!"

I was usually the one staying up-to-date with what was happening in the war, but now that I was locked up and my father was gone, I knew next to nothing. It was maddening.

"I mean, how are you supposed to be king if you don't know what's going on?" Mariela added.

I grimaced. "Don't remind me."

The prospect of being king used to thrill me when I was younger, but now it was the complete opposite. Out of instinct, I reached for the aquamarine moon again. I never used to do that before, but it recently became a source of comfort. It was all I had in my isolation.

Letting the pendant fall against my chest, I asked, "Can you do something for me?"

Mariela nodded vigorously. "Anything."

"Keep an eye on her, will you? Esmé, I mean."

My sister cocked her head to the side, eyes narrowed. "Of course. You know, when you asked me to get her an invitation to the ball, part of me was horrified that you were bringing some fling along. But she's not just some fling, is she?"

I shook my head. It wasn't even a question.

"No. No, she's more than that."

"Do you want me to tell her anything?" she asked.

My eyes flashed as all the words I wanted to say surged through my mind like a tidal wave.

Hello, I'm sorry. Are you okay? I miss you. I think about you every day. I want to see you desperately. I want to kiss you and hold you in my arms. I'm sorry I couldn't keep you safe. I wish I could be there for you. Do you even want me? Would you want someone like me? Should you? Is what I have to offer even enough?

No matter what, it all sounded stupid and trivial to me.

"No. No, I don't think she needs anything from me," I signed.

Mariela audibly scoffed, "So, you're just going to stop talking to her altogether?"

"Until this passes over, at least. She's already going through so much without me fucking it all up," I argued.

"Exactly! She's going through a lot! And you're the only one she knows here, you idiot!" she scolded me in sign language.

"We're not allowed to see each other, Ela!" I contested. "It doesn't matter! Besides, the full moon is coming up, and I don't want to hurt her! She deserves someone better than me anyway!"

It wasn't just the fact that I was becoming a beast or the argument we had. It was more than that. There were things I still held guilt over—things I did in the past that had nothing to do with curses. I didn't want to admit it to her back in the gallery, but some of Silas Calicó's words had truth to them: *the sea is just as deadly as it is beautiful.* I knew that all too well. My fury has followed me much longer than Sebastián has, and I don't know how Esmé would feel toward me if she knew the truth.

My sister glared at me as if she were reading my mind.

"Don't say that. That's not true," she cut the air with her hands to make a point. "You can at least reach out. You have more power here than even she does. You don't have to profess your love for her. You just have to be her friend."

I had the brotherly urge to keep bickering, but was so surprised by her statement that my hands stopped moving. As the stubborn older brother, I liked to think I was always right, but now and then, Mariela would say something that proved me otherwise. She could be a lot wiser than I, not that I would ever admit it out loud. But I'm sure the shameful blush on my face gave me away.

Despite my annoyance, I nodded in agreement and tried thinking of what I could possibly say to Esmé that wasn't insufferably long but also concise. What could I say that could make up for everything? What if words aren't enough?

My hand went to the necklace again, and my last promise came to mind. Struck with an idea, I grinned at my sister and pulled the stone over my head. I held it towards her, and she frowned at the familiar piece of jewelry in my palm.

"Give this to her," I said.

"Why this?"

With the necklace in my fist, I responded, "She'll know what it means. Tell her that my promise still stands and that I... Tell her that if she still wants... I'll be here to answer her call."

My sister's face softened, and with a nod, she took the stone moon in her hands and tucked it safely in her pocket.

"Anything else?"

"No. I'll save it for when I'm finally out of here."

23

The Greenhouse

Esmé

Days passed without a single visit from *Reina* Victoria or my guards. The only person who came during that time was Arabella, who brought me my meals. Otherwise, I was back where I started: locked away in my tower and chained to my bed with nothing but my thoughts—and spirits—to keep me company. I wasn't dead yet, but I had a feeling I was being punished for what I did.

On the one hand, it was a welcome reprieve, but on the other, my remorse was insurmountable. I didn't mean to attack the queen, and I most certainly didn't intend to cause her to break down. But like Canela said, I had no control over my power at all, and my exhaustion must have aggravated that. All I knew was that Savy's words saved me from being thrown in the dungeon or, worse, losing my head. I just hoped that I'd have the chance to apologize.

In my alone time, I found myself so bored and out of it that I started singing songs to pass the hours. I didn't care if the guards could hear me. I simply let the words tumble out of my mouth because music was the one thing that never left my memory. At the very least, the spirits seemed to like it, because instead of grating my skull like a chisel on stone, their voices flew over me peacefully.

At other moments, my mind drifted home.

Home.

The Larimar District, *Teatro Paraiso*, Anelante—no, not Anelante anymore. At least, I wasn't certain.

For the thousandth time, I tried in desperation to recall anything from my forgotten past. *Anything.* Anything would have been better than nothing. But nothing was all I ever received in turn. It was either that or fragments and ideas I couldn't fully grasp. Everything solid in my mind took place in Coáraluna alone, and that was all.

My anxious thoughts, compounded with the isolation, eventually became too much. Despite the size of the room, I struggled to breathe, and whenever I panicked, the whispers grew louder. Up until now, I had been doing my best to ignore them, but after days of imprisonment, a tiny spark of bravery bloomed in my chest. If this was going to be a part of my foreseeable future, then perhaps it wouldn't hurt to listen at least once.

Witchcraft made more sense to me than what the God-given could do, but if this magic truly lived within me, then there had to be some way to reach it. I had no idea how to begin doing such a thing, but in an attempt to do so, I closed my eyes, and instead of pushing the whispers away, I opened up to the sounds around me.

The whispers at the surface tickled my ears, making me flinch on instinct. It was an eerie noise, but the voices were otherwise indiscernible. If I stayed like this, I could pretend I was outside, standing on the street, listening to the conversations of people sitting at a nearby café. They were, I assume, traces of those who once lived in the castle, tied to this place by some emotional connection or unfinished business. Filled with unbridled curiosity, I listened in a little closer, pushing past that layer of indistinct muttering. As soon as I did so, it was as if all the nearby ghosts turned their heads towards me, becoming aware of my intentions. Each one uttered a short, distant phrase.

Who is that? What do you want? Please, please, help me. Poisoned girl, marked by the eye of death. You don't belong here. It was supposed to be the best night of the year. Help me! You need to listen. Keep them safe, please. What are you? You're no commoner. My sweet, little sunshine. You need to kill him. It's the only way. It always gets what it wants. This much power wasn't made for someone like you.

Esmé!

The last voice was so loud, I clapped my hands over my ears. My chains rattled as I sat up and whipped my gaze around, expecting someone to be there, but I was alone in the tower as always. With a groan, I sank back into the mattress, running my hands over my face. It seemed it was still a love-hate relationship between the spirits and me, so it was better to continue singing to keep us all happy.

❊ ☽ ○ ☾ ❊

I don't know how much time passed before my isolation came to an end. All I knew was that the sun was out when Arabella came back once more, bearing positive news:

I would be spending the day at the greenhouse with Paloma.

"Greenhouse?" I replied. "I didn't even know the castle *had* a greenhouse."

"Oh, yes. It's very beautiful and often used for all sorts of botany, alchemy, and magical lessons," she explained.

I raised my eyebrows. Canela had suggested that I hone my power, but I didn't think the queen would take her advice. Especially not after what I did. Yet, by some miracle, I was released from my tower and taken down for my first bath in days.

Once I was clean, Arabella presented me with a beautiful aquamarine dress with an embroidered. It was not only an improvement from the last dress but was also much better than what I had at home. It even fit like a glove and was surprisingly comfortable. The handmaiden brushed my hair, taking her time by the sunlit window and pinned it at the sides to keep it out of my face. The rest of it flowed down my back, soft and clean. If I didn't know any better, I'd say I was back to my usual self, but when I saw my reflection again, my eyes told a different story.

When I met the captain's gaze this time, his green eyes burned with a deeper kind of loathing. I merely pursed my lips and looked away hotly. The cut he gave me scabbed over, but I could still feel the blade. If he didn't hate me before, he certainly did now that I threatened his queen.

I was thankful to be going *away* from the wizard's tower, and I couldn't help but notice that *Castillo* Paricia seemed much lonelier compared to the winter solstice. While it was still breathtaking, the vastness of it was—ironically enough—*haunting*. Occasionally, I'd see a guard patrolling a hallway or a servant running about—some alive and some not. Outside of recent experience, I didn't know much about the life of royals, but I was surprised by the lack of nobility around. It could have been that they all fled after the massacre, but even so, I assumed most royals had a party of ladies-in-waiting or right-hand men trailing behind. Other than a few trusted guards and handmaidens, the Markaél's had none of that. I couldn't help but wonder why.

THE MOON PRINCE

We passed by a set of large windows overlooking the stables and an open training field. In one area, people in armor practiced with spears and shields, while another group trained with swords. I half-expected to see Río among them, though to my chagrin, he was nowhere to be found (*is the castle really so big, or is he actively hiding?*). My keenness and disappointment were embarrassing at this point. However I did spot a different white-haired royal standing before the archery range.

I staggered to a stop. The captain tugged on my chains with a grumble, but I resisted. I wanted to get a good look at the Moon Princess training with her bow and arrow. Rather, *arrows*. She had three of them knocked against the bow and was standing farther away than I would have expected. She ultimately let them fly and I watched as each one landed perfectly in the center of three different targets. In fact, I noticed with a gasp, that a smattering of arrows were sticking out from the bull's eye of every target. Her proficiency moved me.

Until recently, I never stopped to think that the God-given could rely on anything other than their magic. I assumed that if someone was already so powerful, they had no use for such things, but the Markaél's were quickly proving me wrong. Perhaps *El Rey y La Reina* saw benefit in learning how to defend themselves in multiple ways. Perhaps I knew nothing about how the God-given worked at all.

"We don't have all day, Vespertín," the captain growled, pulling at my manacles once more.

I cast a glare in his direction as let the momentum take me away from the view of the training grounds.

My resentment was put on hold when we exited out into a large garden. Sunlight and sea breeze kissed my skin, making me sigh with delight. There were bountiful trees, flowers, and bushes; some were still vibrant with color, while others awaited the spring. Birds chirped, and a few iguanas gathered by a tree. Beautiful fountains with glittering water sat among the greenery, and the grassy space was lined by stone pathways that led down to a giant, domed structure made of glass panels. We walked through it all, granting me the opportunity to admire my first glimpse of nature in days.

Even with my small window, I got little to no sunlight in my tower, and being locked up drained me. I never thought I could take such a thing for granted. Back home, I used to bask in the sun's rays every chance I could get, to the point where Dulce joked I was a reptile. It's why one of my favorite pastimes was crossing the quartz bridges to spend the day at the beach, take a dip in the sea, and watch people surf on wooden boards. Canela once told me that sunshine was good for the mind, and my mind needed all the good it could get. I saw the truth to that now, because my energy doubled in a short period of time.

At the end of the path, I was ushered in through the doors of the huge greenhouse, which was breathtaking in its own right. The interior was supported by marble arches veined with ivy. The entire glass building was filled top to bottom with a collage of lush green hues, dappled with bright, vibrant blooms of flowers. There were plants from all over Avilonía, some of which I had only read of in books. A large pond ran along the center of it all, with lily pads and water flowers floating within. Small bridges arched over the water, connecting the red tile paths running along either side. The place itself smelled like a mixture of sweetness, fresh water, and wet earth, and it filled me with an incredible sense of peace.

"*Buenos días*, Miss Vespertín!"

I whipped my head to the left, where Paloma was coming down the path towards me. The Queen of Storms was nowhere in sight, and my shoulders relaxed.

"*Buenos días*," I returned.

"Oh, the cuffs won't be necessary," she said to the captain. "Queen's orders."

The guard muttered something before saying, "Alright."

He unlocked my restraints and sighed happily as I rubbed my swollen wrists.

The wizard's eyes traced over my face from behind her spectacles. Even though she looked more at ease compared to when we first met, she still seemed cautious in my presence.

"How are you feeling?" she asked.

"Exhausted. Confused. And somehow, not entirely here," I answered.

After experiencing so many mind-boggling things in a row, I was starting to feel a little out of my body.

"Well, hopefully being in this place will help," the wizard said with a smile. "Come."

I began to follow with trepidation, but when she noticed the captain on my heels, Paloma pointed at him like a poorly behaved pet.

"You stay by the door. We're going to be doing magic, Captain. We don't need a repeat of the other night," she said.

Again, he grumbled to himself, but took his place next to the greenhouse entrance.

How did such a childish man get promoted?

Halfway down the path, I leaned in close to Paloma and whispered, "I think he hates me more than anyone else in this castle."

"Oh, don't mind him," the wizard said with a wave of her hand. "He's been through his own troubles lately."

"What does that have to do with me?"

Paloma slowed down, her eyes hesitant. She took a swift glance over my shoulder as if to make sure the captain wasn't listening.

"Whatever took down the king laid waste to his entire ship, Miss Vespertín," she explained, "and he wasn't the only one on board who was lost. A few of the captain's loved ones were there too."

My chest tightened. Of course, he wasn't the only one on that ship. It all started to make sense.

"He blames me," I uttered in realization.

"You're still a royal prisoner, and until proven otherwise, he sees you as a threat. It's his job," Paloma said.

"And you?"

"I, personally, like gathering all the information before making any decisions. So far, you've been lovely, but as I told you, you can't blame any of us for being a bit scared."

I nodded in understanding. If I were in her place, I'd feel the same way.

We approached an open space at the far end of the greenhouse, where the pond came to a stop. The structure ended in a semicircle that was lined with potted rosemary and lavender. Before them were two tables with gardening tools, books, dried plants, and a bundle of things I couldn't recognize from afar. The wizard stood at the center with her hands clasped behind her back, facing me.

I eyed the space hesitantly as I toyed with my malachite ring.

"You said we would be doing magic?" I asked.

"Yes," she said with a bright smile. "That's why I asked them to bring you here. My tower is good and all, but nature is the perfect place to help clear your mind and channel your gifts without getting...*overwhelmed*."

"I thought Canela would be here," I wondered aloud, considering it was her idea.

Paloma pursed her lips ruefully. "Yes, but after what happened, the queen didn't feel comfortable having her around. After all, she disrespected her and threatened one of her guards with a knife."

"Because of me," I muttered somberly.

"I think Canela is very capable of making her own decisions," she assured, adjusting her glasses. "As powerful as she is, we can handle ourselves here just fine."

"Alright." I furrowed my brow then. "You said we're doing magic, but... I'm not a Markaél. My ability is not so straightforward. All I've ever done is hurt people with it. You saw it with your own eyes."

"When untapped, it can be dangerous, yes, but from what I saw, you're quite connected to the spirit world, Miss Vespertín. If I'm correct, you spoke to the Air Prince himself, and you saw the Moon King. You knew he was dead before we did."

"Yes, and?"

"And... most necromancers *force* themselves into the spirit realm. They take control of spirits and their corpses without care. But these spirits seem to flock to you. It can be dangerous, not just for others but for you as well. Still, that is valuable. Or, at least, it *has* to be."

The doors creaked open, drawing Paloma's attention over my shoulder. Her round face instantly brightened, her mouth widening with a grin.

"Oh, perfect!"

I twisted around and saw, to my surprise, *Princesa* Mariela and Echo coming our way. She was out of her training gear, in a pink dress, with no guard or handmaiden by her side.

"Oh!" I instinctively curtsied before waving at her to say, "*Buenos días, Alteza!*"

The princess signed to me, and Paloma translated, "*Buenos días, Miss Vespertín.*"

I mimicked the gesture for the greeting, and the princess nodded in approval.

"I saw you on the training grounds earlier. You're spectacular with a bow," I mused with Paloma's help.

The princess looked surprised by my statement, and her cheeks turned red.

"Thank you. Hopefully it'll come in good use one day," she said.

"Of course. I didn't know you would be joining us today."

After what I did to *La Reina*, I was amazed she was letting her daughter anywhere near me at all.

"*Princesa* Mariela and *Príncipe* Río both started their magical training here in this very building," Paloma said. "No one in Coáraluna has abilities quite like yours, and the only ones who come close live in this castle. Seeing as the queen is a bit preoccupied at the moment, she was willing to let Ela assist in your lessons today."

As far as I knew, there were *three* God-given in this palace. Even though I knew the princess was powerful, I couldn't help but wonder where the *other* Markaél was.

"I'm sorry, but... if you don't mind me asking... what about *Príncipe* Río?" I asked.

The princess's eyes flashed, and despite Paloma's composure, I noticed her briefly tense.

"He's dealing with his curse, no doubt," the wizard said. "He's spent a lot of time in his room. Keeping to himself. They say the first full moon is the worst, so things are taking a turn pretty quickly."

There was a twinge in my heart and a sudden urge to find him pulled at my soul.

"So, I'm guessing we won't be seeing him anytime soon?" I derided.

The wizard shook her head. "No, I'm afraid not. Both he and the queen think it's safer this way. For everyone involved."

"Mmmm, right," I said with an unconvinced hum.

Somehow, whatever remained of my heart seemed to crumble. Even though I was almost certain that if he truly wanted to see me *in his own home*, he would have already. I should have known better by now.

When I locked eyes with *Princesa* Mariela, she shared a pained smile. I could only imagine what it must have felt like to have her brother in such a state after losing her father. That, at the very least, I could feel compassion for.

"Are you sure you want to be here for this, *Alteza*?" I asked apprehensively.

She smirked in a way that made her look like her brother.

"As you know, I can do a lot more than just heal wounds, Miss Vespertín. I'll be just fine."

My face flushed. "Right, of course."

Just because you don't know how to handle your abilities doesn't mean she can't.

"Well, now that everyone's here, I wanted to ask about what happened the other night," Paloma said.

I tensed and immediately started stammering out an apology, "I... I'm so sorry. I didn't mean—"

"We know. It's okay," the wizard reassured with a chuckle. "We just want to know what exactly you did. Can you describe it?"

I exhaled in relief and searched for the best way to put words to the phenomenon.

"It usually happens when my emotions are running rampant," I said. "I hear whispers—the spirits—and they get louder and louder until suddenly I break and then... I don't know how to describe it, but it's like they explode out of me. And the whispers stop."

The princess glanced between me and Paloma as the wizard relayed my explanation to her. I couldn't help but think that she looked mature and incredibly young at the same time. It was different from other girls her age that had I met.

"Yes. You told the queen the last time it happened, you were protecting the prince, right? Could you try doing it again?" Paloma asked.

I pulled my bottom lip between my teeth. "I suppose. It's quite nerve wrecking though."

"If you don't figure out how it works, you're only going to keep hurting people by accident."

Though I knew she was right, the strangeness of my ability still frightened me.

Princesa Mariela softly tapped me on the shoulder, drawing my attention to her soft eyes. She motioned something to Paloma and then for me to listen. I gave her my full, undivided attention as she proceeded to speak in sign language.

"I used to be scared of the ocean. It might sound crazy since I'm the Moon Princess and we live on an island, but I was. I just remember thinking it was so terrifying, and the waves looked like monsters to me. Because of it, I didn't learn how to swim until I was a teenager. I almost drowned one time and probably would have if my dad wasn't there to save me."

The image of a little girl getting eaten by a wave sounded terrifying. Not being able to hear it seemed even worse.

"My parents were very patient, even when I wasn't. I wanted so badly to conquer the water and my fear of it, but then my father told me something that changed everything. He said that the key isn't to fight it or control it, but to embrace it and meet it halfway. You have to be one with it. The waves will only drown you if you let them. So, when I finally started working with the water, I stopped being afraid."

Princesa Mariela stopped signing and walked over to the edge of the pond. She put her hand over it and, with little to no effort, moved her fingers and pulled a stream of water into the air. My eyes sparkled with joy as she made it dance before us like a stream of light. When she was finished, she gracefully placed it back where it belonged and then clasped her hands behind her back shyly as Paloma and I clapped.

"Of course, I still get scared and still have a lot to learn, but I'm not afraid of the ocean anymore," she said.

Never did I think that I could relate to someone as powerful as a God-given, yet the princess's story showed me that we were more similar than anyone could imagine. Her demonstration instilled the right amount of hope and motivation in me that I needed. I couldn't keep letting the wave swallow me whole.

"Okay," I told them, "I'll do whatever you want me to do."

✳ ☽ ○ ☾ ✳

As per Canela's suggestion, I was given a squirrel carcass to practice with. It wasn't how I pictured spending a day at a castle, yet here I was, trying not to feel mournful over the poor creature.

"We wanted to test your...*other* abilities first," Paloma said.

Ah, yes...Necromancy.

Considering the first time was an accident, I had nowhere to begin.

"But how...what do I do?" I asked.

"Do you think you could try and reach out and see if you can sense anything?" *Princesa* Mariela asked.

"I… I can try."

As I placed myself before the dead squirrel, I mirrored the princess' actions from earlier, and I raised my hands over the body. I closed my eyes, and just like in my tower, I opened my mind. The murmurs of the dead were always on the surface, easy to hear if I simply took the time to listen. I focused on them and only them, but when I opened my eyes, nothing changed.

I sighed, "Nothing."

"What if you tried touching it?" Paloma offered.

Even though I wasn't doing that in the ballroom, I was willing to try anything to help the process. With a gentle touch, I put my hand on the animal's soft fur and closed my eyes once more. I reached out and envisioned the squirrel in life, chittering and running around among the trees. The sound of the spirits grew stronger, but I couldn't exactly tell the difference between a human spirit and an animal's. I didn't know what to latch onto.

Nothing. I tried visualizing life going back into its body. Nothing. I thought of the moment Río was bitten by the werewolf. Nothing. Nothing was working.

I groaned in frustration, "I don't know what I'm doing wrong. Maybe it was a one-time thing."

"I highly doubt that, Miss Vespertín," Paloma chuckled. "We just need to find the right steps. The right recipe, you know? We need to get you back to what you felt that day in the ball."

My eyes widened as visions of that night flashed in my mind, making my pulse quicken.

"No, that was life or death. People were dying. I thought Río was going to die. I thought *I* was," I rambled.

"Intense situations can often bring out unbridled emotion," she explained. "What happened that day opened up the door, but that doesn't mean it's closed now. You just need to find another path back to it. It doesn't have to be life or death every time."

I worked at my lip, casting a nervous glance at *Princesa* Mariela. She regarded me with a furrowed brow, as if thinking hard about something.

"What?" I asked.

"What if you just tried talking to the spirits again? Maybe you need to connect with them first," she signed.

"Yes, haven't you tried that before?" the wizard asked.

"Once, in my tower," I replied.

"Then let's try again. Maybe some extra room will help."

Paloma guided me to the open space before the edge of the pond and placed me in the center.

"Think of a place that makes you feel safe and warm. That usually helps," the princess offered voicelessly.

"Safe and warm," I repeated softly.

She and Paloma moved aside, watching me from a distance. I touched my ring and pulled back my shoulders, taking in the beautiful scene before me. And with a deep breath, I softened my gaze.

Just as the princess told me, I wandered to a warm and safe place. What first came to mind was *Teatro Paraiso*, Fabian, and Teo. Then I thought of all of my friends gathered in Dulce's house. I envisioned them all laughing and drinking as music played, my heart growing warmer. Then Río's face came to mind. I thought of his eyes, his smile, and how he looked at me in a way that made me weak at the knees. I thought of hot chocolate, kisses, and blue flowers. I thought of dancing, laughter, and kissing in forbidden spaces. I thought of aquamarine and promises. And as I imagined all of it, I could feel myself vibrating, the whispers building in my mind.

"That's it. Reach into that, Miss Vespertín," Paloma said.

With her approval, I tried holding onto that feeling, reveling in the daylight within me. It was unlike anything I had ever felt in my life. But as always, my wretched mind turned everything sour. I overthought it too much and the happy memories became dark.

My life is gone. I can never go back to *Teatro Paraiso* again. My friends probably think I'm dead, and if I don't do something, the Sun Killer will get to them. If they find out who I am, they'll think I'm a monster. Río thinks I'm a monster, too, and he was never mine. He never will be.

The spirits turned aggressive and violent, screeching at me like crows.

See, she doesn't have what it takes. She's nothing like the God-given. Just a child.

Esmé, they said over and over. Teasing.

"Stop it," I whimpered.

Leave her alone. It was Saévio's voice, firmer than the rest.

"What are they saying?" Paloma asked.

Esmé, focus, the prince stressed. *Spirits get restless. Listen to Ela. You need to meet them halfway. You're the one with the power here, not them.*

"The Air Prince," I whispered.

"What is he saying?"

"He's trying to help me."

"Okay. Try again, but direct them at me this time."

My eyes snapped open as Paloma planted herself a few feet in front of me.

At my blanched expression, she said, "We have to test this out somehow. You didn't do much damage to the queen to begin with, so I should be fine. I have my magic."

She said it to reassure me, but I could see her hands shaking. Green mist curled around her fingers, ready to defend herself from what I may unleash. Even the princess eyed her hesitantly.

"Paloma—"

"Do it now, Miss Vespertín," she stressed.

Wanting to be brave, I swallowed hard, and with my gaze on Paloma's face, I focused on the voices around me.

Help us. She can't *help us. He's going to kill us all. Focus. You control them. You're nothing.* Screaming. Crying. The sound of people dying. It was the ballroom, and it was a battlefield all in one. Massacres and war.

They need you just as much as you need them, Esmé. They're angry. We all are.

The sound was so overstimulating that I instinctively put my hands over my ears to muffle it. My thoughts drifted, and just like in my tower... I started to sing to quell the noise. I kept my eyes glued to the tiled floor as my voice shook with the lyrics. It was a lullaby, a song about a blue rabbit who was friends with the moon.

The whispers hushed around me.

"Miss Vespertín… look up."

I lowered my trembling hands, turning my gaze upwards, and gasped. The spirits, which once appeared to me as shadows, were now made of violet light. They resembled fireflies or fairies. Though I stopped singing, some of them continued to dance through the greenery. Among them, standing on the nearest bridge, was the Air Prince, smiling. The flames from nearby sconces fluttered, drawing the attention of Paloma and the princess, who were utterly stunned.

"Are you alright?" I asked the wizard.

Paloma laughed gleefully, "Oh, yes. I don't know what you did, but that wasn't like last time at all."

I giggled in disbelief, "I think they like it when I sing."

"You met them halfway," the princess signed excitedly.

I made eye contact with *Príncipe* Saévio, and any fear I had left seemed to completely vanish. In its stead, there was a spark in my chest, similar to what I experienced back in the ballroom. I returned to that warm and safe space. I thought of my friends who aren't afraid to speak up and be themselves. I thought of Río's bravery, Mariela's determination, and *Reina* Victoria's love for her family. I thought of how they made me feel. I thought of what I did at the ball and of the cave in my head that was filled with the strange, glowing purple flowers. And I let it all fill me with shimmering daylight.

Behind the prince's spirit, a taller, darker figure materialized out of thin air. My breath hitched, and there was a crack in my skull that made my head throb. Echo went ballistic, now focused behind me towards an eerie scratching sound. Mariela let out a strangled noise and pointed over my shoulder.

I whirled around to see the squirrel, now undead. It sat on its hind legs, its eyes glowing a flaming purple as it stared right at me.

My hands flew to my mouth. "Did I do that?"

Princesa Mariela circled me, looking between my eyes.

"What?" I gestured questioningly.

She took my hand and pulled me toward the pond, pointing to the water. I looked down into its reflection to see a girl staring back at me. Her hair was brown, her skin was bronze, and her eyes glowed a flaming violet.

24

Royal Schemes

Esmé

I was able to release my magic with the princess's direction. The glowing spirits disappeared, their voices hushing as the burning in my chest mollified. The undead squirrel was immobile once more, and I watched in the reflection of the water as my eyes returned to their natural brown color.

"I must report this to the queen as soon as possible," Paloma said excitedly.

"Does this mean that I'll get my memories back?" I asked eagerly.

"I don't know. Can you think of something from before Coáraluna?"

With a little more hope than before, I reached into that empty space, but unfortunately nothing changed. Suddenly, my excitement over was overshadowed by disillusionment.

"No," I replied dejectedly. "No, I don't think so."

The wizard gave me a reassuring smile. "It's alright, Miss Vespertín. These things take time. Now that you have found the path back to your magic, you can strengthen your ability. I'm sure something will come up eventually."

"I hope so. Do you at least have an idea what this means? Now that you've seen what I can do, perhaps you might know where it comes from."

"I think it means that you're incredibly special, Miss Vespertín," Paloma stated, "and we need to figure out why and how. I had a few ideas, but I'm afraid I'm only more discombobulated."

She took off her spectacles and cleaned them off with her skirt.

My shoulders dropped, and a small scoff left my lips. I put everything I had into this lesson, hoping that it would give someone a clue about the nature of my abilities, but to no avail. Though my success instilled a newfound confidence in me, I couldn't help my frustration.

What were they doing while I was locked up?

"Isn't this castle full of some of the most powerful magic-users in the country?" I asked.

"Some, not all," the wizard replied hesitantly. "I'm sorry, Miss Vespertín, but what you have goes beyond anyone's expertise. Anyone here, that is. Any tomes on necromancy or anything of the sort are in Old Avilonía, and even then, I wouldn't advise touching them. For you, I'm going to have to dig into things I haven't touched in years."

"What about Canela? Maybe she knows something."

She hesitated before saying, "If worse comes to worst, then maybe."

I gave her a strange look, suddenly feeling defensive and irked.

"She was the one who found the enchantment in my mind. She's very knowledgeable about the God of Death. She was willing to take me under her wing. Perhaps she knows more about this than—"

"Exactly. She worships the deity of death."

The dark insinuation was obvious, which, at this point, was getting rather tiresome.

"Well, let me help you then," I offered.

She chuckled nervously, "I'm sorry, but no."

"Why not?" I demanded.

"With all due respect, Miss Vespertín——"

"Please call me Esmé."

"With all due respect, Esmé, you are still a prisoner, and the queen has already let us cross her limits this far. I highly doubt she wants you involved in anything more than she's comfortable with."

Something within me finally snapped. Days of isolation mixed with interrogations and experimentation finally pushed me over the edge.

"But this is...this is *my* life you're talking about, Paloma!" I exclaimed. "*My* mind! *My* body! *My* magic! I deserve to look into this just as much, if not more, as any of you. *I* have to live in this cursed vessel every day. If you're not willing to do what it takes to get to the bottom of this, then what's the point? It's hardly fair."

The candlelight swayed with flying with murmurs of the dead, drawing the wary eyes of both the wizard and the princess. Paloma looked at me with that same mild fear as before and spoke as if trying to talk down a wild animal.

"I understand, Esmé. I do. If you want, I'll talk to *Majestad* about it. She might still be frazzled from the other night, so please have patience."

My cheeks burned hot with reproach as I nodded tiredly in response. I didn't want to over speak. Whatever energy I channeled into bringing that squirrel to life was starting to weigh down on me a little.

"I'm sorry for raising my voice, Paloma," I whispered. "I've been locked up for too long."

She almost looked surprised by my apology.

"Don't worry about it, Esmé," she whispered, assuaging my guilt.

Princesa Mariela signed something to Paloma, and the wizard nodded happily before turning back to me.

"She wants to take you for a walk around the greenhouse. I think it will help tremendously."

I instantly straightened up, shooting a grateful smile at the princess.

"That sounds lovely, actually," I said.

I'd do anything to take a walk without my manacles.

The princess hooked her arm into mine and walked me down the stone path, with Echo leading the way. Her keenness to spend time with me was surprising, especially after my tirade, but I appreciated her companionship all the same. Of course, I was nervous considering how little sign language I knew, limiting my ability to communicate with her. Though I had a feeling I wasn't the first person who felt that way.

We traipsed along the back of the greenhouse, passing beneath the canopy of a willow tree. I ran my fingers over its leaves with a soft smile, reveling in the scent and feel of the greenery. Already, I knew Paloma was right about how helpful it would be. I felt myself more grounded in reality and away from the invisible hands of the spirit realm or even my problems. And with how dense the plants were, it almost felt like we were in another world.

I cast a glance at *Princesa* Mariela, who was not admiring the scenery at all but searching for something. My brow furrowed as she took a sweeping gaze at the area and then looked over her shoulder. I mirrored her action, hoping I could see what she was, and realized that both Paloma and the captain were out of sight. From what I could tell, so were we.

The Moon Princess suddenly took my arm and pulled me behind an ivy-covered pillar. I opened my mouth to blurt out a question when she held a finger to her lips, quieting me. She made eye contact with Echo, and without a word, the dog huffed and scampered off down the path. When he was gone, the princess took out a small notebook and a pencil from her dress pocket. I watched her in silent dismay as she scribbled something on the page within turning the notebook towards me.

My eyes slowly widened as I read the script.

I have a message from my brother.

She reached into her pocket again and held her fist towards me. I timidly opened the palm of my hand, letting her place a silver necklace in its center.

My breath hitched in the back of my throat. The last time I saw it was in the queen's possession after she took it from me. I let my fingers brush over the smooth aquamarine pendant as the princess wrote another message.

He wants you to know that his promise still stands and that if you still want, he'll be there to answer your call.

My face softened as my chest filled with warmth.

I know Río didn't mean to bring me harm. Our situation wasn't exactly easy, especially when it came to *me*. After all, *I* was a stranger in *his* home. If anything, he did everything to keep me safe in that ballroom until things took a turn. And despite my better judgment, I missed him dearly. I shouldn't, but I did. However, there were other problems between us, other questions, and things that didn't make sense at all.

I politely motioned for the notebook and pencil, which *Princesa* Mariela gave to me. On the next page, I wrote a message of my own:

260

Then why didn't he bring it to me himself?

She bit her lip as I raised my hands questioningly, her expression troubled. She took one more look at our surroundings, and as far as I could tell, we were still well hidden.

The princess then took the notebook back and said, *Because he can't.*

I furrowed my brow and mouthed the word "Why?"

Her eyes flitted between my own carefully before eventually relaying:

Because he's not where they say he is.

Taken aback, I took the notebook back and frantically scribbled, *What do you mean? Where is he?*

Her next words sent a shock through my system that I couldn't quite describe.

He's in the dungeon.

My jaw dropped, and I mouthed, "Since when?"

Since the day of the ball, she replied.

I gripped the notebook between my hands, staring down at the words in complete astonishment.

This whole time? I thought. *Río's been in the dungeon this whole time? Locked in a cell just like me? And here I thought, like some dumb fool, that he was avoiding me.*

"Why?" I asked again, out loud.

My mom says it's to keep everyone safe, the princess told me.

Great ire prickled beneath my skin. Though I loathed it, I understood why *I* was locked in a tower. I was the girl who could see spirits and raise the dead, but Río was the *Moon Prince.* This was his home. He was supposed to be king one day. What did it mean that we were in the same position?

Echo came barreling towards us, and not a second later, I heard Paloma call out.

"Ela? Esmé?"

Not caring about anything else, I wrote down another message.

I want to see him.

Princesa Mariela's dark eyes grew in size. She shook slightly, and for a second, I thought she would urge me against it.

In a panic, I took her hands and pleaded, "Please, *Alteza*."

"Esmé?" Paloma, repeated more urgently.

"Coming!" I shouted.

I watched as the princess pondered this wild request before writing.

After you've had your next meal, tell Arabella that you'd like another bath. But don't get undressed. Wait for me there.

I nodded vigorously as a newfound hope ran through me. She then shoved the notebook and pencil in her pocket. I stuffed the necklace in mine, and we both stood up straight, pretending to look at the fish in the pond. Echo wagged his tail between us, selling the part. Right then, Paloma and the captain approached.

"There you are. We thought you ran off," the wizard joked.

I chuckled, "No, I was just admiring the pond. Sorry for worrying you."

"Good. Since you're still here, how about we practice something new before you leave?"

✳ ☽ ○ ☾ ✳

With both Paloma and the princess's guidance, I learned the first of many techniques the God-given and other magic wielders used to direct their magic. According to Paloma, everyone eventually found their special technique, but it was a good place for beginners to start. To me, it was a lot like learning dance moves or some form of martial arts, which came easily to me as a performer. When I used it in tandem with my singing, I could almost imagine I was on stage, but with more intention than to please an audience. It made directing my magic that much easier, even if it was only brief. And while I felt like I still couldn't reach what I accomplished in the ballroom, both Paloma and the princess were thoroughly impressed with how naturally it came to me. Apparently, it could take days or even weeks for a technique to work, so it was safe to say my self-esteem went from practically non-existent to the moon in a day. I was only hoping it would last.

When the lesson was over, I could not have been more excited to get my restraints back on and be dragged to my tower. *Princesa* Mariela bid us goodbye with Echo by her side, only stopping to give me a knowing smile. Paloma reassured me once more that she would talk to *Reina* Victoria about letting me get involved in their research before wishing me a good evening as well.

Back in my tower, I scarfed down every inch of food I was given—more than I had eaten in the last few days—and as soon as Arabella returned to retrieve the tray, I told her the princess' lie.

"If it's alright, I'd like to take another quick bath. I did a lot in my lesson today, and Paloma said it would do good for my mind."

The handmaiden looked surprised but nodded in understanding. "Of course. I'll get the tub filled for you with some herbs and come back when it's ready."

When she left, I fished Río's necklace out of my dress and held it in my hand with shaking anticipation. I spent every second that passed thinking about what I was going to say to him. So much managed to transpire while we were apart. I didn't know what to expect, and considering how we left things, I didn't know if he was going to be happy to see me at all.

At the sound of Arabella's footsteps, I stored the necklace in my pocket safely, and was once more led down to the familiar purple bathroom. This time, the tub smelled like lavender, roses, and salt. It was incredibly inviting, and I was almost disappointed that I wouldn't be taking a dip at all, but I had other plans. As always, the handmaiden offered to undress me, which I politely declined. However, I was utterly lost on what to do next.

The princess's instructions only went so far, and I wondered if she took into account that I wouldn't be alone. Was I supposed to distract Arabella somehow? I was the most wanted criminal in the castle; I highly doubted she would believe anything I could conjure up. Should I use my magic somehow?

A well-timed knock came at the door. Arabella got up from her seat and deftly answered it. On the other side, I caught sight of the princess's maid, Mathilde. They exchanged a few words that I couldn't quite make out, but whatever it was, it seemed to be urgent.

Arabella looked over her shoulder at me and said, "There's something important I need to attend to. If I leave you here, will you be alright?"

I nodded. "Yes, of course."

"Good. The guards will be outside. I'll be back shortly."

She disappeared through the door, and all I could do was stare after her, completely gob smacked. I had no idea what the princess did to call Arabella away, but for the first time in days, I was alone *and* unbound in the castle. And just like she told me, I waited. I waited and waited until a strange rustling tore my attention away from the door.

My heartbeat quickened, and I shot upright, listening carefully. It seemed to be coming from the corner of the room, behind a tall screen used for changing. A shadow moved behind the translucent material, and I gasped, thinking it was some kind of entity.

"Who's there?" I whispered.

A scream built up in me as the shadow moved out from behind the screen and into the light, but all that came out was a small squeak. Because the shadow wasn't a shadow. It was *Princesa* Mariela.

I nearly sank to the floor with relief.

She beckoned me to follow her, and I quickly dashed across the room, joining her behind the screen.

"How did you get in here?" I mouthed.

She smirked and then pointed to a square hole in the floor where a large tile had been removed.

My eyes widened.

I'm never taking a bath here again.

The princess motioned for me to watch her and then proceeded to lower herself down through the floor in a dress and all. On hands and knees, I took a peek, and there she was, smiling up at me from what looked to be a dimly lit tunnel. Echo stared back, too, with his tongue sticking out gleefully.

She waved for me to hurry, and with the little strength I had, I followed her lead and lowered myself down until my feet were planted on the ground. I stumbled slightly but quickly regained my balance and brushed off my hands as the princess moved the tile back in place. I blinked a few times in the dim light, taking in the narrow, torch-lit hallway made of gray stone before us. On one end, the stairs went up, while on the other end, the path curved down. From what I could tell, it looked deliberately built for servant use.

Echo nudged my legs, and I happily petted his head. His tail wagged back and forth, making my heart soar.

The princess took out her notebook to write me a note:

Only a few people know about these tunnels. It won't be easy to find us here, but we have to be quick before they start looking for you.

With a firm nod, I let her shepherd the way and followed her and Echo down the slope.

As we made our journey through a series of winding tunnels and stairs, I noticed various doors and openings that led to unknown places around the castle. At times, we'd hear a servant shuffling down one of the paths, and the princess would pull me around a corner until they were gone. At first, I didn't know how she noticed them without sound until I observed how synchronized her and Echo's movements were. There was something about their connection that seemed to go beyond him being a service animal, as if they could communicate without words or hand signals. Another form of magic, I presumed.

At the end of a long hallway, *Princesa* Mariela finally stopped by a wooden door. With a silencing finger to her lips, she pulled it open, revealing what looked like the back of a large tapestry on the other side. The princess reached forward and peeled away a rectangular patch that stood out from the rest of the cloth. It provided a small window into the room on the other side. She looked through it, and I leaned forward in hopes of getting a peek, but she closed it before I could. I straightened up as she turned back to me.

The dungeon is down those stairs, she said. *I'm going to get the guard to open the door and then distract him. On my signal, you run in and go.*

My throat tightened. I didn't think it would be up to me to do this alone.

"Are you sure?" I mouthed.

The princess nodded in reply.

Somehow, I thought I'd have her moral support in all of this. I had a fear that I would mess things up and somehow get caught, but seeing as the palace was so heavily guarded, I understood why this was the only way.

"Okay."

Princesa Mariela crossed her fingers and made a sideways motion with them. In her notebook, she wrote down, *Ready?* I repeated the motion in agreement. *Ready.* She stored the notebook away and signaled to Echo, who took her place by her side like a dutiful servant. The Moon Princess then pulled her shoulders back, raised her head high, and pushed the tapestry aside. She snaked past the fabric, disappearing with her companion.

I approached the tapestry and nudged it aside, just enough to catch her as she approached the guard standing at the top of the dungeon steps. He instantly stood tall and bowed in her presence. They signed to each other—something I didn't understand. There was hesitation on the guard's part, but *Princesa* Mariela was stern, and all of a sudden, the guard was removing the keys from his belt. They disappeared down the stairs, and for many agonizing moments, nothing seemed to happen.

Nothing.

Nothing.

My hands shook as I gripped the edge of the tapestry for dear life, and then...

Echo bolted up the stairs, his loud barking reverberating as he sprinted down the hallway. The guard swiftly followed, with the princess not far behind. She cast a quick look in my direction and waved for me to go as she ran behind them, quick on their heels.

I held my breath and dashed out of the tunnel towards the stairs. I took them two at a time, too scared to look behind me, until I came upon an iron door that was already ajar, the keys still in the lock. With short breaths, I hurried through it and shut it behind me with a resounding clatter.

25

The Necromancer's Vow

Esmé

Two crackling sconces lit the downward staircase leading into the cold dungeon. I pressed my back against the door, both in fear and excitement over what I had done and was about to do. It was unlike me to break away from my confinement and defy orders this way, let alone the queen's. Yet it felt right. It felt right despite the part of me that wanted to stay frozen at the top of the steps or turn back. I swallowed that feeling down and, with my hand on the stone, carefully made my way down.

At the bottom was a large, arcing antechamber. It had a table, some chests, and cases of wine, and the scent of mildew filled the air. From the antechamber branched off two hallways with several cells on each side. A sudden, source less draft shook me from head to toe, and with it came discordant voices. The spirits of the dungeon were especially heavy and suffocating compared to the rest of the palace. Ill-intentioned individuals who threatened the kingdom and crown were locked away in here, some of whom were sentenced to death.

Not only could I hear their thoughts, but I could feel them, what they went through, and what they did to get here. Their voices were more difficult to ignore, so I shoved them away with my hands.

"Stop it," I hissed, making them cease.

"Who's there?"

The voice called out from one of the cells, the sound echoing off the stone. Unlike the rest, I knew this one was real. I recognized who it belonged to immediately.

"Río?" I gasped.

There was rustling, and then, "Esmé?"

My heart leaped in my chest. "Where are you?"

"Over here. To your right."

My body moved of its own accord, going down the hallway to the right until I came upon the only occupied cell in the whole dungeon. As soon as I saw white hair and familiar dark eyes, something within me unwound.

"Río!" I exclaimed.

"Esmé!"

We both dashed forward at the same time. My hands went around the bars, but the prince's chains kept him from getting too close. Of course, it didn't keep him from trying.

Tears pricked at my eyes, partly because of how happy I was to see him, but also due to the state he was in. He looked sick and exhausted. His facial hair had grown a bit, but more pressing were the dark circles under his eyes and the white veins climbing his arms and neck. I knew what a werewolf looked like, but this was the first time I saw what the curse did before the first full moon. It was a sight that broke my heart. Somehow, he still managed to look at me as if I were the brightest star in the sky.

"It's you. It's really you. I thought I was imagining it," he said.

"No, I'm really here. It's me."

"How did you get in here?" he asked with a shake of his head.

I giggled nervously, replying, "Your sister snuck me in."

"W-What? You went behind my mother's back?" he scoffed.

Despite his astonishment, his smile told me he was both impressed and amused.

"I had to," I argued. "As soon as I found out you were in here, I told the princess I wanted to see you."

Río raised his eyebrows. "Really?"

"Of course. Why didn't you tell me your mother was putting you in here?"

He sighed, his shoulders falling. "It wouldn't have made a difference. I didn't want to put more on your shoulders than you already have."

The prince has said similar things to me since we've met. He was always so determined to bear the weight of his secrets and hide behind the facade of the charming young man. I hid my irritation over it, though it only grew to a point where I couldn't take it anymore. Not tonight.

"It would have made a difference to *me*," I replied hotly. "You should've *told* me, Río. You're always trying to spare me from things when I wish you would just tell me what's wrong. Like when you stumble into my apartment and say you're fine when I can see how much you're bleeding."

To my dismay, he chuckled. "And here I thought I was a good liar."

"Maybe when it matters. Otherwise, you're a great deflector."

"Hmmm, and what about you? I at least let you stop the bleeding, but if the roles were reversed, you'd insist on doing it yourself."

I scoffed in disbelief at the well-directed jab. His tone wasn't cold or harsh by any means, yet painfully correct, which is why I couldn't help but laugh despite how annoyed I was.

"You're not wrong," I replied.

Río's expression warmed, softening the blow further.

"I just… I want to be there for you, Río," I said softer now.

It was true yet hard to say out loud.

The prince nodded as he looked between my eyes. "I want to be there for you too, Esmé. You have no idea how badly I do. It kills me knowing the things my mother is putting you through while I'm stuck in here."

"So, your mother *has* told you?"

"Yeah, she's been keeping me updated, at least. If not her, then Ela fills in the gaps."

It brought me a sense of comfort knowing that we weren't both completely in the dark about each other's whereabouts. In equal measure it made me anxious considering the implications of my mystery.

"Then you know about my lost memories," I uttered lowly.

A muscle twitched in Río's cheek, his expression going dim.

"I do. Esmé, I'm so sorry," he lamented. "I wish there was more I could do for you, but I'm stuck in this shit hole. All my authority has been stripped for the time being."

I scowled at that. "How is that possible?"

"Mother doesn't trust me while I'm going through my changes. Nobody does. And to be honest, I don't know if I trust myself either."

"That makes two of us," I muttered bitterly.

There was a deep sense of understanding between us when we looked at each other then. For the first time, I didn't feel as far away from the Moon Prince as I once thought. I felt *seen*. He was always a good friend, but there was always a part of me that was certain of our relationship's eventual demise. I thought we were too different, whether it was because of our upbringings or personalities, but what I once believed to be an irreparable chasm between our worlds was now fused together. We were more alike than I imagined.

To think I was driving myself crazy.

I slipped my arm past the bars and stretched out my hand as far as possible. Río looked at me as if in a daze before he eagerly did the same. As soon as our fingers touched, he clasped his hand around mine, and a wave of comfort seemed to wash over us. He was so warm and familiar, it overwhelmed me with emotion. The prince's gaze was piercing, and even now, he made my heart flutter. He ran it over my face, my wrists, and my neck, and that shimmering light in his eyes seemed to temper.

"Esmé, what have they been doing to you?" he asked.

I snorted, despite myself. "You already know. I'm dangerous, remember? Other than Sebastián Eliódor, I'm the biggest threat to Avilonía right now. I can't walk into a room without anyone thinking I can kill them. At this point, I'm starting to believe all of it."

I didn't mean to throw his words back at him, but it was true. Everyone, not just Río, assumed I was just like the Sun Killer or the Black Death until proven otherwise. The more time passed, the more I accepted my fate.

The prince closed his eyes, and his hold on my hand tightened slightly. The white veins on his skin seemed to pulse and crawl a little higher. My expression slowly fell as he took a few deep, shaking breaths.

"Río? Río, are you okay?"

His eyes snapped open, and he blinked a few times.

"Yeah. Yeah, I'm fine for now," he said. "I'm sorry. It's the curse. It's been happening a lot lately. You should probably leave."

In an act of defiance and loyalty, I pressed myself against the bars so we were holding each other's wrists.

"No. No, I'm not leaving you. Not yet," I protested.

"You should be scared of me, Esmé. You shouldn't be here," he stressed.

"I could say the same about me. You saw what I did firsthand. And we both know which one of us your mother would sacrifice first."

"I wouldn't let her," he said with a glare.

"I don't think either of us has a choice in that matter."

"Esmé…" he said lowly, his eyes boring into mine, "if something happened to you, I would…"

Río trailed off, as if afraid of his admission, but it only intrigued me more. I didn't know how much time we had, which meant every word mattered.

"You would what?" I urged on.

"I would drown the whole world and then myself. I would give in to this transformation willingly and let it consume me. I wouldn't be able to live with myself," he replied ardently.

My cheeks warmed with a blush as I was left completely breathless. I stared at him, eyes wide.

"I didn't know you could be so poetic."

Río smiled. "It's the curse. I fear it's taken away all of my filter and decorum."

"You had those?" I teased.

He laughed in response, which was a sound that made me grin from ear to ear. I was happy to see him happy, especially during times like these.

It was then that I remembered what it was that brought me here in the first place. It wasn't just the prospect of seeing Río but the message that his sister delivered to me. With my other hand, I took the aquamarine necklace out of my pocket and presented it to him. Despite how worn he looked, his face brightened more than it already was.

"Your sister gave me this," I said.

"And?"

I looked down at the stone with an intense yearning that threatened to split me open, and when I spoke, my voice was surprisingly small.

"You know, I couldn't understand why you wanted me to have this again or why you wouldn't bring it to me yourself. For a long time, I thought you hated me. But now that I know you've been here this whole time..." I sighed dejectedly before saying, "I feel so stupid."

"You're not stupid, Esmé," the prince said firmly. "You had every reason to think the worst of me. I'm surprised you went out of your way to come here at all. But if it means anything, I've...I missed you...a lot."

He uttered the words with trepidation, but all I felt was surprise, joy, and relief. We tiptoed around those words quite often, too afraid to say them for one reason or another.

Río looked between my eyes, awaiting my reply.

My heart hammered against my ribs as I said, "I missed you, too."

"Really?" he asked, his shoulders relaxing.

"I always do. Even before now," I told him, tears filling my eyes. "Sometimes I get angry about it, because I feel like I don't have a right to miss you, but I don't want to be angry anymore."

"I don't want you to be angry, either."

"And I don't want you to hate me," I whispered sharply.

"I don't hate you, Esmé," he said indignantly.

"I thought you said I was dangerous."

The prince grimaced. "I know. I know I did, but even then I didn't want to say it. If it were up to me, I wouldn't have left you in that tower. I've had enough time in this cell to know that I could never hate you, Esmé. I spend my hours waiting for the next update from my mother, terrified that one of these days she's going to tell me you're dead."

The idea of him being plagued by the thought of my death stirred something in me to the point of silent tears. I spent so much of our relationship waiting for him or expecting him to come back in pieces that I didn't ponder the possibility of it going both ways. When he worried about my health, did that keep him up at night as well?

"To be honest, I didn't think you ever wanted to see me again after what happened or after I got bitten," he continued. "You have every right to run in the other direction. To be honest, I don't know if I deserve anything else."

I gave him a strange look. It almost didn't seem real that the rogue prince I knew so well could say such things about himself. He was often so confident and capable, but that seemed overshadowed now. It felt wrong.

"That is not true," I scolded him, suddenly emboldened. "Río, you're *amazing*. There are so many things about you that are more than just this curse. You keep telling me to run, but I literally raise the dead. Even then, all I see is you. A little ill and worn out, but so am I."

The Moon Prince took me in with adoration. It took any other words out of my mouth, leaving me speechless. He then leaned towards me, as close as his shackles allowed.

"Esmé Vespertín, you put the moon and stars to shame."

After being treated like a criminal and a monster for days on end, hearing such a compliment from Río did something to me that I couldn't quite put a name to. My gaze flitted between his eyes and then his lips as warm, passionate desire flowed through me.

They're here.

The spirits' jarring whispers dragged me out of the moment. There was the shuffling of feet, keys jingling, and then a door burst open. The prince cursed.

"Gods damn it."

I let go of Río's hand but stayed close as *La Reina* came into view down the hall. She took long strides with her guards in tow, looking livid.

"There you are," she growled.

"Mom, don't," Río protested. "She just wanted to see me. She didn't do anything wrong—"

"Quiet, Río," the queen snapped, raising her hand.

Despite my trembling hands, I stood my ground as she stopped before me and scanned my being with steely eyes.

"I thought I told you that you were not to see each other until the full moon passed."

"That was before I knew he was locked in here," I argued.

"That wasn't for you to know."

"Considering how cooperative I've been thus far, I think I at least deserved that. After all, out of everyone in this castle, he's the one I care about the most."

My accusatory tone came out without remorse despite being in the face of a God-given. The spirits danced around me, making the flames from the nearby torches move. A door was, in fact, opened on winter solstice, and now that I found the path, it was easier to follow it. The guards tensed, and for a moment, I thought the captain would draw his sword again.

The queen bore vicious smile, undoubtedly contemplating whether she should put a lightning bolt through my heart.

"Mom…" Río uttered glaringly.

The people pleaser in me wanted to get on my knees and apologize profusely, but did no such thing. I did this to myself and I will go out dignified. Seeing Río in chains angered me, but that wasn't what I wanted either. Instead, in this moment, I chose to back down. It was less out of cowardice and more out of a refusal to prove her or everyone else in this castle right. I wanted to lose my chains, not earn them.

"He's my friend," I said, more calmly. "I wanted to make sure he was fine. You can take me back to my tower. I won't fight you."

In an act of surrender, I held out my wrists. Without taking her eyes off me, the queen motioned to the captain, who came over and secured the shackles on my wrists. Their unwelcome weight made me want to scream as my short-lived freedom was officially put to an end.

"Goodbye, Río," I whispered.

I expected the same farewell in return, but his gaze was transfixed on the man holding my chains—the captain of the Queen's Guard. I furrowed my brow as he tugged me away from the prince.

"Captain, can I speak to you for a moment?" Río asked suddenly.

Everyone exchanged dubious glance, but of course, the guard didn't disobey an order from the Moon Prince.

"Of course, *Alteza*."

The captain handed my chain off to someone else before striding to the prince's cell, his armor rustling with his movement.

I looked over my shoulder curiously, watching the interaction just like everyone else. And right as the captain was within reach, Río broke his restraints and rushed the bars. With quick reflexes, he grabbed the captain by the collar, took his sword, and forced him against the cell door. I gasped. The other guards yelled, running towards him, only to stop as the prince put the blade against the captain's neck. The man, who was usually large and intimidating, shook beneath his helmet.

"Río!" the queen and I shouted.

Río, however, didn't seem to hear us and ignored everyone's protests as his focus was solely on the man in his hands.

"It sucks being on the other side, doesn't it?" he teased with a wolfish smile.

"Río, stop it!" the queen reiterated.

"Don't worry, Mother, I will. I just want to say one thing." The moon prince leaned in close to the captain's ear and, in a low voice, uttered, "Never lay a hand on Esmé again. Understand?"

My hand fluttered over my neck in disbelief. For good reason, I didn't tell him about the altercation in Paloma's tower, which meant he must have found out on his own. The white veins beneath his skin elongated, and the circles around his eyes darkened. Even when he spoke, he didn't sound entirely like himself.

"She's more special to me than any of you can even comprehend," he said. "So, if you spill another drop of her blood, then by the full moon you'll be lucky to get away with your life, let alone your career."

"Let me go," I said, tugging on my restraints.

"Absolutely not," the queen snapped. "We need to tranquilize him."

"No! Not like that!" I blurted out. "Just let me go, and I'll talk to him. Please."

Reina Victoria rolled her eyes in annoyance. "Miss Vespertín—"

"I'm the expendable one, remember?" I argued.

I looked between her and the guard, who turned to the queen questioningly. *Reina* Victoria glared in confoundment before giving the guard a resigned nod. I thanked her profusely, and as soon as my manacles were off, I turned back towards the prince.

"Río!" I shouted firmly.

The prince finally snapped out of his trance, his gaze instantly finding mine. The fire in his eyes dimmed, and his features seemed to smooth out. I moved toward him steadily, keeping my face open as he watched me. As soon as I was close enough, I carefully placed my hand on his arm.

"It's okay. I'm okay now. You can let him go."

Río searched my face, and all at once, his expression morphed from anger to wide-eyed confusion. Slowly but surely, he dropped the sword and let the captain go. Everyone around us exhaled in relief as the guard stumbled away.

Río staggered back in shock. "Fuck."

"Hey, it's okay," I repeated. "I'm right here."

I reached my hand through the bars once again, and Río took it tentatively. Now that he wasn't bound, he was able to close the distance and rest his forehead against mine between a small gap in the bars.

"I'm so sorry," he uttered.

"I know."

My heart broke seeing him like this. It was evident that the curse was affecting him beyond his control. I knew what that was like firsthand, and that was one of many reasons why I couldn't let it go. I simply couldn't.

On an impulse, I took the malachite ring off my finger and slipped it into the palm of his hand. He furrowed his brow as I closed his fingers around it.

With fire in my heart and soul, I looked into his eyes and whispered, "I will always want you to stay."

They hauled me away before he could say anything else.

26

By Midnight

Esmé

I was practically shoved into my tower, with no one but *Reina* Victoria with me. My wrists were still bound, but my chain was left untethered as we stood at opposite ends of the chamber. The Queen of Storms stared at me with a scrutinization, her arms crossed. I fought to keep my breathing steady, although my heart was pounding at a rapid pace. Only after an eternity of silence did she speak.

"I'm going to be honest, Miss Vespertín, I don't quite know what to make of you." Instead of sounding angry, she seemed almost perplexed, which in turn surprised *me*. "I thought you would take the first opportunity to run for the hills and leave this castle, but instead I find you in the dungeon, talking to my son. Who you were forbidden from seeing, by the way."

I kept my eyes on the floor, taking her words in silence.

"Well?" she asked.

I looked up with a frown. "Well, what?"

"Do you have anything to say for yourself?"

"Me? I thought I didn't have the right to say anything."

"Well, I'm giving you the chance now."

Again, my instincts told me to apologize and be ashamed for defying her. I would've cried over being caught, but that wasn't the case now. Things have changed since then. I had no urge to cry or beg.

"I'm sorry for disobeying you, *Majestad*, but I don't regret what I did," I told her.

She huffed, "Are you sorry for involving my daughter in all of this?"

"She just wanted to help."

"You forget who you are, Esmé," she snapped, making me stiffen. "I set down strict guidelines for you because you are a stranger with dangerous abilities under *my* roof. I should've killed you the day of the ball, but because of Río, you're alive. I've been kind to you despite this, and I've believed your story, yet you still disobey me in my own home, and you continue to put my family in danger."

"With all due respect, I didn't hurt either of them, nor would I ever dream of it," I stressed, shaking my head. "The princess has been nothing but kind. My only intention was to see Río. You can give me the truth serum again if you like, but as soon as your daughter told me that you were holding him prisoner, I took a risk. Punish me for it, but I would gladly do it again."

My words were strong as I spoke them, my conviction and passion growing until I felt I had made my point. Then, all at once, I closed my mouth, panting as I awaited the queen's response.

She glared at me. "Río is *not* my prisoner. Keeping him down there is a precaution due to his condition, which you saw the effects of with your own eyes. I don't like it, but what else am I to do?"

As much as I wanted to judge her for putting him down there, I knew she wasn't wrong, and it pained me. At the end of it all, she was not only the queen but also a mother, two things I was not.

"I understand. I do. I just… I want to help him. Let me help him, please," I implored.

"You are a captive with enough on your plate as it is, and I highly doubt there's much you can do to begin with."

"There's not much I can do with my predicament either, considering my memories aren't coming back anytime soon," I contested. "But if you allow me, I could try. Please allow me to try. I've answered your questions and done what you've asked, but I'm tired of being in the dark about my life and what's going on around me. And it's not fair that you insist on keeping it that way. I may be a prisoner, but I am not a child."

La Reina's eyes glittered with amusement, which threw me off.

"Are you finished?" she asked casually.

"Yes," I whispered, my face flushing.

"You have quite the nerve, Miss Vespertín. I'm loath to say that I admire it." My eyebrows shot up in surprise as she continued, "Paloma is still trying to figure out your memory problem, although she did tell me you made progress today. I didn't bring it up because I was busy dealing with your escapade, but also because I'm still not entirely sure if I should be impressed or concerned. Though we have our theories."

I perked up. "What theories?"

She rolled her eyes. "Nothing that holds much truth."

"Like what?"

"You really want to know?"

"Yes, please," I answered hesitantly.

"Well, I know too well how magical abilities can be passed down from generation to generation. And, well, who was the last person to raise the dead other than Casímir Gedeón?"

My stomach dropped, as if I were free-falling from the sky.

"You think I'm The Black Death's daughter?" I blurted out.

"Maybe not his daughter, but a blood relative of sorts. It would explain why your memory was wiped. Maybe someone didn't want us to know...until the right time, of course. I mean, it would explain how the hounds got in at the ball. Although if that were true, I'm not entirely convinced you wouldn't have killed us by now. Rather, *tried.*"

I think that was supposed to bring me comfort, but it only made me feel worse.

"So how exactly were you planning on helping Río?" she asked with a skeptical eye.

She was expecting a genuine answer, but I didn't exactly have a solid plan. After all, I only just found out he was in the dungeon. I floundered for a moment, thinking long and hard, until I remembered something I pitched to Paloma earlier.

"I'd like your permission to leave the castle for at least an hour."

"What?" the queen scoffed. "Absolutely not. What for?"

"To go to Canela's. Alone."

The queen groaned in vexation, "Please, if she wanted to help us, she would have."

"I know what she did is inexcusable, but I've known her for a long time, and she's a dear friend of mine. She'll listen to me. I know she will."

I pleaded so hard, I was amazed I wasn't on my hands and knees. After being locked up and prodded for so long, this was my one chance to go outside and do something worthwhile. I was determined to see this through more than anything else.

"How do I know you won't truly escape this time?" *La Reina* asked.

"Because I made a promise I intend to keep."

I instinctively touched the place where my malachite ring used to be, which was now in Río's hands.

Reina Victoria pinched the bridge of her nose in an act of exasperation. When her eyes met mine again, she ran her tongue over her teeth seriously.

"You will have exactly one hour." I gasped in surprise, but she didn't let me interrupt. "You are not to be seen. You will not deviate. I don't care how much you miss your friends. The fewer people who know about you, the better. If not for you, then think of Río's safety."

I drooped in disappointment, though I understood her reasoning. If the Sun Killer's people were able to get by as servants, there was no telling where else they could be hiding now that the Moon King was dead. The last thing I wanted to do was risk hurting any of my friends with an ability I only just started to hone.

"Also, you will *not* go alone. That's out of the question," the queen added.

I sputtered. "I hardly think sending a guard with me will be discreet."

"A person of my choosing will come to your door at midnight tonight," she said sternly. "The full moon is approaching. The sooner you do this, the better."

27

The Heart of A Hound

Río

Not only did my restraints need to be replaced following my outburst, but I was also given the luxury of my very own collar. It was uncomfortable, itchy, and limited by movement even more, but I couldn't even fault them. My strength was growing with the impending full moon, so now I was truly like a rabid dog in a cage.

I didn't mean to lose control with Captain Dominic the way that I did. I told myself it wasn't me and that my anger came from the beast that was taking life inside me now, but that wasn't true. It was feeding on something that was already there. All I remember was the *feeling* upon seeing the exhaustion in Esmé's eyes, the bruises on her wrists, and the scar on her neck.

I left her alone in my home for a few days, and this is how she returns to me?

I wanted to scoop her up in my arms and take her away from here. But the best I could do was make one of the culprits pay. That was partially me. I think.

Captain Dominic was good at his job, but he always had a bit of an ego. And Esmé didn't deserve to be treated with such cruelty. That thought alone was enough for the wolf to latch onto and take over when I least expected, and in the aftermath, there was only *my* guilt. I just had to prove my mom right, didn't I? The old Río wouldn't have done something like that, would he? I don't know. Everything was getting blurry.

Memories flashed before my eyes—memories that had nothing to do with war or massacres. No, these took place in a different kingdom filled with color-changing trees, old friends, and a girl I thought I loved. Then, like a slap to the face, I remembered the cove, Ela's screams, my rage, and blood on the stone.

My skin burned with the emotions of that day. It was getting harder to fight the curse with the passing days, yet I closed my eyes and tried focusing on something else. I thought of Esmé because only she served as a soothing balm for my soul.

She risked herself to see me. Not only that, but even in my moment of weakness, she treated me with patience and kindness. There was not an ounce of fear in those brown eyes despite what I had done—despite making a man bleed. No, she was worried about *me*. And regardless of all my self-doubt and shame, she managed to throw it all out the window.

"There are so many things about you that are more than just this curse." That's what she told me.

I held her malachite ring between my fingers, memorizing its flowing lines. It had a silver band that barely fit on my pinky finger. It was well known to me, seeing as Esmé never took it off (we were both sentimental that way). It was the only piece of her past that she owned, or so she told me. Yet for some reason, she slipped it into my hand before they tore her away.

"I will always want you to stay."

It was one sentence, but there was so much depth to it.

I will come back.

It was the same promise I made to her before everything burst into flames. She meant it, too. I could see it in her eyes—that spark and tenacity. I saw bits and pieces of it throughout our relationship. It was what made me like her more. Yes, Esmé could be shy, but she was never *that* shy with me. It enthused me. She always apologized for rambling, but I could listen to her talk all day. I knew she held back, and I often wondered if I would get a chance to hear what was on the tip of her tongue. So, to see her stand her ground against my mother... I couldn't be prouder.

Most people in the court carried themselves around like dolls, but their demure nature was often a farce. They paraded themselves around, following a strict set of rules on how to win over a royal. "Winning" either meant becoming one of us or watching us fall. Regardless of the motive, I knew just how fickle these people could be and how readily they could change their morals at the right price. Unfortunately for them and my mother, I don't abide by such things. I've tangled with enough people in the court and spent enough time at sea to know that I crave *more*.

Esmé may think that what I seek is somewhere across the ocean, away from home. At some point in time, I thought the same, but now I know for a fact that I have already found it. It glows within her, lighting up every room she enters, and she needs no crown or title for it to be true.

28

The Night Before

Esmé

Arabella was the partner *La Reina* chose for my excursion. The woman entered my room holding two cloaks and a dark dress that matched hers. As she helped me dress, I couldn't help but express my shame for tricking her earlier. Though she very pleasantly told me there was no harm done.

"The queen didn't punish you?" I asked.

"No, she's well aware of the princess's part in all of this," she replied with a chuckle. "I was just doing my duty."

"The princess isn't in trouble, is she?"

"No. Well, nothing many of us might consider horrible. Just some extra time studying in her room, I presume. If anything, we're all surprised you're still here."

I furrowed my brow. "Why is that?"

"Well, most prisoners would try to escape confinement, but you didn't. It's also surprising that the queen left you alive at all. Although I do have an inkling why. You're trying to help the prince, correct?"

"I am," I said with a firm nod.

Arabella smiled. "Well, then, that's very honorable of you, Miss Vespertín. I'm more than happy to help."

We tied our cloaks around our necks, and a different guard removed my handcuffs this time. I was boundless anew as I followed the handmaiden down the tower and through the castle. She led me to a tapestry of a deity, not different from the ones I had seen before. This one was of Mikamea, god of creativity, music, the arts, and adventures—also known as The Fool. Similar to the one by the dungeon, this one hid a door that led into the secret tunnels within the palace.

Our exit was the spiraling foyer I came through the day of the ball, which I tried very hard not to look towards. I kept my eyes forward as we rushed outside all the way to the main courtyard with the statue of Marisláni. There, a small wagon with a black horse awaited, as well as its coachman.

I eyed it all with apprehension.

"Are we taking this to *Obsidiana*?"

Entering the district on a horse, no matter how discreet, would draw eyes at any time of day.

"No, just to the first gondola, and we'll make our way down from there," Arabella reassured.

I climbed onto the wagon with the handmaiden by my side, and with a crack of the reins, the horse pulled the wagon forward through the jacaranda trees and beneath the portcullis. This time, I purposefully looked towards the waterfall below as we rode over the bridge and down the hill from whence I came.

Save for the torchlight lighting the way, the tree-lined path was a lot more ominous this time of night. Through the branches, I could make out the Marisláni Ocean once again, painted silver by the moon. We rode mostly in silence with the jostling of the wagon as background noise until I let my eyes flit over to Arabella. Her hood was only half-up, giving me a view of her black hair and welcoming face. She only looked a little older than me, but based on her demeanor and experience, she must have been in her third decade already.

"If you don't mind me asking, Arabella, how long have you worked for the royal family?" I asked curiously.

She smiled softly, her brown eyes glittering. "I think almost 10 years now. I was barely your age when I found my way here."

"And how does one get a job being so close to the God-given?"

"Good references, time, and a lot of patience," she mused. "My *tia* helps make the meals in the kitchen, and when I was looking for a job, she put in a good word for me. I started off mostly washing dishes, mopping, and doing laundry. One day, Mathilde became ill, and because I knew sign language the best, the queen assigned me to the princess in her stead. I must have made a good impression, because I was promoted shortly after. Mathilde is still *Alteza*'s primary, but I do a lot more than wash dishes now."

Considering she made a lasting impression on me, I understood why the queen trusted Arabella. She didn't cower in fear, nor did she think herself above anyone else. She did her job well, and she did it with compassion and a strong backbone.

"And do you like it? Being a handmaiden, I mean?" I asked.

"For the Markaél's? Absolutely. It's chaos in the best way, like when I go home to see my cousins," Arabella replied with a giggle. "I've heard too many horror stories about stewards who work for nobles here or even in the Air Kingdom, and I consider myself very lucky. The queen, though terrifying, is actually a very kind soul. The king loved her very much, and he cared about everyone in the palace. I don't think people realize just how much we workers see. We see them at their best and their worst, and often parts that the public may never get to."

290

I nodded thoughtfully. As someone who has worked what many would deem "lesser jobs," I could always tell someone's true character based on how they treated those serving them. Unfortunately, the better ones were few and far between.

"And what of the prince?"

I almost didn't ask the question at all as I was scared of being too direct and undergoing the embarrassment of letting my feelings show, yet somehow I did.

Arabella cast me a cheeky, knowing smile, making me blush. She didn't let her eyes linger, which I was thankful for.

"*Príncipe* Río is...an interesting young man. Technically, he's supposed to have stewards of his own, but he's been very clear that he wants to do things on his own, so we only ever go into his room for certain tasks. Sort of reminds me of someone I know."

She gave me another pointed look. I opened my mouth to defend myself but simply scowled. The handmaiden chuckled at my expression before continuing.

"He's very intent on carving his own path, which is an admirable quality for someone to have. Especially a prince. He's very kind, funny, and never disrespects the stewards, but...sometimes you just want to... I don't know..."

Arabella held her hands out before her as she tried to find the proper phrase, and in the space between her curled fingers, I knew exactly what I would say.

"Strangle him?" I finished for the sake of her duty.

Both Arabella and the coachman burst out laughing. A grin spread across my face as warmth bloomed in my chest. I've received nothing but rude remarks or fearful stares this past week, but this was the first time I was able to make anyone from the palace truly laugh. Anyone who wasn't Río, that is.

"Yes, exactly," the handmaiden answered with a nod, "and not because we dislike him. No, we miss him dearly when he gets lost at sea. Some of the stewards and even the guards are split on how they feel about his coming transformation, but...those of us who've known him the longest are just praying to the goddess that he'll be alright."

Arabella looked into my eyes and put her warm hand over mine.

"That's why I'm happy to make this journey with you, Miss Vespertín. The queen wouldn't allow this for just anyone, and if she trusts you to do this, then so do I."

I swallowed past a lump in my throat and gave her hand a tight squeeze.

"Thank you," I whispered.

✳︎ ☽ ◯ ☾ ✳︎

I nearly burst into tears when we arrived at the Arts District. We passed *Teatro Paraiso*, Fabian's house, and even though I couldn't see it, I knew Dulce's shop was to the north. And when we boarded the gondola and began the journey down the island, melancholy threatened to drown me.

I missed my city so much. I missed being able to see it from up high with its glittering tufts of firelight. I missed seeing the ocean and the hills, even against the night sky. I missed seeing the stars and going to the beach. I wanted so desperately to find my friends and tell them that I was alive and well, but the waxing moon above was a reminder of just how little time we had left before Río's transformation. The eyes with which I see the world are not the same as before, and I have more pressing matters to attend to. The last thing I wanted was for the queen to send out a search party and take away what little freedom I already had. Especially when she was trusting me with Río's life—a life that I wanted so badly to protect. I simply had to believe that one day I would see my friends again.

Since we were being quite discreet, the path to *Obsidiana* was a lot less familiar to me, but once we entered the major streets with the familiar street urchins, I was able to get us to Canela's shop by memory. A few people were perusing the place, as well as an elderly couple talking to the witch by the counter. Arabella and I pretended to look through the various crystal bowls, hoping to catch Canela's eye. I drifted over to the statue of Micqui, which was lit with candles and adorned with marigolds. Beside me, Arabella shuddered at the sight.

With the jingle of the bell signaling the elderly couple's exit, Canela's voice came up behind us.

"Are you familiar with the God of Death?" she asked warmly.

"I am," I responded, turning to face her. "I've heard he's a symbol for change."

Her auburn eyes flashed in surprise. "Esmé? What are you doing here?"

I held my finger to my lips, whispering, "We need to talk to you in private. It's an emergency."

She glanced between Arabella and me carefully before nodding. "Alright. Go up the stairs to my room. Last door on the right. Let me help some of these customers, and I'll meet you there."

The witch finished decorating the altar before rushing to attend to the counter again.

Arabella and I crept up the stairs, following her directions to a small bedroom with a decently sized bed of white cotton, a purple rug, and a small hearth with no fire in it. There was a vase of dried roses, some books on a shelf, and a table with a smattering of herbs, crystals, and parchments. I paid attention to the chatter downstairs, listening to their farewells and the ringing of the bells, until the shop eventually grew quiet. Only then did we hear a series of footsteps, and Canela came bursting through the door, bearing questions.

"What are you doing here, little songbird? Are you alright? Who is this?"

"This is Arabella," I said. "She's—"

"I'm simply here to accompany her on behalf of the queen," the handmaiden chimed in. "I don't intend to interfere."

"You can trust her," I reassured. "And I'm fine. For now. This isn't about me, but it's very urgent."

Canela furrowed her brow. "What is this about, then?"

"We don't have much time, but it's about Río. He was bitten by a werewolf on the winter solstice, and he's going to turn soon. He's already suffering the effects of the curse, and I just..." I choked on my emotions.

"Ah, yes, I know exactly what happened to the prince," the witch said grimly, crossing her arms.

"Everyone keeps saying that there's no known cure, but I want to help him. There has to be something he can take or something you can do to alleviate whatever he's feeling. Like you did with me. So, if you know anything about werewolves, I'm all ears."

"I'm surprised Paloma hasn't figured something out."

"The queen mentioned that it wasn't her specialty or something of the sort," I told her.

"She's been trying, though," Arabella chimed in. "The wizard's been making an experimental potion for him."

"What does it look like?" Canela asked.

"Black, like ink."

The witch nodded. "Yes, that's one way to deal with the curse, but the results can vary depending on who is making it."

My face lit up. "So you *do* have experience with werewolves?"

"I may have encountered a werewolf bite or two in the past. Not here in Coáraluna, but more inland. How has his rage been?"

Arabella and I exchanged a grimace.

"Not good," I said. "He attacked the captain today."

"Did he?" Canela gasped.

"The captain's fine, thankfully, but… I think Río found out what happened back in Paloma's tower that day. The queen's been keeping him in the dungeon for everyone's safety, and when I found out, I…*snuck out* to see him. When Captain Dominic came down with the queen, it was downhill from there. It's my fault, really."

"You shouldn't take the blame for many moving parts, Esmé. If anything, I commend you for doing such a thing behind the queen's back. I always knew you were brave." Her prideful, cat-like grin made me blush. "Anyways, I think I know something that can help."

Canela beckoned for us to follow her into another room across the hall. It was one that I had only entered a few times before, back when I was her assistant. There were shelves filled with rare ingredients and herbs not at the storefront, but what took up most of the space were books with gold ink on the spines.

Canela perused them carefully as I let my eyes wander around the room.

"You know, the first turn is always the worst," she said casually.

"Paloma said something about that," I muttered. "Why *is* it the worst?"

"The body and mind are undergoing severe, life-altering changes, so everything is amplified. For people like the prince who get bitten so close to the full moon, I can imagine it's rather sudden."

I recalled that brief moment in the dungeon when Río took a moment to compose himself. I saw the way the curse's poison slowly took over his body, making its way up his neck. It was taking over from the inside out.

"He's controlling it, or at least trying to," I said.

"It would take a strong will to be able to do that. His close experience with magic is probably contributing to it."

"He's a fighter," Arabella chimed in with pride.

I met her eyes with a matching expression as that pride filled my heart.

"He is. Although I hate to see him locked up like that."

Canela leaned against the bookshelf to look me in the eyes. "Unfortunately, it's the most common way of dealing with a werewolf, darling. That or killing them. I don't think it's right, but I have to say that the queen's choice to seal him away is more out of love than hatred."

I did not doubt that the queen loved her son, but the injustice of it all left me with petulant irritation.

"Is there truly no cure? Is it that impossible?" I asked.

"Nothing is impossible, especially with magic, but the cure to such things often has a price. Usually, it's a matter of gathering the right components and performing a ritual, but in some cases, those components are a mystery. If you're truly desperate, you can always sell your soul, but then you'd be trading one problem for another."

My gut twisted into knots as the witch returned to her search.

So, Río would either have to spend the rest of his life searching for these components, or he was doomed to be a werewolf forever. That, or he would have to sell his soul in exchange for the curse to be broken. But what did it mean to sell your soul? Who takes the bargain, a demon or the God of Death? Perhaps it could be any deity with the heart to do such a thing. Could Marisláni be forgiving enough of her champion and rid him of the curse herself? How was it possible that such a thing as a curse could be so easily created but difficult to destroy? How are they created in the first place, and if so, how did werewolves come to be? Was *my* magic somehow a curse? Could my lost memories be a symptom of one?

"Aha!"

I jumped at the sound of Canela's victorious cry. She was none the wiser, as she was too busy taking out a red book from the line and flipping through it. Eventually, she came upon a page that satisfied her.

"Since the full moon is coming up quickly, you're going to want something strong," she said, turning the book towards us.

Arabella and I leaned in to read it, but half of the scripture was in a language I couldn't understand.

"What does it do?" I asked.

"It brings together the animal mind and the human mind so that he has a better sense of control. It's especially useful during the first turn or with werewolves who tend to lose themselves more often than not."

My heart soared with giddy excitement.

"That's amazing! How soon can you make it?"

"I need at least a full day, but there's a bit of a catch."

"What do you mean?"

Canela drummed her fingers against the book, working her lip hesitantly. "This particular concoction can only be given...*during* the full moon. When he's already turned."

Arabella gasped, and the blood drained from my face. It shocked us into tense quiet as we waited for the witch to voice another option. When she didn't Arabella broke the silence.

"That's a suicide mission!" she exclaimed.

"It's dangerous, yes, but doable. The potion should take effect almost immediately, and it can help with the transition in the long run," Canela stressed. "I'm sure the queen can find someone fit for the job in a castle full of magic users."

THE MOON PRINCE

I knew firsthand what it was like to face off with a pack of werewolves, and I wish I didn't. I wish I didn't know how well they tore people apart like paper. They were large, strong, terrifyingly fast, and not even healing magic could take away the scars they left behind. Now the prince was to become one of them...and one of *us* had to be brave enough to face one of those creatures again. For *his* sake. I knew it had to be done, even if the idea made me sick to my stomach.

✻ ☽ ◯ ☾ ✻

The queen wasn't happy we had to return to Canela's in a day, but it was outshone with how pleased she was with our success. It was the first time I saw anything close to an earnest smile on her face, which is why it pained me to deliver the instructions for the potion. I wondered which out of all the magic users in *Castillo* Paricia she'd assign to such a daunting task until she decided to do it herself. Even though she was a powerful God-given and Río's mother, I was still shocked by this decision. I don't know why I felt that way, but I bit my tongue lest I overstep again. It made sense though it disturbed me.

In the meantime, my classes were set to continue, which thrilled me immensely. Much to my surprise, *Princesa* Mariela joined my classes again, which was a lovely turn of events considering her involvement in my escape. Her mother assigned her to spend less time doing archery and more time on her technique, which meant she'd be spending less time as a teacher and more as a student beside me.

Not only would I be practicing technique and improving my abilities, but Paloma would also be teaching basic magical knowledge. A lot of it was practical, which I was familiar with from my time in *Obsidiana*, but there were other things that I had been too afraid to dip my toe into until now. If I were to compare the two, Canela's magic was like cooking, and Paloma's was like baking—one required more precision than the other, and both painted a much broader picture than I ever could.

The wizard's specialty may not have been magical beasts or curses, but she had an affinity for the natural world. It was her magic that made the plants grow so abundantly, and why the garden seemed so bright despite the weather. She valued reciprocity, and whatever she gave to the plant life, they let her borrow in turn, fueling her magic. Those like the God-given had an inherent magical ability that recharged with proper care and rest, but others borrowed from the world around them. Charms, talismans, magical weapons, crystals, or anything that Canela carried in her shop benefited everyone. Relying solely on raw power, according to Paloma, could deteriorate the user and have long-term consequences.

Admittedly, it felt good to have power. *Using magic* felt good, and I berated myself for not trying it earlier. For once, my mind and body could be used for something worthwhile. For once, these headaches and shadows had a purpose, and while I still had no clue about their origin, I could at least make them mine. The door was clearer to me now, making my connection to the spirits stronger. I even managed to both reanimate a dead crow and make it fly.

The more I focused, the more I could feel my tether to it as it flew around the greenhouse, like a secondary heartbeat that was smaller than my own. These undead things should have disgusted me, but further we bonded—even in my free time—the more beautiful they became. I dared to wonder if Casímir Gedeón felt such a way or if he only ever saw these souls as a means to an end. Did he see them as souls at all? Did he ponder on who they could have been before their demise, or did he have no such empathy to begin with? No, a man like that couldn't have.

During our walk around the greenhouse (supervised by our new guard), I took the opportunity to apologize to Mariela for getting her in trouble with her mother. She giggled in response and assured me that despite her mother's punishment, she wasn't angry with me at all. Instead, she expressed remorse for not warning *me* before her mother came down to the dungeon. She seemed more preoccupied with getting my side of the story of what happened between Río and Captain Dominic. I did my best to explain the whole ordeal before asking if the prince had ever acted that way before. I knew he could be protective, and he was at the mercy of the werewolf curse, but I wanted to know if there was a way to discern the two.

Princesa Mariela furrowed her brow, staring long and hard at the message I wrote in her notebook. Her eyes took on a storminess that I only ever saw in her mother's. Her expression and apprehension left me assuming the worst. When she finally responded, the message said:

Only once, when we were younger. Some friends were being horrible to me, and Río got angry. It didn't end well, but it wasn't his fault.

She didn't elaborate, stating that it wasn't her story to tell. The only thing she did was reiterate that Rio was protective and always has been. I knew that, and I wanted to continue to believe it, but I also couldn't help but notice that the rumors Dulce told me and what happened between Silas and Río at the ball seemed to be intertwined. It was Río who told me that something "stupid" happened between them. How stupid it was, I still wasn't sure. I just hoped that if I were to ask him again, he would tell me the truth for once.

❋ ☽ ○ ☾ ❋

Paloma was doing everything she could to solve the mystery of my lost memories. She showed me pictures of plants from her books, hoping that one would resemble those in my mind, but none of them matched. Even the practice of my magic has failed to unlock something in me. If I asked the spirits questions, they had no answers to give, and then at night, all I had were strange dreams.

I'd dream about the cave in my mind, with the flowers and the full moon. Or I'd find myself walking in a castle much like this one, except it was darker, colder, and made of black obsidian. Sometimes there would be a black jaguar staring at me with its glowing, feline eyes, and other times I'd see the faceless man in all black. He'd watch me from afar or offer me his hand, only for me to wake up before I could take it. Even more recently, I felt as if someone was cradling me in their arms, but I could never tell who it was.

I relayed these dreams to Paloma in hopes that she could make sense of them, but most of her answers involved symbolism. Traditionally, jaguars and obsidian stones were symbols of protection, which was good news. She also said the nightmares could have been a response to what I went through and that it was normal for my fears to haunt me at night. Still, she wrote them down and promised to let me know if she found something of value.

I clung to that piece of information like a lifeline. As long as I didn't see a demon with red eyes, I had no reason to fret.

❋ ☽ ◯ ☾ ❋

The night before the full moon, Arabella and I left the castle once more to pick up Río's potion at *Obsidiana*. However, when we arrived at Canela's shop, the shutters were drawn and the sign on the front said CLOSED. It was strange. She never closed her shop this early in the night.

We knocked a few times, and I saw one of the shutters move before the door swung open. Canela quickly ushered us within, her eyes scanning the street before closing us inside. Her expression and body language were tense and uneasy, which was unusual for her.

"What's the matter?" I asked.

"Sorry, darling. Things have been a little peculiar around here lately."

"Peculiar, how?"

"The shop has been incredibly busy, and it was worse today. People who live or travel inland have been having issues. Crops aren't growing right, and the water in certain places tastes different. It's making people sick and giving them nightmares. They've been asking me for remedies and I've helped where I can, but many are thinking of requesting an audience with the queen."

Dread festered deep in me.

"What does that mean? What's happening?" I asked.

Canela shook her head. "I'm afraid it's nothing good. It's starting to look a lot like what happened in Old Avilonía, and now that the king is dead... I can only imagine what's happening at The Rift."

Arabella put her hand on my shoulder, and when I turned to her, her eyes were wide.

"We need to tell the queen," she said.

"Let her know what's going on," the witch said with a nod. "I won't be surprised if it's tied to the war somehow. For now, we can help alleviate one of her concerns."

She motioned us over to the counter and quickly hurried behind it. I eagerly approached, awaiting whatever intriguing potion she had in store, but instead of presenting us with a velvet bag or a bottle, she brought forth a small box. It looked like a cardboard pastry box about the size of my hand. I stared at it oddly as she slid it towards us.

"This is the potion?" I inquired, giving her an odd look.

"Something like that," she said with a smirk. "Open it."

I took the box and carefully lifted the lid. Within was not a bottle or a potion of any kind, but something that looked like a round cake with powdered sugar. A sweet and earthy smell emanated from it.

"With all due respect, *Magistra*, are you joking?" Arabella asked.

The witch laughed, "No, I'm not joking. This recipe, although like a potion, doesn't actually come in liquid form. It's made to be easily ingested by a werewolf who is not of sound mind. You'd be surprised how hard it is to get something like a liquid into an animal's mouth. This makes it easier and has herbs that smell and taste delicious to them."

Canela closed the box and tied it off with twine for easy transport before handing it back to me. I carefully slid it into my bag, expressing my undying gratitude.

"Thank you so much, Canela," I said, my heart swelling. "Truly, you've done so much for me since we've met and now for Río…"

The witch took my hands in hers and gave them a light squeeze.

"You're my friend, Esmé, and any friend of yours is a friend of mine. He's a good boy. Always has been. I can tell by what you're doing just how much you care about him. I'm sure he sees that too. There are people out there who dream of being loved in such a way, so don't take it for granted. Don't let it go, no matter what."

Tears stung in my eyes as I whispered, "I won't."

She came around the counter to give us both hugs before bidding us farewell.

"Now, hurry. Be safe, be mindful of the moon, and when the time comes... be brave."

29

The Boy Who Cried Wolf

Río

My skin was on fire.

The muscles beneath ailed with every movement, and there was a thrashing in my skull like a hammer to iron.

This cell was suffocating me. I wanted to tear it apart. I wanted to break my chains, rip these steel bars out of place, and pull away the stone until I was free. I knew I could do it.

Underneath it all was the unbearable anger. I don't know where it came from. I don't know whether it blossomed at some point in time or if it was always present, but it was hungry. It wanted me, and it wanted everything in greed.

I wanted to scream; I wanted to cry; I wanted to... *howl*. Yet there was this one idea that needled away at my mind with every passing minute like a dog begging for scraps:

I want to see Esmé.

My ache for her only doubled with this animalistic fury that was taking over me, and if I didn't see her at least once, I didn't know what I would do.

What *wouldn't* I do?

I leaned against my collar, letting the metal cut into my skin as I yelled,

"Hey! Do you hear me? Come down here! I'm talking to you!"

I shouted until a guard finally came. He looked terrified and made sure to keep his distance. I almost laughed.

"Where's Esmé?" I asked, my voice coming out ragged.

"She's in her tower, *Alteza.*"

"Bring her to me."

"After what happened with Captain Dominic, I'm afraid she is forbidden from seeing you again."

I groaned in frustration, my blood roaring in my ears, "I don't care! I order you to bring her!"

"I'm sorry, *Alteza,* but *Majestad* said not to take orders from you in this state," the guard replied.

He slowly backed away, his voice and body trembling. I ran my hands over my face and growled, the pain worsening.

"Get me the queen, then," I hissed.

"Sir—"

"Bring me my mother, or I will break out of this cell!" I bellowed.

The armored man gasped and nodded vigorously. "Yes, *Alteza.*"

As he scurried out of the dungeon, I sank to my knees, bracing myself on my elbows. Tears fell from my eyes in salty drops on the stone floor as I tried holding myself together, but I was fighting a losing battle. I didn't need windows or a calendar to know the full moon was imminent. And even though I knew it was wrong to let this wrath consume me, the rational part of my mind was getting weaker and weaker. He, too, was locked in a dungeon somewhere in the recesses of my mind.

I reached into my pocket and fished out Esmé's ring, gripping it in my hand as a way to ground myself. And I stayed that way until the queen came at last.

It was peculiar. I could hear her heartbeat from up the stairs and could smell that vanilla perfume she's worn my whole life. I was never able to do that before, and not just with her but with the guards and everyone else who came close. It was overwhelming.

I lifted my head with her approach, my eyes connecting with hers. She looked to be fighting back tears as she took me in.

"Río? They said you asked for me and that you demanded to see Esmé," she said calmly.

I sat back on my heels, my movements slothful. "I did."

"I'm sorry to disappoint you, my love, but you can't see her. Not like this."

"Why not?" I whispered sharply.

The anger was starting to feel like an itch under my skin.

"Because night has already fallen, and any minute now, the full moon will rise," she stressed.

That urge to scream and tear everything apart came back in full force. My blood was rushing in my veins and pounding in my ears. There was just one thing, *one thing* I wanted, and I couldn't even have that.

"I want to see Esmé," I demanded again.

"No."

I lunged, shouting, "Let me see her!"

The stone wall cracked as I pulled on my chains, but didn't completely break. My mother flinched. It was small, but I noticed. Yet she stood her ground, frustrating me even further, and in that moment, my emotions threatened to swallow me whole.

I sank to my knees again and started pulling and tugging at my hot, itching skin.

"I want to see Esmé," I repeated with tears in my eyes, over and over with an inhuman obsession that the logical part of me couldn't quite understand. I said it until my voice didn't sound like mine.

My muscles rippled in odd places, making my breath catch. They expanded and contracted in a painful cramp that was greatly overshadowed by the sudden cracking of bones. My legs twisted and broke, and I fell face forward. The pain was so great, I couldn't help but scream.

I made eye contact with my mother, who looked as pale and terrified as I had ever seen her in my life. In that heartbeat, the animal was gone, and it was just me, looking at my mother in terror as I understood what I was about to become.

"Mom," I choked out as another bone cracked in my arm. "Mom, I'm scared. Please—"

Kill me.

My last word turned into a guttural scream as my spine broke into pieces. My skull and jaw split open, and my hands expanded before my eyes, growing tufts of white fur and claws that could slice through flesh. My cries turned into snarling, and the last thing I was cognizant of was the pain before I inevitably blacked out.

30

Creature of the Moon

Esmé

I was in my tower when I heard Río's screams.

Initially, it seemed like a figment of my imagination or more spirits coming to pester me. It had been a restless day, but in the back of my mind, I knew. I felt it in the center of my chest. The only comparable sensation was when I was in the greenhouse, channeling magic.

I was unbound, sitting at the edge of the bed with a book in hand, when *Reina* Victoria practically barreled through my door. Her cheeks were streaked with dried tears, her makeup smudged beneath her eyes. She fought to keep her composure, but I could see in her face and the shaking of her hands that she was anything but alright. It struck a chord in me.

Putting the book down, I shot up to my feet.

"Did he turn?"

"Yes."

"Did...did something happen?"

"I..."

The queen's lips quivered, and she turned away from me. I took a tentative step towards her, but maintained my distance.

"He was asking for you," she said, finally turning to me.

My eyebrows shot up. "When?"

"Just before he turned."

She looked between my eyes, her steely mask now broken. It was as if she were assessing me for something I couldn't figure out. She then reached into her pocket and took out the small cardboard box containing Canela's potion.

"Here," she said, holding it towards me, "I think you should give it to him."

A gasp caught in my throat.

"Why?" I asked, shaking my head.

Reina Victoria chuckled darkly, "Esmé, I may be a tough bitch, but seeing my baby boy like that... It broke me. That's my shame to bear. But he was calling for *you*, and that might just be what we need for him to listen. I need to be with my daughter. I don't want her worrying about both of us. Not after everything."

I hovered reluctantly, waiting for her to take the potion back, but she stood firm with the parcel out. With a short nod, I took the box in my hands, swallowing hard. I knew this daunting task had to fall on someone; I just never thought I would be at the top of the list.

Río! The water! The city! The spirits shouted.

I briefly staggered and swayed from how powerful the message was.

"What's wrong?" the queen demanded.

Before I could answer, Captain Dominic wrenched the door open, exclaiming, "The city is flooding!"

Reina Victoria and I exchanged a horrified glance before she bolted for the door. With the box in hand, I scurried behind with my heart in my throat, following the captain and the commotion outside and up the ramparts surrounding the castle grounds. The guards, the queen, and I all peered over the edge and gaped at the scene below.

The sea had risen and was pouring into the bottom streets of Coáraluna. Ships were being tossed around and tipped over, and smaller structures were being knocked down. I could hear people screaming, and many of them were scattered around like ants trying to swim or find refuge.

The worst came to mind.

"This isn't the Sun Killer, is it?" I whispered sharply.

"No," the queen shook her head, her face pale. "It's Río."

She lifted her head towards the circular moon, now at its fullest.

My face fell, the dots connecting in my mind. Almost everyone knew that the champions of Marisláni were strongest when the moon was full, just like the rising of the tides. But could it be that attaining the werewolf curse—an affliction that is *driven* by the full moon— could somehow *double* their strength? It seems we are finding out today.

"Could it be…?"

La Reina's expression hardened, her shoulders squaring before pointing at the box in my hands.

"You need to get that thing to him immediately. If we can't find a way to calm him, he's going to take down half of this city. I'll deal with the people. Go!" she ordered.

On the queen's command, I ran back into the castle, rushing towards the bottom floor with Canela's cake in hand. I ran past Paloma, who frantically inquired about *La Reina's* whereabouts and where I was going. I could only shout a few coherent words before we parted.

"She's in the courtyard! I need to take Río this potion!"

"What?" she blurted out. "Oh, moon and stars. Marisláni be with you!"

My only goal was to get to the dungeon as fast as possible and somehow get this magical pastry into the mouth of a beast without dying. There was no plan other than that, and the only weapon I had at my disposal was my underdeveloped magic. It wasn't simply Río at stake, but Coáraluna and the people I loved so much.

I managed to make it to the top of the dungeon stairs when a dreadful scene stopped me in my tracks. Guards stood before me, a few of them battered or bleeding. There were claw marks across one's armor, and another who had slashes on his arm was being tended to by the princess. Echo was staring off down the hallway, growling at something I couldn't see.

As I approached, the hound looked in my direction. Mariela looked over her shoulder at the same time and sighed in relief.

"What happened?" I signed as I spoke aloud.

The guards eyed me cautiously, somehow still afraid of me despite everything else happening. The princess signed her response, and only then did one of the men speak to translate.

"He broke out of his cell. One second we were getting the queen out of there, and the next he was coming up the stairs. Everything happened so fast."

My blood turned to ice. "Where is he?"

"He's in the ballroom," another one replied, "and he took the water with him."

"What water?"

From what I understood, the princess said, "The water from the fountains. All of it."

"What could he possibly need it for?"

Everyone shrugged. Surely, they envisioned the worst, but if he intended to use it against the queen's guards, then he would have been here and not elsewhere. These men, though injured, were not torn to shreds like those from that night. That alone was curious. At least for the time being.

"The city is flooding," I said.

Mariela gasped as the guards muttered words of surprise.

"How?" the princess asked.

"Whatever tie to the moon Río has is stronger now, and as long as he isn't in control, it will only get worse. I need to get this potion to him," I explained with haste. "How do I get to the ballroom from here? By order of the queen."

I made sure to add the last statement lest they decide to withhold anything from me. They all immediately pointed down the hallway, where Echo's attention was.

The princess got up to her feet, saying, "I'll go with you."

"No," I said, shaking my head. "You should go to your mother. Try and help the city."

I used all the sign language I knew to get my point across, and when she tried to argue, I only continued to implore.

"Coáraluna is *flooded*. They need you and your magic. Your mother needs you. I have this. Trust me."

Ela narrowed her eyes at me intensely, not pleased with this decision. There was too much happening at once. We needed all hands-on deck, and the princess was the only tide bender of sound body and mind at the moment.

In the end, she gave in and pointed to Echo. "Follow him."

With a hopeful look, I ran down the corridor behind her animal companion with the box in my grasp.

The entire path to the ballroom was damp, which made it both easier to track him down and harder to keep a steady pace. What a wonder it was that Río was able to use his magic in such a state. I don't know why I assumed curses would negate everything else, especially one that turned you into an animal. Yet it made sense that magic bestowed by gods was far too strong to overpower.

Eventually, we came upon the foyer once again, with the fountain that was now empty and cracked. Some of the tapestries had been torn off the wall, and pieces of shattered vases littered the corridor. And when I arrived at the entrance to the ballroom itself, the doors were torn off the hinges and splintered in half. I came to a sputtering stop at the threshold, almost slipping on a puddle, and was struck frozen at the sight before me.

It was the ballroom as I remembered it—both the good and the bad. The blood was all cleaned up and the bodies were long gone, but the curtains were torn, the walls were stained, and the floor was still cracked. The most gob-smacking thing that put aside any horrible memory was the giant, watery sphere that nearly spanned the entire width of the room. It glowed a magical blue, spinning around like a cyclone yet managing to stay in place. I carefully approached the banister in awe. Apart from the sound of rushing water, a mysterious noise drew my attention. Upon closer listen, I realized it sounded like angry snarling.

Echo whined at my side, and when I glanced over, *Príncipe* Saévio was standing behind him. His sudden appearances didn't scare me as much as before, even if I did wish he would give me a warning.

"He's in there," I said. "I think he's protecting himself."

"Or he's protecting everybody else."

It reminded me of what Canela said. "It's still him."

"It is...but you still have to be careful," he warned. "If I were you, I wouldn't go in there with my bare hands."

I whirled around with an incredulous scowl.

"I am *not* taking in a weapon," I snapped. "This is Río we're talking about. I don't want to hurt him. Besides, I have my magic."

I have more than I did before, anyway.

With a shuddering inhale, I slowly made my way down the stairs.

"Don't worry, I'll still be here when you die, Vespertín," he teased like a true teenager.

"If you're not going to be helpful, then go back to your owner!" I shouted without looking back.

The Air Prince laughed boyishly. "You're a lot braver than you think you are, you know that?"

Despite my irritation, I smiled but didn't respond.

At the bottom of the steps, I tiptoed along the cracked floor towards the enormous orb of water. The more I neared it, the more it gave off a strong breeze that swept up my hair and clothes. I only stopped when I came practically nose to nose with the current. It roared like an angry, coursing river as I stared up at it with diffidence. At first, I resisted the urge to touch it, afraid the water would take me under. But now was not the time for hesitation. I made it this far, and I was going to complete it. Río was in there, and if he was in there, then it had to be possible for me, too.

Still clutching the parcel, I raised my hand, bracing myself as I grazed the surface. The cool water rushed over my fingers with its jarring force, but didn't hurt or take me with it. Instead, I felt the magic within, like the crackling of lightning, but more gentle. I boldly stuck my entire hand through, feeling open air on the other side, much like when I tried uncovering a memory. And with the reassurance I needed, I closed my eyes, held my breath, and ran forward.

It was like diving into the sea, but only briefly, and then I was breaking the surface, coming up for air as I stumbled to the other side. I came out sopping wet, but I was still on my feet with the potion in my grasp. When I opened my eyes, everything was vibrant, glowing blue, as if I were a fish in the ocean. And somehow, the magic felt more powerful than from the outside. Every inch of my skin buzzed, and my heart seemed more alive. I could marvel at it all day.

The floor beneath me shook slightly, and the sound of a low growl drew my attention to the creature in my periphery. My muscles tensed, and my body trembled in terror. A large, seven-and-a-half-foot werewolf with fur the color of moonlight awaited on the other side of the sphere. He stood tall with blade-like claws that could cut through bone just like those beasts that terrorized this very room not long ago. Every instinct was telling me to run, to go back through the watery barrier and never come back, but this was no ordinary werewolf.

This was *Río*.

"Río," I uttered softly, my voice trembling.

He whipped his head in my direction. And when our eyes met—brown meeting glowing blue—he hunched over in a predatory stance. His ears pulled back as he bared his sharp teeth in a snarl. The beast looked nothing like him. Even his eyes were too harsh and brutish, yet I knew...

I swallowed hard, and with a careful step forward, I worked at the twine around the box. Again, I had no plan, but somehow I was called to mention things about his life. Perhaps, in a way, it would remind him of who he is underneath the wolfish exterior.

"Río," I repeated with more firmness, because there was power in a name. "It's me, Esmé. Remember? We met at *Teatro Paraiso* when I performed for your birthday."

He watched me steadily, still on guard, but didn't yet move. *Yet.*

I inched a little more forward.

"Your name is Río Maximiliano Markaél, and you're the Moon Prince. You were born under a blue moon, and you live in Coáraluna. Your sister's name is Mariela, and your mom is Victoria. She's the

Queen of Storms. Your father's name was Marino. He was the Moon King and a brave warrior."

At the mention of his father, he wavered. With hope, I thought I got through to him somehow, but quickly realized my mistake. He went feral—snarling and tearing away at the floor with his claws and teeth. I flinched as pieces of debris flew around.

"Río! Río, stop! It's okay!"

His wolfish face turned to me with fury, and someone in my mind yelled, *Run!*

The white wolf barreled towards me on all fours with terrifying speed, canines out. With a shaking cry, I threw myself out of the way, landing on my side with a groan. I managed to look up just in time to see his claw coming down above me, and I rolled out of the way with a shriek. Pastry still in hand, I scrambled to my feet and put as much distance between Río and me.

I watched him search for me furiously and worked away at the twine as I kept talking. I strayed from mentioning his father or anything that might upset him to keep myself alive.

"You told me you like to surf in your free time. You're horrible at cooking, but you try. And you like to eat mangoes when they're in season. You bring me flowers after every trip you take, blue ones, because they're my favorite. And I remember you once telling me that sunflowers were *your* favorite. I think of you every time I see them."

He lunged at me again and chased me around the sphere until my legs burned. His claws cut the air in vain, just missing parts of my skin. Thinking quickly, I used one of Paloma's techniques, and whipped my hand out towards him. Orbs of purple light flew from my fingers, circling his head in dissonant whispers. The wolf came to a halt, shaking his head as he tried swiping at the spirits with his claws, but they had already vanished. I used the opportunity to run behind him, away from his view. My legs wobbled, and my head was swimming, but I refused to let him catch me.

When the smaller details didn't seem to work, my words started coming from the heart.

"Do you know why I used to avoid saying your real name?" I asked breathlessly. "It's because I was scared the day would come when you'd suddenly decide you didn't want me anymore. It would have broken me, so keeping you at a distance was easier."

My voice wavered as I laid out my confession, and the wolf suddenly stopped. His furious eyes were still on me, but my statement seemed to give him pause.

"In reality, I wanted you so badly, but I was too scared I could never have you. But you were never scared, and I envied you for it."

My voice cracked with my unbridled emotion. These were things that I kept hidden under lock and key. I was too embarrassed to say them to a *prince*, yet somehow, at this moment, it felt safer to say it to a werewolf.

He blinked and shook his head, switching between soft and aggressive. I could tell that he understood me, but wasn't fully lucid yet. The animal side took over again, and he growled at me once more. With the twine finally gone, I opened the box and took the pastry out, letting the cardboard fall to the floor. I held it out before me as he ran with murderous intent, but instead of fleeing, I closed my eyes and started to sing. It was the same lullaby as before—the one about the blue rabbit and the moon—and the same one that made the spirits turn to light.

I braced myself for Río's attack, for the feeling of his claws and teeth on my skin, but the sound of his rumbling footsteps ceased. Still holding the tune, I peeled my eyes open and let out a squeak at the white wolf looming so close to me. His attention, however, was turned towards the wisps of violet light dancing above us. As my singing became softer, the wolf looked down at me. The rage from earlier vanished, now replaced by confusion, curiosity, and then recognition. And in that moment, I saw him for who he truly was. Not merely a wolf, but Río Markaél.

"Río?" I asked gently, still shaking with adrenaline.

He whined in response, and that was all I needed. When his expression seemed to calm, I took a tentative step forward, cake still in hand (though mildly squished).

"Eat this. Please. It'll make you feel better."

Río sniffed it *once* and instantly devoured it out of my hand. I burst into giggles despite my cringe over the feeling. When he was done, I tentatively ran my hand over his head.

"Good boy."

Canela's spell took effect almost immediately. The white wolf straightened up to his full size and glanced around as if seeing the world for the first time. There was something more human in his eyes, and when he peered down at me, there was a solid familiarity there that I've seen many times before. I nearly broke down from joy.

"Hey, big boy," I murmured, "do you remember me now?"

As if in reply, Río reached out his large, clawed paw, face up for me, and I placed my hand on top of it, which was comically small in comparison. He then leaned his head forward gently until I was able to touch him. With a laugh bubbling in my throat, I cupped his large, furry face, which was coarse yet soft at the same time. After the ball, I never thought such a beast could be gentle, yet...

He whined again, and even though he didn't say words, I understood the apology behind the sound.

"Don't worry about it. I'm just glad you're okay. You're safe now. You need to let go and rest, okay?" I motioned to the sphere around us.

The prince looked around, and suddenly, the water stopped moving and slowly opened up like a flower, revealing the rest of the ballroom. It moved away, slithering like a snake up the stairs and out of the room, returning to the fountains from whence it came. And as soon as Río's magic was released, his eyes reverted to their dark brown color.

Never letting go of his hand, my spirits and I led Río out of the destroyed ballroom. And what an odd sight we were, no doubt, to the people waiting out in the foyer. There was a collective gasp, and the werewolf prince took a step back. Everyone, including the queen, was waiting for us with bated breath, their eyes flitting between me and the white wolf beside me.

"We're going back downstairs now," I announced, my eyes locking on *Reina* Victoria.

Both she and Mariela were in complete shock. Savy stood beside them, bearing a look of complete and utter awe.

"Yes. Of course. Everyone, make way!" the queen ordered.

Our spectators was more than happy to scramble away from the large beast in their wake, allowing us the space to walk through.

"It's okay," I whispered to Río over and over.

The queen only stopped me once to look at me with tears in her eyes and say, "Thank you."

I nodded with a smile and kept going until we were back in the dungeon. Río's cell was torn apart but still intact enough to sleep in. I told him to lie down, and he did as he was told, very unlike the beast who tried to kill me earlier. Once I had done what I needed to do, I slowly let go of his paw and started backing out of the cell.

"Goodnight, Río. Get some sleep," I said awkwardly.

I didn't get very far. Something tugged at my skirt, keeping me in place. That something was the prince with my dress between his teeth.

"What are you doing?" I asked with a chuckle.

He tugged me back gently with a whine. Even if he didn't say a word, I could see in his eyes that he wanted me to stay. By all means, I should leave, but seeing the way he looked at me pulled at my heartstrings.

Stay, he told me, and I knew I couldn't leave him like this. After all, I made a promise.

"Okay," I whispered.

Río opened up his big arms, and though it seemed incredibly strange, I got down on the ground and nestled myself into them. It was surprisingly easy to get comfortable like this. He was a monster, a cursed creature, yet he was warm, soft, and safe. Though bigger, his heart was still his heart, and his soul was still his soul. He didn't scare me, and if this is what it took to keep him happy, then so be it.

31

Waking Beauty

Río

I woke up in her arms.

Most of the night was a complete blur, but then all of a sudden, she was there, holding her hand out to me. With her as a pillar, I was able to think clearly again, and all my shame and anguish came rushing back. But she was there, she was there, she was there. The pain returned like a tidal wave as my bones and muscles rippled and cracked back into place. Before I knew it, I was on the floor, slicked with sweat, looking down at human hands. *My* hands. And Esmé was still here.

"Río," she gasped. "Río, are you okay?"

Her gentle hand rested upon the hot skin of my bare shoulder, and when I looked into her eyes, part of me thought I had died and was seeing the afterlife.

"Are you real?" I uttered.

"Yes, I'm real," she giggled. A godly sound.

Esmé pushed a piece of my damp hair away from my forehead with her delicate fingers. The act was so soft, it was almost shocking.

"It's over now," she said.

It's over.

Unable to contain myself, I threw my arms around her and held her tight against my chest. She embraced me with equal fervor, as if with the same intent of never letting go. I buried my face in her brown hair as tears blurred my vision and my body shook.

"You came," I whispered.

"I did."

"You stayed."

"Of course."

With my heart hammering in my chest, I pulled back and took her face in my hands. *Human hands.* And with a sudden fear ripping through me, I scanned her entire body for injuries.

"I didn't hurt you, did I? Are you okay?"

"I'm okay," she chuckled, putting her hands over mine. "You didn't hurt me."

"Did I hurt anyone else?"

Esmé hesitated, and my heart dropped into the pit of my stomach.

"You may have lashed out at a few guards—"

I closed my eyes in shame, dropping my head into my hands. I knew something like this could happen, yet I couldn't escape the horrid guilt it filled me with.

"—but it was nothing too serious. Mariela healed them," she added in reassurance.

Esmé put her hands on either side of my head and tilted my face back to face her. I didn't know when she became so affectionate, but I never wanted it to stop.

"They're alive, Río," she stressed. "Honestly, we all prepared for a lot worse."

"Yes, but I'm their future king. I'm supposed to fill them with pride, not fear," I muttered.

"They've known you for years. I doubt one night will change that."

"You'd be surprised," I said, working my jaw.

Esmé frowned. "I think you underestimate how much people care about you, even your guards."

My brow furrowed as I took her in with curious adoration. Her words helped me see out of the fog of my self-degradation, but there was also something different about her now—the way she spoke and carried herself. She was a little more straightforward and a little less inclined to take back what she said. She was still herself, but shone a little brighter, like a blade that was finally sharpened.

"What?" she asked.

"I like it when you say what's on your mind."

Esmé's shoulders relaxed, her cheeks burning red as she bit her lip shyly.

"You might be the only one," she said softly.

She looked down at her hands and suddenly became serious.

"Río...something else happened last night."

"What? What is it?"

Esmé looked into my eyes apprehensively. It worried me.

"Your tie to the moon got... *stronger* when you turned, and you sort of...flooded the city a little bit," she relayed carefully.

"What?" I blurted out, craning my head back.

"Your mother and sister were handling it, and I think we would've heard if things got worse," she added quickly.

"Still, this whole time, I thought I'd have to worry about *eating* people. It turns out I have to worry about sinking Coáraluna without knowing?" I exclaimed.

I ran my hands over my face and hair in agitation as my worst nightmares were slowly coming true and new ones bloomed.

"You weren't in the right state of mind. If it weren't for Canela's potion, then who knows what else would've happened?"

I snapped my head up with a frown. "What potion?"

"You don't remember?" she asked. "I gave you a small cake that Canela made, which was supposed to help make you feel more...human, I guess. I don't know if *you* felt different, but *I* could tell right away."

I looked back on my hazy memories as a werewolf, and among them, I saw Esmé holding a small pastry in her hand. It smelled so good that I ate it without question.

Like a fucking dog. How embarrassing.

"I do remember, actually," I replied with wonder. "Canela made that?"

"Yes, Arabella and I went to her shop for some help. It was my idea, and your mother only allowed it because it was for you."

My mind and body had just undergone the greatest torment imaginable, yet I couldn't help being enthralled by her. Other than my own family, I have never met anyone so willing to extend their kindness and love to me in such a selfless way. She was my mother's prisoner, yet she was willing to risk herself for me on more than one occasion. She did it despite having every reason to flee this place.

"You didn't have to do that," I said.

"I know, but I wanted to," she replied softly.

Ever since the curse started to take over, my heart was like a rabid, caged animal wanting to tear itself out of my ribs, and somehow, this girl—this woman— tamed it into submission with a softness I had never seen before. She came back. She risked her life for me without knowing if she could return me to who I was. How do you repay someone like that? How do I express the indescribable love and appreciation that I was feeling?

Without thinking, I reached out and ran my thumb over the soft skin of her bottom lip, though I wished it were my tongue instead. Esmé inhaled a shuddering breath and looked at me with eyes that could swallow me whole. We were dangerously close for the first time since everything transpired, and with no bars to keep us apart. It was too enticing not to touch her after being forced apart the way we were.

I let my touch linger on her skin as I looked between her lips and her eyes. In the space between us, I could sense the words she wanted to say.

We spoke at the same time.

"Esmé—"

"Río—"

We giggled, and I let my forehead rest against hers. Little by little, I was starting to remember more things from when I turned. At first was the painful memory of chasing her like a hunter on the prowl. But I chose to linger on a more important memory, one that involved her confession to me.

I brushed my nose against hers. I could hear her heart running wild in response as I hovered a breath away from a kiss. But the dungeon door creaked open, rudely interrupting us.

I sighed heavily. "Shit."

With haste, Esmé positioned herself in front of me to cover my modesty, I presume, seeing as I was fully naked. If this was going to be a regular thing, I needed to purchase more clothing that I wouldn't mind parting with. Or simply not wear clothes at all. During the full moon, at least.

My mother and her guards rushed down the hall towards us, and as soon as we made eye contact, she let out a deep sigh of relief.

"For a moment there, I thought one or both of you were dead," she said.

"Thank you for the vote of confidence, Mom," I replied.

She held her hand out, and one of the guards gave her a blanket, which she tossed in our direction. Esmé took it and helped wrap it around my shoulders.

"Thanks. I forgot clothes were going to be a problem," I muttered.

"We brought those too."

She handed Esmé a stack of clothing as well as a flask. I chugged half of its contents before giving the rest to her.

"So I'm guessing Canela's potion worked?" my mother asked.

"It did," Esmé said with a smile.

"And how did you feel? Did you feel any different?"

"I felt like I was in my body again and like I could think more clearly," I said.

The logical part of my mind was no longer small and locked up, but at the helm, intertwined with the body and instincts of a werewolf. It was utterly disorienting and still felt more like a dream.

Esmé turned back to my mother and asked, "Did you notice a difference? The city. Did it—"

"The water receded, and the city is fine, yes. The lower levels are going to need repairing, as well as a few of our ships, but I guess we'll just add it to the list of worries."

While Esmé rejoiced, I bared my teeth in an apologetic wince.

"Mom, I'm so sorry. All of you... I'm sorry. I didn't know—"

"It's alright, darling. This was the last thing we could've predicted. After all, you're the first God-given to get bitten by a werewolf. I'm sure Paloma will have a field day with all the questions she has for you," she said with a soft smirk. My mother then clasped her hands and nodded curtly. "Very well. Put your clothes on, my love. I want to speak to you soon, but only after you get cleaned up and rest a bit. And Río…"

"Yeah?"

"I think it's time you went back to your real bed, don't you think?"

I tried but failed to hide my excitement and audibly scoffed, sputtered, and erupted into joyful laughter.

"Yes!" I blurted out. "Yes, please. I will do anything."

Esmé giggled, and my mother snorted. She turned to Esmé with her eyebrows raised.

"Esmé?"

She straightened up beside me. "Yes?"

"I'd like to speak with you first, if you don't mind. When you're ready."

"Oh, yes, of course."

My mother led her guards out of the dungeon, allowing Esmé and me some more welcome privacy. With her assistance, we got up from the floor, my muscles aching all over. As I started putting on my fresh clothes, Esmé turned away, playing coy. Even now, it made me grin like a madman.

"What do you think she wants?" I asked.

Esmé shrugged. "I don't know."

"Do you want me to come with you?"

Now that I wasn't in chains and had my power back, I was able to stand by her side in the face of my mother's iron fist. I was more than happy to. To my dismay, Esmé chuckled softly.

"No, it's okay. Things aren't too bad between her and me. For now, anyway."

Now fully clothed, I circled to face her with my eyebrows raised.

"Are you saying my mother likes you?"

"Oh, I wouldn't go that far, but she may have said something similar to that. She threatens my life daily, though."

I nodded. "Yeah, she does that."

"Well, she's going to do it again if I don't go out there and talk to her," she.

Esmé moved towards the broken cell door, and with my heart in my throat, my hand instinctively flew to her wrist.

"Wait."

She looked over her shoulder, her eyes searching my face.

"What's wrong?"

I glance at her lips, and her heartbeat quickened, that blaze in her eyes burning bright. Some part of me expected her to close up or back away. But as I recalled the words she told me in my beast form, I knew I couldn't let her go. Never again.

"Can I kiss y—"

Before I could get the words out, Esmé threw herself into my arms, capturing my mouth with hers. I laughed against her lips and grabbed her by the waist, lifting her against me. She kissed me ardently, making me sigh against her soft skin.

I've craved her touch, her lips, and her familiar sweet scent for so long, and kissing her again was like the first drop of water after a drought. I never thought I'd get to have that again, but here was Esmé, proving me wrong in so many ways that I will forever be thankful for. There were countless things I wanted to say and do to her. There were other places I was hungry to touch, kiss, and worship, but not here and not right now. She deserved better than this dungeon and this haggard body.

Just when things might go a little too far, I disconnected from her gently and put her back on her feet.

"I'm sorry," she whispered through panting breaths.

"Don't ever be sorry," I told her, shaking my head.

The next words that left my mouth were not ones I wanted to say.

"We should go."

"I don't want to," she said, staring up at me with sad eyes.

It hit me then that while I had the privilege of going back to my bedroom, she was still bound to her tower. She was still a prisoner.

"I know, but I'll call for you. Alright?" I reassured.

"Alright."

I intertwined my hand with hers and led her out of my now-destroyed cell, up the stairs until we found my mother and sister at the top.

Mariela gasped, and suddenly she was crashing into me with a warm hug. After giving her a long squeeze, and Echo came running up to paw at my chest and lick my face.

I let out a cackle before saying, "I missed you, too, buddy."

My mother approached with a warm smile and gave me a proper embrace of her own. I closed my eyes and held on to her for a long minute, knowing full well we were both trying hard not to cry.

She took my face in her hands, her eyes piercing mine. "I'm so glad you're alright, my love."

"Me too. I couldn't have done it without Esmé," I said, looking over my shoulder.

Esmé grinned shyly.

"Oh, I know," my mother agreed.

I turned back to my mother and leaned in close to say, as low as I could, "I don't know what you plan on saying to her, but be nice."

My mother scoffed, "What makes you think that I wouldn't?"

I narrowed my eyes at her in response. *Seriously?*

She rolled her eyes. "Okay, yes, fine. I'll be nice. Now go. Please."

I shook my head at her as I walked towards Esmé for one last goodbye. I kissed her cheek and lingered long enough to see her skin turn pink before heading to my room with Echo and Mariela.

32

Forever

Esmé

My lips still tingled from kissing Río, my entire being humming. No matter how much time we spent together, it was always woeful to see him go. In the small wink of morning we shared, I finally had him to myself with nothing to separate us. I wanted so badly for it to last, even if it was in that broken dungeon. We survived so much, and he nearly killed me, yet all I wanted to do was cling to him. It was a deep, pressure-like yearning that I assumed would vanish when the old illusion wore off, but there was no illusion. There was only something a little more raw underneath.

I joined the queen and her two guards to another part of the castle away from the prince. No shackles were put on my wrists, but armored men flanked me, staying vigilant. The chamber I was taken to was a large sitting room of cream, gold, and aquamarine blue. With a charm, the flames in the hearth came to life, and the Queen of Storms excused her men. She stood before me in a dress of such deep violet it almost looked black. It brought out the lilac in her god-touched hair.

"I wanted to take a moment to formally thank you, Miss Vespertín," she said. "It takes a lot of courage to do what you did. I hope you know that."

"I just wanted to help everyone, especially Río," I replied.

"Still, not everyone is so willing to face off with a werewolf, no matter who they are underneath. It's a death wish. Most of them get chained up and left to fend for themselves until sunrise. Yet when Río was running rampant, you didn't let that stop you. And somehow, you managed to come out unscathed."

Her disbelief was well warranted. Other than minor bruising, it was a miracle Río didn't leave me with a scratch. I could give all credit to the fact that it was *him* and not some regular werewolf, but I knew that wasn't totally true. Even *I* was surprised by how well my survival instincts saved me, especially since I had never done anything similar in my life. I was quick, but I was no warrior or athlete. Still, my magic aside, it was I who evaded his sharp claws just before they could slice through me. Even if he somehow hurt me, I wouldn't have held it against him.

"I guess knowing that it was still Río in there gave me the self-preservation and determination to survive," I told her. "I had to get through to him somehow."

The queen eyed me curiously for a pressing moment before saying, "Has anyone ever told you that you have a feline sense of fearlessness, Esmé?"

I blinked in surprise, both at her usage of my name and her incredibly startling question.

"No. No, I don't think I've ever been told anything of the sort."

"Well, I'll be the first to say it then. Felines, like a jaguar perhaps, hunt from the trees, silent and unseen, until it's time to strike. If you go into the jungle naively underestimating the silence, then you've already marked your death. But those who know of the jaguar know to always keep an eye out for the trees," she explained. "I have a feeling that many people have underestimated your silence, Miss Vespertín, even yourself."

All I could do was stare at the queen in astonishment following such deeply profound words. No one, even in my short memory, ever gave me such a ferocious compliment. All that was ever noticed was my politeness, theatrical performance, or my outward appearance, so that was all I ever was. To be told such a thing, and by a God-given who had every right to despise me, held so much weight.

"You saved Coáraluna today," *La Reina* continued. "If Río had lost any more control, who knows what would've happened to the city? And we had Ela on hand because of you, so thank you."

I looked towards the hearth, suddenly overwhelmed with emotion,

"I was just doing what felt right," I whispered, my chest aching.

"I know, and it won't go overlooked."

My vision blurred, and tears spilled over onto my cheeks. I swiped them away, and in that moment, *La Reina* walked up to me and placed her hand on my shoulder with a warm, motherly expression.

"Mark my words, we're going to find out who you are."

"Thank you," I managed as more tears welled in my eyes.

❋ ☽ O ☾ ❋

It was barely past sunrise, which meant it was way too early for magical lessons, but I was too anxious to sleep. The full moon finally passed, but now all I could focus on was the prospect of seeing Río again. He said he would call for me, and I wanted to be awake when he did, so I had an early breakfast and took a nice, warm bath. After the chaos of last night, It was good to be clean and energized.

The best I could do to distract myself was to peruse some literature Canela was kind enough to lend me. She said it was to help with my magic, and I was more than happy to take what she was willing to part with. There were a few books on spirits and the afterlife, as well as mediumship. To my dismay, she also included some on the history of the God-given, as well as smaller booklets on different deities—the core four, as well as the God of Death. I wasn't entirely certain how these would benefit me, but I chose to give her the benefit of the doubt.

Out of curiosity, I flipped through the book of the God-given first. Naturally, the first chapter was on the champions of Solistó: the Elíódor's. Even now, the name gave me with mixed feelings of dread and sorrow. It was a name that once elicited pride but was now a symbol of fear. The Sun Killer was to blame for that. I suppose that was all the more reason to learn of what once was.

Amid the tyrannical reign of Casímir Gedeón, the Elíódor's were the first of the gods' champions, also known as the God-given. Seeing the death and destruction that was befalling their beloved children, the gods chose to bestow gifts to aid them in their ongoing war for freedom. Known as The First Sunrise, the first God-given to be created was a warrior given the name Sol Elíódor. Blessed by Solistó, god of the sun and bravery, the warrior was gifted a ray of sunlight—a piece of Solistó's magic. Thus, Sol Elíódor and his descendants were given the ability to wield fire, heat, and the sun's rays, and had hair as red as jasper stone with eyes that glowed like liquid gold.

Fully intrigued, I continued to read the Elíódor history that named every single one of Sol's descendants as well as their accomplishments, right until the bitter end.

The last true king was Leandro Valentino Elíódor. Though the youngest of two sons, he was dubbed the heir of the Sun Kingdom due to his ability to wield a fire so hot that it burned blue. This was a gift not just any sun champion could master or receive, as the flame itself often chose its wielder. This earned Leandro the title, "The Master of the Blue Flame," as well as the golden crown to the Eliódor throne. On the Day of Infinite Shadow, Leandro was viciously slain by his older brother, Sebastián, in the city of Dragona, along with the rest of his family. Unfortunately, he bore no descendants, leaving his brother, Sebastián Eliódor, as the last bearer of the sun god's gift.

The spirits grew angry at the mention of the Sun Killer's true name.

Murderer. Malvado. King slayer. Usurper.

I didn't fault them for their rage.

On the next few pages were portraits of the Champions of the Sun, all done in watercolor. The first, of course, was Sol Eliódor, who looked every last bit like a warrior. His children followed, and then their children, all with varying degrees of red hair and golden-bronze skin. I was born well after the last Sun King died, but there was something melancholic about seeing the faces of people who belonged to a dead dynasty. Especially when the people who knew them were still alive.

As I arrived to Leandro Eliódor's portrait, my heart dropped. Like everyone else, he had red hair, shimmering eyes, and golden armor. He looked young, barely older than Río is now. *Why are they all so young?* But there was something about the Eliódor's that was different from the Markaél's.

The Champions of the Moon were a little rough around the edges because they appeared as if made by crashing waves and sea salt air. Their power was drawn from the unpredictable ocean and the mysterious moon that dominated the night sky, and they carried those traits with them along with their undying mirth.

In contrast, the Champions of the Sun were fueled by fire and light and seemed to carry themselves with the regality of dragons. Their passion, bravery, and confidence were apparent even through their portraits, yet there was something warm about their eyes. After all, they were born to bear the heat of the burning sun and hold their heads high while doing it.

Still, there was something about Leandro's face I couldn't quite put my finger on. He wasn't someone I thought about often, but I noticed something in his eyes. Perhaps it was the underlying friendliness that made him look surprisingly welcoming. Or maybe it was my own melancholy again. I had a face to the name now, which made his brutal death that much worse, and at the hands of his brother no less.

With apprehension, I flipped to the next page, expecting the remaining Eliódor to be there, except to my surprise—and relief—the portrait had been torn out. In its place was a note signed by Canela.

Though he is part of our history, Leandro Eliódor's brother does not belong in the book of the God-given. It is an insult to Leandro's memory, his family, and the ones who loved him. It is also an insult to the gods and to the people currently affected by him today. His story belongs elsewhere and is written as such. And those who don't know it by now are either too young or willfully ignorant.

I ran my fingers over the torn edge that remained inside the spine as I was left to imagine the Sun Killer's true face. People didn't exactly hang posters of him around town, so his appearance was mostly described in stories so that we may piece him together in our imaginations. Some variation of a monster or a beast was what often formed, though I had a feeling it wasn't entirely so.

A knock came at the door, and I was so enraptured in the book that I yelped in response.

"Sorry to interrupt, Miss Vespertín, but the prince requested to see you."

The change of tone nearly gave me whiplash. I gasped and nearly threw the book aside.

"Did he?"

She bit back a laugh. "Yes, he did."

"A-Alright."

Sliding out of bed, I straightened out my dress and took my hair out of its braid so it fell loose down my back. It was only Arabella who escorted me out of my tower this time. No guards followed along, although a number of them stood at various corners, keeping watch. My wrists were free, though the loss of the manacles' weight was an odd feeling now.

Arabella and I went through a wonderfully decorated floor that was completely new to me and made me wonder exactly how large this castle was. Thick rugs with a starry pattern ran along the wooden floors, and more paintings decorated the walls. Eventually, we came upon a set of double doors with ocean waves carved into them, and I knew then we had arrived.

My heartbeat quickened as we approached, and Arabella knocked three times. Not a second later, I heard Río say,

"Come in!"

The handmaiden pulled one of the doors open and motioned me inside. With bated breath, I smiled at her and stepped inside. The door didn't even shut behind me when I gasped.

"Oh, wow."

While most of the rooms in this castle were cohesive in some shape or form, Río's room stood out above the rest. The walls were painted with a pattern of crashing waves that danced around me. Atop a blue-patterned rug was a large four-poster bed with aquamarine draping and white sheets. In the corner was a small fountain patterned in a collage of blue sea glass. And above was a domed ceiling painted inky black with stars to look like the night sky; among them, a white rabbit chased a shooting star. The room smelled faintly of sea salt and Río.

"Esmé!"

I was pulled out of my admiration for the chamber by none other than the prince himself. He was leaning against the threshold of a separate room, now dressed in casual clothes, washed up, and clean-shaven. He looked so much better and much like his older self now that he was out of that cell and past the full moon. Even his usual smirk was back, and I was utterly breathless again.

"Río," I sighed. "Your room is beautiful."

He rubbed the back of his neck as he made his way toward me. "Thanks. I can't remember the last time I had anyone in here that wasn't my family."

"Oh. Are you sure you're okay with me being here?"

"Yes, absolutely," he said, intertwining his fingers with mine.

His touch always made my heart flutter.

"How are you feeling?" I asked.

"Much, *much* better now. My muscles are a little sore, but I don't feel sick, and I'm steering the ship again. The wolf's asleep. For now, anyway. I'm still dealing with other changes, but nothing that you should worry about."

"Good. It's good to see you looking better. I was really worried."

Río unlaced one of his hands from mine to tuck my hair behind my ear.

"Esmé…" he said softly, "Did you mean what you said last night?"

"What part?" I asked.

"About wanting me but being too scared?"

I furrowed my brow in bewilderment, unsure of what he was referring to, only to widen my eyes. My face flamed in complete mortification.

"You remember that?" I blurted out.

"Of course I do," he chuckled.

"You were a werewolf! I hadn't given you the potion yet! I guess I thought you wouldn't remember."

"I didn't think I would either, to be honest, but...Does that mean you didn't mean it?"

"No! I mean, yes! Yes, I meant it. I... I do," I stammered, feeling even more embarrassed than fearless at the moment.

"And are you still scared now?" he asked warily.

There was an instinctive part of me that wanted to say "yes." Perhaps that was partially true, but it would also be a lie. Before all of this, I was too scared to even speak or act, but now I wanted to do the opposite despite my fear. I wanted to be brave, even if it was hard. Lucky for me, Río made it less so.

"No," I answered simply, startling myself.

There was a spark in his eyes, but that nerves were still there, which was rare for the Moon Prince. For once, *he* was the one having trouble with his words.

"Esmé, I... I'm so sorry," he said.

I frowned. "For what?"

"For hurting you in any way. For making you feel like I broke my promise or like I never cared about you enough. For not protecting you."

I shook my head, squeezing his hand. "Río, it's okay."

"No, it's not. You don't understand, I..."

He cursed under his breath, and I burned with anticipation. When he managed to gather himself, he put his warm hands on either side of my head, boring his dark eyes into mine.

"Esmé, you mean more to me than I have ever been able to comprehend. I don't know why, but from the moment I met you, I knew I wanted to be a part of your life, and I wanted you to be a part of mine. That's not something I've felt with just anyone. I wanted to know your hobbies, your likes and dislikes, your favorite color, and your thoughts about the weather."

I melted then, feeling my heart yearning to spill out anew.

"But as you can see, my world is insane, and I didn't want to drag you into it," he explained. "I thought that if I did, it would ruin everything. It wouldn't be the first time. I thought you would run away or that you would change for the worse, but I was wrong."

As courageous as I wanted to be, I knew there was still one major obstacle in our lives.

"There's still time," I half-joked. "We still don't know what's in my head, Río. I'm an enigma. There's been no progress. My magic is abnormal. I just want you to be sure—"

"*I am*," he said firmly. "We'll figure it out. I don't care. Don't you get it? I want *you*. Not the magic you wield or who you were in the past...*you*. You said that there was more to me than this curse. Well, that statement goes both ways."

I was a crying mess now as I placed my hands on his wrists. All I could muster in this overwhelming devotion was a whisper of his name.

"Río."

He wiped away my tears and kissed me softly on the lips.

"Maybe I shouldn't have done what I did, but I meant what I said to Captain Dominic. I would protect you with my life, Esmé. Because you deserve it. You deserve *everything*, and I want to give you everything," he said fervently. "I'm done hiding. I want you too, and if you want me to stay, I will."

These were the first tears I shed with no sorrow behind them. It was all so surreal, like a dream I was scared to wake up from. What I felt for the Moon Prince was beyond words. There was an overflowing daylight inside me, but this time it blossomed from just how much I've come to love Río Markaél and knowing he felt the same way. He was willing to fight past anything to be by my side, even my self-doubt. It empowered me.

I balled my fists in his shirt and said, "I already told you. I will always want you to stay."

I pushed myself up on my toes, and Río met me halfway, molding his lips to mine. With all of our feelings laid bare and no words left to speak, all that was remained was the complete and utter desire that drove our bodies. I wanted so badly to lose myself to him back in the dungeon, but there was no time or space for us to truly give in to the longing that accrued in us. Even now, I was scared someone might cut our time short and found myself shaking when I found my voice again.

"Río," I panted as he placed warm kisses on my neck. "Río, I don't know how much time we have, but I want—-"

"No one will bother us here," he said, looking into my eyes. "I made sure of it."

My pulse thrummed even faster knowing I had the world—*him*—at my fingertips. My head was empty, but for the need to be at *his* fingertips and mercy—to be ravaged and become one with him.

"You don't need to ask. My body is yours," I said.

Río moaned as if my mere statement undid him, "Yes."

With my help, he took off his shirt and quickly discarded it on the floor. He then grabbed my hips and pressed me against him. His tongue brushed against my own as his fingers tangled in my hair, making me sigh against his mouth. I let my hands explore the familiar facets of his body before disconnecting from him to kiss his neck and chest, suckling so it would leave a mark later.

I inhaled sharply as Río spun me around and began working down the laces of my dress. He did it with equal parts precision and desperation. I ached with every passing second.

He kissed the shell of my ear and whispered, "I'm going to devour every inch of you, and you can be as loud as you want."

I whimpered in reply as a shiver ran down my body.

As soon as I was able to slip out of my clothes, Río carried me to the bed and placed me down on my back. He stayed true to his word, planting greedy kisses all over my skin, but was extra affectionate around my scar. He kissed between the valley of my breasts and then took one in his mouth. With his eyes on me, he circled his tongue around my nipple and massaged the other, eliciting gasps of pleasure from me as he went back and forth. He slowly traced one of his hands down my stomach until it was between my legs, brushing against my core. I instinctively bucked into him with a moan.

He took his attention away from my breasts to look me in the eyes as he teased my wet folds and traced circles around my aching clitoris.

"Fuck, Esmé," he groaned.

I circled my hips against his hand, eager for more. He inserted one finger and then another inside me.

"Río, please," I gasped.

"Gods, I love when you say it like that. But I want you to come in my mouth, okay?"

I nodded, restless and wanting.

I thought it would be me lying on the bed while he devoured me. Instead, it was the prince on his back, asking me to sit on his face.

"Are you sure?" I asked, looking down at him.

"Oh, I'm more than sure."

"Won't I suffocate you?"

Río laughed. "What a beautiful way to die."

I rolled my eyes playfully but did as he asked. I straddled his face and lowered myself down gently until I could feel his hot breath on my pussy and his nose grazing my clitoris. I throbbed in response. Río took hold of my thighs and pulled me down the rest of the way. My gasp was quickly cut short as the prince licked me with his tongue. A strangled moan left my lips, and I immediately grabbed the headboard to steady myself. I glanced down at Río's face between my legs as he smirked with his eyes. I would've glared at him were it not for the completely marvelous image and feeling of him eating me out like dessert on a platter. He was ruthless with his tongue; not an inch of me was spared, and the feeling was so delicious, I couldn't help how loud I was.

I moved my hips against his face, curling my fingers into his hair, but as I neared my climax, Río tightened his grip to stop me from moving. He moved his tongue faster and sucked on my clitoris, building up my pleasure until my orgasm ripped through me in waves and I was crying out.

Río lapped me up as I drooped against the headboard. When he was done, he ran his hand over my thigh lovingly before tapping twice. I carefully got up from his face, and he sat up to kiss me. I could still taste myself on his mouth.

"How was that?" he asked.

"I think I rather like having your face between my thighs," I replied breathlessly.

"It is one of my favorite places to be, yes," he said with a grin.

With a scoff, I kissed him again before letting my gaze trail down to his erection. That heat of desire continued to unfurl deep in me and I was invigorated now, still craving more.

"Can I try something?" I whispered.

"Anything."

"Lie back down again. Please."

His dark eyes flashed with glee. "Oh…why, yes, my lady."

I gave him a gentle push, and Río let himself fall backwards on the mattress with a soft bounce. He rested his arms behind his head, ever the picture of cool and arrogant, as he watched my every move. I made sure not to avert my gaze as I proceeded to straddle his hips and watched his faltering expression. He choked out a nervous laugh, and I couldn't help my smile.

"Moon and fucking stars, Esmé," he uttered.

The prince's calloused hands found my thighs once more, and he gave them a light squeeze. My mouth fell open as I rolled my hips against his length, and a low groan left his lips. What I would do to bottle up the sound for my safekeeping. There was something so pleasing about the effect I had on Río. Seeing him, a prince—*my* prince—pinned under me was an absolute vision.

I splayed my hands against his chest, feeling his strong heartbeat beneath my touch.

"You're so pretty," I told him.

"And I'm all yours."

I clung to those words, reeling.

"Mine," I said aloud, testing it. "And I'm yours."

His eyes were like the night sky as they beheld me.

"Mine," he repeated.

Hearing him say it ignited something in me. I was no one's property, yet I liked the idea of belonging to *one* person like *this*.

I leaned forward, pressing my lips to his and ground against him, feeling him slide against my vulva. I furrowed my brow and let out a whine.

"Say it again," I murmured.

He brushed his nose against mine and repeated, "You're mine. And I'm yours."

I reached between his legs and took his dick in my hand. I lined him up with my entrance before slowly lowering until he filled me completely, both of us moaning in ecstasy. With no more pause, I moved up and down, making us feel good with every stroke as Río seized my hips. He felt so good inside me, so perfect, and I let him know that with every pleasurable sound that came out of me. I felt powerful like this, and I could tell it was exactly how Río wanted me to feel because he relished every second of it.

His hands moved over my stomach, breasts, and neck, kneading my skin.

"That's my girl. Fuck, you feel so good. You look so perfect. I wish you could see yourself," he said in between breaths.

I leaned forward and Río pushed my hair out of my face and traced the soft skin of my lips with his thumb. It all became too much.

"Take me, Río. Fuck me," I begged.

Not needing to be asked twice, he flipped me over so I was under him and thrust into me at a fast, bruising pace. I clutched on to him, digging my nails into his back with nothing but sounds leaving me. There was something primal in the way he moved, his skin slapping against mine. It nearly knocked the wind out of me, but it felt so good, I never wanted him to stop. And with his eyes on mine, we were both pushed over the edge, my body shaking beneath him.

Río let his head fall into the crook of my neck and we melted into each other's arms. Unable to move anything else, I ran my fingers through his hair with my eyes closed as his chest rose and fell with mine. After a few blissful moments, he pulled himself out and lay down next to me.

"Still alive, sunshine?"

"Yeah," I replied dazedly.

When I finally opened my eyes, Río's hair was all messed up and his face was flushed. It was incredibly adorable.

"You're a goddess," he said, pushing my hair out of my face.

I giggled in reply.

He gave me a soft, tender kiss—one that turned me into putty. He then looked into my eyes with a pleading expression.

"Stay."

My lips widened into a feline smile. "Oh, how the tables have turned."

He glared playfully. "Yeah, except this time, neither of us is leaving. I've got nowhere better to go. Do you?"

"No."

"Then stay. Have coffee with me." He kissed my neck before burying his face in it. "Stay. Forever."

His muffled voice tickled my skin, making me laugh, though the request endeared me so. I'm almost certain I was still a prisoner, which meant I technically wasn't supposed to be·here, but who was I to disobey a request from the prince?

I wrapped my arms around him, holding him tightly as I said, "Fine, I'll stay."

Forever.

33

The Dangerous Sea

Río

Trays of empty coffee cups and mostly devoured pastries sat on the bed before us, the majority of which were mine. Despite already having breakfast, I was still ravenous, as if my body was trying to make up for the transformation. Only when I finished every bite did I sit against the pillows with my hands behind my head, feeling giddy.

Esmé looked utterly breathtaking. She'd argue against it, but there was something beautiful about her tousled brown hair and the fact that she was wearing nothing but my shirt. It was the intimacy of it all—sharing the bed, lying in each other's arms, and wasting the morning away. To think I had been missing it this whole time.

Never again.

As if sensing me staring, she took a glance in my direction and furrowed her brow.

"What?"

"I adore you," I said.

She rolled her eyes, looking away as a blush colored her cheeks. My grin only deepened further. I was starting to think that one of my favorite hobbies was flustering this girl of mine.

I hummed to myself. *Mine.* Oh, how I could scream it from the rooftops, but even *I* wasn't that impulsive.

"You know, there's something I've been meaning to talk to you about," she said.

"Oh? What is it?"

Esmé turned to me, cocking her head to the side with mischief in her eyes. As she crawled towards me silently like cat. Thinking it was some playful, sexual advance, I chuckled, but as soon as she was close enough, she jabbed me in the side with her finger, making me recoil. I gave her an incredulous look.

"What the f-what was that for?"

"You didn't tell me you had healing magic this whole time!" she blurted out, pointing to the spot where she poked me.

It was the placement of my latest scar and the one she happened to stitch up. My curse sped up the healing process, but it was the largest one to date and hard to miss.

I cringed apologetically, suddenly stammering, "I-I can actually explain. There's a reason for that."

"Oh, really?" she asked, crossing her arms.

"Yes."

"Okay, then, explain."

Esmé glared at me, but I could tell it wasn't out of genuine anger or betrayal. No, she was obviously irritated and took great amusement in my nerves. And I *was* nervous. I didn't like lying to her, so I didn't do it often. I simply omitted certain details of my nightly excursions. Thankfully, she never asked out of politeness. Although in the grand scheme of things, this lie wasn't covering up anything horrendous at all. Quite the opposite. Somehow, that flustered me more than anything else.

With a deep sigh, I said, "I didn't tell you that I had healing magic because I liked it when you would stitch me up yourself. Granted, I almost told you that the first time, but when you offered to help, I just couldn't say no. It was nice to be taken care of by you, so I never mentioned it."

Esmé's expression immediately relaxed, and she uncrossed her arms, letting them fall into her lap. She stared at me for a long moment, somewhere between confusion and endearment, as I anxiously awaited her response.

"That's why you still have the scar?" she asked, her voice light. Her touch was soft this time as she brushed her fingers over it. "*All* of these scars?"

Her touch fluttered over the places where my skin split open, and she put me back together. I shuddered in response. There weren't many, and some didn't leave a mark at all, but they all meant something. And I could tell she remembered every single one the same way I did.

"Yes," I uttered. "All of them."

"Why?"

I kept my eyes trained on her beautiful face as she continued to map out the scars like constellations. I was so entranced by her affection, her closeness, and the way she simply existed here with me in this way. I almost forgot to speak.

"To keep those memories of you with me," I said.

Esmé looked up in surprise, her brown eyes radiant.

"This whole time I was asking for love letters and flowers, but I think this is probably the most romantic thing you've ever done. Is that strange to say?"

I let out a surprised chuckle and shook my head. "No. No, it's not. At least not to me."

I tucked a piece of her hair behind her ear before leaning in to kiss her softly. She tasted of coffee and sugar—strong, but sweet like her.

She pulled away to point an admonishing finger at me and say, "But please, for the love of the moon and stars, use magic from now on. I would rather you don't bleed out than come to me."

I threw my head back and barked out a laugh.

"Río!"

"Fine," I conceded. "I will. I've got werewolf blood now, so healing will be a lot easier anyway."

"Good."

With her point made, Esmé rested her head against my shoulder and laced her fingers with mine, nestling into me. I rested my head against hers as we both sat in comfortable silence.

In these soft and tender moments, I was always too afraid to move a muscle or say the wrong thing. From the beginning, I took Esmé's boundaries very seriously. I never wanted to push her to do anything she didn't want to, and she didn't seem like the type to initiate affection, so I was always careful to ask her permission first. I was raised a gentleman after all, and my parents would have my head if I acted otherwise. I also knew that my status as a prince could be intimidating, and the last thing I wanted was to scare Esmé away. So, whether or not we crossed a certain boundary was up to her, and a lot of the time, we did. From the first time we kissed, I don't think either of us could ever truly get enough.

Now, the physical touch was almost second nature, and it had nothing to do with sex, either. It was the reassuring touches, the hand-holding, cuddling, and being in each other's space. Something permanently changed between us, and for the first time since meeting her, I could tell that Esmé felt *truly* safe with me. And I knew in my heart that I felt safe with her.

I unconsciously brushed my thumb against the back of her hand.

"How are you feeling?" I asked.

"Right now? Very happy," she replied.

"No headaches?"

"Not at the moment."

"Good."

We stayed like that for a while, in each other arms, until Esmé started to fidget. If I didn't have this strange new sense of hearing, then I would've deduced something was bothering her, but the literally change in her heart was confirmation. I was going to bring it up when she spoke up before me.

"Río?"

"Yeah?"

She hesitated and went quiet again. I furrowed my brow and kissed her on the head in reassurance.

"What's wrong?" I asked.

"I was wondering…What happened with Silas?"

Now, it was my turn to shut my mouth. I shifted uncomfortably as my heart thudded blatantly in my chest.

I knew this day would come eventually. She asked about it once before and I told her it was something stupid that didn't matter, but it did. It mattered a lot, which is why it wasn't easy for me to talk about. But I couldn't keep this part of my life a secret forever, not from her. It was something that still haunted me in many ways despite the years that have passed.

She sat up and looked into my eyes worriedly.

"Río?"

Esmé may know me as a beast and even a rogue, but she didn't fully know the most integral part of *Príncipe* Río Markaél's story. It terrified me to pull the words out, but it was better she heard the truth from the source than left to puzzle out gossip and lies.

✻☽○☾✻

My mother never had a good relationship with her father, the Air King, especially after my uncle died. When she renounced the Vórtice throne to marry my father, that animosity worsened. For many years, they didn't speak to each other outside of council meetings, but following the rise of the Sun Killer, things changed. The Rift was created, and homes and lives were lost, breaking the country in many irreparable ways. So after my sister was born, my mother decided to call a "truce" for the sake of family and country. By some miracle, my grandfather accepted.

From the time I was about five years old, my family spent many years traveling between the air and moon kingdoms. We'd visit the capital city of Nevlina for special occasions, holidays, and birthdays, and my grandfather would visit Coáraluna with the same intent. He didn't always uphold his end of the deal, but when we did see him, he came bearing gifts in the form of criticism. Other times, we'd spend weeks at Lake Respiró, which is where my parents first met when they were kids.

Most of the friends I made in the Air Kingdom were children of high nobility, but there was one particular group I was very close with for years. This group consisted of me, Lorena Silva, Silas Calicó and his cousin, Felix. For a long time, the four of us were inseparable, or so it seemed. In actuality, we enabled each other's bad behavior, which was a recipe for disaster when you were a teenager.

Lorena and I immediately fell into the equivalent of young love and were together from the ages of 13 to 16. She was always the proper lord's daughter while being a fiend behind closed doors. She was also incredibly spoiled, beautiful, and demanding, and got a sense of enjoyment from watching me act on my impulses and risky behavior. At the time, it was a delight trying to impress her and make her laugh, but now I had a feeling she simply liked seeing how far she could make me go.

Silas was the epitome of a daddy's boy in a derogatory way. He always flaunted what he had, even if it technically wasn't his. He pretended like he knew everything, which meant we were always getting into arguments. And because he had no magic and too much money, he liked chasing thrills and inciting chaos where he could. Somehow, we were the best of friends, and I think it had something to do with our competitive nature and adolescent need to fit in. He wanted to be liked by the Moon Prince, and I wanted to be liked by someone who wasn't my family.

Felix, however, was a different story. He was Silas's indolent cousin on his mother's side, who, for the most part, didn't seem to take life seriously at all. He didn't argue like Silas did and wasn't particularly competitive. Most of the time, he was laughing at our antics, making jokes, or drinking too much. He was fun—albeit strange—company to keep, until all of a sudden, he wasn't. He'd get a little too loud, or take a joke too far, or—even worse—flirt with Lorena for fun. It set me off like nothing else, especially when I explicitly told him not to. It nearly resulted in a few physical fights, but Lorena always held me back, telling me it was harmless and amusing.

During this time, I didn't have the best relationship with Mariela. I very adamantly wanted to be a hyper-independent, rebellious teenager who was too cool to spend time with his little sister. And shamefully, I was bitter over her deafness. My parents spent years trying to conceive and were so preoccupied with her that I didn't see the point in having *me* around to watch. The last thing I wanted was to be responsible for her when I had my own priorities, but that all changed when I was 16.

One summer day, my friends and I spontaneously decided to spend the day at Brisa Cove, which was a private beach we frequented. This time, however, my mother insisted I take my 12-year-old sister along for the trip. She had no animal companion yet and had very few friends to begin with, so it was up to *me* to provide them. I was irate and vehemently protested, but my mother threatened to ground me, so I was forced to concede lest the trip be ruined entirely. And with sheer reluctance, I dragged my sister with me to Brisa Cove.

At first, everything seemed fine. In my mind, Mariela was fully capable of taking care of herself and didn't need me to baby her. What we did do, unfortunately, was bicker. She complained about feeling excluded, but no one else but me knew sign language. All the while, my friends would giggle as they watched us engage in silent, frustrated conversation, which, at the time, vexed me greatly. To solve the problem, I started actively ignoring her and chose to have *fun* instead.

While Mariela mostly stuck to the sand, the rest of us swam in the water. We took our boards with us to surf the waves, and to Silas' detriment, I was the best at it (contrary to popular belief, I don't cheat). When we were tired out and finally had enough, we sat around a small fire and talked as we ate and drank. Felix brought out a guitar and started playing, albeit not that well, but it was entertaining nonetheless. Then, at some point, Silas and Felix started talking to Ela with hand gestures that didn't mean anything, which, for a while, seemed to make her laugh. Though she seemed nervous at first, the conversation appeared relatively harmless. She seemed to be having a good time, which, to me, felt like some small mission was accomplished.

Lorena took the opportunity to have me all to herself and turned my attention away from what was happening on the other side of the campfire. We kissed with our backs against a log, and suddenly I was lost. The cove got quieter, things started heating up, and out of nowhere... there was a scream. I stopped what I was doing and snapped to attention. Only realizing then that Silas, Felix, and my sister were gone.

The hairs on the back of my neck stood on end.

"What was that? Where did they go?" I asked.

"I don't know. They probably went exploring," Lorena said.

She tried turning me back to her, but then another scream echoed through the cove. A deep sense of fear hit me like a gut punch, and I pushed away from Lorena, scrambling to my feet. I scanned the entire area around us, searching for my sister and my friends with the little sunlight that was left.

"Silas!" I shouted. "Felix!

"They're probably at the cave," Lorena said, not nearly as bothered as I was.

The blood drained from my face. I should've trusted them. They were my friends, after all, yet every fiber of my being told me otherwise.

I bolted through the sand, making a beeline for the cave I knew so well. Lorena called out for me, but I was already too far gone. I couldn't shake the sense that something was wrong. When I reached the mouth of the rocky opening, I came to a screeching halt. Seawater pooled around my ankles before receding as my eyes found Silas and his cousin a few feet away. They were illuminated by a makeshift torch; their backs were turned to me, sopping wet. Felix was laughing, and they were staring at something I couldn't see.

"Look what you did, you fucking idiot," Silas hissed, smacking him in the shoulder. "Now his royal highness is going to—oh shit."

As if sensing me, Silas turned around, his eyes as big as saucers. With another smack from him, Felix stopped laughing.

"What the fuck is going on here?" I demanded. "Where's Ela?"

"She—We were just having fun and—"

The sound of crying pulled my attention to the interior of the cave, and I stopped caring about what either of them had to say. I pushed past them, and my stomach dropped. There, in the corner, sat my little sister, crying with her knees tucked against her chest. Seeing her look so tiny and vulnerable opened a door in me that was otherwise closed. I ran over and dropped to my knees in front of her.

"Are you okay? What happened?" I signed.

Mariela didn't look physically hurt, but she was sopping wet and shaking with fright. She didn't respond with her words but threw a nasty glare over my shoulder at Felix.

Like a coursing river, a current of rage flowed within me. I straightened up and turned my furious gaze towards them. Lorena had joined the group, looking lost. I was too angry to hear her questions. I was too busy assuming horrible things.

"What the fuck did you do to her?" I snapped.

Felix groaned, "Come on, Max, we were just having fun."

I marched up to him shouting, "What? Did? You? Do?"

The tide flowed deeper into the cave, unnerving Felix. Silas put a hand on my shoulder, trying to calm me down.

"Easy. We were just trying to help."

"Help her with what?"

"To swim."

I craned my head back in shock. Everyone in my family knew that Mariela was scared of the ocean. My friends should have known that. She was getting better about it, but she almost drowned once before. Her lack of hearing intensified it for her.

"She said she didn't know how, but I thought she was lying. So I grabbed her and threw her in," Felix explained casually. "Turns out she wasn't lying at all."

He laughed as if it were the funniest thing in the world, but to me, every word was a nail in his coffin.

"The Moon Princess really can't swim," he added.

My fist collided with Felix's nose with a crack. He stumbled back, his hands flying to his face, where blood dripped down his nostrils. Everyone shouted my name as I shoved him hard.

"Are you fucking stupid? You could've killed her!" I yelled. "If someone told you they're afraid of heights you wouldn't throw them off a fucking cliff!"

Silas grabbed me by the shoulders and wrenched me backwards. "Max, calm down!"

I shrugged him off and pointed a finger at him.

"You're no fucking better. You could've stopped him. Why didn't you? I bet you were hoping that she drowned, huh?" I said, pushing him hard. "I bet that would've been hilarious for all of you!"

I don't know what exactly came over me to react in such a way. All I could think of was my mother and how she lost her brother when she was close to my age. They were always stories to me, but now it was all too real.

"Max, stop it! That's a horrible thing to say!" Lorena scolded.

I raised my hands at her questioningly. "I thought you would take my side."

"Not when you're acting like this."

"Acting like 'what'? Like I'm telling the truth?"

"You don't even like your sister anyway," Silas muttered. "It's not like she can be queen. You and the rest of the kingdom would probably be better off if she were dead."

With an incensed scream, I knocked him down to the floor. The torch fell with a clatter as we landed in a tangle of limbs. The two of us struck each other over and over, unleashing all the true hatred that we covered up in the name of friendship. Blood was spilled on both fronts, until I managed to pin him to the ground. The tide crashed over his face as I growled, making him choke on seawater.

"Río, stop!" Lorena screamed.

Silas coughed. "You're fucking crazy."

Felix came up from behind to pull me away from his cousin. In my blind rage, I swung at him, but as I moved, a wave came along with it and sent him flying against the cave wall. When the water pulled back to the ocean, his body lay crumpled on the floor. His eyes were closed, and a small pool of blood started growing around his head.

Lorena shrieked in horror. My veins ran cold as I looked down at my hands.

"I didn't… I didn't mean to."

That's never happened before.

Through blurred vision, I watched Silas and Lorena rush to Felix's side as they tried but failed to wake him up. Too afraid to see the outcome, I ran out of the cave and threw up at the water's edge. When I turned back around, my body shaking, Mariela was standing halfway down the sand, her eyes wide.

"Is he alive?" I signed weakly.

She nodded. "I healed him, but he's barely breathing."

I heaved a sigh of relief and almost vomited all over again.

I didn't kill him. I'm not a murderer.

Somehow, that didn't make me feel any better.

My sister stared at me with tears in her eyes. She took a few tentative steps forward and then, all at once, ran into me, wrapping her thin arms around my torso. At first, I was too stunned to return the gesture. We never really hugged unless we were forced to, at least not since we were little. Yet, at that moment, the embrace meant something more than words could put together. It was a comfort and the beginning of a new bond.

THE MOON PRINCE

We were the only ones who understood what it meant to be us, and I couldn't let something like that happen to her ever again.

I recounted the story with my head against the pillow and my eyes trained on the ceiling above. It was all I could do to keep focusing on the painted stars instead of Esmé's face, as I was too afraid to see her expression.

I naively assumed I accepted the happenings of that day long ago, but ever since meeting Esmé, I have found myself trying to hide my past. My family was well aware of what transpired, but they never treated me like a monster, even when others did. Esmé, however, was shiny and new in my world, so everything I've ever done seemed twisted compared to her kindness and selflessness. Somehow, turning into a werewolf paled to the decisions I made as a human.

"It was a whole fiasco," I continued. "Because it happened in the Air Kingdom, my grandfather took it to his court. Luckily, my parents are great at arguing, so when Ela and I told them exactly what happened, they were our advocates through and through. My mother was pissed about what they did to my sister and said that my reaction was warranted. But, unfortunately, my grandfather is an asshole.

"Lorena and the Calicó family were all against me, seeing as I tried drowning Silas and nearly killed Felix. And because they were from the Air Kingdom, my grandfather favored them. He said it was... *unbecoming* of a member of the God-given to commit such acts. He said that we shouldn't be using our gifts so foolishly, because it makes us no better than the Sun Killer."

Esmé scoffed, "So... you were punished?"

"As much as my parents would allow. I was banned from the Air Kingdom until I turned 21. Just me. But my parents would have none of it. At the same time, they banned Lorena and Silas's family from setting foot in the Moon Kingdom. My mom said 'fuck you' to my grandfather, cut him off, and we never saw him again."

Even though my sentence ended two years ago, I haven't stepped foot in Nevlina, Valerta, or any of the northern cities in seven years. At least not in the daylight.

I finally dared to look at Esmé, who was cross-legged, watching me with in distress. She was quiet for a while, as if unsure what to say.

"Were you...close to your grandfather?" she asked gingerly.

I shook my head. "No, not really. He's a control freak, was horrible to my mother growing up, and never really liked Mariela and me to begin with."

"Why didn't he like you?"

"As far as he knows, neither of us inherited the Vórtice abilities. He was an asshole about Ela's deafness, just like everyone else. Not to mention, he never liked my father."

My father was my grandfather's opposite in every possible way that mattered, which is why they didn't get along. It didn't matter that my father was a God-given or a respected man. He even opposed his relationship with my mother and didn't attend their wedding. And I think I'm a little too much like my father for Saévio Vórtice II's liking.

Esmé scowled at the whole ordeal. It was oddly comforting to know she felt the same way.

"What happened to Felix?" she asked apprehensively.

I looked at the ceiling again as guilt squeezed at my insides.

"He's still alive, but... he has no memory of what happened. He also hasn't been the same since. Lorena broke up with me after that, saying that I overreacted and she couldn't be with someone like me, which was heartbreaking and disappointing. Silas didn't waste time flocking to her side and providing her a shoulder to cry on. Now, they're married and expecting a child. Figures."

"Sounds like they're perfect for each other," Esmé grumbled.

I snorted. "Unfortunately, even the worst people get a happy ending."

It was ironic how my 'friends' wanted me around because of who I was, but when that stopped being fun, they all turned their backs on me. I tried so hard to fulfill the oxymoronic task of being anybody else with the intent of finding myself, but a reality like mine always caught up. So many people wanted magic like mine, but didn't know the burden it came with. I did not have Felix's luxury of being apathetic. There were more things out there than comparing amounts of money, and there was more to love than constant performance. It cost me greatly to realize that.

Esmé took my hand and held it in her lap. A lump formed in my throat at the utter compassion in she looked at me with.

"I'm sorry that happened, Río. You deserved better than that."

"Yeah, well, some would say that's debatable."

"Not anyone who matters," she derided. "Besides, it's not your fault."

"I mean, at least part of it is. It would've never happened if I took care of Ela. I should've protected her," I argued.

"People make mistakes. You were a child. I hardly think that most teenagers are that aware of their actions."

"Yes, but I should have been!" I sat up now, riled up. "I don't have the privilege of messing up. And I messed up more than once that day. My mom might not treat me like a monster, but I know she's disappointed."

"That doesn't make you a bad person. I don't think your sister would have gone to you otherwise."

My shoulders dropped. Her tone was so gentle despite its firmness that I found it hard to keep raising my voice.

She leaned close to my face, her doe eyes swallowing me whole as she said, "Silas was wrong. I think Marisláni would be proud to call you her champion. And I, for one, like the sea for *all* its traits anyway."

I took her into my arms, pressing her against my chest to feel her close and let her remarkable statement wash over me. She wrapped her arms around my waist and nuzzled into me. There were so many things I wanted to express, but this love was too great to describe, especially when I never thought I would have it, let alone deserve it. I just hoped that one of these days I could find the right words to match its profundity.

34

Fever

Esmé

There was a knock at the door, and Río groaned.

"Who is it?"

"Your mother." *Reina* Victoria's voice was strong through the door.

"Oh shit."

With no other warning, the doors burst forth. I let out a tiny squeak and dove under the sheets to hide the fact that I was half naked. Río snickered beside me, and I peeked out from under the linen to smack him in the arm. The prince sat against the pillows with a grin, completely unfazed, as he was the only one wearing pants.

"Ma, some decorum, please," he said tiredly.

"Please, the two of you have been locked up in here long enough. You wasted no time breaking my rules the second you left that dungeon. Do you ever learn, Río Markaél?"

"Old habits die hard, I guess."

"Esmé is still technically our prisoner, you know."

I tensed at the thought of being bound and forced back to my tower again. Thankfully, Río protested.

"I thought the two of you were okay now," he argued. "Hasn't she proved herself enough? After all, she didn't kill me in my sleep."

"Yet," I whispered.

The prince frowned at me, and when I gave him a playful grin, he shook his head.

He glanced up at his mother and said, "Yet. But if she does, it would probably be my fault."

"That I don't doubt," the queen said. "Still, she has her mind to worry about, and you have a kingdom to attend to. Especially after the full moon."

Río closed his eyes, baring his teeth in a grimace.

"I almost forgot about that."

My eyes widened—*the flood.*

Forgetting my embarrassment, I shot up, still covering my lower half. I quickly brushed my fingers through my hair as I looked at the queen in concern.

"Is everyone alright?" I asked.

"There weren't any casualties, thankfully, but there's still some damage. After all, most of our fisheries and farmland are down there."

"What about *Teatro Paraíso* or the Larimar District? Canela?"

"*Teatro Paraíso* and the Upper Districts are okay. The Obsidian District has a bit more water damage, and the smaller posts aren't doing so great. Canela is fine. She's been helping out where she can. Nothing that can't be fixed, hopefully."

That provided me some semblance of relief, thought I couldn't say the same for Río. He ran his hands over his face in shame and braced himself on the bed.

"It's not your fault," I repeated. "You weren't aware."

"No, but it's the beast's fault, and now I have to clean up its mess," he muttered.

"That's actually what I came here for," *Reina* Victoria said. "Ela went down this morning to help out with the water damage, and anyone who might have gotten hurt. I think now that you're back to normal, *for now*, it would be good for you to join her. They could use an extra pair of hands, especially for repairing."

Río instantly straightened up, his expression brightening. "Yeah. Yes. Absolutely. When?"

"As soon as possible. It'll be a good way for you to make amends. After all, it's what your father would've done. He was never afraid to get his hands dirty."

Río hummed, "Yeah."

Ah, so it runs in the family.

"Is there any way *I* can help?" I asked eagerly.

"No," they both replied.

I frowned, giving the prince a strange look. "Why not?"

"We don't need people getting curious about you, especially not one of your friends," the queen retorted.

"I could wear a cloak," I contested.

"No," Río repeated firmly.

I narrowed my eyes at him. "I know why she's saying no, but why are *you*?"

"Because I know the water is contaminated. I know what that means," he emphasized. There was a sliver of terror in his eyes. "You didn't hear him that day at the ball, but I did. Sebastián Eliódor wanted to take you with him, and he didn't even know who you were or what you could do."

"You're vulnerable, Esmé," *La Reina* stressed, drawing my attention away from Río. "You might be honing your abilities, but until you get those memories back, you will *stay* vulnerable. Especially when faced with a man like him. A demon's magic flourishes in fear, insecurity, and hatred. If you don't have roots, then it will sow its own."

My shoulders slumped dejectedly. When they first told me about the Sun Killer trying to speak to me, it had all been a blur. The idea was so strange that the meaning behind it didn't truly sink in until now. I was so engrossed in helping Río that I almost forgot who *I* was: a nobody and an anomaly all at once. A nightmare for my people and a dream for a dictator. It hit me like a wave, and my throat tightened. The spirits murmured in my ears—a nonsensical noise. My head grew heavy all over again.

Esmé.

Esmé.

Esmé.

"Esmé!"

Río lightly shook my shoulder, and suddenly everything came back into focus. I looked between him and the queen, who were staring right at me.

The prince brushed his fingers against my cheek, his eyes roving over me. "Are you okay? Did you see something?"

"No, no, I didn't," I uttered slowly.

He furrowed his brow and placed the back of his hand on my forehead. "You feel warm. You're not getting sick, are you?"

"I'm fine, Río," I chuckled, pulling his hand away. "I just got overwhelmed. It's hard not to, all things considered."

"You've been through a lot," the queen said with a nod. "Will you be well enough to attend your lessons today?"

"Yes!" I replied excitedly.

"With no manacles, right?" Río asked very poignantly.

The queen rolled her eyes. "Of course not. How will she perform magic with them on?"

She shot him a sarcastic, feline smile before turning away, towards the door.

"Mom," Río sang, elongating the vowel.

"I'll see you downstairs by the stables, darling! And please put some clothes on."

When she left the room, the two of us shared a reluctant look.

"I guess that's my cue to go," he whispered.

It was never easy hearing those words.

Like many evenings past, *Príncipe* Río rolled out of bed and got dressed as I watched him despondently. This time, his attire was somewhere between princely and casual—fitted black pants, a loose white shirt, and a dark blue vest with gold detailing. With a pair of boots in hand, he walked back toward the bed and deflated when he saw my expression.

"I still hate it when you look at me like that."

"I guess some things don't change," I said in a small voice.

He came over to my side and sat down on the edge of the bed, putting the boots down by his feet.

"Things are different now," he said. "I'm only going to be gone for a few hours. Before you know it, we'll be right back here, in this bed, together."

"Promise?"

"I promise."

He went so far as to hold out his right pinky—a childlike gesture that made me giggle. The prince raised his eyebrows playfully.

"I'm being dead serious."

Still chuckling, I held out my pinky and interlocked it with his to seal the deal.

"I believe you," I told him.

Río put on his boots and turned to me again to run his fingers through my hair. I leaned into his soothing touch, my eyes fluttering for a second.

"I'll have someone bring your stuff here," he said. "You're not going back to that tower if I have something to say about it."

I frowned, unsure if that was a smart idea. "Río…"

He shook his head, putting a stop to my protests.

"Esmé, this is *your* room now. Or you can pick any of the empty ones if you want, but I'm not letting you go back in chains again," he contested.

I caressed his cheek, trying to find the words to say as I held back tears. I grew accustomed to my shackles and being hauled around against my will. As a prisoner, I had no other choice, but experiencing a taste of true freedom with Río made me never want to go back. And *he* was giving me a choice not to.

With watery eyes, I kissed Río on the lips.

"I like your room," I murmured.

"Okay." Río nodded, his eyes alight. "Then make yourself at home. I'll be back soon."

✳ ☽ ○ ☾ ✳

Not long after Río left, Arabella came by to drop off my "things." Ironically, I didn't have many things to my name in *Castillo* Paricia, so all they consisted of was the stack of books Canela gave me and some clothes that weren't even mine. My ring and Río's necklace were already back where they belonged—on my finger and around his neck.

I underwent the same routine of preparing myself for lessons in the greenhouse. Since Mariela was down the island helping with the cleanup, it was just Paloma and me this time. It left me with the daunting task of practicing technique all on my own, but the wizard assured that I was more than capable of doing so. She wasn't wrong. I could feel my magic strengthening every day, yet it never felt like enough. The reminder of that ominous cavern in my mind laden me with desperation to improve. Until this morning, I thought I was doing well, only to be told that I was still vulnerable. It was maddening. How far was I supposed to go, then? If my magic was, in fact, the key to unlocking my memories, what then? What did it mean for me, as a necromancer, to keep advancing? It was obvious, yet it was beyond forbidden. Avilonía burned its dead, and I doubted the queen would ever approve of such practices. So, how was I to use this skill practically? How was I to be useful in a way that defied what the Demon King ever did? How was I supposed to prove my innocence?

I didn't even know who *I* was yet.

"Are you alright, Esmé?"

Beyond the muffling sound of spirits, Paloma's voice brought me out of my thoughts. A soft headache pressed between my eyes, but I shook it off with a smile.

"Yes, I was just lost in thought. It's been a hectic few days," I said.

"That's completely understandable. Even if it was *Alteza*, you survived another werewolf attack," the wizard mused.

"That's very true." *You have no idea.*

Near the end of our lesson, *Reina* Victoria walked into the greenhouse with a velvet box in her hands. I bowed as she placed it on the table and turned to face me with a pondering look.

The wizard stood aside quietly with her hands behind her back. She knew the queen was coming but hadn't informed me as to why. *La Reina*'s visits to the greenhouse were brief, but this time felt very different.

"Is everything alright, *Majestad*?" I asked.

"I have a question for you, Esmé," she said.

"Yes?"

"You've improved vastly this past week, and I've heard nothing but good things about your magic so far. The spirits seem to have a positive response to you, all things considered, and I know that one of them was my late brother, Savy."

I nodded in reply.

"So, I guess my question is... have you seen my husband, Marino, the Moon King?"

Oh...

I have seen plenty of spirits around the castle, and the Air Prince was the most prominent one. The Moon King, however, I saw once in the ballroom and haven't seen him since.

"No," I answered tentatively.

Reina Victoria furrowed her brow and shared an odd look with Paloma.

"Strange. I would've thought he'd come home after he passed," she said.

"Well, don't spirits sometimes linger around the places where they...*died?*" I offered kindly.

She winced, and I instantly regretted it. I didn't mean to put the image of her husband's soul being tied to The Rift in her mind.

"I'm sorry."

"No, don't apologize. I just..." She trailed off, her eyes scanning the plants around us. Confusion riddled her features. "It just doesn't make sense."

"What doesn't make sense?"

"My brother died fighting a battle in the dunes of the Sun Kingdom. It was such an unforgiving place that they called it the Gods' Arena. I can attest to it, because I barely survived with my own life," she explained before looking back at me. "That was decades ago, in a place that no longer belongs to us or the gods. So tell me, Esmé, why is Saévio here and Mar isn't?"

The fire from the torches danced in her angry eyes as she awaited my reply. It pained me to have no definitive answer for her. I asked the spirits many questions all the time, but I was not a seer, and they knew as much as I did about current events. Of course, it didn't mean I wasn't curious.

It *didn't* make sense, did it?

"Something strange is happening. That's what Saévio said," I told her.

"Strange, indeed. It doesn't *feel* right either, and I'm not talking about the grief."

I almost wanted to ask what she meant, until she turned to the velvet box.

"Sometimes, witches and mediums use personal items to find people." Her hand rested atop it as she asked, "If you held something of his, do you think you'd be able to see him? His spirit?"

I looked to Paloma then, taken aback by the idea, "I-I don't know. I... I've never tried that before."

"It's something we would've touched on down the line, but considering the nature of the king's death, we thought to give it a go now," the wizard said.

The queen opened the box and took out a beautiful silver crown forged to look like crashing waves. It was similar to the one Río wore, except this one had moonstones around the perimeter.

"This was one of Mar's crowns. They always forge multiple, just in case, but he's worn this one before. So I was hoping that, perhaps, you could see something off of it. Anything."

It was such a daunting ask, and I've raised corpses before.

"I—"

"Try," she demanded, and then more graciously added, "Please."

She marched up to me with the crown resting on her shaking hands. There was desperation in her eyes, reminding me that this God-given was just as much of a human as I was. The country lost a king, but she lost the love of her life and the father of her children. Out of all the requests she's asked of me, this one was personal.

"There's no harm in trying, Esmé. If nothing happens, then it's totally fine," Paloma urged kindly.

My chest tightened. It never occurred to me to do such a thing before, so I wasn't sure if it was possible. But when I looked into the queen's eyes, I couldn't find the heart to deny her. Her raw emotion moved me, and I wanted answers, too.

"Okay. I'll do it."

With hope lighting up her face, the queen handed me the silver crown, which was cold to the touch. The moonstones reflected a fiery rainbow in the torchlight, much like the one around the princess' neck. I was shaking, my heart beating fast, but I closed my eyes and did the only thing I knew how to do: open my mind.

The ghosts danced in circles, but instead of focusing on all of them, I chose to hone in on one. I concentrated on the metal crown against my skin. I pictured the Moon King, using his silhouette and the paintings I saw of him around the castle. I envisioned his scaled armor, his beard, and his moon-touched hair.

"Marino?" I called out. "Marino Markaél?"

Truth be told, I expected nothing. The spirits sounded as they always did, speaking odd messages into my ears, but then they became more frantic and anxious. Their voices quickly turned into screams and cries of anguish that sent a chill down my spine.

Don't, they said. *Don't!*

But it was too late.

The world around me darkened, and I was swallowed by the void. I was no longer in the greenhouse but on a ship sailing on a black sea. The deck and sails were on fire, a blazing inferno in the night. Dark, shadowy werewolves tore sailors to pieces. Everyone was dying or throwing themselves overboard to escape the bloodshed. But I could not escape. I was pinned to the floor, my body among the flames. Out of the corner of my eye, a man with burning red hair and matching eyes walked into view. He towered over me as scorching vines came up from behind him and wrapped around my throat.

"You put up a good fight, Mar, I'll give you that. Your family's always been the hardest one to break, but you're in my hands now."

"That's where you're wrong," I choked out, but the voice wasn't mine. "It's going to take more than just killing me."

The red man chuckled, "You're right. That's why I plan on killing your son. You, however, I have other plans for."

His voice fluctuated as if spoken by two people—one human and one demonic. No name was said, but I knew in my mind, body, and soul who it was. This was the man from the missing portrait. The one responsible for the massacre on the winter solstice and so much more.

The Sun Killer.

I gasped as terror struck me. "No!"

My hands flew to the sides of my head, feeling as if it were about to split open. And when I opened my eyes, I was no longer looking up at the Sun Killer but watching the scene from above as myself. The man with the red eyes snapped his head towards me, and my heart sank. He reached his hand out, and suddenly it was wrapped around my throat, and I was inches away from his face. His fiery eyes pierced mine, threatening to burn me as he crushed my neck.

"You," he growled.

Glass shattered. I thrashed and screamed until, in a flash of blue light, I collapsed to the floor. The crown clattered out of my hands, which were now clawing at my throat, fighting off something that was no longer there.

"Esmé!" Paloma and the queen shouted.

Through my tears, I saw them rush to me and fall to their knees. After a moment's apprehension, I was taken by the shoulders and cradled against someone's chest like a child.

"You're here now, Esmé. Breathe," *Reina* Victoria uttered softly.

Unused to such a maternal act, the queen's gentle affection both startled and comforted me. Her words were a soothing balm, and the scent of her vanilla perfume kept me from spiraling. It was a welcoming contrast to the horror I had just witnessed.

When I managed to sit up, the queen's eyebrows shot up, and Paloma gasped. The queen quickly produced a handkerchief from her pocket and handed it to me.

"Here. Your nose is bleeding."

I used it to wipe my nose and even I was surprised to see it stained red.

"What happened? What did you see?" the wizard asked.

"I saw *everything*," I cried softly, my voice wavering. "I saw what happened on the ship. I saw *him*."

"Who?" the queen asked.

"The Sun Killer."

Her eyes darkened. "What did he say?"

I nearly choked on my next words, tasting bile in the back of my throat.

"He wants to kill Río, and he has plans for the king."

The monarch's face hardened into something marble-like. Not a moment later, lightning flashed, followed by the crack of thunder.

"I think he saw me," I whispered sharply.

The queen looked between my eyes diffidently.

"I think that's enough lessons for today."

I trembled from head to toe as I was practically carried back to Río's room. A migraine pressed down on my skull, and in what felt like minutes, I was struck with a heavy fever that left me retching in the bathroom. It seemed so horrid to do such a thing in such a beautiful room, but my body was working against me. The exhaustion caught up, and I was paying the consequences.

Paloma and Arabella got to work straightaway. The handmaiden returned with a jug of water and didn't leave me alone until I chugged an entire glass. She then swiftly changed me out of my sweat-slicked attire and into a comfortable nightgown. Paloma made me a pungent tea to alleviate the nausea and fever that I was also expected to finish. They both insisted I get some sleep, and when I protested, they threatened to bring my manacles back. I didn't have enough fight in me to argue, and eventually the illness removed any desire to leave the bed at all.

I clutched the sheets around my shaking body, feeling cold yet hot at the same time. I couldn't erase the memory of the Sun Killer from my mind. The tar-like smell of the sea continued to linger, as did the acrid scent of blood and smoke. Whispers of spirits seemed to skitter over me like invisible spiders, their tone more mocking and sinister than ever. *His* red eyes still burned bright in my memory, threatening to obliterate me even now. They were the same crimson shade as the werewolves that attacked the palace. If the vision was real, then I saw the Sun Killer with my own eyes.

It almost made me sick again. Almost.

For you, however, I have other plans.

What does that mean? Why did I see a vision and not the Moon King himself? Why *haven't* I seen his spirit? Did the Sun Killer truly see me, and if so, how? More questions with no answers and more answers that I needed to dig for. My mind went around and around in circles until I eventually fell asleep.

I dreamed of obsidian castles and jaguars with sleek, black fur. The tall man in the dark suit was there. "Hold on," he said. But then everything went from black to bloody red. Pitch-black rivers carried bloody bodies. People screamed. Mountains broke apart. The man in the black suit was gone, and his hair was bloody red now, too. Shadows with red eyes chased me, and I ran for my life. But not fast enough.

You're a mistake, Esmé Vespertín, a voice said.

Sebastián Eliódor towered above me again, looking down in disgust with his flaming red eyes. He held a sword in his hands, with a black diamond glittering on the hilt.

"We don't need heroes like you anymore. I'll take it from here."

He plunged the sword into my chest, and I screamed.

I grasped my chest in panic. Hands fell on my shoulders, and in my agitated state, I started shoving them away, afraid that the man with the red eyes was coming back for more.

"No!"

"Esmé."

"Get away from me!"

"Esmé!"

Someone shook me, and as my eyes adjusted, it became clear that I wasn't looking into red eyes but dark ones. Río's eyes, watching me in dismay. I looked around, taking in my surroundings. I was in Río's room, and he was back just like he said.

My jaw dropped as I came to, my vision blurring with tears.

"I'm so sorry," I whispered. "I thought...I was dreaming and then..."

His face softened, and he pulled me against his chest. "It's okay, sweetheart. You're safe now. It wasn't real."

"It felt real," I mumbled against his skin.

Just like my vision.

"I know, but you're here now. It was probably just a fever dream," he murmured.

The nightmare aside, I was still unbelievably ill. I couldn't remember the last time I was this sick, but it would explain the strange, vivid dream. My mind was already a minefield to begin with.

We sat here in the dim firelight as Río held me against the pillows and caressed my hair. I basked in his comforting touch, letting the sound of his steady heart ground me.

"I didn't even hear you come in," I said.

"I did my best not to wake you. I know you needed to rest."

"And then I rudely woke you up. I'm sorry."

He chuckled, "It's okay. I don't mind."

I tried getting up, but my head swam and stars danced before my eyes. My hand shot out to use Río's shoulder as an anchor as I awaited any indication that I might throw up again. He looked at me seriously.

"Did they push you too hard?" he asked.

I shook my pounding head.

"It's fine," I mumbled.

"No, it's not," he said sternly. "What did you see?"

It was obvious they told him about his father's crown and what happened at the greenhouse. I wanted to find some way to describe it, but the memory of a father's final moments was too horrible for a son to hear.

"It's nothing you need to know. The Sun Killer was there. It was terrible. End of story," I whispered. "If anything, *I'm* the one who's been pushing myself too hard."

"I don't blame you for being scared of him, Esmé. But if you're going to use magic like that, you need to take care of yourself. It's not meant to be an unlimited source. It can fuck you up. Look at you!" He touched my forehead and hissed. "Hold on."

Río looked around before hopping out of bed. He disappeared into the bathroom before coming out with a small washcloth. He walked over to the small fountain in the corner of the room, dipped the towel in, and wrung it out.

"Healing magic can't fix a fever, but I know something that can help."

Río came back to bed, and told me to lay back against the pillow. He held the damp down in his hand for a second and I watched as it frosted over slightly. Without protest, I let him place the cold cloth against my forehead. It was startling, but it did a fine job at soothing my aching skin.

"Is that okay?" he asked.

"Mhmmm."

Río moved the cloth around my face and chest gently. It alleviated the heat and pressure that weighed me down all day.

My heart seemed to overflow as I stared at him. He offered to help me in many ways since we met, but I never allowed him to. Of course, it never deterred him from trying. And now that he was taking care of me in this state, I understood why he came to me when he was injured. It was nice to be taken care of, especially by someone you cared about so much. It gave me a better view of the tender side I loved very much.

"How are you feeling?" he asked.

I smiled at him softly. "Better. Thank you."

He gave me a quick kiss on the lips, making them tingle.

"Always."

❊ ☽ ◯ ☾ ❊

The following morning, I was still relatively unwell. No matter what argument I gave, everyone insisted I continue to be bedridden. I hated the idea, but my very protective Moon Prince was unyielding. He even offered to stay with me, but I urged him to keep helping with the cleanup. The idea of keeping him away when he was needed didn't sit well with me, and as always, he promised to come back soon.

After breakfast, I slept most of the morning away. It was all my body wanted to do. The only things that woke me were my meals and checkups. During one of those checkups, Paloma came in with a thick book in hand and an uncharacteristically vacillating expression.

"I know you're not feeling well, so I won't keep you for long, but this was too important to wait," she started. "With everything going on, it took a while for me to find those flowers you've seen in your mind. There aren't many native flora with the description you gave, and it stumped even me, which was very infuriating. There are quite a few that glow in certain parts of the country, but in the end, what I *did* find wasn't anything...*real*."

I frowned. "What do you mean?"

"You can take a look at this book," she said, placing it before me. "I bookmarked the page for you, but if your description is correct, then the flowers you described belong to a realm that isn't in our world."

Part of me expected Paloma to burst out laughing and tell me she was joking, but the punchline never came. Instead, she very seriously urged me to open the book. I immediately flipped to the bookmarked section, and right there, taking up the entire page, was an exact pencil drawing of the bushes in the obsidian cavern—star shaped, bright purple, and long stems. At the bottom, there was a label that read LAELIA, and beside it was a note that read:

A rough sketch of the legendary plant that is said to grow in the domain of the God of Death, also known as the Underworld.

I read the sentence over and over, as if it would change before my very eyes. The world around me seemed to fade beneath the blood rushing in my ears, making me dizzy.

"The Underworld?" I finally blurted out.

The wizard eyed me nervously, as if handling something fragile.

"Maybe you saw them in a book or a painting somewhere. No one's ever seen them in person. It can't be possible," she said.

"Then who drew this picture?" I demanded.

"A witch. Perhaps a seer of some kind. One who was blessed with knowledge."

I scoffed, "But I'm not a seer or a witch! What does the God of Death have to do with *me*?"

The wizard worked her hands ruefully as she tried but failed to produce an answer.

"I… I don't know…"

With my growing sickness, everything sounded as if I were underwater. Should it have surprised me that I was tied to the God of Death somehow, considering my magic? Perhaps not. Whether that tie was created with nefarious intentions was a mystery. I may know Canela's opinion of Micqui, but I also knew how the queen viewed him, and unfortunately, fear often overshadowed truth. My relationship with her may have improved over time, but this piece of information could be enough evidence for her to return me to my tower, if not sentence me to death itself.

"Does the queen know?" I asked.

"Not yet. I wanted to tell you first," Paloma replied.

I relaxed, if only a fraction. For that, at the very least, I was grateful.

"Well, don't tell anyone yet, please," I implored tremulously. "I know your loyalty is to *Majestad* and her family, but if you could just…give me some time. At least to learn more."

Paloma's face softened in what I assumed was compassion.

"I'll do what I can. I want to solve this just as much as you do, Esmé. I love the queen very much, but in this case, I'm willing to...*omit* certain things for the sake of answers, because this affects everyone, not just you. Clearly, pieces of this puzzle are still missing, and one shouldn't make choices without the full picture."

"Thank you," I sighed.

"Of course. There's only so much time I can give you, but I really think you should look into those books Canela let you borrow. I have a feeling you might find something good. Something *true*. The God of Death wasn't always a bad omen; even I know that."

"You're not the first person to tell me that," I uttered warily. "I hope, for everyone's sake, that it's true."

"I have to believe it is."

We stared at each other in tense silence—her gaze pleading and mine exhausted in every possible way. Eventually, the wizard excused herself, and for a long while, I stared down at the picture of the Laelia intensely. The heat in my skin rose with my fear and deepening self-doubt, making everything heavy again. But I couldn't sleep. I refused to sleep until I found more answers.

Through my feverish haze, I searched through Canela's books with trembling hands until I found the one about Micqui, the God of Death.

Known by many names, Micqui, the God of Death, is said to have been forged out of obsidian stone at the peak of a new moon. Needing someone to oversee matters of the afterlife, the gods of the sun, moon, earth, and air appointed Micqui ruler of the Underworld. Though many believe that Micqui himself is a harbinger of death, he is more of an usher of spirits. Even more so, he is widely known to those who worship him as a protector of lost souls, a purveyor of transformation, and a bringer of justice. Thus earning him the title of "The Adjudicator." Nothing is hidden from the God of Death, for he is merciless in his judgment. He brings decay to nurture the new.

There were more paragraphs about symbolism, worship, and finally, the Underworld itself.

According to legend, the Underworld is divided between what is known as the Virtuous Forest and the Black Mirror. The Virtuous Forest is the land in which the righteous souls come to rest in the afterlife of their dreams. The path to the forest is said to be lined with Laelia flowers, a glowing plant that sprouts from the very cracks of Micqui's obsidian domain. The Black Mirror, however, is a black, lightless sea in which wicked souls are judged before its reflection, drowned, and forced to live their worst nightmares for eternity. The God of Death himself is said to live in a third neutral space within the Underworld, where he resides in a castle made of volcanic glass.

I must have re-read that paragraph about a hundred times. Although the Black Mirror was new to me, I knew about The Virtuous Forest. How I could have missed the part about the glowing flowers completely astonished me. If the Underworld was made of obsidian and the path to the forest was lined with Laelia, what did that make the cave in my mind? Was I seeing into the Underworld somehow? If so, how?

Refusing to stop there, I moved on to the other books in the pile and ingested every piece of information on deities and spirits that I could. Though I wasn't entirely certain I retained any of it given how sick I was. Eventually, I circled back to the tome about the God-given from the other day. I flipped to the page about the champions of the sun once more and stared at Leandro's portrait. Now that I knew what his brother looked like, the contrast was unnerving. No wonder Canela ripped his page out. Sebastián had no light in his eyes. He was the antithesis of what the sun champions were, and he was using Solistó's gift for evil. It angered me in a way that was bewildering.

Eventually, I let the weight of my body take me down so I was laying on my side, book still open. I scanned the words over and over, looking for some hidden message until I dozed off again.

❋ ☽ ○ ☾ ❋

I was on the burning ship again, both as myself and as the king. The Sun Killer's eyes burned into me, and I could hear his voice echoing.

You're supposed to be dead.

A girl like you shouldn't have survived this long.

Then I was on the floor in a castle of red and gold, and he was plunging a sword into my chest.

I dreamt of obsidian castles, red eyes, and black diamonds. Suddenly, I was on horseback, panting as I made my way through rocky mountains. Then I was in a sea made of sand with tall spires standing in the distance. More and more and more and—

I was jostled awake from my fever-induced slumber. With my heart in my throat, I instantly snapped upright, thinking I had been thrashing again.

"Río? What is—"

He held his finger to his lips to shush me, but there was no visible agitation in his eyes. For some reason, he looked excited about something.

"What's going on? Why do I need to be quiet?" I asked.

"I want to show you something," he whispered.

I rubbed the grogginess from my eyes with a frown. "Show me what?"

"It's a place on the grounds that I've been meaning to show you. By the water."

I swept my gaze around the chamber, trying to discern what time of day it was from the drawn curtains.

"Is it still night?"

"Yes."

"And you want to show me this *now*?"

The prince shrugged. "I know, I know, but it's the perfect time. Everyone's asleep, and no one will bother us. But we have to be quiet because we don't need the guards getting into our business."

I furrowed my brow, glowering skeptically. "I thought I was supposed to rest."

"This will make you feel way better. Trust me. I wouldn't show it to you if it made you worse." When I took too long to respond, he took my hands in his. "Please? It'll be quick. I promise."

After a pause of bewildered silence, I rolled my eyes and shrugged.

"Fine, but let me put on something decent."

I'd take any chance to feel a little normal again.

35

Connection

Río

Río.

Río, wake up.

Wake up, Río!

Wake up. Wake up. Wake up!

A voice shouted in my ear, rousing me from bed with a gasp. My heart thrummed in my chest with panic until I recognized my familiar painted ceiling. I relaxed against the pillow with a sigh and put my arm over my eyes, staying that way until the feeling passed.

I instinctively reached over to check on Esmé, but her side of the bed was empty. I raised my head from the pillow and stared at the rumpled sheets for a long, puzzling moment.

"Esmé?" I called out, thinking she was in the bathroom.

There was no answer, only the eerie silence that filled the entire room.

Oh, gods, I hope she's not sick again.

I got out of bed and walked over to the next room, calling out again, "Esmé, are you okay?"

The bathroom, however, was completely dark and vacant, with no sign that Esmé had been in there at all.

Alarm bells sounded off in my head as I suddenly entered a panic. Esmé was ill and could barely walk by herself without nearly fainting, so where could she have gone in the middle of the night? Why didn't she wake me? Something deep inside told me something wasn't right. I could sense it in the sudden, stale, frigid air. It was different and more sinister than the usual cold winter nights, and I knew better than to ignore such things now.

The sound of barking came down the hall, drawing my attention to the doors, which I barely noticed were slightly ajar. I crossed the room to look outside, and as soon as I pulled the door open, a tar-like scent flooded my senses. My hand flew over my nose as I stumbled back in disgust, and my heartbeat quickened with a fear that came from memories of not long ago. Memories of a blackened sea at the shore of a decaying kingdom overrun by soulless soldiers. It was the stench of Old Avilonía, black magic...and Sebastián Eliódor.

Mariela and Echo approached the threshold as I was stuck frozen in shock. My sister was in her robe, bearing an expression of bewilderment as she used her teardrop necklace to light the way. She waved a hand in my face until I finally looked her in the eyes.

"What's wrong?" she signed.

I shook my head, briefly curling my shaking hands into fists.

"Esmé's gone. I think she's in danger," I said.

Mariela's eyes flashed. "That's why Echo brought me here. He said someone was in danger. What happened?"

"I woke up and she was gone."

Echo barked again, calling our attention to something he was sniffing on the ground. I crouched down to see pieces of a shattered green rock by the doors. My mouth went dry as I beheld the final confirmation of my worst fears.

Malaquita. Pieces of Esmé's ring.

She once told me that if it broke, it meant the stone used all its magic to protect the user from danger. It was something Canela told her, and I trusted that witch more than most magic users I've ever met.

I thought back to the voice that awakened me and that rotten feeling that's been hard to ignore since Esmé became sick. It had less to do with the illness at all and a lot more with what caused it. Paloma and my mother made me well aware of what they asked her to do with my father's crown as well as the vision she had of my father's final moments. Esmé didn't tell me the details of what she saw—to spare me, no doubt—but I knew enough.

"We wanted to see if she could do it. She was willing to help," my mother told me.

Of course, she was willing to help! I wanted to scream. *That's who she is! She doesn't know any better!* You *should!*

Fighting the anger rising inside of me now, I put the broken pieces of malachite into my pocket before straightening up. Springing into action, I rushed to my wardrobe to throw on a shirt and some shoes.

When I was face-to-face with my sister again, I said, "We need to find her. *Now.*"

36

Changeling

Esmé

I couldn't help my anxious hyper-awareness as Río guided me through the castle. As always, he was the confident one, whereas I was keeping an eye out for any guards who might catch us. Although the halls of *Castillo* Paricia seemed especially silent and empty tonight.

"Where is everyone?" I whispered.

"Asleep, most likely."

"I meant the guards. I'm surprised Captain Dominic isn't out here like a hound dog."

"Ah, don't worry about him. Brutes need their beauty sleep, too."

I giggled. "Are you going to tell me where we're going?"

"Not yet. I told you it's a surprise," he said with a sly smile.

Perhaps it was my paranoia, but there was a change in his overall demeanor that I couldn't put my finger on. I couldn't quite put my finger on it, but there almost seemed to be less *spark* to him. Not to mention his protective fussiness from over the last few days seemed to water down all of a sudden.

"Are you okay? Did something happen down in the city?" I asked.

Río stopped in his tracks and turned to me with a tight-lipped smile. He pushed a piece of hair behind my ear, his expression turning grim.

"No, it's fine. I just… I've been thinking about my dad. I miss him."

The corners of my mouth turned down as I rested my hand on his arm.

"I'm sorry," I said. "Have you been to the moon temple since the funeral?"

"No, I haven't. It's a little too painful, still," Río replied. He then put his hands on my shoulders, holding me at arm's length. "Right now, I want to focus on you. Okay?"

I nodded apprehensively. "Okay."

With that, he turned around and pushed a set of doors open. To my astonishment, we somehow made it to the garden, which I took no notice of in my feverish state. Whenever I was here, the sun was high in the blue sky; its light brought the colors of the garden to life. Now, the sky was a starless, inky black curtain, giving the space an air of mystery and wonder. Usually, I found the night mesmerizing, but the more I looked at the garden, the more nervous I became. I didn't know why.

"Come on. Follow me," Río said, taking my hand.

In a fleeting moment, I swore his voice sounded like two.

37

Running Out of Time

Río

The stench of tar continued throughout the palace, which only I could smell due to my new, heightened senses. With Echo's help, I realized that there was a trail of it, which made our pursuit of Esmé that much easier. Along that path were two unconscious guards who were barely waking up by the stairs. I questioned them, but all they remembered was seeing Esmé walking by in a nightgown with her eyes closed. When they tried speaking to her, their vision filled with red, and suddenly they were waking up on the floor. The rest of the men we found recounted similar stories, contributing to the haunting puzzle.

Esmé couldn't put a person to sleep, but there was someone else who could.

But where was he taking her? Why wasn't she dead yet?

It wasn't one to spook so easily, but I could feel myself unraveling. If anyone tried talking to me, I could not hear them. I was too focused on finding Esmé before disaster, too focused on the demonic scent in my nostrils leading me into the unknown. Only when Echo barked at me and my sister smacked me in the arm did I snap out of it to meet her eyes.

"I've been trying to catch up to you," she signed in exasperation.

"Sorry, I'm not really here right now," I snapped.

"I understand, but I've been trying to tell you that one of the guards saw her walking towards the garden."

I perked up. "Really?"

"Yeah, come on!"

Mariela took my hand and pulled me onward, continuing down the trail I was following. Echo heralded the way when all of a sudden, he started barking incessantly at some tall windows. We ran to his side and looked down towards a girl with long brown hair dressed in a white nightgown. She was walking barefoot through the garden like a ghost in the night.

"Esmé!" I shouted before dashing towards the stairs.

I refused to stop, leaving Echo, my sister, and the search party behind until I bolted through the doors into the open air. The smell of pollution was stronger here despite the sea and flora. I was frantic, but with the curse came a gift, and it was my newfound stamina and speed. The unfamiliar feeling had me stumbling like a newborn deer, but I picked myself back up again, refusing to give up.

"Esmé!" I called out again, but she kept her trajectory towards the greenhouse, as if unable to hear me.

My gaze remained locked on her figure as I wound through the garden, heading towards the building made of glass, until she veered left. My heart stuttered because I knew very well that the only thing in that direction...was the edge of a cliff.

38

Prince of Darkness

Esmé

A disembodied voice shouted behind me.

I looked over my shoulder, half-expecting to see someone there, but there was no one. The voice was distorted, and I couldn't quite tell who or what it was, but when I heard it again, there was a strange ache tugging at my heart, telling me to go in that direction.

"What's wrong?" Río asked.

"I don't know. I think it's the spirits again, but this one feels different."

"It's probably because you're sick. Magic can get weird when we're physically unwell."

I turned back around with a nod, remembering what he explained to me the other night.

"Yeah, maybe you're right."

Considering our trajectory, I assumed we were paying the greenhouse a visit until he urged me to the left through the grass, down a path I'd never been on.

"Are we not going in there?" I asked with a frown.

"No, not today. I have something different in mind."

An odd skepticism was taking root within me, and I couldn't quite shake it. The prince's tone and curtness toward me were making me nervous. I didn't know if I had done something wrong or if there was something wrong with *him*. Was the fever making me delusional? Perhaps. Regardless, I followed.

He took us to the edge of the palace grounds that overlooked the Marisláni Ocean. There was an outlook with a short wall made of stone. I placed my hands on it looked down with curiosity. The hill came to a sudden, steep drop below us into treacherous waters below. I stepped back timorously, afraid I could fall at any moment. Río put his hand on my arm with a chuckle.

"It's okay, Esmé."

I glanced up at him warily. "Why did you bring me here?"

I heard the voice again. This time it sounded like they were calling my name. Again, I glanced towards the palace, but saw nothing.

Río took my chin and turned me back towards him.

"We're going to jump," he said with a smile that didn't reach his eyes.

"*Off the cliff?*" I blurted out. "Are you insane?"

"I've done it many times before. You'll be fine. I'll be right next to you."

"I'm sorry, but I am *not* doing that," I argued, shaking my head. "I don't care if the cold water will make me feel better. I just want to go inside. Can we go inside, *please?*"

I hugged myself tightly against the cold winter wind, wishing to be rid of this building dread inside me. I felt like I was losing my mind.

Río rolled his eyes. "Come on, Esmé. Don't be a coward."

I gaped at him, blinking as if that would help how stunned I was. Not only was his statement completely unlike him, but so was his voice. I thought I had imagined it before, but now I was certain that it was as if two people were speaking at once. It was similar to something I had only heard in visions and nightmares.

There was barking. The voice behind me was loud and clear, but this time, I knew *exactly* who it was.

"Esmé, don't!"

Terror rattled me to my core as I stared at the person before me, finally seeing him for who he wasn't.

"You're not Río," I whispered sharply.

I took a step back, but in a wink, I was standing on top of the railing, with no recollection of climbing up there myself. As my body teetered forward, I let out a shuddering cry and stuck my arms out to keep my balance. The figure grabbed my wrist, his touch like a hot brand against my skin.

"How did you—? Let me go!" I shouted, fighting against him.

The man who wasn't Río kept a firm grip on my arm, refusing to release me even as I tried to pry his fingers off. His face morphed into something skeletal, and his irises burned a deep scarlet.

He glanced over my shoulder with a scowl.

"Love is so irritating," he muttered before shoving me forward over the cliff.

39

Possession

Río

He is trying to kill her. He just wants to put on a show.

"No, no, no, no. Esmé!"

I picked up speed, barreling toward her as she approached the cliff's edge. She stopped for a moment, lingering there. I could hear Echo barking behind me in time with my beating heart.

"Esmé, don't!" I shouted.

As I passed by the side of the greenhouse, I reached out my hand, energetically latching onto the cold water of the pond. Esmé climbed up the stone railing, and everything after that happened fast. Glass shattered as I pulled on the water and an invisible force pushed Esmé over the precipice. As if holding a whip, I wrapped the stream around her waist, stopping her in midair, and forcefully tugged her towards me. I raced forward just in time to catch her in my arms and hold her tightly against me as we tumbled to the ground. Pain shot through my shoulder. The water from the greenhouse dispersed into a brief rainfall, but all I cared about was the relief surging through my chest.

Fuck, that was close.

I got up to my knees, the world tilting for a moment as I looked down at Esmé's face. Her eyes were closed, but she was still breathing.

"Esmé," I said, pushing her hair out of her face. When she didn't respond, I tried shaking her. "Esmé!"

Her eyes snapped wide open, but instead of beautiful, chocolate brown eyes looking back at me, red *smoke* filled her irises. A big, anomalous smile spread across her face.

"Hello, Río Markaél," she said in a voice that wasn't entirely hers.

The blood drained from my face.

The Sun Killer.

"Shit!"

With a feral scream, Esmé lunged at me and knocked me on my back with all her might. The wind left my lungs, and she tried wrapping her hands around my throat, but I grabbed her wrists to detain her. She bore a dark, murderous expression that didn't belong to her at all. I never thought I could loathe anything about her, but this wasn't her at all.

I shouted, trying to get through to her.

"Esmé!"

"Esmé isn't here right now," she growled.

I threw her off and rose to my feet, all while keeping my eyes trained on the demon pretending to be her. She rolled a few times before getting back up and chuckling lowly. When *his* crimson eyes found mine, he pulled her shoulders back, held her head high, and clasped her hands behind her back the way I've seen many men of high stature do. The smell of tar was ever-present.

"How was the full moon, Moon Prince? Or shall I say... Moon *Beast?*" the Sun Killer teased. "You *are* a half-beast now, aren't you? Otherwise, how else would you still be alive when I wasted my best servants trying to kill you?"

The fact that he was using her body and voice enraged me like nothing else, and for the first time since the full moon, there was a burning itch beneath my skin.

"How did you get to her, you piece of shit?" I hissed.

We circled each other in the open grass, me keeping a distance while he tried to catch up.

"Esmé shouldn't have stuck her nose in things that aren't her business," he said, his voice shifting between tones. "I felt her *watching* me. And I don't like being watched."

"What she saw happened nearly two weeks ago. It was a memory!"

"A memory she shouldn't have seen!" he bellowed, the demonic tone rumbling.

I wavered slightly in my steps, as the insinuation startled me. My confusion hardened into something deadly.

"What did you do to my father?" I demanded.

He huffed, "Mourn your father, Markaél. He's already dead."

"What the fuck did you do?" I spat.

The Sun Killer stopped moving and watched me from across the lawn with his head cocked to the side like a marionette.

"You don't even know what she is, do you? Not really. But I do."

I scowled. "What the fuck are you talking about?"

He hummed before saying, "We share a lot in common. We were born of the same magic and blood."

My body went rigid. The implication was clear, but I refused to believe it.

"You're lying."

He laughed, "I'm not."

"If you share so much in common, then why would you try and kill her?"

The Sun Killer smiled, but if he ever deemed to answer, I would never know.

A large black dog dashed from behind me and lunged at him with a snarl. My eyes widened as I tried but failed to stop him from sinking his teeth into Esmé's arm. Sebastián cried out and, with some struggle, managed to throw the hound off of him. Next to me, my sister appeared with a bow and arrow at the ready, but I reacted just in time to block her path.

"No! It's still Esmé's body! You'll kill her! It's what he wants!" I signed frantically.

In my moment of distraction, Sebastián charged at me again and, with whatever demonic power he held, was able to take me down with Esmé's small frame. We wrestled in the grass, until I ultimately pinned him down. He bit and scratched at me, but my newfound strength kept him at bay.

Echo made a move towards us, but I motioned him away.

"Stay back!"

"You can't do it, can you?" Sebastián drawled, mixing her voice with his. "That's why you haven't called the water. That's why you haven't *turned.*" He sang the last word like a taunt and then whispered, "You're afraid you'll kill her."

I clenched my teeth, unable to deny his accusation as he struggled against my hold.

"Let the beast out, Markaél. Let your anger consume you. What's one girl in the face of power? What is she compared to Avilonía?"

"You shut the fuck up!" I barked.

My body ran hot with that clawing, wolfish fury, but I refused to let go. I couldn't hurt him without hurting *her.* I couldn't give him the satisfaction.

"You should've stayed asleep and just let me do it," he hissed. "But now I'm going to have to kill you *and* your family with her bare hands!"

He threw his head forward, hitting my nose with a painful crack. He clambered upright as I clutched my face in the grass. I felt my sister's hands on my shoulders as she helped pull me to my feet. Anticipating another attack, we both looked towards the demon, who suddenly halted in his step.

"No!"

His face contorted in agony with the scream. Except it wasn't the Sun Killer at all, but Esmé herself. The red smoke in her eyes dissipated as she clutched her head in pain.

"Leave him alone!" she screeched, almost to herself.

My eyes widened. "Esmé?"

Her hands dropped, and her eyes rolled into the back of her head, knees buckling. She fell into the grass, and I dashed towards her, taking her in my trembling arms. I tried calling out to her, but neither she nor the Sun Killer responded. Instead, she started to convulse, and short, pained gasps came out of her mouth.

I don't know what she did, but it was enough to gain some semblance of control back from Sebastián. He wasn't trying to kill me anymore, but he still had control of her somehow. The only way to help her was to get rid of him. *Fast.*

I hoisted her up into my arms and got to my feet. My sister stood by seriously with her bow at her side, her eyes going from Esmé to me. I walked past her with steel in my spine and a smoldering resolve like no other. She and Echo trailed silently behind through the garden all the way to the castle exterior. The entire staff stood on the steps, watching from afar. My mother was at the front, with Paloma and Captain Dominic at her sides, as well as a dark, threatening storm hovering above.

"Esmé's possessed. I'm taking her to Canela," I announced with my approach.

"Wait, what?" my mother exclaimed.

The stewards around us gasped.

Canela was a witch whom many in this city trusted, including me. She was Esmé's closest friend and helped both of us in many ways that I will be forever grateful for. She was also well-versed enough in dark magic and curses to be the only one who could help me now.

"Wait, what?" my mother exclaimed. The stewards around us gasped. "Possessed? How?"

"Her vision. Sebastián said he could *feel* her watching, and he latched onto her then."

Tears sprung to my mother's eyes. I held onto Esmé tighter to keep her and myself from shaking.

"If I don't take her to Canela right now, then she and who knows how many others will die. And if you try to stop me, I will never forgive you," I said in a harsh tone.

I half expected my mother to yell and argue, but to my chagrin, she never did. No, I kept seeing that guilt, along with what I assumed were empathy and *pride*.

"Go," she said, "but I'm following closely behind."

40

Exorcism

Río

The horse's hooves clattered against the cobblestone as I bounded down the island. My heart thudded ferociously as I clutched the reins and Esmé for dear life. The entire journey, I drew the attention of everyone, especially in *Distrito Obsidiana*. At first, I thought it was the speed I was going at until I heard my formal name being used. Apparently, in my rush, I forgot to throw a cloak on, so now my white, moon-touched hair was on display, drawing eyes to me and the strange, bound girl in my arms. At the very least, it gave me a wide enough berth to move quickly through the narrow streets towards my destination.

Eventually, I came to a halt in front of the witch's shop and hopped off the stallion while carefully hoisting Esmé over my shoulder. She was still writhing, but her wrists were tied, and the Sun Killer hadn't tried to kill me thus far.

People whispered among themselves around me.

"It's the prince!"

"Why is he here?"

"Who is that he's holding?"

The growing circle of citizens was making me more nervous than I already was.

I raised a warning hand. "Stay back, please. This is royal business. Go back to yours."

I was past the point of caring about my image when there were other things at stake. At the very least, I had authority, so they kept their distance. They knew better than to anger a tide bender like me.

At the storefront, the curtains were pulled shut, and the sign on the front read CLOSED. I ignored it and raised my fist to pound on the wooden door. There was no answer. I knocked again, my worry heightening.

"She just closed half an hour ago," a man said.

"I don't care. This is a matter of life or death," I replied. I adjusted Esmé on my shoulder and knocked again. "*Magistra* Canela!"

Just as I was thinking of breaking it down, the lock clicked, and the door swung inward. The witch came out with a vexed look, mid-rant.

"I have half a mind to hex you for—*Alteza?*" Her eyes widened. "What's wrong? Is that—"

"Canela, I need your help," I stressed in a whisper. "It's Esmé."

The witch's expression fell, and she stepped aside, urging me into her shop.

"On the counter," she said.

As Canela uttered a few calming words to the people, I rushed inside to place Esmé on the counter. For safety purposes, I bound her hands and ankles with rope before leaving the palace, which hurt me as much as everything else. Her face was pale, her skin hot and slick with sweat. Now and then, she'd convulse or whimper as if in pain.

I ran my hand over her hair and swallowed against a lump in my throat.

It was supposed to be a fever. That was all it was supposed to be.

Canela closed the door and ran to the other side of Esmé to get a good look at her.

"Sweet moon above. What happened?" she exclaimed.

"Sebastián Eliódor," I seethed.

"What? How?"

"She… She had a vision that she wasn't supposed to see. My father's final moments. The Sun Killer was there and he saw her. She immediately got sick with a fever, vomiting, headaches, and then…" I recalled everything with a sharp whisper, my voice shaking. "A voice woke me up earlier tonight, and she was gone. I had this horrible feeling... The next thing I knew, I found her in the garden, trying to walk off a cliff. I saved her, but he already had control of her body. He tried to kill me."

The witch's horror was clear on her face as I recounted this.

"He couldn't use her abilities, but he did try to tear me apart," I added.

"Perhaps it has to do with him only being part demon," she offered.

"Yeah, but he was very strong. If it weren't for my curse, it would've been a lot harder than it already was to defend myself. And to save her. If I wasn't fast enough, then he would've…"

I wavered, not wanting to finish the thought.

There was a commotion outside as well as the sound of clattering hooves and whinnying horses. Voices talked over each other, and suddenly another knock came at the door.

"Who is it now?" Canela demanded.

"My mother," I answered, already going to the door.

Our eyes met in a fearful gaze as soon as I opened it. My mother pushed past me, with Paloma and my sister in tow. Mariela stopped to hug me around the shoulders—a welcome, calming embrace.

"Where's Echo?" I inquired about the hound's absence.

"I didn't want him to freak out again, so I left him outside to keep watch," she signed. "He really didn't like that demon."

"That makes two of us."

"You didn't tell me you invited a whole troupe to the exorcism," Canela said.

"Exorcism?" we all exclaimed.

The witch scoffed, "The Sun Killer has taken possession of this girl, which means we need to expel him. *Exorcise.* So if any of you are uncomfortable with that, I suggest you leave now. Otherwise, help me clear that table so we can put her on it. We need to move fast. The more bodies, the better."

With no hesitation, Paloma and Mariela started taking potions, crystals, and herbs from a table in the middle of the shop and carried them off to where Canela directed. My mother, however, stood around aimlessly. She seemed conflicted, and was clearly annoyed with being ordered around.

"If you're going to argue, please leave," I told her before she could complain.

She gave me an incredulous look. "I'm not going to argue. And if you think I'm leaving you alone with that bastard's influence so close, you have another thing coming."

She took off her coat and proceeded to roll up her sleeves. With mild relief, I moved past everyone to move Esmé again.

"Strap her to the table with this," Canela ordered, holding a black rope.

Once Esmé was on the center table, my mother and I worked together to cut her loose and rebind her. As if sensing she was free, Esmé started swiping at us with an angry snarl. Between the two of us, we managed to restrain her, but it affected me enough that I had to step away.

This was unlike anything I've ever experienced before. I've watched people die in horrifying ways, but this was different. This was a new, personal kind of horror for me. It was Esmé, but it wasn't. It was her body, but her very soul was held hostage by the being who killed my father. The worst of it all was that I couldn't protect her. My magic was useless to me now.

I pressed my palms against my eyes, inhaling to fight back tears. But the more I fought them back, the more my insides twisted. A low groan escaped through my teeth in anger, fear, and sorrow. I quickly wiped my eyes and stared off towards a candle-lit altar with a three-headed statue of the God of Death.

Behind me, I could sense my mother hovering over my shoulder.

"I thought she was safe," I uttered. "When she got so close to that stone...I was so scared that something like this would happen. But she was still herself, and everything seemed fine. Things went crazy, but she was still fine. I was sleeping *right next to her*, and then... I didn't think he would go this far."

"If anything, it's my fault, Río," my mother said. "I was so worked up about your father's death that I thought—I *hoped*—that something good would come out of it. She's strong, but I pushed her too far. And I'm sorry."

I looked over at her as she blinked back tears. The coil of anger in me unwound when I saw the remorse and grief in her eyes. They were the same ones I carried with me, and I understood exactly where they came from.

Her gaze trailed to the statue.

"You know, before we were married, your father nearly lost his life."

I mentally staggered at this startling piece of information.

"You never told me that."

"Yeah, well, it was a pretty painful day for me," she explained. "He proposed to me earlier that day, and like a stubborn idiot, I said no because I thought *he* was being an idiot. It was war, so we had plenty of near-death experiences, but this one was... *brutal.* I didn't even stop to think. I immediately rushed him to safety—in the middle of battle, no less—and my father thought I was stupid. But I did it anyway. Not even a minute after your father woke up, I accepted his proposal."

Despite the tone of the story, I couldn't help but smile.

"Why am I not surprised that's how the proposal went?"

She snorted. "He was a hopeless romantic, your father. Of course, he would do such a thing before running into the jaws of death."

Our laughter came out soft and melancholy, and I found myself missing him again.

"I just want you to know that I know how you feel, darling," she said.

We shared a somber look.

My mother was a great parent. Even if I didn't always see that, and we had ups and downs, I wouldn't trade her for the world. After all, I wasn't always the easiest son to have. I knew my mother to be ambitious, distrusting, and unforgiving, especially when it came to her family or her kingdom. After everything she survived, I couldn't truly blame her. I knew she wanted us to be safe. But the thought of her breaking so many rules to save my father's life—personal and not—allowed me to see her in a different light. Perhaps we weren't as different as I thought we were.

She took my face in her thin hands and said, "Don't beat yourself up for not knowing the inner workings of a demon, my love. People like him know how to hit you where it hurts, and they will stop at nothing to get what they want. Whether it takes years or days, they are ruthless. She's lucky that you found her in time and that you're alive to help her now."

I closed my eyes with a nod because that was all I could do without breaking. My mother wrapped her arms around my shoulders, making me bend at the waist.

"My sweet little rabbit," she whispered.

My lips quivered. It was something she called me since I was a child, though not as much now. It reminded me of how much I missed such affection from my mother now that I was older.

"Sorry to interrupt, but I need everybody around the table now!" Canela shouted.

My mother slowly let me go and patted me on the shoulders before ushering me back towards Esmé, who was now surrounded by a thick layer of salt. I placed myself by her head as everyone else gathered around the table. The anticipation rushed back into me in full force.

Black and white candles were scattered all around the room, as was an array of herbs and crystals. Canela burned a bundle of leaves and scattered the smoke until the room smelled of rosemary and sage.

The witch took a quick glance around the room before saying, "Whatever you do, don't touch the salt. It's for protection, and if you break it, it breaks the seal."

When everyone understood, she looked to my mother, Mariela, and me.

"I know the God-given are used to channeling their magic into a single target, but right now I am asking you to dig deep and channel it into this ritual and into helping Esmé. Whatever ocean, lightning, or deity lives in you, tap into that."

My family and I nodded without question.

"We'll do whatever we have to."

41

The Sun Killer

Esmé

A scream ripped out of me as I flew over the cliff's edge, plummeting to my crushing death. My stomach dropped, my dress and hair flying as the roiling waves of the ocean grew closer. I was meeting my untimely end, and there was absolutely nothing I could do to stop it. The handful of memories from my short-lived life flashed before me in the seconds before the rocks came, only to never meet them. The hillside, the castle, and the ocean disappeared as a black void swallowed me whole, and I fell into nothingness.

I couldn't tell if I was floating, falling, or some mixture of the two, but after what felt like an eternity, I landed hard on my side. I choked out a groan as pain reverberated through my ribs and, only after a dizzying moment, managed to get myself on my hands and knees. Something sharp cut into my palms, and with startling confusion, I looked down to see that bits of glass pierced my now-bleeding hands. When I finally took a sweeping glance around to see where I landed, I was shocked to realize that I had been here before. Many times.

It was that cavern from the recesses of my mind, but all wrong. The Laelia was dead and rotten all around me, emitting the bitter scent of decay. Shattered glass littered the stone floor, and the obsidian itself seemed to glow red from within. Even the full moon above was bloody crimson, yet the air was as cold as ice. I couldn't help but hug myself.

What happened? Am I dead?

"Esmé!"

I gasped as Río's voice echoed through the cave. It was distant, but I knew it was him.

With my heart racing in my chest, I shouted, "Río?"

My voice bounced against the stone as I awaited a response to no avail. I called out again but received nothing in return. With dirt and blood all over me, I walked forward with my arms out, feeling for the invisible wall...but there was *nothing*.

My breath hitched with a mixture of unease and excitement as I now understood where the broken glass originated from.

What does this mean?

My eyes swept around the scene, beyond the bushes, and into the dark caves I was never allowed to enter before. The barrier was gone, which meant I was finally free to roam. Even more so, I could learn if the rest of my memories truly lie beyond.

Only one way to find out.

With trepidation and curiosity, I took my first step forward and instantly sank into the ground. I screamed as blackened and charred vines coiled around my legs and pulled me under. They wrapped around my entire body, suffocating me until there was nothing but darkness. I couldn't breathe, couldn't scream, and couldn't move. Scorching heat emanated from them, threatening to cook me alive.

And then I heard his voice.

"What she saw happened nearly two weeks ago. It was a memory!"

By some miracle, I managed to force my eyes open. Through my hazy vision, I saw Río standing before me in the garden at *Castillo Paricia*. He was looking at me with disdain.

"A memory she shouldn't have seen!" a voice bellowed.

The voice was so loud, it shook me, as if coming from inside. I tried calling and reaching out to Río, but my own words were stifled in the back of my throat. Yet, to my horror, my body moved, and through my lips, someone who wasn't me spoke. Someone was *using* me, and I was doomed to watch as a third-party observer.

This isn't real, I tried telling myself as I squeezed my eyes shut. *This isn't real.*

But it was. I knew it was real. A long time ago, Río told me this could happen, but back then, we assumed I was safe. Now, I was a prisoner in my own body.

"You don't even know what she is, do you? Not really. But I do."

Río scowled. "What the fuck are you talking about?"

The conversation faded in and out as I was pulled in and out of the darkness. With my sheer will, I forcefully waded through it, pushing myself through the curtains that this demon wanted closed.

"If she's your blood, then why would you try and kill her?" Río asked.

Echo came out of the darkness. My controller and I cried out as he sank his teeth into my arm. There was a tussle, and then I had my eyes locked on Río again, who was looking at his sister, distracted. As if through a dream, I watched myself attack him as I internally screamed bloody murder. It did nothing. I fought within my mind to regain control, but the heat and the darkness choked me back. I called to my power, but the spirits were completely gone, and it frightened me.

"Let the beast out, Markaél. Let your anger consume you. What's one girl in the face of power? What is she compared to Avilonía?"

"You shut the fuck up!" the prince shouted.

"You should've just let me do it. But now I'm going to have to kill you *and* your family with her bare hands!"

There was a struggle, but as soon as those words were uttered, something within me exploded. My eyes snapped open, and the world around me turned from black to blue. When I screamed, I felt it come from my mouth, and for a few short seconds, I was in enough command of my body to wrench myself away from Río.

"No! Leave him alone!"

The voice snarled in my head, I was shoved back, and suddenly I was falling into darkness again.

Falling.

Falling.

Falling.

Until I crashed face down on something wet and soft. The air here was even more bitter and rotten. With a grunt, I crawled up to my knees, my muscles singing with pain. My hands were covered in mud and tar.

"I should've known you were stronger than you looked."

I snapped my gaze up and scrambled backwards with a cry.

Standing above me against the backdrop of a decaying forest was what appeared to be a smoking, shapeless entity with red eyes. However, within that smoke was a man. His long, jasper-red hair was streaked with gray, his face was slender, and his skin was paler than those who shared his name. Though it could've been due to the translucent nature of his face, making his skull partially visible. He wore charred, blood-red robes that emanated mist, and a familiar black diamond hung around his neck with a pulsing glow like a beating heart. Unlike his kin, there was no daylight in his eyes, just pure, scarlet rage.

Sebastián Eliódor, the Sun Killer.

Both he and the smoke engulfing him studied me with their glowing eyes. Seeing him so close outside of visions and dreams froze me in place. I've died by his hand more than once in those nightmares, but we've never personally met until now. This was more than just a man; he was a horror within himself, for this was someone who took everything and left nothing but death.

"You," I whispered.

I was almost too scared to move.

"Me," he said, cocking his head to the side. "Do you know who I am?"

I tried keeping my distance as I wobbled to my feet, but if I thought about running, I wouldn't get very far as there was a large wall of flames trapping in with him.

"Of course I do. Everyone does," I answered shakily.

He chuckled. "Do you know who *you* are?"

My teeth clicked together as I shut my mouth. I knew better than to tell a powerful magic user anything about me, but my silence only seemed to amuse him. He stepped forward, and in a flash, he was three feet before me. I yelped and stumbled backward into a blackened tree.

"There's no point in trying to hide anything from me, Esmé Vespertín," he snapped. "That *is* your name, isn't it? Allegedly, anyway."

I swallowed thickly. "W… Why would you say that?"

"It's your name, but given to you by whom? Not your parents, I don't think."

He spoke to me with his back straight and his hands clasped behind his back, emulating the prince he used to me. I lifted my chin curiously, suddenly intrigued.

"What do *you* know about my parents?"

"As of late, more than you."

He turned away from me, and I made to put more distance between us. A flaming vine shot up from the ground and curled itself around me, keeping me from straying. I shrieked as it raised me off my feet, high enough to hold me captive. I fought against its hold, but it only tightened, its thorns stabbing into my skin. I tried reaching for that door to my magic, I knew so well, hoping it would aid me.

"Let me go!"

"Your spirits can't help you here, Esmé. This is *my* domain," he said. The wretched man scowled in disgust. "You shouldn't even have that power. A girl like you shouldn't be able to raise the dead, yet you do. *Why?*"

The Sun Killer pulled me closer to shout in my face.

"I've tried for years, *decades*, to do what you do, and you just appear out of nowhere and do it in a night. No training? No memory? No *stone?*"

An oppressive wave of heat emanated from his every pore, growing with his fury, and all I could do was turn away with a whimper.

"Hardly seems fair," he added.

I refused to look at him, as if somehow I could make him go away. Of course, it didn't deter him, forcing me to face this villain on my own.

"I'm sorry you feel that way," I muttered, "but if you're here looking for answers, you're not going to find any. Believe me, we've already tried."

"Oh, I know. You are a puzzle even I was not able to crack, Miss Vespertín. Only now have I been able to grasp a small piece, but there are still many things I can't see in your head. It's beyond infuriating. Do I need to crack your skull open myself? Is that it? How did she do it?"

Out of everything, his last question took me aback. I eyed him sidelong as he stared at me with complete and utter disbelief that was wholly strange to me.

She?

I knew absolutely nothing about magic, my missing memories or the barrier in my mind, let alone if the person involved was a woman.

"Who are you talking about?" I asked.

The Sun Killer leaned back to look me in my eyes and say, "Your mother, the witch. Evaliná Calthá."

My eyes grew wide as I trembled with his sudden revelation.

"My...my mother? A witch?"

I was raised into the air once more, turning my question into a gasp as my stomach dropped.

"You're not even supposed to be alive," he rumbled, "but I know for a fact she must have done something to hide you from me. She ruined a lot of plans for me that day. Avilonía would've been mine if it weren't for her."

This piece of information was like a jolt of lightning striking my body, and despite my fear of this monster, I knew this was the only opportunity I had to learn more.

"How did you know her? What was she to you?" I asked.

There was a part of me that was afraid of the answer.

The Sun Killer's gaze veered off, going somewhere far away.

"She was married to my brother. Dear little Leo."

His voice seemed to soften at his younger brother's name, and his eyes flickered between gold and red.

I froze, feeling a mixture of bewilderment, disbelief, and astonishment. I sifted through every piece of information I read from Canela's books. Nowhere was it mentioned that the Sun King had a wife, let alone a child. As much as I wanted to cling to Evalina Caltha's name, I had no reason to believe that the Sun Killer wouldn't lie to me now out of pure cruelty.

"I don't believe you," I said. "He didn't have any children. I don't wield fire or have red hair. Either you're mistaken or you're trying to trick me!"

"Believe me, this is no mistake, Esmé, and I have no time for games," he barked. "You think a spell that can erase memories can't erase traces of your appearance as well? You've read the books. You've seen the visions. The glowing eyes. Flames are affected by your presence. Perhaps you have an affinity for sunlight. I sensed it the second I entered your little head. I might not know where your dark abilities come from, but what I *can* see is one thing: you are an Eliódor."

"How can you possibly know that?" I whispered.

"The God-given and their descendants are all marked by whatever deity touched them. It's in our souls and our *bones*. I don't know where you think you came from, Miss Vespertín, but you are a God-given. We share the same blood."

My vision darkened around the edges as I started to panic. More slithering vines wrapped around me, and one tightened around my throat. The red-eyed smoke chuckled in response, amused by my suffering.

"As much as I'd love to keep you around, darling niece, I can't have you or your hound of a boyfriend fucking up my plans," the Sun Killer said.

He raised his hand, ready to crush me into ash, when all of a sudden, his form flickered in and out of existence. He winced in pain and snarled viciously at the sky.

"Fucking witch."

There was the sound of chanting in the distance, making me pause. The earth violently shook in response, and the vines loosened their grip. Seeing the opportunity, I gathered my strength, inhaled, and thrashed in anger. With that rage, a flash of blue left me and incinerated the vines to dust.

I fell to the floor, staring at my hands in shock.

"The blue flame," the Sun Killer gasped.

When I looked into his crimson eyes, I could almost say he looked *envious*.

I bolted for the blackened forest, not entirely certain of where to go. The Sun Killer growled and hurled balls of fire that swept past me at dangerous speeds. I took cover behind the trees, but a few managed to catch my skin. I somehow made it halfway to the flaming wall before another vine wrapped itself around my legs and knocked me down. With one glance over my shoulder, I saw Sebastián's smoking form flying towards me. He was slower, but still closing in. I kicked, screamed, and clawed, trying to break free from the vine. For a second, I was convinced I never would. But the chanting became louder. He howled in rage, I was released, and I basically sprinted for the fire wall not daring to look back.

I didn't have a plan as I neared the flaming barrier. All I knew was that it was better to be burned alive than fall into the hands of such a villain. I was willing to brave those flames if it meant my freedom. This was *my* mind, after all. Perhaps, if I managed to get out of this horrible place, I could find my way back to myself. I had to *try*.

I stuck my hand out to graze the flames, ready fall into their embrace. Something pierced my stomach, stopping me in my tracks with a strangled gasp. I looked down to see a root sticking out of my body and pain like never before spread through me. The Sun Killer circled to face me with a cold glare as a sob fell from my lips.

"Not this time," he said.

He wrenched out the stake, letting me collapse the ground. Blood oozed from my gaping wound, seeping through my dress. I tried putting my shaking hands over it in a desperate attempt to apply pressure, but it was no use.

"This isn't real. This isn't real," I whispered through tears.

The Sun Killer stood over me with a look of condescending pity.

"I'm afraid it is."

42

Love You To Death

Río

Everything was going right. I could feel it. I could *see* it. Esmé stopped whimpering, and her thrashing abated. She appeared more focused now, with her brows drawn together. Now and then, she'd twitch or gasp, but overall was like she was returning to herself. We all kept chanting, following Canela's lead. The candles burned bright, and then for a moment, they flashed blue. Even then, our concentration on the ritual never faltered.

Then, Esmé's eyes snapped open. Her back arched off the table as a choking gasp left her lips. It was a brief, startling moment before her eyes shut, and she lay there motionless once more. At the same time, there was a strange feeling in my chest as if something was severed with a blade, followed by a sense of free-falling into a chasm. I stopped chanting, and my hand flew to my aching chest. The feeling quickly disappeared, leaving behind gaping emptiness.

"Esmé?" I uttered.

I wanted to believe that we succeeded—that the demon was out and she was free—but with my eyes locked on her form, I quickly noticed that her chest wasn't moving. My heart sank.

"She's not breathing."

Mindful of the salt, I rushed to her side and I lifted her to search for a pulse at her neck. Nothing. Even worse, I couldn't *hear* the beating of her heart. That plummeting sensation returned. My eyes brimmed with tears as I shook my head.

"No, no, no, no, no." I took her face in my hands and said, "Esmé! Esmé, wake up!"

Her body was as limp as a rag doll, even more than before, and her skin was already losing warmth. My skin started to burn, but I resisted it. Instead, I leaned into my instincts.

"Cut the rope," I said.

"*Alteza*, we don't know if he's still in there—"

"Cut the rope, now!" I ordered.

Canela gave me a wary look before taking a dagger from her boot and severing Esmé's restraints. I pulled them all away, letting them fall to the floor. With the knowledge I learned living by the sea, I used mouth-to-mouth to put air into her lungs, but no matter how hard I tried, her chest never moved on its own, and her heart didn't start beating.

I whirled around to Canela, who had tears in her eyes.

"Isn't there anything you can do?" I asked.

She shook her head. "I can't bring people back to life, *Alteza*."

"Can't you look into her mind, something?" I shouted in desperation.

"With a demon in her body, I can't do that without making things worse."

With a frustrated groan, I turned to my sister and signed with shaking hands, "What about you? You can heal her, can't you?"

Ela was already a puddle of tears, and her lips quivered as she replied.

"If she had a physical wound, I could heal her. Otherwise, my magic doesn't work that way, Río. I'm sorry…" she said before covering her mouth.

Everything seemed to slow down around me as I lost touch with reality. My mother put her hand on my shoulder in an act of comfort, but it was too painful.

"Río…"

"Don't!" I pulled away, turning my attention back to Esmé.

Tears rolled down my cheeks and onto the wooden table as I took her beautiful face in my hands. I couldn't help but notice that she looked more peaceful than before. She looked like she did when she was asleep next to me. Safe. Or so I thought.

I brought her against my chest, clenching my jaw to keep myself from breaking apart altogether. I squeezed my eyes shut and ran my hand over her soft hair, picturing one of the last times I held her like this. It was in the bed we now shared. She was sick, but she was alive. She was alive, and she was holding me under a dome of stars. And she was warm. And I remember thinking that I would do anything if it made her feel better. I would never use my powers again if it meant she would be okay. I would take a silver blade to the heart or let myself drown. Because nothing felt more right than having her there by my side, whether it was in bed, the garden, or the sea.

No. No, she can't be gone. She can't be dead. Not like this. I promised I would protect her. I said I would give her everything, and I would. She saved me in that ballroom. She pulled me back before I lost myself and sank the city, and this is how it ends?

"There was so much more I wanted to give you. So much I wanted to say. So much I wanted you to see," I whispered sharply. "We were just getting started. I know it's stupid, but I wanted to grow old with you. I wanted to marry you. I should've been there. I should've been by your side from the beginning. I'm so sorry."

I choked out my last words.

I'm not done. I don't want it to be done.

43

Daughter of the Blue Flame

Esmé

The rot enveloped me, as if squeezing away my life and decomposing me at the same time. I was a mouse in the belly of a viper. The crimson eyes of the smoking entity surrounding the Sun Killer burned into mine with wicked glee, taking pleasure in my death. I was unsure of it before, but if the stories held true, then this dark being was none other than Casímir Gedeón's soul, or what became of it. He and my supposed uncle moved as one now, bound by the black diamond—darkness, and flame intertwined. And now I was to join the long list of names of those they murdered, bleeding and helpless, just like Río's father...and mine.

Though it was hopeless, I looked into the Sun Killer's eyes and whispered, "Why?"

He huffed in amusement. "If there's one thing I've learned in this life... it's that there's no such thing as luck or fate, Esmé. There is only what you do or don't take. The God-given have squandered their gifts long enough. They don't know the first thing about true power, and I intend to show them."

"*Squandered?*"

The question was meant to be incredulous, but in my weakening state, it was barely above a whisper.

Is that the history you've painted for yourself?

"Yes," he replied.

With my life draining from me, I found a sliver of bite still left.

"We were at peace before you came along," I choked out. "The only one who squandered their power was you."

The Sun Killer's eyes flickered between red and gold as his lips twisted with a scowl. I wasn't one to find joy in making people angry, especially not anyone as powerful as him, yet I felt a spark of it at the thought of hitting a nerve.

"You know nothing," the demonic voice rumbled before smoothing out. "You are an abnormality, Esmé. The first of my mistakes. You know nothing of what it's like having to claw your way out of the darkness of someone's shadow for an ounce of light. But the great thing is that I did not need that light. What I needed to do was embrace the shadow itself. Only *it* gave me power. Only *he* believed in me, and now I am more than I ever could have been."

I wanted to tell him that I *did* know. I did know what it was like to live in shadow, but it would have been futile. Someone else's voice more beautiful voice filled the space before I could.

"There was so much more I wanted to give you. So much I wanted to say. So much I wanted you to see."

It was Río speaking to me from beyond, completely broken. Only then did I know that I was dead out there, too.

"We were just getting started. I know it's stupid, but I wanted to grow old with you. I wanted to marry you. I should've been there. I should've been by your side from the beginning. I'm so sorry."

It shattered me to hear him that way.

"Río, no," I cried.

"I love you. Please don't go."

My aching body shook with grieving.

"I love you too," I replied hoarsely.

"Don't worry," the red-eyed king said coldly, "You'll see each other again."

I shot him the deadliest glare as a hatred I never harbored before burned beneath my skin.

"He's going to kill you," I hissed.

"He'll certainly try."

With a flick of his hand, a sharp root came out of the ground, aimed at my heart. Again, my life flashed before my eyes as I prepared for death. I thought of Río, Mariela, Canela, and my friends. What will become of them? What will happen to my body? Will the Sun Killer still be able to use me as a puppet to hurt those I love, or will he be gone with my death? What will happen to Río and his curse? What will happen to Avilonía? I didn't get to warn them. I didn't get to say goodbye. I didn't even get my memories back. I didn't get to do anything. I will die an anomaly and haunt that shadow forever.

I wanted to close my eyes to avoid watching my own murder, but was glad I didn't. The charred root that was flying straight towards my chest froze in midair and crumbled to ashes. Though I was too hazy to react, both the Sun Killer and the Black Death looked taken back. A murder of crows appeared overhead, their cries growing louder as they got closer. They gathered in a spiraling swarm, melding together into a tall man with jet-black hair wearing an all-black suit.

The Sun Killer's breath hitched.

"You're not welcome in this vessel," the figure stated in a booming voice.

With shocking speed, he closed the distance and grabbed the Sun Killer's face. The wretched king and his smoking companion let out a monstrous, agonized scream as they glowed a deep violet. Then, with little to no effort, the black-suited man threw them backwards, rendering them to ash and dust. The vines encasing my body crumbled along with them, releasing me from the Sun Killer's crushing magic.

I remained with my back against the darkened soil, still bleeding out, my eyes trained on the man in black. He strode over to me and took a crouch by my side. Considering the dramatic entrance, dark attire, and imposing presence, I assumed another demon came to take over until a soft smile spread across his face. That alone sparked a sudden recognition in me.

"You. You're the man from the shadows. The voice," I managed to say.

"I'm glad you at least remember that." His voice was borderline monotone, yet silky and smooth. He then held out his hand in a friendly gesture. "You're not dying today, Esmé."

My gaze flitted between his hand and violet eyes before graciously taking it. The man gave me a light squeeze, and in the blink of an eye, my stomach dropped. I was flying in midair, but before I could scream, I was landing on my feet in a new place. I cursed under my breath as I nearly teetered to the ground. Fortunately, the man caught me before doing so.

"Sorry, I should've warned you about that," he said.

"It's...fine," I said dizzily.

I stepped away as my blurry vision adjusted to my surroundings. We were back in the obsidian cavern, now far away from the decaying forest and my wretched uncle. Never did I think I would be happy to be in this tiny cave, yet seeing it look just as it did before filled me with a sense of relief. The glass was gone, the flowers were back in bloom, and the moon was silver-white once more. Even I was all cleaned up, with no wound, no blood, and my strength fully regained. I ran my hands over myself in disbelief before looking at the man who just saved my life.

He was slender and incredibly tall, even more than Río. He had spotless sand-colored skin, almond eyes that were the color of violets, and straight jet-black hair that was pushed back. His suit was reminiscent of those someone of high nobility would wear, except it was made for a funeral with details of silver and obsidian. At certain angles, the material was revealed to have hidden violet embroidery.

With his hands in his pockets, the stranger took me in with a fondness that was oddly familiar. It softened his otherwise striking expression.

"Thank you for saving me, sir, but... who are you?" I finally asked.

He cleared his throat and shifted his weight, as if the answer required a readjustment.

"My name is Micqui," he replied.

My eyes nearly popped out of their sockets.

"Micqui? As in the God of Death?" I exclaimed.

He chuckled. "The exact one."

I put my hands over my eyes, squeezing them shut, before taking a peek through my fingers. Given my history with hallucinations and other strange things, I thought perhaps I'd wake up in bed or that he might disappear, but he never did. All he did was watch me curiously.

"Do you want proof?" he asked.

"What kind of proof-Oh, moon and stars!"

Mid-question, he shape-shifted into a black jaguar before my very eyes. I instinctively hugged myself as he came towards me, though he merely circled the flowers, posing no threat. Underneath the moonlight, I could make out spots hidden in his dark fur.

"Maybe something smaller?" he asked in my head, making me jump.

The jaguar shrank down into a black house cat. He stretched out before me and sat down with a meow. I crouched down with a delighted scoff and ran my hand over his smooth fur. A small bell hung from a purple ribbon around his neck.

I gasped. "Midnight? *You're* Midnight?"

In a cloud of violet mist, the God of Death turned back to his human form, his eyes alight. I stood straight up with a squeak.

"Perhaps."

"I've been keeping the God of Death as a pet this whole time?" I blurted out, gaping at him.

"For the record, you're a very lovely caretaker."

"But… *why*? Why were you watching me? Why was this place and this flower from your realm in my mind? Or the glass?" I asked, gesturing to the cavern.

"To protect you from something like *this*."

"Why would *I* need to be protected?"

"Unfortunately, I think our friend over there might have spoiled that answer for you," he said with grim vexation.

My shoulders and expression dropped. "So it's true? I *am* an Eliódor."

"You are," he assured.

"How? I can't recall any of the other sun champions being able to see spirits or raise the dead. I don't wield fire or the sun's rays. I don't have red hair. I don't…"

"But you did see the blue flame, didn't you?"

I faltered, unable to deny the burst of blue light that came from me in that dark forest.

"I know it's hard to believe, Esmé, but that's only because the reality I created was meant to keep you safe. You're not supposed to know the truth unless I allow it. I can explain it all, or... I could just show you."

"How?"

"By giving you back your memories."

My heart leapt in my chest as he offered his hand to me once more. After everything I've been through—all the mystery and pain— the answer to all of my questions was in the palm of Micqui's hand. Micqui, *the God of Death*. After what the Sun Killer said, I had half a mind to run, but no. I had to be braver than that. I *am* braver than that.

I walked forward and placed my hand in Micqui's.

"Please."

He seemed pleased by this answer and then told me to close my eyes.

✻ ☽ ○ ☾ ✻

My name is Esmé Vespertín. I am 21 years old, and I am an orphan.

My parents were Leandro Eliódor, the former Sun King of Avilonía, and a woman named Evaliná Calthá. Evaliná was a witch and spirit healer from the southeastern coast of the Sun Kingdom who prayed to the God of Death. She and Leandro met after the fall of Casímir Gedeón, when the Sun King started suffering from dreams of the war. While on a visit to the city of Pantera, he came upon her shop by chance. They instantly connected, and Evaliná offered to help him with his nightmares.

Leandro spent many days traveling back and forth between Dragona and Pantera, taking whatever the witch provided him. It started with potions, charms, and spells, and then eventually, her company. They fell deeply in love but both chose to keep their relationship private until their first child was born. The Sun King wasted no time in proposing, and they eloped in a private ceremony with only a few of their friends and families present. Evaliná moved to Dragona, and a few months down the line, she became pregnant.

The pregnancy itself was a peaceful one, as both Leandro and Evaliná were excited to welcome their first child and start anew in this era of peace. Unfortunately, when it came close to giving birth, Leandro's brother acquired the first Eye of Gedeón. Being a witch with a connection to the spirit world, Evaliná always knew that Sebastián had an aura of bitterness and envy about him. Leandro was bestowed the gift of the blue flame and became king before his older brother. It was something she often voiced to her husband, but Leandro was too blinded by his love for Sebastián to truly see it.

Sebastián's insecurities ultimately made him susceptible to The Black Death's influence, and he quickly started to change. His negative thoughts were amplified and exacerbated by the parasite that found a home in him. It whispered its ideas, and without his compatriot's knowledge, Sebastián took the black diamond and fixed it into a magically crafted sword. Then, one night, with his envy and wrath boiling over like an erupting volcano, he murdered his brother and the rest of his family in cold blood. The only person who managed to escape was Evaliná Eliódor.

When two beings blessed by magic shared a sacred bond, their souls became intertwined. It is a connection that goes beyond the physical and, in many cases, enhances their abilities. Energy can be exchanged, healing magic works faster, and protection spells are twice as strong. Telepathic communication is not uncommon, and it is said that in some cases, a curse given to one may be broken by the other. And it was this very bond that let Evaliná know her husband was murdered.

THE MOON PRINCE

The Sun Killer overlooked this, and while his back was turned, Evaliná Eliódor stole the sword, scabbard, and all, and fled on horseback. She raced through the Colibrí Desert and into the mountains, all within a matter of hours. With a few followers already at his beck and call, Sebastián was hot on her heels and tore through the terrain to find her. Despite her swollen belly and the contractions that threatened to break her, Evaliná was relentless in her mission to destroy the sword once and for all.

She searched through the rocky mountains, led by her magic, until she came upon a ravine. It was the deepest in all of Avilonía, said to go down into the core of the earth. Without hesitation, Evaliná threw the blade in. It went down so far that she didn't even hear it land.

Still in labor, the witch found a cave at the top of a snowy peak, and with no one but herself, gave birth to a baby girl. Her hair was as red as jasper stone, and her brown eyes glittered with gold. Even as a newborn, she radiated daylight like a trueborn Eliódor like her father.

For the few minutes of joy that Evaliná had over her healthy daughter, there was a never-ending, suffocating terror that shook her. She could feel that Leandro's brother was close, and as soon as he found them, they would both be dead. Evaliná could do nothing but cry. She cried, prayed, and begged to anyone who would listen. She dug her fingers into the ground, reached deep into her magic and, in an act of desperation, offered her soul in exchange for her daughter's life. As long as her daughter was alive and Leandro's magic could continue through her, then she was willing to make the sacrifice. A god answered her mighty cry and that god was Micqui.

The gods did not grant their mercy in abundance. They did their jobs, ruled their realms, and bestowed gifts only when necessary, as they believed humanity had a right to free will. Micqui was no different. He was the Adjudicator, a neutral spectator, as death was a natural process of life. Even so, being the ruler of the Underworld and a judge of sorts, he knew firsthand the chaos and destruction that Gedeón wreaked upon the world. People like him and Sebastián thought themselves deities when in reality, they had no respect for anyone but themselves. They cared not for balance or the natural processes of life. They needed to be stopped at any cost, so Micqui saved the last true heir of the Eliódor name.

The God of Death adopted the Sun Princess and took her to the safest place he could think of: the Underworld. Though it wasn't the most welcoming place, nothing could touch her there. No prying eyes, dark magic, or demons—a god's domain was impenetrable. For her safety, Micqui kept her given name a secret and chose an alias instead.

Esmé Vespertín, the first of her name.

From the moment she was born, Esmé was special. She was shy but very curious and had a lot to say when she wanted to say it. She was incredibly creative, had a strong sense of justice, and a deep love for animals. Not only did she inherit her father's gift to manipulate fire, but she also had her mother's natural affinity for connecting with spirits. Living in the Underworld enhanced both, which equally excited and worried the deity.

Like a surrogate parent, Micqui tried his best to provide a normal upbringing for the princess, despite how impossible it sounded. He created a room for her in his castle made of obsidian and educated her on humanity and death. He gave her books—real books—about nature, baking, and astronomy. He even elicited the help of Mikamea and his twin to teach her how to dance and sing. She was a shining light all on her own and managed to carve out a place of her own in both the Underworld and Micqui's heart.

Of course, the years ticked by, and living in isolation stopped doing her favors. Esmé was still a mortal and a champion of the sun god at that. She needed sunshine to thrive, and there was only so much an immortal deity could teach her about the real world without solid experience. It pained him to even think it, but Micqui knew that the day would eventually come when he had to let Esmé go out on her own and figure out humanity for herself.

He took this as an opportunity to do something no god had done in generations. He knew the fear surrounding himself and his line of work, but it wasn't always that way. A long time ago, Aviloníans dedicated a week to celebrating the dead and the souls of those who passed on. The festivities were vibrant and colorful, filled with music, pastries, connection, and *love*. But when Casímir Gedeón came along, people started viewing spirits and death with terror. The Aviloníans started burning the fallen, celebrations of death faded away, and spirits became lost and unable to pass on.

The God of Death was forced to begrudgingly accept his new reputation and fate...until Esmé came along. She was a muse of sorts that opened his eyes to the idea that perhaps the God-given needed a something more. What if the only way to fight Gedeón's magic was to take it back? Leandro's brother and the demon that fueled him were powered by darkness, destruction, and forceful decay. So, what is a better antithesis to such a thing than the embodiment of light? Esmé carried Leandro's blue flame and Evaliná's magic, so why not give her an extra push and let one breathe into the other? Why not give the dead a second chance and let the tide turn in Avilonía's favor?

Why not?

So, with a gift to help her survive, Micqui erased Esmé's memories. He put a barrier in her mind and cast an illusion to hide her God-given traits from everyone, even herself. He then set her on a course towards one of the surviving kingdoms of New Avilonía and the nearest God-given he knew he could trust—the Markaél's.

Everything else is history.

✷ ☽ ◯ ☾ ✷

"But... why did the barrier break? Why was he able to get into my mind now?" I asked after he was done showing me the truth.

My head was spinning, my mind was reeling, and I was buzzing with adrenaline all at once.

"The Moon Prince," Micqui replied with a sigh.

"What about him?" I asked defensively.

"I didn't know this when I unleashed you onto the world, but the two of you are...*destined* to be together. Tonalli, the Goddess of Fate, let me know that, albeit a little late. She has a thing about timing and free will. But I knew then that I had made the right choice."

I scoffed, trying not to linger on the fact that he was casually friends with the gods of fate, love, and creativity.

"Destined? But that doesn't explain how—"

"When he brought the stone into your home, it fractured the barrier I placed in your mind," he explained. "I was furious about it, but you know... His blatant disregard for the rules is both admirable and infuriating. The stone didn't possess you, but that fracture was enough to release the power you naturally have. The queen's poking and prodding only fractured it further. Before I knew it, what I put in place to keep you safe made you vulnerable.

"Having those cracks overlapped with the self-doubt over your lost identity was a feeding ground for dark magic. The vision you had with Marino's crown let Sebastián see through those cracks. He wormed his way in and took over your body."

He looked between my eyes and uttered the next words apprehensively.

"You died, Esmé. When your uncle stabbed you, your body stopped breathing, but your soul was still tethered long enough for me to take you into my domain. Río's love and presence strengthened that tether."

My heart dropped into my stomach as I recalled those mournful words Río said in my final moments.

"Wait...am I still dead? Does he think I'm dead?" I asked, shakily.

"Not for much longer. You're very much alive, Esmé. Like I said, you don't get to die today. Fate and, ironically, *death* will it," Micqui said with a smirk.

My shoulders relaxed, if only a little. "What about the ring? I've had that ring for as long as I can remember. Where did it come from?"

"It was your mother's," he replied. "She put extra protective magic into that stone. You don't know it, but it warded off quite a lot."

He held out his hand, and sitting right in the center of his palm was my ring—my mother's ring.

"It shattered when that parasite possessed you, but it was an easy fix."

My gaze met Micqui's in awe, his violet eyes sparkling. I gingerly took the ring and placed it back on my finger. The weight and familiarity provided an immediate sense of comfort.

"Thank you. For everything," I said.

"Of course."

There were only so many words to express my gratitude, but I hoped he understood. He was a guardian who stepped in when my parents' lives were taken. He gave me a home. He taught me how to read, sing, dance, and bake. He gave me freedom. There were 18 years' worth of memories between us, and they were only just now settling into my mind. I could almost cry from the sense of relief now that this mystery was solved and the chasm was no longer empty, yet in equal measure, I could cry about all the horrible things that were also true. But not yet.

I had so many questions, yet none of them would come out. Except for one.

"If you gave me this name to protect me, then what's my real name?"

After a contemplative moment of silence, Micqui smiled.

"Your name is Aurora. Aurora Eleanora Eliódor."

44

Sunrise

Río

I couldn't let Esmé go. I didn't have the strength. All I could do was whisper words I never had the chance to say.

I love you. I always have.

Some delusional part of me thought I could will her back to life with my magic, while another was simply too afraid to accept this horrible fate.

The silence in the room was deafening, the grim tension palpable. I could feel my heart wanting to explode as my skin started to burn. The beast within longed to tear through my skin and break the world apart—to find Sebastián and make him pay. I almost let it consume me. I was ready to. There was nothing else I could think of to assuage this feeling in me.

Just as I stepped towards the edge of that metaphorical cliff, the aching nothingness in my ribcage filled with what I could only describe as an overabundance of daylight. My eyes snapped open, and I pulled Esmé away from my chest with a bewildered frown.

"Esmé?"

As I stared down at her face, her eyes still closed, I watched as Esmé took in a deep breath. Everyone gasped in response, and suddenly I shook with an opposite emotion. Though I didn't need to, I put my ear against her chest to hear and confirm the undeniable sound of her beating heart. My knees almost gave out from overwhelming relief.

"No fucking way. She's alive!" I exclaimed.

With cries of joy, my mother, sister, Canela, and Paloma all rounded the table once more as I gently laid Esmé back down. They were puffy and teary-eyed, but hope and excitement returned to their once somber faces. Mariela and my mother took places on either side of me, each taking one of my hands. I gave them a soft squeeze.

"Is he gone?" my mother asked.

Canela shook her head. "I don't know."

As if in answer, one by one, every flame turned from a warm amber to a bright, unwavering blue. A gentle breeze circled us, carrying the sound of dissonant whispers that sent a chill down my spine. I quietly sniffed, expecting that familiar smell of tar, but got nothing but rosemary and incense.

Paloma gasped, "Look!"

We tore our attention away from the candles to where she pointed towards the table. Esmé's skin returned to its warm, golden color, and her hair, which was once chestnut brown, transformed from the root to the ends into a rich red. We were all completely mystified, but no one was as affected as my mother.

"Oh my gods," she whispered, letting go of my hand.

I looked over my shoulder just as she took a wobbling step back, tears glistening in her eyes. I instantly strode over to her, putting my hands on her shoulders in comfort.

"Hey…What's wrong?" I asked.

My mind spiraled with every possible horrible conclusion, until she finally uttered a name she rarely ever spoke.

"Leandro. The Blue Flame."

She gestured to the candles around the room, and suddenly I understood.

"Esmé!" Canela exclaimed.

"Where am I?"

I spun around at the sound of Esmé's voice, completely forgetting any thoughts of blue flames or Leandro Eliódor. Time seemed to stretch as I beheld her, now fully awake and utterly confused. When her eyes found mine, she stilled. Her expression softened, and tears pooled in her eyes. As soon as she said my name, it was like everything was right again.

"Río."

"Esmé."

She sat up, and I practically flew to her. Just as I was within reach, she threw her arms around my shoulders and I enveloped her in my arms, pressing her against me. This time, she squeezed me back and buried her face in my neck as she cried. I ran my hand over her hair, reveling in her warmth, smell, and touch. Only after a long minute did I take her face in my shaking hands as tears formed in my eyes. Tears carved paths down her cheeks, and I wiped them away with my thumb.

"You were dead. You died. I thought I lost you," I said hoarsely.

"I know, I know, but I'm back. I'm here," she said, touching my hands and chest as if to prove to me that she was real. "He's gone. It's just me. I promise."

But she didn't need to prove anything to me. I could see it in her eyes. They were brown with gold flecks in them now, but above all else, they were full of that undeniable love and vibrancy that was unique to her.

"It's really you," she gasped.

"Of course it is."

I kissed her passionately, not caring that we had an audience, only that I was able to do it again. When we disconnected, I pushed a lock of hair behind her ear and then paused at the vibrant hue.

"Esmé…your hair is red."

She frowned. "What?"

I ran a finger through it and pulled a piece forward for her to see. Esmé's mouth fell open in astonishment. As if unable to believe it, she grabbed her hair by the fistful to stare at it in awe I found adorable.

"I guess the illusion's gone," she whispered.

"'Illusion'? What did you see?" my mother asked.

Esmé looked around the room and then at me, as if only just noticing there were others present. She smoothed out her hair as a haunted look passed over her face. Whatever she experienced with Sebastián Eliódor couldn't have been anything short of traumatizing.

I offered my hand, and she took it without question.

"I was in the Sun Killer's domain," she said wearily, and my insides clenched. "It was a dark place made of fire and tar. My magic was useless to me there."

"What did he do?" I asked, resisting a scowl.

Esmé closed her eyes and shook her head. When she opened them, she looked nowhere but at our joined hands.

"He said a lot of nasty things," she muttered, "but above all else, he wanted me dead."

"Why?" Canela asked.

"Because I'm…"

Esmé trailed off, her mind going somewhere else. I ran my thumb across her skin.

"What's wrong?" I asked.

Her gaze trailed to a group of candles, their flames still glowing bright blue. There was a tormented look on her face, and I ached to rid her of it.

"I'm Leandro Eliódor's daughter."

A mixture of shock, comfort, hope, and fear washed over me all at once. Shock, for obvious reasons. Comfort, because I had a fear she might be the Sun Killer's daughter instead. There was hope, because for the longest time, the last known Eliódor was Sebastián, and he was no Champion of the Sun. If Esmé truly was the last Sun King's daughter, then there was hope not just for me but for everyone. But it also terrified me because it officially made her Sebastián's number one target.

"I should've known," my mother said.

Her attention was glued on Esmé as she approached the table with a vibrant spark I hadn't seen in a long time.

"Evaliná, your mother, was pregnant when your father died. When I heard she was killed, I thought Sebastián killed you too," she said, signing at the same time.

"Wait, what?" I blurted out. My sister looked gob smacked. "You never told me she was pregnant."

"There are a lot of horror stories from those years that I didn't want to subject either of you to. Though killing infants isn't beneath the Black Death or his influence, I'm glad at least that was wrong."

"You can thank my mother for that. My...*uncle,* on the other hand, is very unhappy about my existence," Esmé grumbled. "He killed me, and the only reason I survived was because of...my..."

She grimaced, struggling with her words.

"This is going to sound insane."

I rolled my eyes. "We really need to stop saying that. Esmé, my sweet little angel, you were possessed and almost died. I think the most insane thing *has* already happened today."

Esmé narrowed her gaze, but everyone around the room nodded or made noises of agreement. After a moment of hesitation, she finally put us out of our misery.

"The God of Death saved my life."

What's another crazy thing to add to the list?

✳ ☽ ◯ ☾ ✳

Esmé proceeded to explain everything that the God of Death told her about her parents, how her mother fled from the Sun Killer, and the deal she made to save her life. Micqui hid her in the Underworld until he inevitably erased her memory and released her into society with a new identity. As of today, Esmé had all her memories back, and the Sun Killer was permanently banished by the God of Death himself.

While it did sound insane, I wasn't entirely fazed, considering everything that's happened thus far. It ranked pretty low beneath possession and Esmé dying, right next to my girlfriend being an Elíodor. As a God-given, my awareness of gods speaking to humans was pretty high. Of course, it wasn't every day that one of us was raised by one. If anything, I was more concerned about Esmé. While she seemed to be holding it together in front of everyone else, I could see in her eyes and the way she fidgeted that she wasn't doing well at all.

"Why did Micqui's protection stop working?" I asked after some thought.

"I asked the same thing," Esmé replied in amusement. "He said it was...uhhh...he said it was you."

I craned my head back. "What? *Me?* How?"

"Not you directly, necessarily. The day you brought the stone into my house, it broke something. The more magic I used and the stronger I became, the more it broke and the more vulnerable it made me."

I ran my hands over my face with a pang of guilt. "Shit."

Esmé put her hand on my arm and shook her head.

"Don't. He also said that you and I were...*fated*. And if it weren't for you, he—my uncle—would've done much worse much sooner. You saved me, Río," she stressed. "You helped bring me back."

I rested my forehead against hers, accepting her reassurance.

"Fated," Canela repeated, drawing our attention to her. "Romantic or not, a connection like that breeds strong magic. Just like your parents, Esmé, or even yours, Río. Apart, you are strong, but together, you can be powerful."

"It's true," my mother said. "My brother and I had a bond like that, and when I married Marino... it was something else."

Esmé and I looked at each other, and I could tell she was recalling every interaction we've ever had since the beginning. My birthday at *Teatro Paraíso*, and then running into her in the Obsidian District. Me walking her home, followed by her offer of hot chocolate in her house, and then coming back almost every night after that. The night I came back with the stone. The night in the ballroom. Her calling my name. Her coming back to me in the dungeon and facing me in my monstrous form. And everything else leading up to now. Fate or not, I would be a stone-cold liar if I said I didn't think Esmé and I were meant to be.

"And what does that mean for us, exactly?" I asked.

My mother grinned. "Hope, Río. For the first time in a long time, we have hope. You were right. Try not to let it get to your head."

Mariela snorted, and I threw her a sneer. Esmé giggled, a sound I was ecstatic to hear, even if it was at my expense.

45

Eclipse

Esmé

Paloma gave me a cloak to wear, both for secrecy's sake and for the fact that I was still in my nightgown. Mariela was able to heal Echo's bite on my arm, but I was still dirty from the altercation in the garden.

I stared down at myself in discomfort and suddenly had trouble breathing. Even though it happened internally, I couldn't help but feel like the dirt on my skin was remnants of the Sun Killer's domain. He was long gone now, but the weight of everything was settling in. My mind was burdensome, my body ached, and I was filled with an immense urge to cry all over again.

Río put a finger under my chin and tilted my head up so I was looking into his eyes instead.

"Hey," he said softly, "you're okay. We'll get you cleaned up when we get back to the castle."

"I don't even have shoes on," I muttered.

"I can carry you if you want," he offered.

Before all of this, I would've protested and insisted on walking on my own, but I was so exhausted on so many levels that the thought of letting Río—the real Río—carry me in his arms sounded like the relief I needed. And after what transpired, I think he needed it too.

"Yes, please."

With a tender grin and as much care as possible, Río lifted me up into his arms. I kissed his cheek before wrapping my arms around his neck and resting my head against his shoulder. We both sighed in each other's warm embrace, eased by each other's firm presence and closeness. He kissed my hair and I closed my eyes, recalling those words he said in my death.

"You should probably hide your hair, little bird," Canela said behind me.

My eyes snapped open as I remembered who I truly was.

"Right," I whispered, pulling the hood over my head to cover my new hair.

"Welcome to the club, Red," Río sang.

I threw him a playful frown, but his smile was all too contagious. Even though the change would take some getting used to, there was solace in knowing I wasn't alone.

There were quite a few onlookers outside Canela's shop. A few of them I recognized from beneath my hood, and for a moment, I swore I saw Ignacio. Apparently, Río brought me here on horseback with no disguise and I'm sure a carriage full of royals and their guards was not something the people of the Obsidian District witnessed often. The strange girl they carried around with them didn't do the gossip any favors either. Considering how secretive his family was, I couldn't help but take the blame for the whole ordeal.

For my sake, we rode back in the carriage, and Mariela took Río's horse with Echo to lead her way. The royal carriage was a lot like the one that took me to the ball, except larger and with a lot more gold. Nobody spoke the entire journey as we were all drained from the traumatic experience. I sat nestled against the prince, with his arm draped around me. Even if it was a little, I hoped to get some sleep, but every time I closed my eyes, I saw my uncle with his burning red eyes. I tried focusing on the grooves of my ring, just like I aways have, but all it reminded me of was my mother now. That alone threatened to break me.

At Castillo Paricia, everyone seemed to be waiting with bated breath.

Río stepped out before me and, to someone I couldn't see, said, "I want a healing bath drawn in my room immediately."

"Right away, *Alteza*," they replied.

The prince assisted me out of the carriage, and immediately, there was a sharp gasp from the stewards present. I looked up sharply as they all gaped at me as if seeing a living deity before them. I felt around my head and realized my hood had fallen off. I instinctively took a step back, but Río kept a firm hold on my hand.

"Hey, look at me."

My eyes locked onto his dark ones, affectionate and encouraging enough to let him guide me down. Before my bare feet could touch the courtyard, the prince scooped me up, his gaze only on me.

"I've got you," he whispered.

Río carried me up into the castle, through the many stairs and hallways, and didn't put me down until we arrived safely in his chamber. He placed me down by the foot of the bed, locked the doors, and proceeded to check every corner of the room, as if searching for some kind of threat. Meanwhile, I stared at the large bed, the scene of the crime.

My books were put away and neatly stacked on a small table across the room. The bed was made, but my last moment here was still alive in spirit. The heaviness of it all crushed me as the events of the night danced before me in a macabre show. Those memories, though horrifying, would never truly belong to me. No, I shared them with the Sun Killer and the Black Death. I was forced to be a spectator as they wreaked havoc on the world in this body—this *vessel*.

A vessel was merely an empty container meant to be filled with something. Never in my life did I think I would have anything in common with an inanimate object. Even if I did, I never would have wanted someone *else* to decide what did or didn't live inside me. It was violating. It stripped me in a way I never imagined. And I felt completely and utterly stupid for letting this happen.

"Hey, the bath is ready," Río said, but I was too lost in thought.

"He pretended to be you," I told him. My vision blurred, and the more I spoke, the more everything hurt. "He said he wanted to show me something. He wanted to make me feel better, and I just...followed him like nothing. I barely questioned it at first, but I thought it was you. I thought it was you. I thought—"

My words tumbled out of me in a desperate attempt to exorcise these emotions, but Río refused to let me crumble alone.

"Don't," he said, shaking his head. "Don't do that to yourself, Esmé."

He was by me in quick strides and wiping away my tears. There was something furious in his eyes, but it wasn't towards me.

"He used us against each other, Río," I cried. "He was so powerful. My magic wasn't enough. I was so helpless. I couldn't stop him."

"I know. I know, but we're still here. You're still here," he argued fervently.

"This time," I whispered.

It wasn't the first, and it wouldn't be the last. Not now. Not anymore.

The prince's eyes darkened grimly.

I ran my fingers through my hair and looked down at the vibrant red color. It was a color that belonged to my father and his cursed brother, just like the blue flame and this shadow. Yes, I was still alive, but at what cost? I knew the entire truth, but all I felt was hopelessness and despair.

"Everyone is so happy that I'm an Eliódor, but why can't I feel it?" I asked, my voice frail. "I thought I would feel better when I got my memories back. Better about my life or myself, but now I'm just…"

My emotions boiled over, and my chest heaved, the next words coming out as an agonized sob.

"I'm so sad."

I put my face in my hands and let my knees buckle. Río caught me just in time and lowered us both to the floor, holding me in his arms as I cried uncontrollably.

"He took them from me! I'm still an orphan. I have no home. Everything's broken. It's just loss and decay. He took away everything. How is it possible that the only family I have left is a monster?"

I never experienced such grief before. Not like this. It pierced right through the marrow of my bones.

"How could he do something like that? How can I come from such evil? He was supposed to love his brother, but it didn't matter. His family didn't matter. *I* don't matter. I'm an anomaly to him. A mistake to be erased. Maybe I am."

"No, no, no, Esmé, stop." Río put his hands on the sides head to look me dead in the eyes and say, "Listen to me. You are *not* a mistake. I'd kill him just for saying that. *He* is the one who failed, not you.

You're the exact opposite. You're a precious gift. You're magic. You are *everything*."

His voice cracked and he swallowed thickly. There was disbelief in his impassioned statement, as if he couldn't fathom what I was saying. He looked so distressed with his red-rimmed eyes.

"Sebastián doesn't even know you or doesn't care enough to try, so don't listen to him. You matter to me and to the people who truly care about you. Even the God of Death himself. I'm sorry for what he did to you, to your family, to mine, to my mom, and to *us*. I don't know why people like him exist, but you're nothing like him. And maybe that's exactly why he wants you dead."

I clutched onto his shirt as I stared into his beautiful, umber eyes. There was a real, ardent love that someone like the Sun Killer could never replicate. It cradled me like a warm blanket. He was so undeniably Río that I knew for certain I would never allow myself to think anything else.

"I love you," I whispered.

My voice was small, but my feelings could flood the whole world twice over. We both said those words when we thought I wasn't coming back, and now I wanted to say them in life before it was too late.

Surprise, adoration, and happiness cycled through Río's face. He kissed me softly on the lips before repeating the words back to me.

"I love you...*so much*."

Río picked me up from the floor so we could take a relaxing bath in the salt and herb-filled waters of the tub. He took particular care of me, and I was more than glad to let him take the reins. I was simply content to be alone with him again and to finally be rid of the filth and mire. Tiredness aside, my illness was completely gone, so I was finally coherent enough to enjoy this time with my prince.

Neither of us was inclined to do anything sexual at all since we were both feeling incredibly fragile. All I asked of him was that he hold me tight and never let go, which, according to him, was one of the easiest requests I could ever make. He was soft and gentle, but his arms were firm around me, keeping me grounded as we lay beneath the sheets. We exchanged kisses and soft words, as well as a few more I love you's.

"My real name is Aurora," I told him. "Aurora Eleanora Eliódor."

"Aurora," he sang. "I like that name. Do you want me to call you that instead?"

I hummed thoughtfully. "I'm not sure yet. I've only ever had one name before."

"You can try it out and see how you like it."

I pulled him tighter, somehow nervous over such a small yet grandiose thing.

"Okay, but I only want you to say it. I'm not ready for everyone else to know."

"Don't worry, your name is safe with me... *Aurora*."

Maybe I *did* like the sound of that.

46

Broken Mirror

Esmé

The following day, *Reina* Victoria pronounced me a free woman. I was no longer a prisoner and was free to come and go as I pleased. Within the castle, that is. Everywhere else was to be...*discussed*. Only a few trusted individuals knew about my identity and were to keep their mouths shut for my safety and the safety of the country. Among them were the royal family, Paloma, a few stewards and guards, and, of course, Canela. Everyone else who came in and out of the palace for training or meetings was to be doubted.

The biggest issue was my red hair. The Markaél's debated among themselves the best way to obscure who I was, with a scarf being the most popular solution. Thankfully, Micqui resolved the issue with another smaller gift. It was a beautiful necklace with circular obsidian stone that had intricately shaped golden petals all around. It reminded me of a sunflower, which was intentional, according to the God of

Death. Within the necklace was a charm that, when touched, would turn my hair brown to hide my Eliódor appearance. It could last a full day and can only be undone by me, and me alone. I knew better than to overuse magic now, so I kept my usage for the daytime.

It was strange to rise from being a captive of the crown to a princess who wore a crown (figuratively). To those who knew, at least. To everyone else, I was proven innocent of my crimes and have become an ally to the God-given. Though I could always tell who knew I was a princess based on their exuberance. All of them addressed me as "*Alteza*" and "*Princesa* Esmé," including the Markaél's themselves. Even Captain Dominic went out of his way to apologize for his behavior and vowed to make up for it (which pleased the prince). Like many changes in my life, the surge of respect was going to require some adapting on my behalf.

My lessons were put on hold until I fully recovered from my fatigue and the lingering effects of my possession. In all honesty, I was grateful for it. What happened with my uncle left me hollowed out, and desolation followed me in the days that ensued. I used to believe that the scariest thing I could encounter was a ghost, but they were merely dust motes compared to the power of a demon. They only ever played games with me at the start of our relationship, but even then, they never sought to strip me of my autonomy. I had a hard time trusting myself since then and was overcome with a sense of paranoia. I was terrified that he would come back or that I'd lose my mind again somehow. Savy was particularly kind in this time, and sometimes I would hear Micqui's voice in my ear, telling me I was safe. The only one who truly understood how I felt was Río.

When he wasn't helping with the cleanup, we spent nearly every waking moment together, whether it was in his bedroom, the castle's private beach, or the garden. If he were on the training grounds, I'd lean over one of the balconies and watch him practice with a sword or spear. I could tell he liked showing off when I was around, which was both amusing and alluring. I often wondered if he was capable of being bad at anything until I remembered how terrible he was at making hot chocolate. Was it the same thing as being a fighter? Not at all, but knowing it made me smile. One day, if I dare, I'd like to ask him to teach me how to wield a weapon, because I was starting to understand that perhaps it *was* a good idea to have options.

With no shackles, no tower, and a newfound liberty, the castle felt more like another home. Even when Río was gone, I used the greenhouse for leisure and spent much time between it, the gardens, and the library, catching up on my family history. I grew closer to Mariela, Paloma, Arabella, and even the queen. Yet I couldn't help but feel like something incredibly vital was still missing from my life.

Dulce, Camilo, and Flora. Even Fabian and Teo came to mind. Not a day went by that I didn't think about them, and now that I was able, I longed to see them. But when I expressed this to Río and the queen, they were extremely reluctant. It was too much of a risk for me to go into the city as an Eliódor, which was irritating. Somehow, I managed to argue well enough that the queen offered a compromise:

I can invite *one* friend to the castle and talk to them in a private room.

I raised my eyebrows at that. "You'd be willing to let one of them come here?"

"Do any of them use magic?" she asked.

"No. Not at all."

"Good. It'll be safer if they come here. One thing goes wrong, and we can deal with it."

"That won't be necessary," I reassured, but agreed to her terms.

It pained me to choose between my friends, but if I were obligated to, my first choice would be Dulce. Out of the three of them, she was the friend I've known the longest, and the one who promised to check up on me when I returned from the ball. I can only imagine her distress at finding out I never returned, so it was only fair I let her know I was alive. As much as I could be, at least.

The queen sent out a formal invitation, and on the day of the meeting, I was an anxious mess. I spent hours making sure I looked nice and proper and even picked out the prettiest rose-colored dress from a collection the Markaél's had made for me. Arabella applied some light makeup and braided my hair in two plaits that she twisted into two buns above my neck. With Micqui's charm in effect, Dulce wouldn't even know that I wasn't still the Esmé she knew.

"I know it's too much of a risk, but I wish you could meet her," I told Río.

I was pacing back and forth in our room when he suddenly caught me by the shoulders with a smirk.

"One day I will," he said, "but I'm still trying to keep you to myself. I don't know if you want the extra spectacle if she tells someone about us."

"Dulce wouldn't…well…"

I bit my lip. As much as I loved her, I wasn't entirely certain Dulce wouldn't say anything to our friends. She loved gossip, after all.

When the time came, Río took my hand and walked me down to a private parlor where my friend was waiting. He stopped us down the hall from the doors and whispered to me in a gentle tone.

"I'll be right outside if you need anything. You don't even have to yell. Werewolf senses and all that." He kissed me on the cheek and said, "Good luck."

I squeezed his hand, and headed towards the chamber doors. The man standing guard bowed his head and pulled it open so I could slip inside.

The parlor was like many rooms in Castillo Paricia, all satin, gold, blue, and white. It was filled with several chairs and couches for sitting and socializing. There were also clay statues, beaded figurines, beautifully woven tapestries, as well as potted greenery. Tall windows let in bright sunlight, and a warm fire burned in the hearth. I could feel its energy even from far away—a new thing that I was constantly aware of. Standing by the windows was a familiar, petite woman with black hair, wearing her best olive-green dress that she no doubt made herself. Her hair was in a braided crown around her head.

"Dulce," I gasped.

"Esmé!"

We both ran into each other's arms. I immediately burst into tears, feeling a mixture of joy and longing as we held each other tight. It felt like an eternity since we last saw each other. Her face was the last I saw from our group of friends, as she bid me good luck and promised great things. I wonder if she imagined her words would come true in such a twisted manner, the same way I could have never guessed that my first prayer to Micqui would lead me here.

With a sniffle, we pulled apart while still holding each other's hands.

"You're alive!" Dulce exclaimed.

I giggled breathlessly. "I am!"

"How?" she asked, shaking her head in disbelief. "Esmé, we thought you were dead! After the ball—the *massacre*—you never came back, and then these armed people went to your apartment. Camilo didn't want to believe it, but Flora was a mess. And now you're here in *Castillo* Paricia, of all places?"

Armed guards? Nobody told me about that.

"I... I know. I'm sorry. I can't even imagine what it was like for you guys to be in the dark," I replied.

"You-you were there, right? Did you see... *everything*?"

"Yes...I did."

Dulce put a hand over her lips with a gasp.

"Are you okay? How are you still alive? Have you been here this whole time?" she rambled.

"As of right now, I'm okay," I told her with a nod. "I was hurt during the winter solstice."

I pulled down my sleeve to show her the spindly scars from the werewolf's claws.

"Moon and fucking stars, Esmé. You survived a full-blown werewolf attack!" she said.

I nodded, adjusting my dress. "Narrowly. They healed me and have been keeping me safe here."

"That's amazing. I didn't think the God-given were so generous," she mused. "Do you think they'll let you come home now that you're healed?"

Dulce's expression and tone oozed hope. It stabbed into my heart like a knife. I wanted so badly to affirm those desires, but knew I couldn't. I knew *why* I couldn't.

"N-No, Dulce. I'm not," I told her, my voice thin.

Her jubilance slowly disappeared.

"Why not?"

"I can't."

It hurt me not to tell her the truth, but after what happened with my uncle, it was dangerous to do otherwise.

My friend scoffed, fixing me with a strange scowl. "That's the only answer I get?"

"It's complicated, and I don't want to drag you or anyone else into this more than I have to."

"Well, that's not ominous at all. What about Camilo and Flora? Are you going to tell *them* about this? What about *Teatro Paraiso*? Everyone's been asking about you."

"I'm not going back, Dulce," I told her, my voice on the verge of breaking. "You're the only one I'm telling."

She took a sweeping look around the room, as if seeking prying eyes. When her gaze met mine once more, she rested her hands on my arms and leaned forward to speak in a whisper.

"Are they keeping you prisoner here? Is that why? What did they do to you? Is it the queen? Is she forcing you to keep your mouth shut about what really happened at the ball?"

Even if it were true, her questions caught me completely off-guard. I couldn't help but back away from her touch.

"I can tell you firsthand that you have no idea what you're talking about," I said.

"Well, then, tell me what's going on, because I'm starting to get worried. I mean, you invited me here after being gone for weeks, and now you're just being vague. The entire city has been freaking the fuck out ever since the winter solstice. The king's dead, werewolves attacked the palace, and then the prince nearly drowned the city."

A wave of frustration ran through me at her callous mention of Río.

"Dulce!" I snapped.

"What?"

The flames in the hearth swayed, turning blue before going back to normal. Her eyes flashed at the brief change.

"The flood was an accident," I told her, forcing politeness into my words.

"And how do you know that?" she asked.

"I just do."

She narrowed her eyes at me skeptically, and I could tell that she was piecing something together. It felt as if I were walking on eggshells, which was not something I expected to endure today. I found myself hiding behind a wall that I only ever used with people who *weren't* my friends and whom I *didn't* trust. It wasn't what I wanted to do, but it was the only way to keep her from finding out the truth.

"Oh… you've been seeing him around, haven't you?" she asked slyly.

"It's hard not to, in a place like this," I replied curtly, dodging her insinuation. "You were wrong about him."

She didn't look too convinced.

"Wasn't he bitten by a werewolf?" she derided.

The image of Río getting bitten flashed before my eyes. It was so brief, yet it was enough to quicken my heartbeat and turn the flames blue again. How strange that it came so naturally, despite my lack of practice.

Dulce's gaze snapped to the hearth, her face paling. "How is that happening?"

"Who told you that?" I asked, ignoring her question.

"Which part?"

"The part about the prince."

"There were survivors, Esmé. They saw things," she stressed, facing me with biting curiosity. "Based on your reaction, I'm guessing it's true."

"Does it matter?"

"It matters because he's supposed to be the next Moon King," Dulce contested. "You know how people feel about werewolves. And after what happened at the ball, he doesn't stand a chance. We're at war, and the Moon Kingdom is crumbling before our very eyes."

"Crumbling?" I blurted out.

It was complete and utter nonsense to me. Is this what it was like to know the truth of something firsthand yet have the outside world completely twist and misunderstand it? Did I suddenly know too much?

"Who said the Moon Kingdom is crumbling?"

"Isn't it obvious?"

"No," I chuckled in disbelief. "Dulce, we're at war with one of the most dangerous men in the world, and you're praying on the downfall of one of the only people who wants to bring him down."

"I'm not 'praying' on his downfall," she protested.

"Well, you clearly find joy in it."

"I just don't want another Sebastián Elíodor on our hands. That's all anyone is worried about. It's happened once. Who says it won't happen again?"

Something broke like that once-familiar wall of and my emotions spilled over. I was too incredulous to care. This recent wound of mine was still too raw, and my love for Río was too great. I could not allow her to speak ill of him in such a foul way.

"You know nothing of Sebastián Elíodor, Dulce, the same way you know nothing about the prince," I hissed. "Trust me, you don't want the Moon Kingdom to fall. You don't want another Anelante or Dragona. That's precisely what *he* wants. It doesn't matter how much you love being right or how much you hate the God-given or werewolves. None of that will matter when we're dead!"

The blue flame grew in size and brightness with my anger, painting our faces like waves of the sea. Funny, I couldn't recall ever being this furious before. Not before the ball, and not towards the people I held so dear. But now there was something within me that I could no longer contain. The events of the last few weeks have left me cracked and frayed at the edges.

Dulce blinked a few times at my sharp tone. Her eyes flitted between me and the flames as she cycled through a myriad of emotions. When she spoke, she uttered a question that's been repeating in my mind since all of this began:

"What's wrong with you?"

There was nothing but earnest affection in her voice.

I hummed wearily. *What isn't?*

"There are things you don't know. I'm different in ways that I can never come back from. And it's nobody's fault but fate, really," I muttered bitterly.

That's not true. It's my uncle's fault, but she can't know that.

Dulce's shoulders drooped as the passion and fury left her. She took tentative steps towards me, and when I didn't back away, she took my hands in hers once more.

"Esmé…" she uttered, her eyes brimming with tears. "Esmé…just tell me. I won't tell anyone, I promise. I'm just…I'm so worried about you. You know I love you, and I… I hate to see you like this. Please…"

My lips quivered as I whispered, "I can't."

"Why not?"

"I… If I tell you, I would only be putting you in danger. You have to understand. I just wanted you to know that I was alright. It was the one thing I could risk," I explained, already crying.

Sorrowful tears raced down her cheeks, falling onto the floor as she squeezed my hands in the silence.

"I wish I could help you," she said when she found her voice.

"You can help me by surviving. Maybe you should think about getting out of Coáraluna sometime in the future."

Dulce shook her head. "Wait, what? Why?"

"I have a feeling that the bad things are only just starting, and I don't want you or anyone else to become another victim."

Again, she gawked at me. I could tell she wanted to keep probing for answers even though I couldn't give her any.

"Please. Trust me," I stressed.

Dulce rolled her eyes with a groan but inevitably nodded. "Okay, okay, okay. Fine."

We embraced each other again, this time holding on for twice as long.

"Does he treat you well, at least, your moon prince?" she asked.

I couldn't help but laugh because, of course, she could tell.

"Yes," I answered with a blissful sigh. "Yes, he does."

She then leaned back to give me a skeptical look. "Is he the one who gave you the very expensive necklace?"

My cheeks burned red, making it impossible to hide much of anything now.

Dulce gasped, "You sneaky little bitch. I should've known you had juicy secrets."

The laugh that came out of me was genuine and profound, and managed to alleviate most of the remaining tension between us. The hearth glowed orange-red, save for the occasional blue flicker. If Dulce had any pressing questions about the behavior of the fire, she didn't ask them. No, instead, we sat together a little while longer as she caught me up on everything that's happened with our friends and her shop. I gave her as many minor details as I could spare, most of which I agreed upon with Río. Though I would have loved to keep her around, eventually we had to part ways. We hugged and cried again before saying our final goodbyes, with promises that I would tell her the truth when the time was right.

✸ ☽ ◯ ☾ ✸

When I exited the parlor, Río was waiting down the hall for me as promised. He looked into my eyes carefully.

"What happened? Is everything alright?"

"Yes, everything's fine," I replied.

"Are you sure? Because I heard yelling earlier and saw the light turn blue. I was this close to barging in."

I sighed heavily, my shoulders falling. "I just got a little agitated. No objects or people were burned, I promise. Sorry for worrying you."

"My love, how many times do I need to tell you that you don't have to apologize for everything?" he asked with a smirk. "Also, you can't control how much I worry about you because it's a symptom of how much I absolutely adore you."

I rolled my eyes bashfully as a blush spread across my face. Río grabbed my face and kissed both my cheeks and mouth, making me giggle. He placed my hand on his arm, and the two of us walked side by side back from whence we came.

"Are you happy you got to see her?" he asked.

"I am," I replied wistfully. "For a moment there, I almost wasn't, but...she's still my friend. She still cares. And I care about her."

"Do you guys usually yell at each other, or...?"

I snorted. "No. This is the first time. I don't know what's gotten into me lately. It's like I'm on the verge of erupting more often than not."

"Do you need me to list off everything you've been through this last month or...?"

"I guess I just didn't expect it—how much I've changed. Or at least I didn't realize it until I talked to Dulce again."

We strolled into the fresh air of the garden and sat at the edge of a fountain with a small statue of a water dragon. I traced my fingers through the cool water, letting my mind drift. I could feel Río staring at me. It warmed my heart when he did that.

"Do *you* think I stand a chance? As king?" he asked suddenly.

I looked up at him sharply. It was an earnest question. Of course, he heard my conversation with Dulce. He swore he wouldn't eavesdrop, but considering how loud we had been, I'm sure it was hard to ignore.

Río didn't like talking about becoming Moon King very often, if at all. He viewed the prospect like another impending doom, just as he did his first turning, and while he was usually so fearless and sure, this was a major wound for him. It was why I got so angry with Dulce in the first place, and it broke my heart that Río had to hear some of his insecurities confirmed.

"Of course I do," I replied vehemently.

It wasn't even a question.

"You're not just saying that because you love me?" he asked with an eyebrow raised.

"No, I'm saying it because I love you *and* because it's true."

"You don't think being a werewolf affects things?"

"Some people might think that, but not me. There's also your family and the people of this castle. I mean, they respect you so much." I interlaced his hand with mine as I looked at him. "You care so much about Avilonía. You've spent the past year risking your life to help with the efforts against the Sun Killer. I mean, I've seen your wounds firsthand. You don't do it for praise; otherwise, you wouldn't let everyone think you're this horrible person capable of cold-blooded murder. You literally helped rebuild after the full moon. What noble has ever done any of that?"

He snorted. "Not many. That's for sure."

"Exactly. You know, it used to infuriate me how easy it was for you to live life without a care, but the truth is, you actually do care. It's admirable how far you're willing to go for the people you love. I would know. You do what needs to be done because it has to be, and you'll do it yourself because you want to. You're funny and charming and... you know. All of that makes you a king in my eyes. I would follow you anywhere, but again, I'm biased."

I shrugged, shooting him a playful smirk. The prince took me in fondly before leaning in close.

"I love you so much," he said.

"I love you, my sweet prince."

He kissed me ardently before saying, "You'll make a great queen someday. I know you will."

I instinctively cringed and had the urge to curl up into a ball. Whereas Río spent his whole life trying to become a ruler, the concept of being royalty was novel to me. It was practically a joke.

He laughed at my expression. "What? It's true."

"I'd rather not think about that right now."

"Baby steps, then."

"Baby steps," I repeated.

The teardrop light at his hip flashed, drawing our attention away from each other. Río's smile vanished as he took it in his hand, his dark eyes going wide. Somewhere within the castle, Echo started barking.

"What is that? What does it mean?" I asked.

He took my hand and pulled me to my feet.

"It means we need to go inside. *Now*."

47

The Betrayers

Río

Esmé and I practically ran through the garden towards the castle, following the sound of Echo's barking. We barely made it past the doors when Arabella came rushing towards us with the hound in tow, and my sister was nowhere to be seen.

"*Alteza!*" she called.

"What's wrong? Where's my sister?" I asked.

"She's upstairs with Paloma. Her healing magic was needed."

"Why? For who?"

"No one from your family, *Alteza*," she assured, sensing my unease. "They both sent me to find you. A survivor from your father's ship has arrived."

To say I was taken by surprise would be an understatement.

"*Who?*"

"Yara Volpes. You might remember her from your training sessions. She washed up on the shore earlier today, and the guards brought her here. Paloma and the princess are tending to her, but from what I saw, she looked barely alive and like she hadn't eaten in days."

It wasn't often that I was left at a loss for words. All we've ever been told since my father's death, time and time again, was that there were no survivors. Considering how treacherous The Rift could be, we hardly questioned it. No one person could endure it by themselves, let alone Sebastián Eliódor's wrath. If Yara's mind were still her own, then it would be a complete miracle.

Esmé—*Aurora*—lightly touched my arm, and when I looked at her, she was as stricken as I was. She knew better than I did what happened on that ship. No doubt she was imagining it now.

"Where is she now?" she asked Arabella.

"Your old tower, *Alteza*," the maiden answered with faint amusement. "*Majestad* doesn't trust that she's of sound mind, so Yara will be staying there until she's interrogated."

I scoffed, "Not the dungeon? Mother's feeling generous. Thank you for the message, Arabella. We can take Echo from here."

"Of course, *Alteza*," she replied with a chuckle before going off to do her next task.

I crouched before Echo to run my hands over his fur and kiss him on the head, thanking him for doing a good job. He wagged his tail and licked the side of my face in return. Aurora came around to kneel beside him and pet him along his back happily. My eyes lingered on her face before hovering over the obsidian pendant hanging from her neck. It was the one thing keeping her from looking like an Eliódor and, therefore, keeping a target off her back. It was for her safety, yet I couldn't help but feel a pang of guilt for forcing her to hide.

"Aurora," I whispered.

She tore her attention away from Echo to look at me.

"Hmm?"

I chose my next words carefully, not wanting to upset her.

"When you had that vision of your uncle on the ship...did you see a young woman?" I asked.

Her gaze shuttered slightly, her brow furrowing. Suddenly, it was as if she wasn't looking at me at all but at something distant. Eventually, she shook her head.

"No. No, I... I didn't see many faces. The fire and darkness made it hard to tell and..." She faltered, working her lip. "The ones I did see were dead or dying."

I nodded grimly as that ache in my chest returned. "Yeah, that's what I thought."

"I'm guessing you don't trust her either?"

"I want to, I really do, but I know better than that. This whole thing sounds too good to be true."

Not only was I my father's spy before all of this, but I am also my mother's son. As much as I tried rejecting certain parts of my upbringing, mistrust was inherent in me. It warred with my optimism, and I only learned to truly hone it once I started "playing vigilante" (as my mother put it). And as much as I wanted to trust Yara and whatever answers she could give us, I knew there had to be another shoe waiting to drop.

❋) ○ (❋

Yara Volpes and I spent time together on the training grounds and on my father's ship, so I knew her well enough. She was barely a year older than my sister and was born and raised in the farmlands east of Coáraluna. She was one of the best swordsmen we've ever seen, which is why my mother chose her to become a warrior instead of a guard. Seeing as I couldn't be on the front lines with my father, I vouched for Yara to go with him in my stead. Once he saw how talented she was, he kept her on his ship indefinitely. The fact that she was still alive after it went down was either convenient or proved how much of a fighter she was.

Emilia Mondragón

My mother was going to conduct her interrogation in the evening, which further proved she was as impatient for answers as I was. Even then, I preferred not to attend them unless necessary. Interrogations were tedious work, and pulling information out of people was not something I liked to do. It disturbed me, especially when a truth serum was involved, so I often waited for the debrief from my mother when it was over. Some might call it a weak point in my spine, but it didn't offend me.

Aurora and I were passing the time in the bedroom when Arabella came by to tell us that my mother requested our presence in Paloma's tower. We practically ran there, eager for whatever information may await us. The two of us spent the last few hours speculating about what we would learn from Yara, as it was all a big mystery. Even Auror didn't have the full picture of what happened on that ship, so having another piece of the puzzle would alleviate confusion for all of us.

Like always, I expected a summary of the interrogation from my mother, but when we arrived, Yara was still bound to the iron chair under the effects of the serum. Her breath hitched when she saw me.

"*Alteza.*"

She bowed her head, which was about as much as she could do in her situation. My befuddled gaze went from her to my mother.

"What's going on? I thought you were going to call me when you were done."

"I was, but I had a feeling you would want to hear this truth for yourself."

I noticed then that my mother was visibly seething, her eyes like daggers. It was like seeing storm clouds approach. I know she didn't harbor disdain for Yara, at least not before today, so whatever cracked her icy exterior must have been serious.

"What truth?" I asked.

My mother only jutted her chin towards Yara, motioning for me to ask her myself. I shared a dubious look with Aurora, who nodded in reassurance from her place beside the queen. I worked my jaw seriously and I took my mother's place in front of Yara and the iron chair.

Whatever wounds Yara Volpes may have had before her arrival were now gone, but the evidence of what she endured was still clear to those who knew. Her copper skin was mildly sun-scorched, and her long raven hair, which was once half-shaven on the side, was starting to grow out. Despite her warrior-like musculature, she was more gaunt than before, and there was a new, thin scar on her face, slicing across her chin. She seemed to freeze in my presence, as if she had seen a ghost. It took me a second to understand why.

I look like my father.

I cleared my throat and crossed my arms to hide how much the thought affected me.

"Hey, Yara. I'm glad you're alive. When we heard the news, we were almost certain we had lost everyone."

"I don't blame you," she said. "For a while, I didn't think I would make it."

Her answers were instant now that she was at the mercy of the serum.

"Then how exactly *did* you survive?" I asked.

"Your father, the king saved me. He threw me overboard with his magic. I swam to the nearest lifeboat, and... I prayed."

Aurora scoffed over my shoulder, and I knew exactly what she was thinking.

"You *swam* through the Rift?" I asked incredulously.

The Rift was a polluted deathtrap. Dark creatures lurked within, waiting to devour anything that fell beneath the surface.

Yara shrugged. "It was either that or die. I managed to row far away until I got lost at sea. A storm hit, and I was almost certain I would die from starvation. Eventually, the nymphs found me and helped me get to Coáraluna. Who knew they were so kind?"

A delighted chuckle left my lips, softening the interaction if only for a moment. The fact that the nymphs were still helping our people was monumental, considering our tumultuous past with them. I owe them a lot for what they've done.

"Did you see him?" Aurora chimed in. "The Sun Killer?"

The warrior tensed, a bit surprised by Aurora's presence, but the potion didn't allow her any hesitation.

"No. He hadn't boarded the ship yet, so I didn't see him with my own eyes. But I think *Rey* Marino knew he was coming when the werewolves appeared. That's why he threw me overboard."

I cast a sidelong glance at my mother, wondering if this was it, but all she did was urge me forward with a motion of her head. For some reason, she wanted *me* to figure this out, and I had no clue as to why. It filled me with dread.

Again, I looked into Yara's eyes, now fearing my next question.

"How did the werewolves get on the ship?"

The warrior's eyes darkened with anger in a way that defied her youthful nature.

"It was Captain Calicó, *Alteza*," she grinded out. "He sent a message to the king, asking him for aid on the coast of Old Avilonía. When we got there, he and his supposed crew boarded the ship, only for him to announce his allegiance to the Sun Killer. A fight broke out, and then his crew started turning. It was a massacre."

Tears filled Yara's eyes as she relived her waking nightmare. At the same time, the animal in me seemed to unfurl from itself. Its snout was seeking, claws scratching, as the answer I had been searching for was now in my hands. Yet it was an answer I did not expect.

Aurora gasped, "Captain Calicó. Is that—"

"Silas' father," I rumbled, far away from myself.

"It was him too!" Yara exclaimed. "The captain said that you and your family would be dead come the solstice, the same way the king would be. He said his son was walking in his footsteps by fulfilling the other half of the plan. I wanted to get the message to you, but it was too late."

My heart thudded like hammer on steel, the sound echoing in my ears. White-hot fury singed my skin as that unbearable itch returned once more.

Silas.

His name echoed like the bark of a hound.

No wonder his father couldn't go to the ball that night. No wonder he was so bold.

They're the reason my father is dead.

The edges of my vision darkened, and I could hear nothing but the sound of people screaming. Real screams from that night mixed with my anguish.

"Río?" My mother's voice was muffled to my ears.

If I don't leave, I'm going to hurt her and everyone here.

"I need a moment," I choked out, my voice ragged.

I made a beeline for the tower door, ignoring everyone's protests. My legs guided me through the castle until I was outside before the garden once again. As soon as I was in the dark shade of night, I doubled over and sank to my knees in the stone courtyard. I clutched my head, willing the monster down as I screamed into the ground in anger, frustration, and pain. My muscles twitched as the wolf begged to be let out—to run, to find, to tear to shreds. I knew where Silas lived. I could get there if I wanted to.

This is his *fault.*

"Stop," I hissed. "Stop it. Stop it. Stop it."

I should've killed him back then.

"I SHOULD HAVE KILLED HIM!"

Claws grew out of my nails, and the hair on my arms thickened. My muscles rippled with more aggression, and my spine felt on the verge of breaking.

"Río!" Aurora called behind me.

She was beside me in seconds with her hands on my shoulders.

"Don't," I said, trying to push her away. "Don't. I'll hurt you."

"No, you won't."

Despite the claws and signs of my looming transformation, Aurora wrapped her arms around me and held my face firmly against her chest. There was a part of me that wanted to lean into my wrath, but as soon as I was in Aurora's arms, it quietly receded. In that beautiful voice of hers, she started to sing so low that only I could hear. It was a song from my birthday, and the dam within me broke. I wrapped my arms around her waist and buried my face in her stomach as I cried tears with no end. Everything I withheld since Fort Adelfa to almost losing Esmé came flooding out. It spilled over. All because of one bastard from my past that should've drowned years ago.

"I'm so sorry," Aurora cried softly. "I'm so sorry."

When the well was dry, I sat back on my heels and let Aurora wipe my face. My mother, who had been watching from afar, came to join us. She sat down beside me and caressed my cheek somberly.

"There was no easy way to tell you, my love, but I didn't want to keep it from you. I would rather you hear it from the source with the truth serum," she said. "I guess I just didn't expect it to trigger the curse. I'm sorry."

I shook my head. "I don't blame you. I blame Silas and his family."

My outrage hardened into a glare.

"I'm going to kill him," I said.

That same cold resolve turned my mother's irises into storms.

"I know."

When I met Aurora's gaze, she gave no protest and displayed no fear. No, she shared a similar expression, but instead of storm or ice in her eyes, the burning gold in her eyes intensified. We were all connected in that moment by the same determination to rectify the injustice that had been done.

48

Pillars

Esmé

Yara Volpes was proven innocent of any connection to the Sun Killer. After her interrogation under the truth serum, Canela was invited back to corroborate the story with her magic. When it was known for certain that the warrior's story was true, the queen called for us to meet her in the war room early the next morning.

Us. *Me*. She wanted *me* to attend the important political meeting. I couldn't understand why until Río reminded me that I was a princess now—*the* Sun Princess. My existence was vital to the future of Avilonía; therefore, I needed to play my part in it. I don't know what I was expected to say, but I was grateful to be included in the conversation for once.

I assumed we were meeting with strange political figures or warriors of high rank, but when Río and I arrived, there were only familiar faces. The Markaél's, Echo, Paloma, Canela, Captain

Dominic, Yara, and even Arabella. Despite my bewilderment, the tension in my shoulders unwound. They all bowed upon my entrance, including Yara, whom I lingered on the longest. My hesitation was quickly assuaged by the queen.

"You may remove your disguise, little Eliódor. You have no enemies here."

I knew by now that the Queen of Storms didn't put her trust in just anyone and picked her allies well.

Río's hand rested against the small of my back in a gentle act of reassurance as I carefully touched the obsidian pendant resting against my chest. The only confirmation that it worked was the reactions that followed. There were a few soft gasps, and everyone's faces gleamed. Yara looked especially awestruck, which was unsurprising considering we only just met. When I looked over my shoulder at Río, his eyes were already on me, glimmering with devotion.

We each took a seat around the circular marble table, and I stole a sideways glance at my prince, who took everyone in curiously. Aside from a few private moments, he's been dismal and much quieter since finding out about Silas and Captain Calicó. It saddened me, though I understood why. I saw the result of Captain Calicó's betrayal in my mind's eye and barely survived what his son caused at the winter solstice. But, like his mother, I also wasn't prepared for the curse to come into play. I didn't realize just how closely tied one's emotions could be to such a thing, yet, like all magic, I suppose it made sense. The wolf in him was as wild as the fire in me. I knew it was absurd to approach a werewolf on the verge of transformation, but it hurt so much more to leave Río broken and alone in that garden.

As if sensing me staring, Río looked at me, and his expression immediately softened. He laced his fingers with mine and kissed the back of my hand. Knowing that we had an audience, I only briefly leaned against his shoulder before straightening to face everyone else.

"I know some of you are wondering why I've gathered you all here," the queen began, standing with her back against the window. "Well, as of today, you're the only ones I can fully trust. You've taken care of my family, you've seen what happens behind these castle walls, and you care about what happens to this country. That to me means more than your class or ranking, because as we all know, it's all bullshit.

"The Calicó family may not have been from our kingdom, but at the end of the day, we are all from Avilonía. To ally yourself with a dictator who has killed thousands of our own in the name of the Black Death makes you a disgrace to Avilonía itself. Not only is the Calicó family responsible for the death of your king and the warriors on that ship, but also for the deaths at the winter solstice. This betrayal has occurred right under our noses, and I refuse to let history repeat itself. I refuse to run. I refuse to be lenient. No treacherous deed will go unpunished, that you can all be sure of."

Her words seemed to rumble, as if she were casting a spell or calling upon a storm. I could feel it deep within me, just like I did in that courtyard.

"How will they be punished?" Río asked.

"When the time comes, I'll deal with Captain Calicó myself," she replied. "Silas, on the other hand, I'll leave for you to decide, my love."

The corners of Río's lips quirked up deviously. There was no dark chuckle or smart remark, only a thoughtful resolve that mirrored his mother's. It confirmed to me that his silence was not only sorrow but something dangerous as the deep sea itself. He knew *exactly* how he planned to kill Silas, and some dark part of me was curious to know the answer.

"In the meantime," the queen said slowly, filling me with anticipation, "we must prepare for war."

A few of us, including me, exchanged befuddled expressions.

"But we're already at war, *Majestad*," Canela said, voicing our thoughts.

La Reina shook her head grimly. "Not like this."

It was an ominous warning, as if she were seeing something we were not. Everyone at the table expressed varying degrees of alarm. All except Río. The prince looked completely unperturbed, as if he had been expecting his mother to say this. They must have talked about it in one of their private conversations prior to the meeting. I had no problem with that in most circumstances, but I once again felt left out of something extremely vital.

"What do you mean, *Majestad*?" I asked.

"What goes on at The Rift is merely an effort to avoid what used to be. The war our ancestors fought. The one my father, my husband, and I fought in. When we killed Casímir Gedeón and finally entered an era of peace, so many of us started to build lives, and... when a new threat came, we were too scared to lose any of it. We focused more on keeping the monsters out instead of fighting them, but the walls are coming down, and it's only a matter of time before Sebastián Eliódor reaches us. We need to be prepared for when that happens. We need to be prepared to fight."

"All of us, *Majestad*?" Arabella asked dubiously.

"All who are willing and able," the queen replied. "Don't be mistaken, fighting does not require magic or brute strength. Healers, craftsmen, farmers, and people who protect those who cannot fight are all as important as warriors. Though I do recommend self-defense lessons for all of you. Especially you, *Alteza*."

The Queen of Storms looked at me then, and I was overcome with a burst of excitement. A smile spread across my face as I nodded vigorously.

"Yes. Yes, I would love that."

She returned my smile, her eyes alight. "Good. Río and I would be more than happy to assist in that."

The prince himself seemed more awake and like his own self as he shared my enthusiasm.

"Yes, absolutely."

Across the table, Paloma raised a hand to say, "*Majestad*, how else shall we prepare?"

The queen crossed her arms and shook her lilac hair.

"We need to work fast. The dark magic of Old Avilonía is seeping into our rivers and ruining the crops and livestock. We need to gather our allies and strengthen our armies. That includes the Air King."

Both Mariela and Río groaned. I school my features, hiding my own displeasure. It wasn't merely the stories that Río told me that did it, but the fact that Silas and his father were from the Air Kingdom, too.

"Are we sure he doesn't know about Captain Calicó?" the prince asked. "I mean, considering his history."

"I know he's not the most ideal ally to have, but your grandfather wants Sebastián dead as much as we do. His army is strong, though we'll need to have a conversation about how trustworthy they are when the time comes," his mother assured.

Río sighed dramatically and grumbled, "As long as you don't sign me up for it."

"Do we even know where Silas and his father could be? Did they run?" I asked.

"Captain Calicó is nowhere to be found, *Alteza*, but we assume he's in Old Avilonía," Captain Dominic answered.

"Silas wouldn't run," Río added. "He's a coward. Probably too much of a coward to go to Old Avilonía. He'll cling to Valerta and the Air Kingdom as much as possible."

"That should be easy, then, right?" I asked.

The prince grimaced. "At a glance, maybe, but if they've been planning this for a long time, then it might not be. Storming in with an army wouldn't exactly be smart."

"Why not?"

"People get lost that way. *He* could get lost that way. Since we don't know where he's hiding, he could use opportunity to flee."

I nodded in understanding, wishing I had something to take notes with, because strategy was another skill I had to hone.

Mariela raised her hand before signing, "What about the Isle?"

The room grew quiet. Río raised his eyebrows at his mother expectantly.

She bit her lip apprehensively. "I may or may not send a message to the Isle, but don't get your hopes up."

"What's the Isle?" Yara and I asked.

"The Isle of Sierra. *Reina* Montserrat's territory," Río explained, meeting my gaze.

My jaw dropped. *Reina* Montserrat was the last Earth Queen and champion of the Earth god, Terrakán. No one knew what happened to her after The Great Divide, only that she lost her wife to the Sun Killer and disappeared without a trace. Everyone assumed she was murdered by my uncle or met some other horrific demise. What did it mean that she was still alive, and people knew?

Micqui didn't tell me that.

Canela laughed jubilantly, no doubt in disbelief, while the rest of us processed in stunned silence. Only the Markaél's were unfazed. Of course.

"She's been alive? This whole time?" I exclaimed.

"Yeah."

"Where?"

"A chain of islands going southwest," *La Reina* explained. "Once The Rift was created, she fled with the little family she had left and built a fortress in the middle of the ocean."

"She cut off all connection with Avilonía," Río said bitterly. "She...*renounced* her title as a God-given. Even though that's not possible."

"You've met her?" I asked, taken aback.

"No, but I know enough. My dad tried getting through to her, but…"

"She stopped taking messages," the queen finished. "The champions of Terrakán are a different level of intense. They're sturdy, steadfast warriors, and they're incredibly stubborn. Montserrat was not the best at opening up about her feelings, but we all knew they ran deep. I think that's why losing Sierra broke her the way it did. I don't blame her."

"I don't blame her either, but her help could be the difference we need from losing more people. She's not the only one who's lost someone they love. There *will* be more if we lose," Río argued.

"Well, if she's been ignoring your letters, then maybe someone should to talk to her in person. I'm sure there's a way to sail to the Isle, right?" I asked.

The prince perked up. "Actually, there is. I'd be more than happy to go. Mostly because I really want to see it for myself."

The queen scoffed, "That woman would probably have you speared through for arriving unannounced."

"She wouldn't be the first person to try. I'll take my chances."

The prospect of meeting the Earth Queen herself thrilled me. I've never been outside of Coáraluna before, and the Champions of the Earth were the final piece of a puzzle that was slowly forming in my mind.

"Better yet, I'll send her another letter and hope she responds. We'll add that to the list of possible allies and many things to accomplish," the queen said. "Other than the nobility of this kingdom, do we have any other ideas?"

"Mic-My...My patron!" I answered exuberantly.

"The nymphs," Río said in tandem. "There are more than enough of them who are willing to help. I mean, they helped Yara."

"They were very kind, *Majestad*," the warrior chimed in with a nod.

Even though it pained me, I resisted the urge to rattle off every question I had about said nymphs and the prince's affiliation with them. Otherwise, we'd be here all day. I knew of their existence and that they had their own society, particularly in the northern ocean. A king ruled there in a castle made of coral and rock, though I didn't know much else.

Arabella spoke up again.

"If I may, *Majestad*, you spoke of possible evacuation. Will it come to that?"

"It could," the queen replied with a nod. "Nothing is for certain, which is why we built tunnels that lead out of the city in case of an emergency. I'll be placing guards near the entrances for when—*if* the day comes. I know it's a terrifying thought to have, but I know far too well the patterns of war. It's best not to ignore them."

The handmaiden swallowed thickly. "Should we inform our loved ones then?"

"You can. A light notice will be sent to every family in the city, but if you want to tell your loved ones ahead of time, I merely ask that you do it discreetly. I don't want to cause mayhem prematurely."

I was suddenly very glad I warned Dulce ahead of time. It didn't even occur to me that a mass evacuation would be happening in the future. I just knew what my uncle was capable of, and I had a feeling we angered him quite enough.

Río ran his hands through his hair and leaned forward on the table. He held his hand out and started listing things off as he counted on his fingers.

"Okay. We have Grandfather, the nymphs, Esmé's patron, and possibly a lost Earth Queen who lives in the middle of the ocean. We need to build our army and hope that people will want to fight. We need to go to the Air Kingdom and kill Silas, find his father, and kill *him*. And on top of that, we need to find the remaining eyes of Gedeón and finally kill Sebastián Eliódor. Am I missing anything?"

He flashed his mother a facetious smile and she rolled her eyes.

"No, I believe that's all for now."

I anxiously toyed with my ring as a sudden panic rose in me. With every task Río named, I truly started to grasp the arduous, bloody future that awaited us. This fight was no longer in someone else's hands but also mine. *I* was one of four pillars in this God-given journey, and the weight of this country was heavy.

Río looked at me with a furrowed brow, and I replied with a shy smile. While the rest of the conversation continued, the prince sat back in his chair smoothly and let his arm fall gently around my waist. He leaned over me with his mouth at the shell of my ear.

"Are you okay?" he whispered.

Those werewolf senses truly worked wonders.

"I will be," I answered. "Just a little overwhelmed."

"Do you want to take a quick walk?"

While I was thankful for the offer, I politely shook my head. The last thing I wanted was to walk out of my first political meeting because I was a little nervous.

Instead, I focused on his eyes, letting the rest of the room fade away. You would think it was the first time we ever saw each other, when in reality, we could never get enough. We were each other's reprieve when we needed a moment to breathe. Even if this was Río's whole life and he had more experience than I did, I could tell it was a lot for him, too. We were both pillars now, and the future that lay ahead was daunting for us both. If it meant it would make things easier for him, then I was willing to bear the burden.

49

By the Sea

Esmé

Reina Victoria asked Río and me to stay behind after the meeting was over. Once everyone else was gone, she stood across the table from us with a strange, wary energy. The war room seemed more tense in the emptiness as the attention was no longer spread out. I was on the edge of my seat.

"There's a more private matter I wanted to talk to you two about," she said.

"What's wrong?" Río asked with a tone of dread.

"If what the God of Death said is true, then the two of you are fated. Love and connection are powerful things, which is why people like the Sun Killer seek to destroy them. Though not many of us can say the same thing, you survived not one but two close encounters with him—the winter solstice and Esmé's possession. First of many, surely. Despite our plans, nothing is ever certain, but what I do know is that you, Río, will be king. And Esmé, you will be queen."

My insides clenched at how factual she was with the statement. I couldn't even imagine myself anywhere near her level, yet it was a title I was meant to bear.

She continued, "I know I wasn't the biggest supporter of your relationship at first, but you can hardly blame me considering the circumstances. But even before we knew who you were, Esmé, I saw your love for what it truly is. What you two have is beyond what the seers and gods say. Which is why I believe that before we truly move forward, it would be best for the two of you to...*seal* your bond."

I tilted my head to the side, not understanding what she meant. Río, however, seemed to understand perfectly.

"Wait what?" he blurted out.

"What does that mean?" I asked.

"A marriage ceremony, Esmé," his mother said simply, yet not at all.

I opened my mouth, but no sound came out. I snapped my gaze to Río, who looked pale and on the verge of panic.

"You're joking," he said.

"No, Río, I'm not."

"When?"

"As soon as possible."

The Moon Prince stood up and leaned forward with his hands on the table. The chair shrieked across the floor with his sudden movement. All I could do was watch him in stunned silence.

"No. No, you don't get to do that. You don't get to decide that. Not now," he snapped.

"I don't plan on forcing you or twisting your arm, but this is more than just spectacle and facade. I don't care about parading you two around or planning any more balls. Not right now. This is about the ritual. The bond that you both have. I thought out of everything I've asked, this would have been an easy decision for you," she contested.

"It's not about that."

"Then what is it?"

As Río and his mother argued about this vital part of my future, I felt myself shrink a little. Sure, the idea of a spontaneous wedding was jarring, but I didn't expect Río to react in such a visceral manner. It hit me in a way I didn't expect. Marriage was more of a faraway fantasy than a solid reality for me. I wanted it, but kept my expectations low to save my poor heart. When I met Río, I started imagining his face in the picture. Of course, I thought it would happen many years down the line, but at the very least, I assumed he wanted the same. He *said* he wanted the same.

Perhaps he changed his mind.

"So you *don't* want to marry me?" I choked out.

The prince whipped his head towards me, and he went bright red. Horror, guilt, and regret washed over his face as he sat back down to face me fully.

"No, no, no, that's not what I meant at all," he said, taking my hands in his.

"Then why are you so angry?"

"I'm not angry at *you*. I love you. I love you so much. I just hate..." He groaned before looking at his mother. "I hate the idea of this being another strategy. You made it very clear when we were kids that we had the freedom to marry as we pleased. Esmé has the right to that too."

"Yes, and I choose to marry *you*," I stated.

Río's brow softened when his eyes met mine once more.

"Even like this, all rushed?" he asked. "I at least wanted it to be the right time. I wanted to get you a ring, get down on one knee, and buy you a nice dress. You've already been through so much. I don't want you to feel forced."

I've never felt so endeared yet so exasperated at the same time.

"Río, I don't need any of that, and you wouldn't be forcing me to do anything," I protested, my face moist from crying. "Marrying you would be the easiest thing I will ever have to do!"

He wiped my tears away affectionately, a smirk gracing his lips.

"I didn't know you could say something so romantic in such an annoyed tone."

"Well, maybe if you asked me first, I wouldn't be so annoyed. How are you supposed to know my answer if you don't ask?" I blubbered dramatically.

He and his mother laughed. She always had quite a show with our antics.

"But what about courtship? I thought it was what you wanted," he said.

"You've already won over my heart, and we've been through quite a lot together, so we're well past courtship at this point. We have the queen's blessing, so I think all you need to do is ask the big question."

We both turned to the queen, who was watching us curiously.

"Ma, can you leave us alone for five minutes?" the prince asked.

La Reina sighed, already making her way to the door innocently.

"Five minutes," she said before disappearing.

Río got out of his chair and pushed it aside so he could get down on one knee. My heart fluttered like a hummingbird's wings he took my hands and his dark eyes pierced mine. He was shaking just as much as I was.

"Aurora Elíódor," he said, making me smile.

"Yes?" I whispered.

"Obviously, I didn't expect to do this today, but honestly, I think it makes sense for us. It's just you and me with no one around. What would make it better is us being in your apartment with some hot chocolate and your cat, who was secretly a god this whole time. Can't believe I missed that one."

A giggle bubbled in my throat, but I didn't dare interrupt.

"Gods... I love everything about you. I always have, even when you assumed I didn't. It's like breathing for me at this point. It's second nature, and I will spend forever making sure that you know that. It's the kind of love that can fill oceans and makes me feel like I can do anything. You make me want to be a better person, or at least the person that you see when you look at me. I know that our future looks scary right now, but I know that as long as we're together, it'll be okay. And when the scary is all over, I want to be there with you too. Forever. I want to laugh with you, hold you when you cry, take baths with you, sing with you, and fight demons. Fated or not, I will *always* choose you. So, will you choose *me*...and be my wife?"

Río's face had long blurred before my eyes from genuine, unadulterated joy, and the candles around us burned bright blue in response.

"Of course I will!" I exclaimed.

Río cupped my face and kissed me ardently. I clung to him, savoring him and the beautiful moment I only ever hoped to find in dreams.

"I think I like it when you call me Aurora," I told him between kisses.

"Do you?"

"I do."

Río smirked. "Okay...*my* Aurora."

THE MOON PRINCE

Río and I were to be married within the next few days. Most royal weddings were year-long spectacles, with a myriad of events leading up to the ceremony itself, but for the sake of everyone's safety, the queen thought it best to have a private ceremony. Despite Río's initial guilt and how rushed everything was, the two of us were actually relieved to have an intimate ceremony. It was how my parents got married, and from what I was told, their love was powerful.

For the second time, I was questioned about dress designs and had my measurements taken. The night before the ceremony, I was dragged into a separate chamber on the opposite wing and wasn't to see the prince until the ritual. The day of, it was like the evening of the solstice, but twofold. Arabella and two other trusted handmaidens spent most of the morning making sure I was fed and prepped for the event to come. I was bathed, scrubbed, and waxed with the finest products I had ever seen. My hair was brushed before the hearth and pulled half-up into a braided crown around my head with golden ribbon. Arabella let a few pieces frame my face and placed some red flowers within the plaits themselves. Brown powder was applied to my eyelids and my eyes were with charcoal. And my lips, the boldest of them all, matched the red color of my new hair.

The centerpiece of it all was of course, the dress. It was traditional for any couple of high stature to wear their family colors to the ceremony. Since Río was next in line to be Moon King, he would be wearing white. As a newly found Eliódor, I chose to wear red.

It took a lot of convincing, but with the queen's permission, I sent a letter to Dulce requesting that she make the gown for me. Even though it wasn't easy, I kept the letter vague and mentioned nothing of weddings, only that I needed the gown soon. She replied swiftly, saying that even though she was deeply curious, she was more than happy to make another gown for me. When it arrived, Arabella refused to let me see it until the day came. And only she insisted.

Emilia Mondragón

My wedding dress was a glittering crimson jewel made of beautifully woven lace and shining beads. The neckline was off my shoulders once again, with sleeves that went down to my wrists. The skirt was an A-line that was more comfortable to move in. Beads of varying shades of red were sewn into the lace itself, and many more hung from the neckline, waist, and sleeves in teardrops. My jewelry was made of gold metal inlaid with glittering red stones, and by the grace of the gods, I was gifted a golden tiara. Whereas Río's looked like crashing waves, mine resembled curling flames. Together with my hair and lipstick, I looked like a crackling fire.

Taking in my reflection, I had to bite my cheek to keep from getting too emotional. There was something different about this dress compared to the one Dulce made for the ball. It was just as magical, but this day was more personal and therefore more special. And when I looked in the mirror, I no longer saw Esmé Vespertín but Aurora Eliódor. I saw my father like I did in his watercolor portrait, and I saw my uncle, whose eyes burned as red as my dress. There was good and evil in this color and in my bloodline. I almost wished I had chosen gold instead, but if I let the Sun Killer have that, then he could take anything from me.

✴ ☽ ○ ☾ ✴

Before sunset, I was escorted towards the back of the island to a private beach. We took a tunnel and a series of stone steps that led out into the natural greenery. From behind some trees, a black jaguar appeared out of the shadows, making us stop in our tracks. I bit back a gasp, startled by his sudden appearance.

"You look like a true Eliódor," he mused.

The feline's mouth didn't move, but I could hear him as clear as day.

"Micqui!" I exclaimed with joy. "I can't believe you're truly here."

"I raised you. Of course, I'd be here."

I giggled blithely, though Arabella and my guards looked terrified.

"Río said he wanted to talk to you before the ceremony...to get your blessing," I said tentatively.

"Yes, we had a bit of a talk earlier in his room."

My eyes widened. "And...?"

Somehow, the jaguar shot me a derisive look.

"If I had any major objections to your relationship at all, we wouldn't be here. Trust me. As your guardian, I think he's frustrating, but as the God of Death, I think he's exactly what you and this country need. Río is a good man. He'll make a great husband and a great king. I wouldn't trust anyone else with your heart."

I looked to the sky to keep any tears from ruining my makeup. Arabella rushed to my side with a handkerchief at the ready.

"Oh, Micqui," I whispered, "I'm not even at the altar, and you're making me cry."

The deity chuckled warmly. "Sorry. From what I've seen, it's pretty normal."

In a swirl of violet mist, Micqui transformed into his tall, human form. Arabella and the guards yelped. The god paid them no mind as he approached me with soft violet eyes and handed me an embroidered handkerchief. With an amused giggle, I used it to dab under my eyes.

He was less and less a stranger with every passing day as years of fondness were now within reach. I may not have my parents here with me today, but I at least had someone who may as well be.

In a burst of affection, I hugged Micqui around the waist and squeezed him lightly. He slowly but surely enveloped me in his arms, as if unaccustomed to such things but still willing.

"Thank you," I whispered.

"No need to thank me. I'd move mountains for you, little dragon."

We continued through the trees with Micqui resting as a crow on my shoulder (to be less intimidating) until the dirt trail turned to sand and the beach began. The sun was starting to sink closer to the Marisláni Ocean, warming the blue sky with golden light. The usual breeze was still, and I had a feeling the Queen of Storms had something to do with it.

We were greeted by her and Mariela first. *Reina* Victoria wore her honorary violet color, and Mariela wore sapphire blue. They beamed at me, their gazes flitting to the black crow. Echo was stock-still, only whining at the corvid. Behind the hound, Savy looked every bit a scared teenager in the face of the God of Death.

"You look beautiful," the princess signed.

"Thank you!"

"Are you ready?" Victoria asked.

"Yes," I replied, despite my nerves.

"Come on, then."

They took me further along through the sand until we rounded a large pile of rocks. The beach widened, and that was when I caught my first glimpse of him. *My prince.* He was standing by the edge of the water, watching the waves. With a few words of encouragement to me, Micqui took flight.

"Río, your bride has arrived!" the queen called.

She and the princess moved aside as Río turned around.

My breath was immediately taken away. I've only ever known Río in the dark leather attire he wore on his voyages or the princely blue vestments from the palace. He was a rogue, a prince, or a mixture of both. But the Río before me now was something entirely different. He was wearing a jacket much like the one at the ball, except this one was the color of fresh snow. With the matching pants, knee-high boots, and his white hair, he almost looked like moonlight incarnate. Even the beaded waves on his shoulders were an iridescent white, shifting in the sunlight. The only splashes of color were the chain of moons across his chest and the silver crown on his head. He looked somewhere between prince and king, human and deity.

My future husband.

With a sudden rush of giddiness, I grabbed my skirt and ran to him. Río met me halfway down the sand. His dark eyes danced over me in complete awe, and when he raised his hand to caress my cheek, it was as if he was afraid to ruin me.

"You look breathtaking," he said.

I smiled bashfully. "So do you."

He furrowed his brow seriously then, reducing his voice to a whisper.

"You're still sure you want to do this, right? I mean, you're not just getting a Markaél. You're also getting a werewolf."

"Of course I'm sure. I've met you as a werewolf, remember? I think I know what I'm signing up for. I'm the one who's a necromancer with a demonic uncle. We do this *together.*"

Río grinned with adoration. He then raised a finger before digging through his pockets. Out of one, he took out a small box and opened it for me to see. Inside was a gold-banded ring with a circular moonstone, surrounded by a cluster of flowers with aquamarine stones in the center. I've never seen anything like it.

"Río, this is gorgeous," I gasped. "When did you get this?"

"It was stressful, but my family knows a jeweler who's been making our rings for generations. I had this idea for a while. It's Markaél tradition to use moonstones, but I added the aquamarine to make it a little more personal."

Like his necklace and the flowers he used to give me.

"Oh, Río, I love it. It's perfect," I choked out, trying not to break down. "What about *your* ring? I didn't have time to get you anything."

"Already taken care of."

He dug into another pocket and brought forth another box. Within this one was a larger gold ring with a red, square jasper stone in the center.

"So I have my little Red everywhere I go," he said with a smirk.

The corners of my lips turned down as I stared at him with such unadulterated love. He put so much thought into these rings without me having to ask, which meant so much more than any other material he could have given me.

"I could kiss you," I said.

He leaned in close to our noses barely touched. "We'll have time for that later."

Among our tiny party of wedding guests were Micqui, Paloma, Arabella, Mathilde, Captain Dominic, Yara Volpes, and—much to my merriment—Canela. My wonderful witch friend was going to be performing the marriage ritual for us this evening, which made the event even more perfect. Everyone gathered around in a semicircle as Río and I faced each other in front of the ocean and the setting sun. Canela stood next to us with a basket carrying a goblet, wine, a book, a dagger, a pink cord, and a smoking bundle of dried herbs. She lit the bundle and doused us in smoke as we held hands and took turns repeating vows from her book.

"Though you do not own me, I am, in all forms, undoubtedly yours. Though you do not command me, I will care for and serve you when you require. And though we do not share the same body, you and I alone share the same soul. I will be your partner in day or night, dawn or dusk, waking and sleeping. I will carry that which you cannot find the strength for, and I promise to soften life's blows. I will embrace your darkness and be your shining light. I will love you, hold you, and fight alongside you in this realm and every realm. Forever and always, in life and death."

By the time we finished our vows, the floodgates truly opened, and our faces were tear-stained. We exchanged our personalized rings, and Canela presented us with her crystal dagger. She explained that to finish the ritual, we must spill blood into a goblet of wine, drink from it, and then bind our hands.

As I listened intently, a freezing chill skittered down my spine, forcing me out of my bubble of joy. The breeze picked up again, but what I felt had nothing to do with the cold. No, a sudden fearful dread took over me. The spirits in the air began to cry. They whimpered and shouted in terror.

Upon my stark change in demeanor, the witch stopped speaking, and Río grew serious.

"What's wrong?" he asked.

I shook my head. "I don't know. Something's happening."

The feeling and the noise didn't abate. It triggered something deep within me, making my body shiver. I knew in my soul that there was only one thing that could make me feel this way. It was the same darkness from the ball and the one that nearly killed me from the inside out.

"He's—" I almost didn't want to say the words out loud. "He's here."

The blood drained from the prince's face. "What?"

"Something's coming," Micqui's voice echoed in my head.

His jaguar form was sitting on a rock not too far away when he snapped his head towards us.

"Moon Prince," he called in a booming voice.

Río jolted around, cursing under his breath. The god narrowed his violet stare at him.

"Keep her safe. I'll be back."

My husband and I shared a frightfully look as the god dispersed into a murder of crows and flew into the sky. Everyone around me made statements of alarm as their excited energy shifted. Thunder cracked, startling us all and drawing our attention to the queen.

"I promise you, that wasn't me," she assured. More thunder rumbled, and Victoria looked over her shoulder. "It's coming from inland."

"Sebastián," I whispered, suddenly panicking.

"How do you know?" Río asked.

"I can feel it."

If I didn't know any better, I would've thought his apprehension meant he didn't believe me, when in reality, it wasn't a lack of belief, but a wish that it wasn't true. It was something we both undoubtedly felt on this day that was supposed to be ours.

A muscle twitched in the prince's cheek as he nodded seriously.

He turned to his mother and said, "We need to get back to the castle. We need to see what's happening."

"Let's go. Now!" she demanded, moving back the way we came with Mariela behind her.

I ran alongside Río, holding my skirt in my hands as he kept his hand on my back. We barely made it through the garden when Mariela stopped and pointed to the sky.

Black, roiling clouds moved over Coáraluna at a pace that defied nature. They glowed with an orange-red fire as scarlet lightning danced within them. Echo barked at them as if it would make a difference.

"I can't stop them," the Queen of Storms said in frustration. "No matter how hard I try, I can't command them."

"That's because this is dark magic, *Majestad*," Canela said. "The gods didn't make this."

50

The Fire & the Flood

Esmé

I touched my necklace as Río pulled me straight through the castle interior, with everyone following closely behind. We practically sprinted to the main courtyard, past the statue of Marisláni. The guards were already frantic, muttering things to each other as we ascended to the ramparts above. It gave us a full view of Coáraluna and the dark storm lumbering over the hills like a beast.

I clutched Río's arm, and the queen started barking out orders.

"Alert the guards. Tell them to initiate full evacuation now. Everyone else in this castle who cannot fight is free to leave as well."

Captain Dominic bowed. "Yes, *Majestad.*"

A pack of guards trailed behind their captain with spears in hand, their armor clattering in their wake. Canela approached the queen then with a look of determination.

"I can help. I'm close with many people down there," she said.

The Queen of Storms nodded. "Yes, thank you, Canela. Take them through the tunnels. The captain will show you where."

With a firm nod, Canela turned to me and pulled me into a hearty embrace. I clutched her tightly, suddenly unsure if or when I was going to see her again. Tears threatened to choke me, but I swallowed them down.

"Congratulations, little songbird," she whispered.

"Thank you. If you see my friends...take care of them, will you?"

"I'll do my best."

She gave me another squeeze before running back down to the courtyard and following the guards. As if waiting in line, Yara came rushing to *Reina* Victoria with her hands clasped behind her back.

"What do you want me to do, *Majestad*?"

"Miss Volpes, I know you've been through a lot, but are you willing and able?"

"*Sí, Majestad.* I'll do anything."

"Then go and make sure you're geared up. Be prepared for anything. And take my daughter with you."

"Right away!"

The queen signed for her daughter to follow, who nodded firmly before trailing behind Yara.

Watching her give out orders with little time to prepare was like attending a masterclass on how to rule. Beneath her pristine exterior was a trained warrior who fought many battles in her youth. It reminded me of something her brother told me, about how young they were to be fighting in such a war.

"Is this it?" I asked. "What about our other plans?"

She bent over to loosen a ribbon around her ankle and used it to tie her lilac hair into a ponytail. It was a casual thing, as if she had done it many times before.

"One thing you should know about fighting in a war, *Alteza*," she spoke, tightening the ribbon, "is that you need to be adaptable. We can never predict *when* our enemy will attack, but what we *can* do is learn from them and think quickly when they do. Our plans are still the same, just not in the order we hoped. I will not let our people die because of some petulant man-child who doesn't know how to lose."

I recalled my uncle's tirade in that tar-stained forest with a huff. He may be a petulant child, but a child with the power of a demon was a danger to all.

"He didn't lose to just anyone," I argued. "My survival means he lost to his brother *again*. There's no telling what he'll do."

"That's why we need to get our people out of here," she stressed.

The dark cloud circled the entire city in a swirl. It flashed crimson lightning, and the thunder that ensued was guttural. The wind and thunder stopped, leaving behind an uncanny silence. Then...it started to rain.

A warm, sizzling drop fell on my shoulder, hotter than any rain I've ever felt. When I looked down, it wasn't water at all but thick, black tar. Río touched it with his finger, a look of disgust twisting his face. Another drop fell on his hair, and then another landed on his jacket. More and more black tar fell until our clothes were stained with large spots, and the air reeked of it. Río tried using his magic to shield us, but it did nothing. he took off his jacket and held it over our heads in a futile attempt at protection.

I looked down at my sullied hands, and was taken back to that scorched, rotting forest. I shook to the core. The sound of screams echoed from below, drawing our eyes back to the city. And what was once peaceful Coáraluna was now a stained tragedy, with people running and screaming from something we couldn't see. Beside me, Río's breath came out ragged.

"Everybody, get out of the rain!" he ordered. "Now!"

He put his arm around my waist and guided me down from the ramparts. The rain was so heavy and viscous that it stuck to everything—my skin, clothes, and hair—making it hard to run at full speed. Even Marisláni's marble body and *Castillo* Paricia's facade were a soiled mess.

We were halfway to the palace entrance when Río stopped with a shout.

"What the fuck?"

I looked over my shoulder, and to my horror, a small black vine formed out of a puddle and wrapped itself around his ankle. Río stomped it out with a snarl until it finally let him go. I wrenched him away from it, heading for the stairs, but stumbled back with a scream. Río crashed into my back with a grunt as I watched a tall figure grow out of the tar. Its body stuck together from the muck and rose into the shape of a hulking, crimson-armored figure with smoking red eyes. In his hands was a large, heavy sword, raised to swing.

"Get down!" Río shouted.

We threw ourselves in opposite directions as the dark warrior's blade hit the floor with a solid, metal scratch. I snapped my head towards him, panting as his scarlet eyes found mine. In a past life I would've feared them, but what I felt now was only pure loathing.

"Move, Eliódor!" the queen shouted.

White lightning flashed in the heavens, and with a gasp, I rolled out of the way. A bolt of crackling light struck the dark entity, sending him splattering across the courtyard.

"There are more of them!" *Reina* Victoria yelled in panic. "They're tearing the city apart. We need to move."

Río helped me to my feet, and we dashed towards the palace entrance. I swept my gaze across the courtyard as more dark warriors spawned, attacking anyone in sight. Mariela sent arrows flying through the dark rain as Yara slashed at enemies with her sword. Another one appeared at the top of the stairs, already charging at us. Río raised his hand, but somehow my instincts were faster. I reached into that well inside me and whipped my hand out with a scream. A streak of bright blue flame burst from the tips of my fingers and latched itself onto the warrior like tinder. It burned his upper body until it crumbled to the ground in ashes. I gawked at my hand as Río grabbed the other and pulled me inside.

Only when we were in the safety of the castle did he display his surprise.

"I don't think I've ever seen anything like that before."

He tried wiping away the muck from his body in irritation and pushed his hair back, which was now caked in black.

"I probably should've practiced when I had the time," I grumbled, wiping at my face.

"No better thing to practice on than these things."

"What are they?" I asked.

"Sebastián's army," Río replied. His eyes were trained on the commotion outside, where the creatures were banging on the doors. "I've seen them before. My dad said they're not technically alive, but they sure can kill."

"Spirits?"

"More like lesser demons. Still, I didn't think they could get this far so fast. Sebastián's been saving up his worst. Wait here."

Río approached the large entryway fountain and dragged every last bit of water out with an intense expression. It followed him out the door, back into the fray. I wrapped my arms around myself and watched. The sounds of bloodshed turned my blood cold. I was torn between wanting to help and not wanting to get in the way. I wasn't combat-trained by any means, but I wanted so badly to be useful.

Before I could make up my mind, everyone, including *Reina* Victoria, came rushing inside. The remaining guards barricaded the doors, and Río used the water to freeze them shut. Through the cracked windows, I could see not only the shadows of my uncle's dark soldiers but also fiery vines crawling up the walls. It was only a matter of time before they made their way in.

"There are too many of them," I uttered.

"They're all over the grounds," Mariela signed. "They got in through the rain."

"We can't let them cage us in here. That's what he wants," the queen argued.

"We have to fight our way out then," Río said.

All I could think about was the people down below and the sounds of their screaming. Even if we managed to save ourselves, there was still all of Coáraluna left. With the clouds spanning out past the hills, there was no doubt in my mind that these lesser demons were terrorizing the entire city or even the whole kingdom. An evacuation order didn't matter if they never made it out alive.

"What about our people? This place is a fortress, and those things managed to get in. They don't stand a chance down there. We need to help them," I contested.

Coáraluna is my home. *Our* home. My friends, his family, our people...

"Agreed," the queen said. "The fight doesn't end once we get out of here. I can only imagine what's going on down there, and quite frankly, I don't want to waste any more time."

"I'll go," Río stated, resolute.

"Me too," I seconded eagerly.

He gave me a strange look, but his mother looked borderline ecstatic.

"Good. It's been too long since we've had another firebender on our side. I know we haven't had the chance to train you, but often the best way to learn is by doing. Río, I trust that you'll guide her and get our people to safety."

"Of course."

"Then go quickly. I'll delegate the rest."

She pulled her children aside, the three of them exchanging words with their hands before embracing one another. I tried not to blatantly stare but stole a couple of glances in their direction. The whole interaction pulled at something melancholic in me. Their bond was so pure, and their love was so true.

"Whatever you do, don't hesitate," the queen announced when they broke apart. "If we lose each other, go to the Air Kingdom. I'll find you there."

Río and I bolted for the stairs, only for his mother to call out once more.

"Río?"

He stopped mid-step, looking over his shoulder. "Yeah?"

"Don't hold back. The time is now," she uttered carefully.

I eyed my husband as a muscle feathered in his cheek and he simply nodded. We continued up the stairs, through the palace, desperate to get down to the city.

"Was she referring to your curse?" I asked.

"Yeah," he replied grimly.

The prince removed his crown and rolled up his sleeves. In contrast, I was too sad to discard my new but dirty tiara.

"I know it scares you, but I agree with her. My uncle attacked the palace with his pack. Why not do the same to his army?"

Río sighed, "I know it makes sense. I would probably be saying the same thing to someone else, but I'm scared of losing control again. A werewolf that's out of its mind is just another enemy for you to avoid. I don't want to hurt you."

"I understand, but...this isn't the first turning anymore. Besides, I'll be there with you. I don't think—"

Río stopped abruptly and pivoted to face me. For some reason, he seemed hesitant.

"My love… I think you should go."

"Go? Go where?"

"You should evacuate with everyone else. Go with Canela."

I threw him an incredulous look. "Absolutely not. I'm going with you."

"No." He shook his head, putting his hands on my shoulders. "Get to safety. Leave through the tunnels, and I'll find you. I promise."

"Río, I'm not leaving you behind," I argued.

"Micqui said to keep you safe."

"He said to keep me safe. He didn't mean I couldn't fight! Your mother agreed that I should!"

"Aurora—" he started.

"Don't!"

The flames in the sconces danced as I raised an admonishing finger, but Río didn't even flinch. He only seemed to grow more agitated.

"He almost killed you! He *did* kill you! You were dead in my arms!" he shouted before stilling himself. "So much has happened since the full moon, and I've almost lost control already. I'm scared that if something happens to you again, I won't just turn; I'll lose *myself*."

My irritation eased with the reminder of my death, but I refused to budge. That day ruined both of us.

"My love, you don't need to protect me from everything. I *want* to do this. This is my fight just as much as it is yours. I'm tired of watching from the side and letting things happen to me and the people

I care about because of *him*. We made a vow to fight beside each other, so either you take me with you or I'll find another way."

We stared at each other with matching stubbornness, our wedding attire now ruined. More shouts came from beyond, along with more lightning and rattling the walls.

Río ran his hands over his face and let his head fall back. With his eyes on the ceiling, he heaved a guttural, aggravated sigh. Somehow, when his eyes met mine again, a smirk played on his lips.

"Not even an hour into marriage and we're already arguing," he said, holding out his hand. "Come on. Let's go."

Despite the circumstances, I couldn't help but smile as I put my hands in his.

We ran as fast as possible, though Río had to tear a piece off my dress to stop me from tripping on it. We eventually arrived at a door that led straight to the stables. Inside, the horses were bucking and whinnying in distress, riled up by the sound of slaughter and the flames crawling up the walls. The rain had long stopped, but what it left behind was now terrorizing everything in its wake. Smoke stung our eyes and filled our lungs, blurring our vision and choking our very breath.

I almost stumbled again, but not because of my dress. There was a body I hadn't seen—a young boy. He was a jovial stableman I had seen a few times before. Now, he lay covered in muck and blood, his eyes open and lifeless. I clapped my hand over my hand as bile rose in my throat. Río immediately veered us away.

"I know. Don't look," he whispered. "Help me with this."

He started opening every stable door, and I did the same on the other side until all but one horse ran off to safety. The prince placed a saddle on the remaining brown stallion's back. I kept my eyes on the barn door as the sound of growling grew closer. Rio held his hand down to me, and I quickly took it, letting him help me up on the rear.

I wrapped my arms around his waist, my gown bunching up around me, and with a snap of the reins, Río urged the horse forward. My body lurched back from the movement, and I tightened my hold. A few red-armored warriors appeared through the doors, coming our way. Río kicked one of them in the face and sped past the rest, riding like a beast through the palace and down the hill.

✹ ☽ ◯ ☾ ✹

Coáraluna was an inferno.

Everything was covered in grime and ash. Black, thorny vines slithered up the houses, cracking at the stone and breaking the windows. Lightning struck a crowd of dark soldiers as people ran away screaming. Some of the royal guards were trying to get citizens to safety, while others had their weapons raised at a row of assailants with red eyes. The guards charged them, inciting a bloody fight they couldn't win. Whatever magic Sebastián put into these beings was powerful. They withstood the harshest of blows and pierced through armor like it was nothing. Our stallion nearly bucked us off in fear, and as soon as we dismounted, it ran off through the chaos.

"Stay close to me!" Río shouted. "Watch my back and I'll watch yours!"

He grabbed whatever clean water was left in the nearby canal and started using it as a spear. As soon as it hit its target, the weapon would melt and reshape into another spear to be thrown again and again.

For once, I didn't have to merely observe or leave him behind. I *chose* to be here, so I had to prove that Paloma's lessons were worth something. This battlefield was the opposite of a greenhouse, and my emotions were running rampant, but I knew very well that such things are what sparked my magic in the first place.

I let the whispers get loud, connecting my anger to theirs as they begged to be set free. It was almost as if they were joyful to have a target worth attacking. Who was I to deny them? I raised my hands to the sides of my head, and I flicked them out with a grunt. Wisps of blue light surrounded a group of red soldiers and turned their bodies to ash. I did it again and again until no enemies were blocking our path.

I stood proud of what I did with sweat dripping down the side of my face, and in a gown no less.

"Get as many of our people to safety. If you need to take any of them down, aim for the head. It's the only other way to disarm them. We'll be here to aid you," Río told the guards before turning his attention to me. "You think you can help me with these?"

He pointed to the thorned vines that clawed out of the ground like hands. They nearly killed me once, but I also knew they weren't indestructible.

"I can try," I replied hesitantly.

"If you can't, then just keep doing what you're doing. You're doing great," he said earnestly.

Río picked up a sword from the ground as well as another weapon, which he held out to me. At a glance, it looked like a regular spear, except with a longer, curved blade. I examined it in with a mixture of trepidation and eagerness. Somehow, the prince chuckled.

"You said you wanted to learn how to defend yourself, right?"

I nodded. "Yeah."

"This is a *gladio*. It cuts like a sword without having to get too close."

I took it gingerly from his hand and tested the weight. It was taller than I but a lot lighter than I expected.

"Use both hands and stab with the sharp end. We'll worry about technique later. I just don't want you to be empty-handed."

"Thank you," I said, clutching the gladio tightly.

Río cupped the side of my head affectionately, his eyes ablaze.

"Use this fire to your advantage. Get angry."

I matched his expression, feeling his fury like the flames around me.

"I will."

We moved through the district, fighting through the bedlam. With the *gladio* in my hands, I was given a newfound grit. I could feel the embers all around me—not just their heat, but their *magic*. It tingled beneath my skin, not in a scorching or oppressive way, but in a manner that reminded me of light. I tried using it to produce a pure flame. The path was hard to find with my fraught emotions, but I did enough to break down some of the vines in our wake.

The image of *Teatro Paraíso* was the only thing that brought me to a stuttering halt. The familiar exterior of the place I once called home was now blackened and engulfed in flames. I let out a small cry and I averted my eyes to save myself the pain, but in the other direction, the Jade District looked no different. Even if I couldn't see it, I knew Dulce's shop was being reduced to cinders. It took everything in me not to imagine her, Fabian's, or Teo's bodies in the fire. Or to run forth and find them.

Focus, Eliódor, I heard Micqui say in my ear, though he was nowhere to be found.

I dried my tears and forced my attention forward with a new, eerie numbness and caught up to Río. We moved down the hill, ushering people to the evacuation tunnels while fending off warriors and sentient vines. Wielding a weapon was never in *Esmé's* realm of imagination, but *Aurora* found that the *gladio* served as a great outlet for despair.

No matter how much I fumbled, I didn't let it stop me. A flaming vine came for me, and I instinctively slashed at it. A blade of fire shot out from the *gladio*, slicing through the vine. I gasped as it disintegrated. Even Río looked surprised.

"I think that weapon might be made for you," he said.

"Don't get your hopes up, because I don't think I'll be able to recreate that again."

I made my best attempt at focusing despite my home being a waking nightmare. Even the Larimar District was destroyed. The people who weren't heading for the tunnels were either dying, screaming or crying over dead bodies. I tried guiding them to safety and provided what little protection I could, but it never felt like enough. Vines were crushing Aviloníans into nothing, and enemies were cutting them to bits. Corpses littered the streets—people whom I used to pass by every day. Winter solstice decorations were now reduced to ash. New spirits were joining the old ones—people who should've never died. There was so much blood and darkness, and with every piece of my magic that I used, it only worsened. Overwhelming would be an understatement.

"Aurora!" Río shouted.

It's too much.

A scorching root came up from behind me and wrapped itself around my torso. I screeched as it lifted me into the air, and my *gladio* fell out of my hands. Río yelled and started hacking away at it with his sword. I fought against the feeling of helplessness and impending suffocation. My heart pounded in a frenzy as panicked, yet as the vine squeezed tighter, that burning feeling in my chest grew in size.

With a roar, a circle of blue flames burst from me. The vine disintegrated, and I fell to the cobblestone with a pained groan. Stars danced before my vision, and when everything refocused, I was met with a face I hadn't seen in a long time. It belonged to a young woman in a blue dress with chestnut hair. Her emerald eyes, which were once full of life, were looking right at me, now open and devoid of light.

It was my last straw.

"No," I sobbed.

Río fell to his knees next to me, frantic with worry.

"Are you okay?"

I sat up, never tearing my eyes off the body. When he saw my expression and my friend's corpse, his expression darkened.

"Flora!" I cried.

The fire surrounding her turned blue—a small pocket of my magic amid my uncle's flames. Río cradled my head against his chest, providing me a semblance of comfort in the chaos.

Moments from the past three years flashed in my nearby memory. Meeting her for the first time at my audition and then working with her through brutal rehearsals. Evenings spent at Dulce's house. She liked her lists and her order, but she was fun and vibrant and always incredibly kind. Theater was her love and pride, and now she'd never see another show again.

She was supposed to get out.

"I did my best to protect you from the cruel side of humanity, little dragon." Micqui's jaguar form appeared from the shadows and came to sit by Flora's corpse. "While it's important for you to see it, I wish you didn't have to learn like this."

Though he was a deity of death, remorse was genuine.

Glowing purple flowers bloomed around my friend, giving her some of her light back. They grew in a trail, connecting her to the other bodies on the street, which connected to the bodies all over the city. There was magic to them. I could feel it in my chest as if I were tethered to them, too. The whispers danced around me, their presence strengthening, like other limbs attached to my being. Even the embers were present in me. It was angry and devastated all at once.

"I can feel them. All of them."

Aurora, they sang.

"Listen to them, Aurora," Micqui said. "They want vengeance just as much as you do. That is the justice I will give."

Aurora, they repeated louder.

I looked over Río's shoulder. Standing in the street was a crowd of people—*spirits*. *Príncipe* Saévio was there, as were Flora, the stable boy, my mother, and many others that I knew or didn't know. A soft blue glow emanated from each of them as they awaited some kind of response from me. A *command*.

"What do you see?" Río asked.

"I can see her. I can see all of them," I whispered.

He tensed. "What do they want?"

"I think...they want to come back."

My gaze flitted between my wedding ring and then my mother's before meeting Río's eyes.

"Remember what they said about soul bonds?" I asked, suddenly thrumming with hope.

He furrowed his brow curiously. "Yeah."

I nodded before grabbing his face and kissing him. I wasn't entirely certain if my idea was going to work, but I hoped I wasn't wrong. All I knew was what Micqui told me about my parents and how strong their bond was. I thought of the Moon King, *Reina* Montserrat, and the creation of The Rift. I let the spirits wash over me, crying and screaming, enraged as I felt the daylight in my soul build. And as Río kissed me back, I felt the crashing waves of his magic too. There was wrath in me, and there was hope. There was grief, and there was love. I thought of the color blue and everyone I lost. I thought of Micqui and how he bestowed the gift to breathe life instead of death. I let my feelings and my magic intertwine as Río grounded me to reality.

When I finally pulled away, the entire city was aglow with cerulean flame. There was an aching moment of nothingness, and then we heard the bodies move. Río's face fell as, one by one, the corpses rustled to their feet. I connected to them, feeling them not just close by but all around the city, from the palace to Larimar to the fishing ports. All of their eyes were a blue flame.

Tear them apart.

They followed my command and sprinted forward, towards the nearest dark warriors. Río and I clung to each other as they rushed past, afraid they might knock us over in their wake.

After a moment of stunned silence, Río tore his attention away from the horde to look at me in awe.

"You did it," he marveled.

"You helped."

We rose to our feet as there were suddenly no more enemies in proximity. Río trained his eyes down the island towards the horde and what felt like hundreds of soldiers that remained. There was a look of conflict in his eyes, as if weighing something heavy.

"Guess it's my turn then," he uttered.

I frowned. "What do you mean?"

He backed away from me, and when I made to follow, he held his hand out.

"Don't. Stay away from me. When I come out, you better run."

Barely a second passed when Río doubled over with a strangled cry. The veins on his neck turned white. He was finally giving in. My heartbeat quickened. Seeing him in pain like that, my instinct was to comfort him, but I stopped myself.

Río peeled off his clothes as he staggered further away from me. I picked them up, keeping my eyes glued on him until he inevitably fell around the corner with a groan. The echoing sound of inhuman snarls and bones cracking echoed through the night. Against my instinct, I backed away, watching his shadow grow larger and larger, until all of a sudden, there was a howl. A large white werewolf jumped into view and ran right past me, barreling behind the corpses on all fours. I watched in awe before Micqui approached, suddenly two sizes larger.

"Get on. You won't be able to keep up on your own two feet."

Still clutching Río's clothes, I mounted Micqui's back and held on to his fur as best as I could as he raced through the streets of Coáraluna. His movement was much smoother than a horse's and even faster, but it made the task of hanging on that much more difficult. I made it my duty to check every remaining street and alleyway for citizens left behind. The walking dead and large werewolf didn't help alleviate their terror, but they were smart enough to follow my orders at least. Half of them were shaking, while others looked like they saw a walking miracle.

We followed the path carved by burning corpses, Río's claws, and his strengthened water magic. Our biggest problem wasn't even the soldiers but the vines. They curled themselves around everything, set the houses on fire, and burned everyone's skin. I did my best to keep them at bay, but with my energy split, I was starting to become drained the further down the city we went. The *gladio* was my savior, though my arms were getting weak.

With our large group of survivors, we finally arrived at the docks when thunder cracked, drawing our attention towards the top of the hill where *Castillo* Paricia was now in flames. Thorny branches like claws curled around its walls, crushing the stone and glass. A shuddering scream left my lips at the horrifying sight. The queen was up there, and as far as I knew, so were Mariela, Paloma, and Yara.

"No," I uttered. "No, no, no."

Río was immediately distraught and started running back up the hill. I was already behind him when Micqui jumped in our way.

"If you go back up there, you'll die," he snapped.

Río hunched over, ears pulled back, and teeth bared as he growled at Micqui. I stepped between them with my hands out.

"Micqui, his family is up there. We can't just abandon them!" I argued.

"I'll make sure they are safe. But if any of you—his sister included—get caught by Sebastián Eliódor's army, then it will be the end of Avilonía. I can assure you of that. Go!" He jutted his chin towards the bridges. "Drown them and go. I know how to find you."

The jaguar disappeared in a murder of crows again and Río growled in his direction. Despite my grief, I put my hand on his furry arm and pulled him back towards the docks. His demeanor softened as he looked at me and let out a sad whine.

"I know, but we need to trust him. We need to get them to safety," I said, motioning to our trembling group of survivors.

"There's more!" one of them shouted.

They were pointing past the quartz bridges, where a swarm of red-armored warriors was roaring their way towards us from inland. A dizzy spell made my world tilt, a symptom of overwhelm and exhaustion. Río nudged me with his snout.

"I don't have much left," I said. "I've never used this much magic in one night before."

I looked from the swarm to the still-burning city and the palace above it all. As much as I wanted to find another way, Micqui's warning echoed loud and clear. There were too many of them. And the queen was a powerful woman. I had to believe she and the rest of them got out somehow. I had to believe she would understand.

We can come back. We will come back.

"Drown them," I said, looking up at my white wolf. "Flood it all and get us out of here."

Río's eyes flashed in surprise before settling into a fierce smolder. He nodded and stepped forward so he was standing in front of all of us.

"Stay close together!" I ordered the people behind me.

With shaky whimpers, they clutched onto each other for dear life. I angled myself to keep an eye behind us, and in one last attack, I threw out my hands and sent the corpses forward over the bridge. As soon as they collided with the Sun Killer's army, a tremor shook the ground. Río raised his claws, and with the power of the moon, the water receded far back into the sea and then came rushing back in a massive tidal wave. With a roar, he swiped them, and the waves crashed down. They obliterated the army as well as the quartz structures that connected us inland as if they were made of clay. With the momentum, the waves hurled back toward us, making everyone scream, but Río maneuvered them toward the inner city. The water flooded everything, putting out fires and taking out whatever assailants remained.

The Moon Prince then turned towards us and scooped me up in his big arms. I clutched onto his fur as he led us down by the water. With one last gust of power, the waves around the island picked up and flooded each district, flushing everything out. At the top of the hill, *Castillo* Paricia was left a charred, broken mess.

Río whined, and I leaned against him.

"I know," I whispered with a broken heart.

Keeping me in his arms, the prince turned towards the sea and created a large pocket in the water for us to walk through. On my order, we all stepped within and disappeared beneath the ocean waves, heading to the northwestern coast to safety.

Acknowledgments

It is May 27th, 2025 and I am writing this from my bed after finishing the final draft of this book. It's a bit surreal. The fantasy genre and all of its creatures have been friends to me since I was a child. They held my hand and made me feel less alone even when others wanted to tear them from me. I refused to give it up and I'm glad I didn't. I'm glad I let my imagination run free until I was able to create a world of my own. So in that regard, I'm acknowledging my younger self. Writing this was like letting her run free, while my older self trailed behind, refining her work. I created a colorful world inspired by my culture and others like mine, with people who look like me and the ones I love. And even though there's a lot of darkness in this story too, the pure love in it healed something in me.

This book was finished long before Daywalkers was even published, and there came a point where I wasn't even sure if either of these stories would leave my hands at all. I'd like to acknowledge my sheer spite, but I would especially like to shout out my brother, Ollie. He's always there to listen to my ramblings about whatever story I'm working on. He's the first who gets to hear the story and he's the first one to knock some sense into me when I'm convinced I'm a horrible writer who should never write again.

My lovely friends Lani and Kami, who were my alpha/beta readers for this story, thank you! We've come a long way from tumblr.com and I'm so happy that some of us are still together. And the fact that you guys support my original work even now makes me so grateful. You guys are the coolest. Just know that I would go to war for you!

To Mintaii, my cover designer, who is so incredibly talented and amazing. I am obsessed with your work and you brought my vision to life and more!!

As a queer Mexican-American living in the U.S., these times have been horrific. It can feel especially dystopian having to continue on and promote things on social media, but I know I'm not alone. I'm so happy to be a part of a Latine community that cares about each other and also connect with other BIPOC, queer, disabled people online. By your sheer presence and determination to exist, you've inspired me to live the same way. And you've inspired me to create the stories that I want with characters that look like me, share experiences like mine, and come from my culture. When I'm comparing myself to others (especially those significantly more privileged than me), I find solace with all of you. I keep writing because of you and I allow myself to rest because of you. I can only hope to contribute to that however I can.

Of course, I would be nothing without my small but growing community of readers and writers alike! It still baffles me that you guys genuinely like me and my work, but know that your love is appreciated. Especially everyone on the ARC team!! It has always been a dream of mine to gather a community of like-minded individuals who love to write, read, and spread kindness. Whether you have followed me since Daywalkers or only recently, thank you so much! It could be five of you or it could be thousands, I love you all the same.

Love,

Emilia Mondragón

About the Author

Emilia Mondragón is an independent queer author from Southern California. She is the daughter of Mexican-immigrant parents and is a lover of all things horror and fantasy. Over the course of her life, she has dipped her toes in many creative fields such as film, theater, singing, acting, and dancing, but ultimately decided to pursue her lifelong dream of becoming an author. She also self-published a vampire urban fantasy called DAYWALKERS.